CW00922988

THE PERSUADER

RICHARD PENNELL

authorHOUSE®

AuthorHouse™ UK Ltd.
500 Avebury Boulevard
Central Milton Keynes, MK9 2BE
www.authorhouse.co.uk
Phone: 08001974150

First published by AuthorHouse 8/19/2010

ISBN: 978-1-4490-7856-0 (sc)

This book is printed on acid-free paper.

Bobby Parsons is a normal, happy boy living in East London in the 1950's. He lives with his mum, dad and sister and, plays football with his mates in the local park and supports West Ham. Then his father is implicated in a scam to embezzle money from his employer and is sent to prison.

The family is supported by a dubious character who comes to play an important part in Bobby's life. When his father is released from prison he finds life very difficult and to make the situation worse for him he discovers that his actions have effected Bobby's career prospects.

Bobby is offered the chance of revenge on the person who he believes set up his father and is responsible for his plight. This action leads an adult Bobby into the world of criminals where he develops his skills as The Persuader.

The story progresses to tell how he becomes more deeply involved and lives a duel, split life, and how matters are eventually resolved.

CHAPTER 1

February 1959

Bobby Parsons ran out of school, as he did almost every day, down Lancaster Road, right into St Anthony's Road, past the corner shop and into his house. "Hi Mum" he shouted out as he made straight for his bedroom to put on his football kit and his new football boots, a Christmas present from his Gran. As soon as he was changed he shouted, "Going over the park Mum" as he left the house as quickly as he had entered and ran to West Ham park to meet with his mates who had also run out of school and done exactly the same thing. Football was played with a tennis ball that was the prize possession of Paddy McGuire. Goalposts were jumpers. If it wasn't raining this was the normal post school activity for Bobby and his mates. Bobby was eight and he wanted to be a footballer when he grew up. His dad had already taken him to Upton Park several times and he and his Dad had talked about the games they had seen for days afterwards. Bobby knew that he was not the best footballer in his group. He couldn't run as fast as Jimmy O'Connell, he couldn't kick the ball as hard as Tony Owen, he couldn't tackle as well as Liam Marriott but that didn't matter. He didn't want to be like Vic Keeble or John Dick and score goals, or like Mike Grice or Malcolm Musgrove and run fast down the wing, he wanted to be like Kenny Brown, the centre half. Bobby liked him best because he always had a smile on his face and joked with John Bond who played at right back for West Ham. People told Bobby that he was tall for his age, certainly he was the tallest of all his mates, so he could head a ball well and he knew that a centre half had to be good at heading.

It was the same most evenings after school, football in the park then home to tea. Bobby's home was a house that had been divided into two flats. Bobby, his mum and dad and sister Jane lived downstairs. He and his sister shared a bedroom; there was one other for his parents, a sitting room and a small kitchen. There was a toilet which was outside the back door. His dad had built a lean-to so that they could use the toilet without getting wet if it was raining. His Gran lived upstairs and sometimes, if his Mum was out working, his Gran would get his tea. He liked his Gran's teas, she would cut the bread very thick and put loads of butter on it and fill the sandwich with great chunks of cheese. Today though Bobby's Mum was at home. She was a comptometer operator. She worked for an agency that usually brought work to the house to do, but occasionally she had to go out temping in an accounts office of a company.

Bobby's sister was five and had just started school at St Anthony's. Sometimes she got on Bobby's nerves as she kept on talking about school and how good it was and telling Bobby and his Mum all about things that Bobby already knew. Jane was talking about Miss Cuthbert and her reading cards and about Father O'Leary the priest who had visited her class that day and what he had said them. "He says the same to all of the small kids" Bobby said, "and reading cards are only for people who can't read properly, we have proper books". "That's enough" said Mum. "You had reading cards too before you had books". Anyway while you are both here I must tell you that next week and the week after I am going to work at the Plessey factory in Ilford so Gran will get your teas for two weeks. I don't want any arguing or bad behavior while I am out". "I will be home at about 6 O'clock in the evening so I should be in just before Dad".

Bobby and Jane's Dad, Robert, worked as an accounts clerk at West Ham Corporation. Everybody said that was a good job, very secure and with a pension. Bobby didn't understand any of that but he loved his Dad and although he went to bed soon after his Dad had finished his dinner during the week he spent as much time as possible with him at weekends even getting up to go to mass with him at 8 O'clock on Sunday's. Bobby's Mum and Jane went to 10.30 Mass but Robert said that he wanted to get it over and done with.

Life for Bobby, Jane and his Mum and Dad was very routine and very comfortable and it never occurred to Bobby that anything would ever happen to change it.

Two weeks later, when Bobby's Mum was out working, as usual he ran home to change into his football kit, shouted "Hi Gran" up the stairs as he ran into the house. "Bobby come here" his Gran shouted down to him. "I'm just going over the park" Bobby shouted back. "Come up here when I tell you- now" Gran shouted back. Bobby stopped. His Gran never talked to him like that. He went upstairs. "What's the matter Gran"?

"Sit down Bobby" said Gran.

"What's the matter"? Bobby said again.

"There's been a problem with your Dad. I'm sure it's a mistake but the police went to where your Mum is working to tell her that they have taken him to the police station on the Romford Road. It seems that some money has gone missing from his works, and they think that he might know something about it. She has gone there to see him so you must stay here until she comes home. Jane will be home in a minute and I don't want her upset so I am just going to tell her that Mum is working late tonight. OK? It's our secret".

When Jane arrived home, Gran greeted her and she didn't notice anything was wrong. Bobby thought that this was funny as he hadn't gone out as usual and both he and Gran were very quiet. The evening passed very slowly, at last it was bedtime and Gran put Bobby and Jane to bed.

It was almost midnight when Bobby's Mum arrived home. Jane was fast asleep but Bobby had not been able to sleep because he wanted to know what was happening. He crept from his bed and into the sitting room where his Mum and Gran were talking. "What's going on Mum?" said Bobby. "What are you doing up? asked his Mum. "I can't sleep. Where is Dad, what's going on?" "Sit down and I'll tell you and Gran what I know" Mum said.

Mum then explained what she had been told. There was over twelve thousand pounds missing in the Corporation accounts. The accounts in question had been dealt with by Robert, but he says that the alterations he had made had been done so at the instruction of his two bosses. They had also been arrested. Robert claims that he didn't know what was happening and was only doing what he was told. The police didn't believe him. "Dad has got to appear in the magistrate's court tomorrow and then we will see what will happen" said Mum.

CHAPTER 2

The following morning Mum got the children up, made breakfast and off they went to school as usual. As soon as they had gone Mum got ready and left for the magistrates court in Stratford.

After a normal, uneventful day in school Bobby ran home as usual and was delighted to see his Dad sitting in his usual chair. "Dad" said Bobby as he ran up to his Dad and threw his arms around him. "I knew everything would be alright" "Of course it will" said Dad, "Don't worry".

Now that everything was OK again Bobby got changed and ran over to the park to play football. Everything was alright again, everything was normal.

The next day when Bobby went to school everybody was talking about his Dad. The case had been reported in the Stratford Express and all of his friends parents had been talking about it over breakfast. Bobby explained to them that it was a mistake and that his Dad was home now and that it was over. During the lunch break though one of the boys in the year above Bobby started to pick on him.

"Your Dad's a thief Parsons. My Dad says that he's stole from all of us."

"He's not a thief" shouted back Bobby, "it was a mistake

because he was only doing what he was told and now the court has let him go. He's at home now".

"Yeah, he's at home on bail. He ain't working is he? He's been sacked from 'is job and he's got to go back to a bigger court to be tried for all sorts of things. 'e stole council money, that's money that all of our parents pay in rates, so 'e's stolen from all of us."

"No he hasn't" Bobby said, almost crying, "he hasn't done anything.

"Thief, thief, thief" some of the older boys started to chant. Bobby ran at them, fists flaying, he caught two of the group with hard punches before they got hold of him and started to twist his arm. Just then the headmistress Mrs. Andrews, who had heard the chanting, arrived on the scene and marched Bobby and the other four boys involved into her office.

Having heard what each of the boys had to say, and sending the two boys that Bobby had hit, one with a bloody nose, the other with a split lip, to Miss Cuthbert to be cleaned up, Mrs. Andrews kept just Bobby in her office. "I read about your Father in the paper at lunchtime Bobby, I know what is going on". "But it's all over Miss, Dad was away yesterday but he's back home now, it's all alright"

"Not really Bobby" said Mrs. Andrews, "he still has to stand trial for the three charges" Bobby was shattered, Mrs. Andrews wouldn't tell fibs. Why hadn't his parent said something? Mrs. Andrews could tell that Bobby was confused by the look on his face. "What did your Dad say to you Bobby"? asked Mrs. Andrews.

"Nothing really" said Bobby. "He was home when I got in from school yesterday so I thought it was all OK as he wasn't in prison. We all had tea last night and then we sat a bit and listened to the radio and then I went to bed. This morning I just got up as usual and came to school, everything is the same as it always is".

"Bobby, I'm going to take you home now and have a chat with your Mum and Dad" said Mrs. Andrews, getting up and putting her coat on.

It was only about a four minute walk from the school to Bobby's house, he could run it in two, but today the walk with Mrs. Andrews seemed like hours. Although the front door was never locked during the day Mrs. Andrews knocked on the door and Bobby Mum looked very surprised when she opened it and saw Bobby and the head mistress standing there.

"Can I come in please Mrs. Parsons, we need to discuss the situation I think" said Mrs. Andrews.

"Of course" said Bobby's Mum, standing aside and letting her into the hall.

Bobby was sent to the bedroom he shared with his sister, not as a punishment his Mum explained but they only had one sitting room and this talk was for adults. Bobby tried to listen through the wall but the adults were talking in low voices.

After what seemed like hours but was in fact about thirty minutes, Bobby's Mum and Mrs. Andrews came into the bedroom. "Goodbye Bobby and good luck" said Mrs. Andrews, "I think that your Mum and Dad will explain everything to you now".

Mum saw Mrs. Andrews out of the front door and then said to Bobby "come on into the living room young man and let's talk about this". Mum and Dad explained to Bobby that Dad had been released on bail. They explained what that meant and that Dad would have to go back to a court in a few weeks time to face trial for conspiracy to theft, false accounting and fraud. He had tried to explain to the magistrate that he did not knowingly do anything wrong but he was told that it would be for a jury to decide. In the meantime it would probably be better for Bobby or Jane not to go to school but instead to go and stay with Auntie Mavis, Mum's sister, who lived in a place called Woodbridge, miles away in Suffolk. Bobby thought this was brilliant. He had been there once before and there were boats and a beach and woods and all sorts of things and he could play with his cousin Bernard.

Two days later Bobby with his sister and Mum were on the train from Liverpool Street to Ipswich and then changed to another to Woodbridge to stay with Auntie Mavis and Uncle Len. It was a bit of a squeeze in the house, it only had two bedrooms and there were now four children, but what an adventure. It was good fun and Bobby liked Auntie Mavis and Uncle Len as well as Bernard and his other cousin Betty. But soon he was missing home, his Mum and Dad, Gran, his mates he played football with and going to see West Ham with Dad. Uncle Len took him to see Ipswich Town play but they weren't his West Ham and all of their supporters had funny accents when they cheered.

Auntie Mavis would take Bobby and his sister to a phone box down by the quay every three days and phoned a number where Bobby's Mum was. Bobby couldn't ask all the questions he wanted to because Jane did still not know that there was any problem, she just thought that they were on holiday. Bobby did find out that that his Dad was due in court very soon and that as soon as he was, Mum would come up to Suffolk and see them both.

CHAPTER 3

The day of the court case arrived. Robert was in the dock with two of his bosses. The court was told that the Chief Clerk, Mr. Wilkinson had a gambling problem. He had run up a large debt with a local bookie that had made threats against him and his family unless he paid him the amount he owed. With interest this amount was now more than fifteen thousand pounds, more than three times what Mr. Wilkinson earned in a year. His assistant Mr. Holmes was in on the plan, Mr. Wilkinson was to pay him £1000 when the money was paid. Robert did not know anything about the problem and explained that he was only doing what both Mr. Wilkinson and Mr. Holmes told him to do. The jury did not believe him and found all three men guilty. Robert was sentenced to seven years in prison, Mr. Holmes ten and Mr. Wilkinson twelve.

Bobby's Mum arrived in Woodbridge the day after the trial. She sat Bobby and Jane down in Auntie Mavis's sitting room and told them what had happened. She told them that they would be staying with Auntie Mavis for another two weeks and then they would be moving somewhere else to live and going to a different school. Jane didn't seem to react at all, she just thought it was all a big adventure. Bobby was devastated. All of his friends were in Forest Gate and went to St Anthony's school. He wanted to go home, he knew when he explained what had happened to his mates it would make no difference. After a lot of discussion it was agreed that Bobby would go back with his Mum to Forest Gate and Jane would stay with auntie Mavis until things were settled. Bobby was sure that he could convince his Mum that they shouldn't move.

They arrived home on Thursday evening and Gran had a meal ready for them. Bobby's Mum explained to Gran that Bobby did not want to move and thought that there would not be any problems. She said that she would go and see Mrs. Andrews in the morning and talk about Bobby going back to school.

Mrs. Andrews was not happy when she was told about Bobby wanting to return. "We have good children in this school but there has been a lot of publicity about your husband and I think that Bobby would be victimized by some of the older children".

"That's a chance I will have to take. Bobby wants to stay here at St Anthonys' so we need to find out whether he can deal with the problems or not"

The following Monday Bobby was back in class. As he walked into the playground everybody looked at him and all of the talking seemed to stop. The bell rang almost immediately and the pupils filed into the classrooms. The teacher welcomed Bobby back and told the class that whatever Bobby's Dad had done it was nothing to do with Bobby.

"My Dad hasn't done anything wrong" shouted Bobby, "it is all a mistake, he was just doing what he was told to do by his bosses".

"That's enough Bobby, I am only trying to explain that whatever has happened is nothing to do with you and nobody here should take it out on you".

At playtime Bobby went into the playground with the rest

the class for his milk. Even his special friends were a bit quiet and pupils from other classes looked at him strangely. Playtime was soon over and it was back into class for a writing lesson.

It was soon lunchtime and as usual Bobby had a sandwich, he didn't like school dinners. As Bobby went to sit down at one of the tables, the two boys already sitting there got up and went to sit somewhere else. Bobby sat down but nobody came and sat down at the same table. After lunch, in the playground one of the older boys stuck his foot out in front of Bobby and he fell over it. "Oh look, blood on your knee. Little bloody Bobby. You are not wanted here, your Dad's a thief and you know what they say, like father like son". None of his friends came to help him up and ask him how he was.

The afternoon came and went and Bobby left school to go over the park as usual. As he walked along Lancaster Road to go home his best friend Tony Owen came up and walked beside him.

"Look Bobby, this is real problem but all of our Mums and Dads have told us we are not to have anything to do with you"

"Why? I haven't done anything"

"I know, I don't understand it, but it's not just mine, it's probably every parent of all of the kids. The newspaper said that the three men took money from the public so they think that it is their money".

"But my Dad didn't get any of it Tony, and me and mum certainly didn't, so why pick on me"?

"Grown ups!" said Tony, "but the problem is that it has happened so you will not get any support at school or anyone to play with and that goes for football over the park, we are not allowed to play with you".

"Not play football?"

They had now arrived outside of Bobby's house, Tony looked at him and just said "Bye Bobby, good luck".

CHAPTER 4

Two weeks later Bobby, his Mum and Jane moved to a flat in house in Kingston Road in Ilford. Mum had explained the need to move to Jane and also that she was going to tell the neighbors that she was a widow. Jane seemed to just accept the whole thing which Bobby found amazing. He decided to put it down to the fact that she was very young and also stupid. Bobby on the other hand decided that he would have to go along with it although he hated what was happening and hated his Mum for telling people that his Dad was dead. The flat was on the ground floor of a house which had been extended. It had a kitchen, just big enough for a small table. The bedroom for his Mum and a bathroom and toilet were in the extension that had been built on the back of the house and what had been a large room had a dividing wall install so that Bobby and Jane had small but separate bedrooms. The front room of the house was a good size lounge.

The agency that Bobby's mother worked for was based in Ilford so she started back at work immediately. She arranged for Bobby and Jane to go to St Peter and Paul's school but as it was the end of June when they moved it was decided that they would start in September.

Jane seemed very happy, there were other girls of a

similar age in the road. They seemed to feel sorry for Jane not having a Father. She had made new friends but Bobby did not want to meet with anybody. He spent the next two month in his bedroom or in the sitting room reading. Fortunately the library was very close so Bobby had an endless supply of books. He had never read so much in his life, thrillers, history, life story's, but best of all he liked the "Just William" books, he read the whole series. William was a renegade, single minded, he knew what he wanted. Bobby decided that that was what he needed to be. He was almost nine years old but felt that he was on his own and whatever happened in his life was up to him.

CHAPTER 5

B obby stared his new school in September 1959. He was in Mrs. Jackson's class. She introduced him to the class but said nothing about his Dad. Maybe she knew, maybe she didn't. Jane also started at the school but in the two months that they had been in Ilford she had really annoyed Bobby. She seemed to thrive on the fact that her Dad was 'dead', saying that she was a half- orphan. Sometimes Bobby could have hit her. He told his mum what she was doing and was told that she was very young and it was her way of dealing with it. Bobby's way of dealing with Jane was to ignore her. Bobby' class mates seemed friendly enough. At morning playtime while they drank their milk they asked him questions about himself. He told then that he liked football and was a West Ham supporter as most of them were but was very careful not to say much because he did not want to get into a conversation about his Dad. He had not told anybody that his Dad was dead like both his Mum and sister had. Bobby felt bad about actually saying it, it seemed like somehow he was letting his Dad down and what would happen when he came out of jail.

The lessons at the new school were more interesting than at St Anthony's. Bobby found the geography lessons to be very interesting and also the arithmetic lessons were harder but better. During the second week Bobby went to the library on his way home and got out geography books so that he could learn more about what they were talking about in the lesson. The lady in the library remembered him now and was very impressed when he asked for the geography section. He also asked about books on arithmetic but she told him that they had none in the children's section and those in the adult section would be much too hard for him.

Bobby thought that reading about other countries and what they did and how they lived was brilliant. He told his Mum that one day he was going to visit lots of different countries but she told him that you needed to be very rich to go abroad.

"Then I will be very rich" he said, " 'cos I'm going".

At St Peter and Paul's, pupils came from all over Ilford and as far away as Gants Hill and Goodmayes. There was nobody living near Bobby to play with after school. Bobby didn't mind that, he just wanted to be on his own and read. If friends meant what happened in Forest Gate then he didn't want them. Apart from at school the only time that he saw any of the other boys was at mass on Sundays. They would say hello after mass but then would all go on their separate ways. Some of the parents had cars, some of those who walked to church would go for a coffee or an ice cream at Rossi's café just past the Regal cinema in the High Road. Bobby never asked to go as he did not think that Mum would be able to afford it.

At the end of the school year in July 1960, Bobby's school report was excellent. The headmaster Mr. Murphy's comment was "as you will see from his class teacher comments Bobby has settled in very well and is an exemplary pupil. We are all very hopeful that Bobby will pass his 11 plus". Bobby's Mum was very happy although she had been getting a bit concerned about the amount of time that he was spending in the bedroom on his own. At the parents evening at school the teacher had said how well Bobby was doing and how well behaved he was but also mentioned that he had not made any close friends but was friendly with everyone.

On the last day of term Bobby turned into his street after school and noticed a large car outside of his house.

"Blimey, that's a Jag" he said to himself and ran to his house and in the front door. He just knew it had to be something to do with his Dad.

"I've got a surprise for you Bobby" said his Mum. Bobby saw a man in the living room as he walked in. He was very tall, with broad shoulders and thick black hair that sort of curled on top. The man was plugging in a television. A few of the boys at school had one but Bobby had never actually seen one working.

"This is Mr. Constantine" said Mum. "He's a friend of mine……..and also Dads, and has organized for us to have this" pointing to the television.

"Wow! How does it work"? said Bobby.

"Here, I'll show you" said Mr. Constantine. "Here is a switch to turn it on or off and here is a tuning knob. You turn this to get the programme. Look, this is BBC, and this is ITV. You can get both channels. I have put an aerial on the roof so the picture should be good". Mr. Constantine had a funny accent. Bobby thought that he must be a foreigner but he thought it would be rude to ask.

"Great" said Bobby gazing open mouthed at Robin Hood on the screen.

"Just in time for your school holidays then" said Mr. Constantine.

"Yes" replied Bobby only half listening.

"What do you say Bobby"? said Mum.

"What?" said Bobby looking round at her.

"How about thank you to Mr. Constantine"

"Oh yes, thank you Mr. Constantine".

"That's alright" said Mr. Constantine as he walked from the room.

After Mr. Constantine had left Bobby told his Mum that he thought that Me Constantine had a funny voice.

"He's from Greece. He fought with the British Army during the war and when it finished he came and lived in England" said Mum.

"So he is foreign then, I thought so" said Bobby proudly.

The six weeks school holidays were a bit of a drag. Fortunately Jane had plenty of friends living nearby so she was almost always out. Bobby now hated his sister and wanted nothing to do with her. He completely ignored her even if they were having a meal together. He could not understand how she had forgotten their father so easily. Mum had spoken to him about it. He had explained how he felt and Mum, although she seemed a bit surprised about what he had said, didn't mention it again and seemed to accept the situation. Jane didn't even seem to notice, she was so wrapped up in her own world.

Bobby spent his holidays reading and watching television when it started in the afternoons. There were some lunchtime programmers, Rag Tag and Bobtail, The Woodentops and other, but these were for kids. He got a book from the library about Greece and found out about the country Mr. Constantine had come from. He asked the lady at the library for books about Greece in the war but she said that they were for adults only.

CHAPTER 5

Back at school in September the class was being prepared for the 11 plus examinations. All the teachers and the priests who came into the classes from the church next door, and all of the parents kept saying how important it was to pass and to go to grammar school. The children were told to pray at mass on Sundays to ask God to help them pass. Bobby prayed and asked God to help him pass but he also asked God to send his Dad home. Bobby sometimes wondered if anybody else ever thought about his dad.

A new school lesson was added this year, swimming. Once a week, on a Wednesday morning, the class would line up and march in two's along Ilford High Road to Ilford Baths. The Baths had two pools, the biggest, known as the first class pool, closed in the winter and only the smaller second class pool stayed open but in September the first class pool was still open. The class split into three groups, the non-swimmers, those who could swim a width and those that could swim a length. Bobby had never been swimming before so he joined the non-swimmers. He was given a float, a rectangular piece of polystyrene, and he and all of the others in his group got into the pool and lined up about six feet from the pool side. They were told to hold the floats out in front of them and kick their feet and swim to the edge. Bobby found it very easy. They did it about six times and then the instructor asked if anybody would like to try and swim the six feet without the float. Bobby put up his arm and easily swam to the side of the pool.

"Very good, now move back a bit further and swim to the side" said the instructor. Bobby did this and then repeated it from about twelve feet away. He splashed a bit but made the side.

"Maybe next week you should try for the width, you seem a natural" said the instructor.

The following week Bobby tried the width swim but could not get across without putting his feet down but the week after that he tried again and made it across. He got a little yellow strip to sew onto his swimming trunks. One month later he swam a length and got a red strip for his costume and within three months he swam one hundred yards and got a white strip. By Christmas he was the best swimmer in the school, and he loved it.

The term passed quickly. Mum worked at home all the time now, she didn't go out to visit companies. She had turned a corner of the living room into a little office. Other than Mr. Constantine she didn't seem to have any friends. Mr. Constantine came round sometimes to check that the television was working and he would usually bring them all some fruit. Gran would visit us about every two weeks but it was not the same as when she had lived upstairs. She asked things like how was school, what were we doing, but we didn't really have much to say. She would watch Whirlybirds on the television, she liked the stories about the helicopter pilots.

Mum said that Gran was coming for Christmas and would stay for a few days. Bobby was pleased about that. He decided that he needed some money for presents for Mum and Gran (Jane could go without). Just before the end of term

Bobby mentioned this to Mr. Constantine who had come to the house again to check on the TV (as they now called the television).

"I'll tell you what Bobby, you are tall for your age, could you reach the roof of a car?"

"I would think so, why?

"I have a car sales pitch in Manor Park, right on the High Road. I need someone to keep the cars clean. Nobody will buy a dirty car. Come to my car showroom and I will give you two shillings for every car you clean. They must be done right though. I'll clear it with your Mother if you like."

"Yes please" said Bobby.

It was a long walk from Ilford to Manor park for a ten year old but the following Saturday Bobby walked there and started to clean the cars. Along Manor Park High Road many of the shops had been turned into second hand car showrooms and Mr. Constantine owned four of these shops together.

Bobby walked into the shop that said 'Sid's Car Sales' which Mr. Constantine had told him was his. Inside the shop was standing a huge man. Mr. Constantine was big but this man was huge, huge body, huge hands, and huge head.

"Whadder yer want" the huge head said.

"I've come to see Mr. Constantine" said Bobby.

"That's OK Stavros" said Mr. Constantine as he came out of an office at the back of the showroom.

"Bobby, this is my driver, Stavros, he's in charge if I am not here. Stavros, this is Bobby, he is going to clean some cars for us" Stavros looked at Bobby but said nothing. Bobby couldn't understand why Mr. Constantine needed a driver, he could drive himself, and he always did when he visited Mum. There was another man there, a short man with ginger hair and a funny smile. He had on a creased brown suit, a beige shirt and brown stripped tie. Bobby realized that

Mr. Constantine always looked smart and as big as he was, Stavros had a nice suit and shirt on too. This man was a bit scruffy Bobby thought. But he had a big smile and a real cockney accent.

"This is Colin, he's here to talk to the customers". Mr. Constantine introduced Bobby to Colin and told him that Bobby was to clean cars. As tall as he was Bobby did have a bit of a problem reaching the roofs but he quickly worked out that if he did the roof last, he could turn the bucket upside down and stand on it and if he left the rag very wet there was enough water in it to wash the roof. Mr. Constantine had twenty cars in his shops. After doing three of them Mr. Constantine brought Bobby out some orange juice from his office at the back of the lot.

"That's great Bobby, that's six shillings I owe you".

"I haven't' finished yet. I need a pound by Christmas so I need to do five today and five next week, there's only two Saturdays left before Christmas".

"I just thought that you were tired and had had enough. I thought that you would want to go home for your lunch".

"I will go home when I am finished", said Bobby moving to the next car, a big Austin Westminster.

When Bobby had finished five cars he took the bucket and cloth into Mr. Constantine's office.

"That's five car's I've done, five more next week and that will be a pound, I will be owed".

"I'll give you your ten bob now."

"No, keep it and give me the whole pound next week please."

"OK Bobby, if that's what you want. I'll get Stavros to drive you home. See you next week then".

Stavros appeared at the door and Bobby followed him to the Jag parked in the road. Bobby was pleased of the lift because he was tired after cleaning the cars but anyway he wasn't going to turn down a lift in a Jaguar. He hoped that somebody he knew would see him.

The next Saturday Bobby was back at the car showroom cleaning another five cars and walked out with a one pound note in his pocket.

On Christmas Eve he went to British Home Stores in Ilford and brought two large boxes of chocolates, one for Mum and one for Gran. They were eight and eleven pence each so he still had more than two shillings left. He decided while walking home that he would save that money. He had never had any spare money in his life and he had realized how important it was to have some put aside. He decided on that walk home that he would never again not have money somewhere.

He got home and hid the chocolates under his bed, he went downstairs just as Gran arrived, it was tea time and was looking forward to Christmas morning.

CHAPTER 6

Bobby was up early on Christmas morning but when he went into the kitchen he found that Gran was up even earlier. She was sitting at the kitchen table drinking a cup tea having her first cigarette of the day. It wasn't that long ago since Gran had lived upstairs and Bobby had seen her every day. But now, for the first time, Bobby thought that she looked old. Her hair was more grey and thinner than he remembered and her shoulders were a bit more round. She seemed to take longer to get out of a chair and was generally slower.

"How are you Gran, it's great that you are here for Christmas".

"I'm fine, but how are you Bobby?

"I'm fine too".

"Are you now? Really? No problems at school, missing your Father? It was the first time that anybody had mentioned Bobby's father for ages.

"I do miss Dad, and talking about him. Mum and Jane tell everybody that he is dead. What's going to happen when he comes home? He has nobody, only us, Mum has you and us but Dads father is dead and his Mum lives in Ireland, maybe he will go and live there and I will never see him again".

"I'm sure that you'll see him again Bobby. I know your Dad well, he's a good man, he would not leave you and Jane".

"Tell Mum that and ask he what she is going to do when Dad gets home, whenever that is". Bobby felt tears in his eyes as he heard his Mum come out of the lounge where she had been sleeping as Gran had slept in her bed. He quickly wiped his face with his sleeve and put on a big smile and said "Happy Christmas Mum".

"Happy Christmas to you too Bobby" she said as she went to the cooker to put the kettle on.

Then Jane arrived, all noisy and jumping up and down, "where are my presents then---where are my presents"? she shouted. Bobby couldn't stand her, she was so greedy, so selfish, he just got up and went into his bedroom to get dressed and think about what his Dad was doing on Christmas Day in prison. He came back into the kitchen when he was dressed with the two boxes of chocolates and gave them to Mum and Gran. They were very pleased and both gave him a big wet kiss to thank him. Jane asked where her present was but Bobby just ignored her which got a withering look from Gran.

"Come into the lounge children" said Mum, "let's see what Father Christmas has brought you".

Mum pointed to a big shape in the corner covered with Christmas paper, it was a bike. There was a note on it saying it was from Mum and Gran.

"Fantastic" said Bobby "I can join the swimming club now because I can get there on time. Thanks very much Mum and Gran, it's just.........brilliant" Bobby was stunned, he ripped off the paper, it was full size BSA, yellow and black.

Bobby was happier this Christmas than he had been for

ages. He liked Gran being there and his Mum seemed happier with her around too. Jane had shut up once she had got her new doll and dolls pram and had played with it quietly and away from Bobby. There has been some good programmes on the television including some very funny programmes on Christmas night that Bobby had been allowed to stay up late too watch. The only bad time was when Gran had tried to talk to him about his attitude to Jane. Bobby had dismissed it but Gran persisted saying that she was his sister and he should be good to 'family'.

"What, like she is to Dad? She tells everybody that he is dead and all of her friends feel sad for her. That's what family means to her. I read in a book from the library, what you sow you reap, that's what she is doing. Ignoring Dad, so I'm ignoring her".

"Sometimes Bobby you are a bit too old for your age" Gran said.

Christmas was over too quickly for Bobby and it was time to go back to school. Bobby wanted to ride his bike to school but was not allowed to. To cycle to school you needed to have your cycling proficiency badge so Bobby told his class teacher that he wanted to be tested for it and it was arranged for a Saturday morning in two weeks time.

When he came home after his third day back at school Bobby told Mum that he wanted to join Ilford Swimming Club. A boy in his class, Jim Robins went, it was on a Tuesday at 6 O'clock and cost two shillings a week.

"I don't want you to pay for it Mum, I will pay for it by working. I am going to see Mr. Constantine on Saturday and ask if I can clean cars every Saturday. That will get me plenty of money".

The next Saturday morning Bobby cycled to Mr. Constantine's car lot and it was agreed that he would clean cars for two shillings each.

"Thanks, but I'll be late next week 'cause I have to do my cycling proficiency test so I will come and maybe only do three".

"OK son" shouted Mr. Constantine to Bobby's disappearing back.

"I don't know why you are bothering with that boy" said Stavros.

"Just a feeling. I think he may be an investment for the future"

CHAPTER 7

Most of his life was great for Bobby. He had his bike to get around on. He had a job that made him ten shillings a week, far more than he could spend, he was swimming at Ilford Swimming Club on a Tuesday and the to top it all the lady in the library would let him look at some of the grown up reference books sometimes, like when he said he wanted to know how a car engine worked. He was doing well at school and never got into any trouble so apart from when he thought about his Dad, he was very happy.

A funny thing happened the first Saturday when Bobby had finished cleaning the cars. Mr. Constantine had been out all day, only Colin was there talking to customers and trying to sell the cars. Mr. Constantine had come into the shop at about 2 O'clock just before Bobby had finished the fifth car and gone into his office. When Bobby finished he went into Mr. Constantine's office and said "I'm off now, I've done five so that ten shillings you owe me"

Mr. Constantine reached for his wallet and took out a ten shillings note. "That's alright you can owe it to me and give me a pound next week"

Mr. Constantine stood up and said in a voice that sounded a bit cross "Son, I am going to give you a valuable lesson for life. If somebody offers you money – take it. Don't let then owe it to you. What would happen if I fell under a bus this week, I would be dead and you would never get your money? Take it now and put it in the post office or something"

Bobby went across the office and took the ten shilling note. "Thank you" he said, and left quickly.

That week he went into the post office in Ilford High Road and opened a post office account and deposited the ten shillings.

Bobby loved the swimming. After only four weeks he was moved up a group and asked if he wanted to go to the extra club swimming on a Saturday morning. He said he couldn't because he had to be in Manor Park by about 10 O'clock but was told that this was OK because the club had the pool at 6.30am. So on a Saturday Bobby went swimming before going to clean cars.

Easter holiday came and Bobby revised for his 11 plus exams. He actually found the work a bit boring so was also spending a lot of time reading books from the library. He had read all of the Famous Five and The Secret Seven books and at the suggestion of the lady in library was now reading science fiction books really meant for teenagers. He felt very grown up when he went in there now.

Back at school after Easter the final revision for the 11 plus was being done with the whole class doing previous exam papers to prepare.

The first exam day arrived. It was called a 'general paper'. You had to put in missing words and select shapes. Bobby found it fairly easy and when he got home that evening and Mum asked, he told her that he thought that he had done well.

Two days later was arithmetic. This was one of Bobby's favorite subjects. He looked at the paper and was pleased to see how easy it was. He finished it in about half the time than it should have taken. The teachers had always said that if you finished the paper early then you should check it, so Bobby checked it. It all looked fine to him so he got up to leave the hall. His class teacher Mrs. Brown was sitting at the door and she followed him out.

"What's the matter Bobby"?

"Nothing. I finished, I checked it and there was nothing else to do".

"If you are sure then that's alright. You can go home if you want to because there are no more lessons today".

Bobby ran to his bike and cycled home. He would be nearly an hour early; Mum will be surprised he thought. As he turned into Kingston Road he saw Mr. Constantine's Jaguar parked outside of the house. He opened the front door and immediately felt that there was something not right. He stood still and listened and then he heard a moaning sound. It was coming from his mother's bedroom. He walked as quietly as he could up to her bedroom and opened the door slowly. He peered around the door and saw Mr. Constantine with no clothes on, lying on top of his mother, pushing up and down and breathing heavily. The moans were from his Mum, he was hurting her! Bobby sprang across the room, launched himself onto the bed grabbing the man around the neck and pulling as hard as he could. It caught Mr. Constantine by surprise and I fell sideways as Bobby held on tighter.

"Bobby what are you doing" yelled Mum.

"Getting him off you, stopping him hurting you".

"He is not hurting me Bobby, go into the kitchen and put the kettle on, I will be there in a minute".

Bobby was very confused but went into the kitchen and did what his mother said. A minute later his mother came into the kitchen wearing her dressing gown.

"I saw him hurting you" said Bobby not knowing what else to say.

"This is difficult to explain Bobby because you are too young to understand but he was not hurting me. What we were doing is something adults do sometimes because they enjoy it. The sound that people make when they do it are actually because they enjoy it not because it hurts" Mum was right, he didn't understand at all. Just then Mr. Constantine's walked into the kitchen.

"Are you OK Ari"? Said Mum.

"I'm fine. You are a little tiger aren't you son, protecting your Mother like that. You are strong too for somebody so young. That may be useful when you get older".

Mum had called Mr. Constantine Ari. This was the first time he had ever heard him called by another name.

The next Saturday Bobby went to Manor Park to clean cars as usual and Colin was there. Mr. Constantine didn't usually come any more but Bobby hoped that he would this week as he wanted to talk to him about what had happened. Bobby was cleaning six cars now and was paid twelve shillings for his work. When he had finished Colin gave him his money and said goodbye.

"Colin, did you know that Mr. Constantine's name is Harry?"

"It's not Harry, its Ari without the 'H', short for Aristotle. But don't let him hear him call you that. Only his family and very close friends call him Ari."

"Do you call him Ari Colin?"

"Not on your life. He would sack me if I did. He's Mr. Constantine to me, we ain't friends".Bobby was cycling home thinking about what Colin had said. Mum must be a good friend of Mr. Constantine if she could call him Ari. He wondered whether he was a friend of his Dads as well, he thought he remembered his mum saying that he was.

CHAPTER 8

Bobby came in from school. "Mum, I passed my eleven plus, the teachers told us today. There are letters being sent out to tell parents what to do next. They will arrive in the next few days they said".

"That's great Bobby. Did you do well enough to go to St Ignatius? "

"I don't know, they didn't say. I suppose it will be in the letter".

"Well, well done anyway Bobby, it's very good that you are going to a grammar school. You are a clever lad and it will make a big difference to your future."

Three days later the letter arrived, address to Mrs. Parsons. It confirmed that Bobby had passed his eleven plus exam but had not gained sufficient marks to be offered a place at St Ignatius. The boys that passed their eleven plus at St Peter and Paul's had a choice of two schools to choose as a preference. St Ig's as it was known, was the better of the two and was located in Tottenham. They only took the top 10% of pass marks from many schools over the catchment area. Bobby was not in that 10%. Those who did not go to St Ig's from St Peter and Paul's went to St Bonaventure's. St Bonaventure's was located in St Anthony's Road, Forest Gate, right opposite the house that the family had moved from. When Bobby got home his mother gave him the news.

"That's OK" said Bobby, "it's easier to get to than St Igs and who wants to go to Tottenham anyway, Dad always said they had a useless football team".

"You don't understand Bobby, it's not the school, it's where it is". Suddenly it dawned on Bobby what she meant. All of the boys from his old school would be there and all of the pupils would know that his Dad was in prison and would bully him as they had started to do before they moved.

"What are we going to do?" said Bobby.

"Leave it to me, I will go to the school and see the Head and explain the situation and tell him why you cannot go to school in Forest Gate" Bobby went to his bedroom and while changing his clothes and thinking about what his Mum had said he started to get angry. He was sure that the school knew nothing about the situation with his father and felt as though it would have been different if his mother had been truthful.

A week later Bobby's Mum told him that she had seen Mr. Murphy, the head teacher and Canon O'Leary at the church but there was nothing they could do about the school. It appeared that the school had been aware of the situation, records had been sent from St Anthony's, and Mr. Murphy had spoken to the priest who dealt with admissions at St Ignatius but there was no flexibility in the rules. What was even more annoying was that Bobby had missed the top 10% by only two marks.

"What are we going to do now" said Bobby.

"Mr. Murphy said that you would be welcome at Canon Palmers."

"That's for people who failed the exam, it's a secondary modern, I don't want to go there".

"Leave it to me I will have a think about it and see what I can do".

School lessons now were a bit boring. Everybody had sat the exam, the results were out and everybody knew what school they were going to. Bobby didn't speak to anybody about his position. He would go swimming after school most afternoons and then read well into the evening. He could now swim a mile and was considered to be one of the best under twelve's in the club.

One day in the middle of June Bobby came home from the pool to be greeted by an exited mother. "We have an interview for a school next Tuesday."

"What do you mean" said Bobby.

"There is a very good grammar school in Stepney called Reins. They will accept you provided both you and I pass an interview. We are seeing them next Tuesday. We have to be there at ten. Best shirt and trousers my boy". Mum seemed really excited about it.

Tuesday arrived and Bobby and his Mum got the 25 bus from Ilford Broadway to outside Stepney Green Station and then walked the short distance to the school. "One thing Bobby, I know that you don't like it but we have to say that your Father is dead if we are asked. I know that you don't want to lie but if they think he is in prison they may hold that against you".

Bobby nodded.

There were six boys for interviews that morning. The parents were sat in a large hall and 3 of the older boys in the school, prefects they called themselves, collect the six boys and took them on a tour of the school. Bobby was amazed. It was so big with so many rooms and the subjects that they taught were so different. They had laboratories for science and rooms for art and geography and history. Bobby definitely wanted to go to school here. When he returned to the hall his mother was still sitting there.

"Mum, this is brilliant. There are all of these different rooms you go to, not one room like at school now. I want to come here". His mother explained that she had had one interview already. That there were three men, the head teacher and two governors, who asked questions. She told Bobby that she had told them about him and agreed to ensure that he came to school on time and would respect the school rules.

Soon it was Bobby's turn. He felt very nervous when he went into the room despite that fact that his mother was with him. The three men looked very serious and the one in the middle had a black cloak thing on. They asked him questions like, did he like school, what did he do in his free time, did he read a daily newspaper, how many days had he been away from school sick, to all of which Bobby gave short quick answers. They then asked what he had thought of the school when he had been taken around it by the prefect. Bobby couldn't stop talking about it, how he thought it was brilliant, how he loved the library, the laboratories and all of the different rooms, he was so enthusiastic that the two men sitting on either side of the man with the cloak started to smile.

Bobby was still talking when the man in the middle said "thank you Mr. Parsons, I think that will be enough. We have got the essence of your opinion of the facilities we offer". Bobby didn't understand what he was saying, he thought it sounded very posh. "We will advise you in writing within the next three days if your application has been successful".

"Do you think that they will let me in?" said Bobby as they left the school and walked to the bus stop.

"I don't know" said Mum, "but I don't think that you could have done any better.

Three days later the letter arrived offering Bobby a place at Reins from September 1962.

CHAPTER 9

Bobby couldn't wait for the school holidays to be over so that he could start his new school. He has been out with Mum and Gran to a clothes shop in Mile End to get a school blazer, cap and tie. They had got him two new pairs of grey trousers, two new white shirts in the new drip dry poplin material, new black lace up shoes, white shorts and T shirt for PT and blue shorts and a red shirt and socks for football. He also had a new pair of football boots and white plimsoles which he was told were birthday presents, his birthday was on 1st September, the week before he would start school. Gran brought him a satchel for his birthday, she said that at his new school he would have to carry books home with him.

Apart from cleaning cars on a Saturday and swimming every day, he also went to the library every day as well. He had noticed that they had newspapers in there and if he was asked if he read a newspaper when he started school, he wanted to be able to say yes. However what started as something he thought he should do, soon became a pleasure. He loved to read all of the things that were going on in the world and although he didn't understand all of it he would make notes about the stories and then look things up, such as where Russia was, and Cuba and try and find out more about President Kennedy and what a teddy boy was and why they seemed to like to fight.

The day came and Bobby set off for school. He felt very grown up going on the bus all that way on his own. He arrived at school in plenty of time and walked through the gate into the playground. There were little groups of obviously new boys. The first year boys had to wear short trousers, after that is was optional so most of the others had long trousers on. The new boys stood around in little clusters saying hello but not really talking. Bobby walked up to one of the groups and said hello. About ten minutes passed when a teacher wearing a cloak walked into the playground and rang a bell shouting, "any first year boys starting today please follow me". Bobby and his little group followed the man though a door and up some stairs to the hall area that he had waited in for his interview. Names were called out and when it was their name they replied "yes sir". That pupil was then given a form number, Bobby's was form 1H. They were then told where to go to find their form rooms and sent off so the teacher could return to the playground to collect the next group of new boys to arrive.

Bobby and others entered the form room. "Good morning boys, find a desk and sit down please" said a teacher standing at the front of the classroom. "My name is Mr. Hughes, I am your form teacher, and hence you are in Form 1H, 1 for year 1 and H because that is my initial. That means that you should not get lost".

A few minutes later some more boys came into the room and Mr. Hughes said the same thing to them. "It looks like you are all here so I will call the register to check".

Everybody was there. Mr. Hughes then explained the form system of the school, the fact that they moved from room to room for some lessons but had some in the form room. He put the term timetable on the blackboard and made them all copy it out onto paper he gave them. He explained the school rules about wearing caps and ties and the standard of behavior that was expected outside of school as well as in it. Mr. Hughes was a French teacher so he told them that he would take them for French but not for any other subject but as form teacher he would deal with any problems they may have.

Break came and Bobby's head was spinning. He was please to get to the playground for some fresh air. "Hi what's your name?" asked the boy who had been sitting behind him.

"Bobby Parsons, what's yours?"

"Geoffrey Rosenberg. Where are you from?"

"Ilford. You?

"Stoke Newington."

"Where is that?"

"Near Tottenham, not far. Ilford is out to the east isn't it."

"Yes said Bobby, East London and keep going and you'll get there".

Reins wasn't a big school, only sixty boys in each year, but it seemed big to Bobby after his junior school. All of the boys seemed friendly and all asked the same sort of questions as Geoffrey had, trying to get to know their class mates. Bobby answered the questions but did volunteer any other information; he still remembered what had happened at St Anthony's. As a result Bobby was friendly with everyone and everyone was friendly with him but he was not part of any of the little groups that were formed. He enjoyed school very much and worked hard. He always did his homework on time and was above average in all of the lessons except French, he could not get to grips with that. On Tuesday afternoons his year group went to sport activity. The school had no playing fields of their own so the boys would go in two coaches to Dagenham, to Gorsebrook playing fields. Bobby hadn't played football since he had left Forest Gate and soon realized that he was not as good at it as he had thought. There were some very good footballers in his class, he was only average, but he nevertheless enjoyed his Tuesday football game.

His life fell into a routine, school all week with some homework in the evenings, swimming on Tuesday and Thursday evenings too, swimming on Saturday morning then cleaning six cars and going home to watch the football results on the television. On a Saturday evening he would sit in the kitchen and do homework. His Mum would watch TV but he didn't like the Billy Cotton Band Show or The Black and White Minstrels, he preferred the music on Radio Luxemburg and AFN. On Sunday the family would go to mass and then home for a roast dinner. Sometimes Gran would come for Sunday dinner, sometimes it was just Mum and Jane.

Christmas came and went, Mum bought him some clothes and Gran brought him a duffle bag for his swimming gear.

In January the school held trials for the swimming team at Mile End Baths. Bobby was the best swimmer in his year. He could swim faster and further than any of the others. All the boys at the trial were asked how far they could swim.

"I don't know" said Bobby when asked, "a mile? Two miles?

The coach told him he had better get into the pool and start swimming now then so that rest can catch up later. Bobby didn't realize that the coach was being sarcastic, not believing Bobby's claim to be true.

"Better stop now, don't want you wearing yourself out

before the time trials" said the coach after about three quarters of a mile.

"That's OK" said Bobby in a matter of fact voice "I'm not tired".

"OK then, six of you on the blocks, 100 yards. You up for that this soon Mr. Parsons?"

"Yes, fine." Bobby was 10 yards in front of the second place boy at the finish. From that point on the coach took him very seriously. The following week he trained with the school swimming team on Monday lunchtimes.

In May Bobby represented the school in the East London Schools Gala at Poplar Baths. He was entered in the relay and the 100 yards freestyle for under 13's. He won his freestyle heat easily. In the semi-final he had strong competition, but finished first in a new London Schools record. He came second in the finals, being beaten by only one tenth of a second, the winner breaking Bobby's new record. He was very disappointed until the coach pointed out to him that the winner was nearly 13 years old whereas Bobby was only 12.

"Next year, you see. You will win everything".

Summer came and the only real change was that instead of football, the Tuesday afternoon sport was cricket. Bobby had never played cricket before and could not believe that anybody could enjoy such a boring game. You either were sitting around waiting for a turn to bat, which never came because the other side had to have a turn, or when the other side was batting you stood miles away from the wicket in case a ball came in your direction. He had brought himself a watch and on Tuesday cricket practice it was looked at about every three minutes, willing the time to go faster.

His first year passed quickly. His end of term report was very good in all subjects. Only Mr. Hughes for French had a less than good comment "tries hard when in the mood, but has no natural aptitude for languages". The head teacher's comments were a bit more profound "Bobby is a pleasure to teach, always polite and attentive. However although he is friendly with all of his colleges he is developing tendencies of a loner, often preferring solitude to the company of others. This may cause social problems in later life".

CHAPTER 10

The summer holidays arrived. Most of the boys at school were going away on a holiday but Bobby knew that he wouldn't be, Mum couldn't afford it. He was surprised therefore when Mum announced that they were going to spend a week with Auntie Mavis in Suffolk. She had moved from Woodbridge to a small village called Alderton, which was near the coast. She had a much bigger house in the main street so Mum and Jane could share a room and Bobby slept on the settee, usually with the new pet Labrador, Flossie.

You could walk to the sea from the house or get a bus to Bawdsey Quay where the beach was sandy and you could sit and watch the small boats go up and down the river. There was a ferry across the river to Old Felixstowe and on the other side there was a café. Bobby, Jane and Mum went there twice for afternoon tea and a cake. Best of all though was that you could walk up the river bank and nobody else was along there.

Bobby enjoyed his week in Suffolk but at the end of it he was pleased to be going home. He missed the swimming pool, the library, his bike and his own room. Somebody had told him that there was an outside pool in a nearby park, Valentines Park. He wanted to check that out. When he got back, instead of car cleaning just on a Saturday morning Bobby would also clean on a Thursday, that meant he was doing twelve a week, one pound four shillings, a fortune to him. Almost all of the money went into his post office account although he did keep a bit back to spend on ice cream and pool admission fees.

Soon it was September, back to school and happily for Bobby, back to football on a Tuesday. He was now in 2B, his form master was Mr. Bruce who took them for English Literature. This was a subject that Bobby loved, they read 'proper books'. They started the term with The Rover by Joseph Conrad. Bobby had never read anything like this before and read it in a week. He didn't tell Mr. Bruce because it was supposed to last a term. He could not get into Shakespeare, their play for this year was Twelfth Night but surprising himself he did like The Poems of Walter De La Mere.

He was now borrowing books from the adult library in Ilford so looked for others by Conrad. The villages of Dorset in the books fascinated him, he put them down as another place he would visit when he was older.

His second year at Grammar School seemed to fly by. He liked most of his lessons, was popular with the teachers and his peers, although still he had no close friends. He liked football but hated cricket but it was in the swimming pool that he excelled. His coach at Ilford swimming club had been teaching him the butterfly stroke. He was told that it was a very tiring stoke but Bobby had developed strong, broad shoulders and upper arms as well as toned stomach muscles as a result of years of regular swimming. With his physic he did not find the new stroke a problem. He was also excellent at breaststroke and backstroke as well as crawl.

In the East London school gala that year he won the under thirteen individual medley, helped the team win the relay coming from third to first place on his leg, he won the 100 yards freestyle and came second in the 400 metres freestyle. His success made him a cult hero at school.

July came around again and Bobby wondered if his mother had arranged a holiday in Suffolk again. He did not see Mr. Constantine very much these days but he felt that he still visited his home. He could faintly smell cigar smoke sometimes and only Mr. Constantine smoked cigars that he knew. Some of the boys at school talked about sex. Bobby didn't say anything but he thought back to the time that he found his Mother and Mr. Constantine in bed and thought that sex was what they had been doing. He wondered if they still did it when he wasn't there.

Term ended and Bobby arrived home with all of his books and lots of work to do during the holidays.

"Hello Bobby" his Mum called out as he closed the front door. "Come into the kitchen I want to talk to you, I've got some news for you"

"Is it about Dad?"

"Dads dead" chipped in Jane.

"Shut up!" shouted Bobby.

"Bobby, don't talk to Jane like that. No, its not about your Dad. We are going to move next week"

"Moving? I don't want to move" Bobby was appalled. Apart from the problem with his Father Bobby was perfectly happy.

"What about school, what about swimming, what about my car cleaning?"

"We're not moving far, only to Seven Kings. It will be better for you. It's nearer the swimming pool, and it's near to the station so you can go to school by train instead of by bus, it will be quicker. Don't worry it will be fine."

"Why do we have to move?"

"It's a much bigger house, with three big bedrooms, a

lounge, a dining room a big kitchen and a nice garden. It will be much better for us, more room, and nicer area".

"OK" Bobby could think of nothing else to say.

Two weeks later a lorry arrived at the flat and three men loaded all of the furniture, clothes and Bobby's bike into it. Just as the loading was being completed Mr. Constantine arrived. Bobby hadn't seen him for at least two months and was surprised to see him there now.

"Hello Mr. Constantine, we are moving today" said Bobby.

"Yes I know, it's a nice house that you are moving to. I've come to drive you there and make sure that my men look after your furniture"

"Your men?"

"Yes, this removal company is one of my businesses so I am helping your Mother". Bobby thought that was nice of Mr. Constantine.

With the furniture in the lorry, Bobby, Jane and his mother left the house. His mother locked the front door and gave the key to Mr. Constantine. "Into the car then" said Mr. Constantine "Bobby you are the man, you sit in the front." Bobby felt good at that remark and walked to the car. As he approached he noticed that it was not the Jag but a shiny black Mercedes Benz.

"Is this a new car Mr. Constantine? said Bobby.

"Yes it is, do you like it?" he said as Bobby climbed in the front seat.

"Its very nice, one day I will have a car like this."

"I rather think that you might young Bobby" said Mr. Constantine thoughtfully.

The new house was in Cambridge Road. Bobby did have a much bigger room and there was room for a desk as well as his bed and wardrobe. The lounge was bigger and the table could go into a dining room. The kitchen too was much bigger, Mum had been right. It was a much bigger and nicer house.

After a couple of days Bobby had his bedroom organized. He had taken some money from his post office account and bought a desk from a second hand shop in Seven Kings High Road. Mr. Constantine had somehow found out about it and organized collecting it from the shop and getting two men to put it upstairs in his bedroom. He had walked to the station and found that it only took five minutes. There was a library not too far away and Ilford swimming pool was nearer his new home that his old, once again Mum had been right. The only problem was the car cleaning, Manor Park was probably too far to go from home now. A few days later Mr. Constantine visited to see if they were settling in Bobby explained the problem.

"That's no problem at all Bobby. If you want to carry on cleaning cars I own a car lot here in Seven Kings High Road. If you go to the top of the road and turn left as though you were going to the library, on the right hand side is a big pub called The Seven Kings Hotel. Just before it is Ace Cars. That's mine. You can work there if you like".

"That's perfect" said Bobby.

"Good. The man to see when you arrive is called Martin. I will tell him to expect you next Saturday then". So Bobby resumed his routine life in Seven Kings. He thought that he hoped that his Dad would know where to find them when he came out of prison.

CHAPTER 11

Bobby and Jane were having tea one evening towards the end of August when Mum said "Gran's coming to stay next week to look after you". For some reason Bobby felt alarmed.

"Why, where are you going"?

"Mr. Constantine has to go away and do some business. He needs some help so has asked me to go with him. I will be going on Monday morning and will be home by lunchtime on Saturday. It will be nice to have Gran here, she will enjoy that. It means that I won't be here for your birthday Bobby but Gran is going to bake you a cake". Bobby felt reassured; Mr. Constantine would look after Mum.

Gran arrived on the Sunday and Mum left on the Monday. Since the move Jane had spent more time in the house. She had had lots of Friends who lived nearby in Kingston Road but there didn't seem to be anybody of her age nearby in Cambridge Road. Gran seemed to feel sorry for her and Jane played on this and kept on to Gran to do things with her. This was really annoying Bobby so he made sure he spent as much time as possible out. He spent a lot of time in the library. One day he was in there looking at an encyclopedia, looking up 'Shakespeare' when he noticed the word 'sex' in the index. He wanted to know what the boys at school were talking about and what he suspected Mum and Mr. Constantine had been doing that afternoon two years ago, so he turned to that section. He read the whole chapter about sperms and eggs and how it was the way that babies were created.

"Were mum and Mr. Constantine trying to make a baby?" Bobby said to himself. "I don't want another sister". Bobby wanted to talk about it to someone, but whom? He was rather disgusted with the thought of somebody putting their willie, which he had read was called a penis, into the front of a girls bum. He couldn't think why adults wanted to do it because it was nice, that is what his mum had told him. Bobby decided that he couldn't talk to anybody about it, he would have to wait until he could read some more about it another time.

Mum was home when Bobby came arrived from car cleaning the next Saturday. For some reason Bobby was relieved and was pleased to see his mother. She was pleased to see him too and she and Gran had prepared a lovely dinner of chicken, roast potatoes and vegetables with ice cream for pudding. Mum looked great. Bobby noticed that she had some new clothes on and her hair was different than usual.

Dinner was a success, everybody seemed to be happy. Bobby even sat in the lounge with Mum, Gran and Jane and watched the Morecombe and Wise Show, something he would not normally do. Actually he found it very funny and thought that he would probably watch it again next week.

Jane went to bed at eight thirty; Bobby being older was allowed to stay up until nine thirty on Saturday's. Just as he was going from the room to go to bed he turned at the door, "are you going to have another baby Mum?"

"No of course not. Why do you ask?"

"Nothing I just wondered" he said as he left the room.

"You need to talk to that boy" Gran said to his mother after he was gone. "He spends too much time on his own thinking, he still misses his father and he reads too much. He is now 13 years old and maturing. Behind it all he is insecure. You need to sit down with him and talk to him about his problems and about growing up".

CHAPTER 12

Bobby was pleased when it was time to go back to school a few days later. He went by train and although he had to change trains twice, at Stratford and again at Mile End, it was quicker that going by bus. He enjoyed it more too. There were other boys from Reins on the trains as well as others from a school in Whitechapel, Davenant Foundation. There were girls too from Coburn in Mile End and on the way home girls from the Ursuline Convent in Forest Gate got on the train, some of whom had gone to St Peter and Paul's. Bobby noticed that some of the girls had breasts but he was careful not to stare.

He was in form 3R, Mr. Rosen who taught him physics, was the form teacher for this year. Mr. Rosen told the form that this third year was very important because at the end of it all pupils would need to decide which subjects they were going to take at GCE reducing the current 15 subjects to between 8 to 10.

On the third day back at school Mr. Rosen brought a new boy into the form and introduced him as Nicolas Mead. Nicolas had just moved back to the South of England was starting today. He placed him in the desk next to Bobby.

"Can you please take Nicholas under your wing Bobby

and show him how things are done please. You can guide him with travel as well please, he lives near you in the East." Nicholas sat down, nodding to Bobby while registration was called.

The first lesson was history which the boys stayed in the form room for. The history teacher Mr. Harris entered and said "I hear we have a new boy today, Mr. Mead please raise your hand". Nicholas put his hand up so that Mr. Harris could identify him.

"Goodness me, who put you two boys together, you could be twins." Bobby looked again at Nicholas and realized that they did indeed look very similar. Both were tall, both had thick black hair, both had deep brown eyes and the same shape of head and face. Bobby was much broader shouldered and had thicker arms and legs but at first glance he could see what Mr. Harris meant.

At break Bobby led the way to the playground. "Call me Nick, only my mother calls me Nicholas."

"Everybody calls me Bobby but - Hi Nick. I'll show you where the toilets are and if you follow me after the break I will take you do the chemistry lab, that's our next lesson".

During the lunch break Nick told Bobby that he and his mother had just moved to Ilford. Nick had been born in Stevenage where his father had worked for a company making computers, ICL. Nick explained that his father had died earlier this year so his mother had decided to move to Ilford because that is where her sister had lived and she had liked the area. Bobby listened and was pleased that Nick did not ask him about his situation. Bobby did say that he had lived in Ilford until recently but now lived in Seven Kings. He said that he would travel home with Nick as far as Ilford.

Bobby had never heard of computers but Nick made them sound interesting. Bobby decided that he should find out more during one of his trips to the library.

Over the next few months Bobby and Nick became very good friends. Both were quiet and studious and similar in character. Nick was not a good swimmer but joined Ilford swimming club. The two boys chatted about their lives, school, interests and families. Bobby admitted to Nick that his father was in prison. Nick was flattered when Bobby told him that he was the only person that he had ever told. They talked about girls, especially those that they saw most days on the train home. On one of the journeys home Nick told Bobby that he seemed naive about them.

"What do you mean?" said Bobby.

"Bobby, they all look at you. They all think that you are good looking and fancy you. You look a lot older than you are, probably about sixteen and they stand there hoping that you will chat them up"

"If they fancy me they must fancy you as well. Everybody says we look so a like".

"Maybe we do a bit but you are more filled out than me and look older".

Bobby looked around the carriage as they left Forest Gate and the convent girls had got onto the train. As he caught some of their eyes it seemed that maybe Nick was right, the girls did smile at him.

CHAPTER 13

It was a Saturday in November and Bobby had left the swimming pool, gone home for a quick bacon and egg sandwich and then cycled to the car lot to start cleaning the cars. He noticed Mr. Constantine's Mercedes parked in the front of the lot. This was unusual, he hadn't seen him for months. "Hello Bobby. How are you?"

"Fine thank you Mr. Constantine".

"Get in the car, I've got something to show you".

Mr. Constantine drove towards Ilford, turning left off of the High Road and then right into Kingston Road. "Where are we going, this is where I used to live?"

"It's a surprise, just a couple of more minutes". The car stopped outside of his old house. Bobby followed Mr. Constantine up the path and into the hall of the flat.

"Go into the lounge Bobby" Mr. Constantine said. Bobby was really confused but did what he was told, he walked into the lounge and there, standing in the middle of the floor, was his Father.

"Dad" was all Bobby could say as he rushed up to him and hugged him as hard as he could.

"I'll leave you two alone. I'll be back in a couple of hours to take you back to the lot Bobby".

Bobby was overcome, he couldn't speak for several minutes. Finally they broke apart. "I thought you would be in prison for seven years, it's not been that long."

"No, I have served more than half of my sentence so I am on what is called parole, which means that I have been let out early but have to obey certain rules and report to the local police station each week".

"That's great. Are you coming back to live with us?

"No Bobby, that is not possible. Your mother needed to move on after the trial so she divorced me, we are no longer married". This was a bombshell to Bobby. He had always assumed that they would all live together again when his father was released. Bobby and his father then sat and talked for two hours. Bobby told him about school and swimming and cleaning Mr. Constantine's cars to earn money. His father would not talk about his time in prison but told him that he had been visited by Mr. Constantine when he was first arrested and the whole story about how the situation had arisen. Before telling him though he made Bobby promise never to tell anybody what had happened. Bobby promised.

CHAPTER 14

While Robert had been awaiting trial Mr. Constantine had visited him. He had told him that the reason that Mr. Wilkinson had stolen the money was because he owed it to Mr. Constantine. He had many legitimate businesses but he also arranged some poker games where the players would gamble large sums of money and he also had a bookie business betting on horse and dog racing. Both these were illegal. Mr. Wilkinson had bet on horses and lost and had then played poker to try and win the money back but had lost again. The money he had lost he had borrowed from Mr. Constantine. He had owed him more than £15000. Roberts's solicitor had already told him that his case was weak and Mr. Constantine offered to pay the legal bill for Robert is he did not say anything about the gambling to the police. In return he would also make sure that Roberts's family were looked after while he was in jail and find him a job when he got out. "Mr. Constantine owns this house, that is why he was able to let you move so quickly".

"Are you going to live here now?"

"For the time being. I have got a job serving petrol at a garage that Mr. Constantine owns, Greens Service Station in East Ham, on the Barking Road. I'm working the night shift so it is convenient to live here and Mr. Constantine is charging me a good rent". Too soon it seemed Mr. Constantine returned to take Bobby back to the car lot.

"Can I come and see you soon Dad?" said Bobby as he was leaving.

"You can come and see me whenever you want to Bobby. Just remember that I am working nights, I will get home at about half past seven, have some breakfast and then go to bed, so afternoons would be better than mornings".

Bobby was very quiet back in the car. This was a big change in his life and he needed to think about what was happening.

"Thank you for looking after my Dad" said Bobby. "Maybe one day I can pay you back". Ari Constantine looked at him, smiled and said nothing.

CHAPTER 15

Bobby only managed to clean three cars that day but he didn't care. He was quiet when he got home going to his bedroom and lying on his bed thinking until his mother called him down for tea. As Bobby, Jane and their Mother ate baked beans on toast Bobby quietly said "I saw Dad today; he's living in our old house in Ilford".

"Don't tell lies" said Jane, "He's dead". Without any warning Bobby's right arm shot out and his fist caught his sister on the side of her head knocking her off the chair and across the floor. It was the first time in that Bobby had ever hit anybody apart from the scuffle in the school playground shortly before he left St. Antonys'.

"Bobby" yelled his mother standing up so quickly that he chair fell over behind her. "Go to your room". Bobby stood up and turned to leave. "He's not dead and he's living in Ilford and I am going to see him again and tell everybody the truth". As he left the room he heard Jane start to cry. He knew that he should not have hit her but for some reason he felt pleased that he had hurt her. Somehow it seemed to be for his Dad.

About an hour later his mother came into his bedroom. "I'm not going to say sorry because I'm not" he said as she closed the door behind her.

"What you did was very wrong Bobby. I understand that you are upset but it can never be right to hit a woman".

"Maybe but she deserved it. She has always said that Dad was dead when we all knew that he was in prison."

"That was her way of dealing with it Bobby, we are all different".

"Well I think that she is wrong. Dad did nothing wrong, I know that. He is our father and until he was taken away was very good to us. By the way why didn't you tell me that you had divorced him? That's why he can't live here with us."

"It a difficult thing to discuss with you Bobby, maybe when you get older you will understand".

"I wish people would stop saying that, I understand plenty, and I am going to see Dad again and soon. Are you going to marry Mr. Constantine?"

"No Bobby" his mother answered after a pause, "I am not going to marry Mr. Constantine and you should see your Dad whenever you want, he is still your father". There seemed nothing else to say, his mother got up and walked to the door. Just as she was about to leave she turned towards Bobby, "I would be happy if you would apologise to Jane". Bobby just looked at her and she saw a determination on his face that she hadn't seen before and without him saying anything, she knew that he would never apologise for what he had done. Bobby didn't leave his bedroom that evening except to clean his teeth before he went to bed. Sleep was difficult. His mind kept thinking about what had happened that day. The next morning they went to mass as usual on a Sunday. Since moving to Seven Kings they went to St Teresa's church in Newbury Park. Bobby noticed a large bruise on the side of Jane's head and again he felt pleased that he had hurt her even though he felt guilty, not about hitting her but about being pleased about her pain; sadistic was a word that he had read about this sort of thing. He hated his sister. At mass Bobby prayed for his father and asked God to keep him safe and make him happy. The day passed with a strained atmosphere at home and Bobby was pleased to get to bed in the evening.

When he met Nick on the train on Monday morning he felt relieved and he was back in his routine again. He told Nick all about the weekend and meeting his father again. Nick seemed genuinely pleased for Bobby and asked could he meet his father. Bobby was delighted with his friend's reaction. He was the only person in the world who Bobby felt that he could talk to.

The following Sunday afternoon Bobby called at Nick's house and took him to meet his father. Robert was pleased to meet with Nick and also that Bobby had a friend to confide in whom he obviously trusted.

Bobby and Nick got closer over the following months. Nick told Bobby all about his father and that he died from a rare form of liver decease, Bobby explained to Nick how his sister had denied his father being alive and how his mother seemed to support her; Nick told Bobby how his mother had changed since his father had died and how she was always wanting to know what Nick was doing and where he was going and how much it was getting on his nerves.

Soon it was Christmas. Gran came again which somehow Bobby felt was a good thing. He had saved a lot of his earnings over the last year and had almost eighty pounds in his post office account. He was able to treat both his mother and Gran this year both brought them both an expensive scarf which he thought they would like. Both said that they were thrilled with them. For Nick he bought a dynamo light set for his bike. Nick liked cycling but always seemed to run out of batteries in the lights on his bike. His mother noticed that he had bought nothing for Jane.

Greens Service Station shut on Christmas Day. It was the

only day in the year that it did. As his Dad was not working he asked his mother could he come to Christmas dinner. His mother said no because she didn't think that Jane could deal with it. The thought of his father spending Christmas alone made Bobby more angry with Jane. He thought about it and told his mother that he was going to see his dad after lunch. Bobby was very surprised when his mother said she thought that was a very good idea and even more surprised when she offered to ask his father if he could stay the night "there are three bedrooms there you know, I am sure that he would like you to stay if you want to". "Yes please. That would be brilliant" Not only was Bobby surprised at the suggestion but it hadn't occurred to him that his mother and father spoke to each other.

Christmas afternoon arrived and Bobby cycled to his fathers. When he arrived he gave his father his present, an expensive bottle of whisky which Nicks mother had agreed to buy for him when he explained what it was for. Bobby and his father settled down for the afternoon and the time passed very quickly. Although they saw each other often they didn't have time for long chats, this was different. Bobby told his Dad all about school, he subjects that he liked and the ones that he didn't. He told him about his swimming and about Nick and his father dying. About how he travelled on the train and Nick saying that the girls were looking at him. His Father told Bobby about working at the garage and how much he hated prison although not actually what happened even though Bobby asked him. He told him how much he had missed Nick, his Mother and Jane while he was away and still missed them now.

"Bobby, I hear that you punched Jane a while ago and hurt her."

"She deserved it".

"Not really, but even if she did, you shouldn't hit girls".

"Maybe not normally, but she did deserve it".

"It should be me that is more upset than you Bobby. It's me she has shut out. To her I am dead" said Robert sadly.

Bobby felt so very sorry for his father. "Who told you, Mr. Constantine?"

"No Bobby, your Mother did, she keeps me informed about what is going on". Again Bobby was amazed that his mother and father would still talk about such things.

"I didn't know that you and Mum still spoke to each other".

"Of course we do. We were in love once, we grew up together, I have known her since she was five years old. We still have affection for each other and we still have you and Jane in common to consider".

"When do you talk to her? Neither of us has a phone although we are going to get one early next year, we are on the waiting list Mum says".

"She comes here to see me during the afternoon sometimes. I am usually up by two o'clock so she comes around for an hour or so after that". It never occurred to Bobby that his parents actually met.

"Do you go to bed with each other"? It was out of Bobby's mouth before he thought what he had said. His father looked him for what seemed like ages and then said calmly" Sometimes. Why do you ask"?

"Just wondered" said Bobby, wishing now that this conversation would end.

"Anything that you want to talk about?" said his father.

"Not really. Some of the guys at school say that that is how babies happen".

"Well that's true, if you let it, but that's not the only reason. Two adults making love is enjoyable if they have affection for each other and also adults have certain needs. You will understand when you get older"

"I wish people would stop saying that me" said Bobby wanting to change the subject. Suddenly Robert realised that it was eight o'clock. They had been sitting talking for four hours. Bobby realised that he was hungry so they went into the kitchen and made some sandwiches with ham that Robert has bought for tea.

The next morning they chatted again and Robert told Bobby that his nights at the garage were now going be regular. Up until now he had not known which nights he would work until the beginning of the week but now Mr. Green the manager had got somebody to work every Saturday night so Robert would always have that night off.

"Great that means that I can see you every week at a regular time".

They had another ham sandwich for lunch the next day and then Bobby left. The garage was open again today and Robert said that he wanted a rest before he went to work.

Bobby arrived home in a very happy mood and both his mother and Gran seemed pleased to see him and pleased that he had had a nice time. The next day he cycled to Nick's house and told him all about the time he spent with his dad. He felt sorry for Nick. He had had a nice Christmas with his mother but Bobby sensed that Nick missed his father more than he let on. Bobby knew what this felt like.

Before he went back to school Bobby visited the library one day. He went to the reference section and looked up 'computers'. He was very surprised that there we so many of them all over the world. They were used by governments, the American Army and many large companies. He read about IBM the big American producer that was much bigger than ICL who were the biggest producer in Britain. There was so much to read and so many book and magazine articles that he decided to come back to it later in the term.

CHAPTER 16

Christmas holidays over it was back to school. Nothing much changed but in Biology the subject dealt with 'human reproductive system'. Although it was all diagram's and scientific terms such as 'penis' and 'fallopian tube' Bobby could at least understand what was meant by sex, although the teacher didn't say anything about enjoyment as both his mother and father had said, and he didn't understand how it could be nice.

On the first weekend of the term he went to the car lot as usual. This Saturday he gave Martin a letter to pass to Mr. Constantine. He told Mr. Constantine that he wanted to stop cleaning cars on a Saturday. His father had the day off and he wanted to spend Saturday afternoons with him. He asked Mr. Constantine if that would be alright and when he could stop working.

The following Wednesday he arrived home from school as usual and saw Mr. Constantine's car outside of his house. He was in the kitchen with his mother having a cup of tea. "Hello lad. How are you? Haven't seen you in a while".

"I'm fine thank you. Did you get my letter?"

"Yes, Martin gave it to me today when I called into the lot. I think that it is a good idea that you should spend time with you father. Families are very important. I wish my father was still alive". This was the first time that Bobby had ever heard Mr. Constantine talk about any of his family.

"What did he die of?" he asked.

"It's a long story Bobby, one day I will tell you. It happened many years ago, in 1943 in Greece so it will wait a bit longer to be told". Bobby went upstairs to change from his school uniform. Something made him go to his mother's bedroom and peek in the door. The bed was not made, she always made it in the morning. He knew what Mr. Constantine had really come to the house for. He wondered how often he came when he was at school. Bobby went downstairs just as Mr. Constantine was leaving.

"Bobby. You will still need some money from time to time so I'll tell you what. You can clean cars during the school holiday if like. That way at least you will have some money for Christmas presents next year".

"Thank you" said Bobby. He hadn't really thought about money when he said he wanted to give up work. He had over forty pounds in his Post Office account but he knew that would not last him until next Christmas.

CHAPTER 17

Easter approached, Bobby had fallen into his routine, school, swimming two evenings a week, and homework. Sometimes there would be a gala on a Saturday and Bobby would be swimming in it. His Dad would always go and see him an often Nick would go too. Sometimes even Mrs. Mead would go with Nick. Bobby thought that it would be nice if his Dad and Mrs. Mead got together, they both seemed lonely. Bobby talked to Nick about this.

"Look Bobby, don't take this the wrong way but your Dad has been to prison. I know that he was innocent but I don't think that my mother would go with somebody who had been to prison" Bobby didn't say anything, he needed to think about what his friend had said.

During the Easter holidays Bobby and Nick went to the cinema. They went to see a James Bond film, Goldfinger. Nick had been to the cinema a few times before but only to children's films, Bobby had never been. Both of them thought it was terrific. They were actually too young to be allowed in but both of them looked much older so they did not have a problem. Although Bobby hadn't been to Upton Park to watch West Ham since his father had been imprisoned he always looked out for their results and read the match reports. They now had a very different team from the one he had seen and they seemed to be doing quite well. They had a new manager, Ron Greenwood, they were in a good position in the league, and doing well in the cup.

Back at school the pressure was on for the end of term exams. Again Mr. Rosen explained how important they were because of the selection of GCE subjects. "The subjects you take at GCE will shape your whole future" he would say every time he spoke to the class about them.

Lessons were interrupted by the East London Schools Gala at Poplar Baths. Bobby was again swimming in four races including the relay. He had gained a reputation among the swimming fraternity and was welcomed by the other competitors. The gala was held on a Wednesday evening and Bobby was over the moon when his father told him that he had got the evening off work so that he could watch him. His pleasure was even greater when his Mum said that she was coming too and that Mr. Constantine had lent his father a car so he was driving them all to Poplar.

"I didn't know that Dad could drive" said Bobby when his Mum told him of the plans.

"Neither did I Bobby, but he has been learning since he got out of prison so that he may have an opportunity of a better job." Robert drove them to Poplar picking up Nick from his home on the way.

Bobby won the under fifteen 400 metres freestyle, 100 metres butterfly, 4 x fifty metre individual medley and Reins won the 4 x one hundred relay with Bobby swimming the anchor leg. It was the schools most successful gala ever and Bobby's too. He told his parents on the way home that he had done it for them.

Bobby was congratulated by the headmaster at morning assembly the next day and was the hero in school all day too. Even the teachers he met said well done.

Going home on the train was getting more interesting especially when the convent girls got on the train at Forest Gate. Bobby and Nick had got friendly with some of the girls even finding out their names. They would board the train and talk to them about school that day and what subjects they had had. On Mondays they would talk about what they had done over the weekend and giggle whenever they spoke about boys. There were also a couple of boys who were at St Bonaventure's who Bobby knew from St Peter and Paul's.

CHAPTER 18

One afternoon Bobby and Nick were idly chatting when Nick said that he wanted to buy a new racing bike so would need to earn some money during the school summer holiday. This reminded Bobby that his savings were dwindling fast. He now only had less than £20 left in his post office account.

"I had a mate that was three years older than me and when he was our age he went pea picking. He earn't lots of money". Bobby found out that there was a farm on the Eastern Avenue, just past Whalebone Lane that employed pea pickers every year. It was hard work and you got paid for how much you picked. Bobby decided to give that a go when he broke up.

In the meantime it was exam time. After the physics exam, the class was leaving the physics lab after Mr. Rosen had collected in the papers. "I hope that you will be taking Physics as a GCE subject Mr. Parsons" said Mr. Rosen as Bobby passed him.

"I like physics Mr. Rosen so probably I will. Will we be doing anything to do with computers?"

"Computers? What do you know about computers?"

"Not much, but I have been reading about them and I

think that they are very interesting so would like to learn more".

"Mr. Parsons, I think that computers are our future. I think that in years to come computers will be involved in many of our lives. Regretfully we will not be learning about computers in Physics next year but I would be pleased to have some lessons after school with you and we can see what we can find out together."

"Nick may be interested as well Mr. Rosen. Did you know his Dad worked for ICL?"

"No I didn't. Maybe we will have an after school computer club. We will see".

Bobby's end of term exam results were excellent all except for French. Nicks too were very good and he got 93% in French, it was his best subject.

"We won't be together on that one will we" he said as they discussed their reports on the journey home. Bobby had told Nick about his conversation with Mr. Rosen and Nick was very interested in joining them. "My Dad always said computers were our future too. He said that in many years time computers would be much smaller and would be in factory's and be involved in production where the process was simple and repetitive".

Bobby had read that also being said by somebody from IBM. He was becoming even more interested in computers.

CHAPTER 19

The summer holiday came at last. On the first day Bobby got up early and cycled to where he thought the pea picking farm was. There was a man in the field checking the crop but no pickers. The man explained that the peas where not quite ready and needed another week. "Come back next Monday" he said.

The following Monday at 8 o'clock he was back and was surprised to see so many people there. Almost all of them were women and their children. They were already hard at work even this early. The foreman explained the procedure to Bobby, gave him a sack and said to fill it almost to the top. "Bring it back here, I weigh it and check that it is 56 pounds and for every sack you fill you get a token. At four O'clock the farmer comes and loads the sacks and he stays then until about 7 o'clock. Once he is here you can exchange the tokens for cash, five shillings each".

Bobby had filled four sacks by lunchtime and stopped for a sandwich and some orange squash that his mother had made for him. He sat some way from the group of other pickers but could still hear them. They were what his mother would call rough women, swearing at each other and the children.

After a short break Bobby started picking again. After a while he noticed a girl from the group had left them and was picking peas on the opposite side of the row to him.

"Hello" she said, "my name is Rose, what's yours?"

"Bobby".

"Bobby what?"

"Bobby Parsons".

"Where ya from".

"Seven Kings, you?"

"Deptford".

"Where's that?"

"Souf London. You're a bit posh to be doin' this aren't you?"

"I need the money."

"Oh, like us all luv. How old are you?"

"Sixteen" he lied. Everybody said he looked old for his age so now he would put it o the test.

"Thought so, same as me". She smiled at him and carried on picking. As she leaned over the plants Bobby could see the shape of her breasts. He realized that she had a thin v – necked t-shirt on and no bra. She looked up and smiled again. He quickly looked away, he felt himself blush and thought that she must know exactly what he was thinking.

At six o'clock the group from Deptford started to leave. There were three women, eight young children, two others who were about twelve or thirteen and Rose. They all travelled in an old van that had once been green but was now more rust coloured.

"Bye" shouted Rose, "see you tomorrow".

Bobby hoped that he would.

He prepared to leave when he had finished the sack, his back was hurting a bit and he felt very tired. His spirits were lifted however when the farmer said that he had picked nine sacks of peas, that was two pounds five shillings. Bobby had never earn't that much in his life.

He arrived home at half past seven, ate his dinner and went to bed. He set the alarm for six o'clock and then fell asleep almost immediately. He dreamt of Rose and her breasts.

The next day Bobby was picking at seven o'clock, just before the old van arrived. He was relieved to see Rose climb out of the back door, he realized that he had been holding his breath. She came straight over the row that he was picking. "Hello Posh Bobby" she said with a big smile as she started to pick on the opposite side of the row to him. She was a very fast picker, which made Bobby pick faster too. He didn't want Rose to think that he couldn't keep up.

Lunchtime arrived and Bobby went to sit on the opposite side of the field to Rose's group. She came and sat with him. "What do you do then, still at school?" she said.

"Yes, You?"

"I left a year ago. Worked a bit in Woolworth's, did a bit in a pub although I'm not really old enough, but we'll work the farms in the summer, better money". Bobby was looking at Rose as she spoke. He thought she was beautiful. She had long dark hair, bright blue eyes, lovely white teeth and her breasts, they were so gorgeous he could hardly take his eyes off them. She was wearing a short cotton skirt and another v-necked t-shirt on today. She finished her sandwich and lay down. Her breasts seemed even larger to Bobby. He felt his willie start to grow and get hard, he couldn't stop it.

"Well, that's being a bit naughty isn't it" said Rose laughing. She put her hand over his erection. "We'll have to try and think of a cure for that" she said as she took her hand away and got up to go back to work.

"Sorry" Bobby mumbled as he followed her to the peas.

"Whadya sorry for yer fool, its only natural" she said

with a voice that Bobby thought was wonderful. They picked all afternoon and at six o'clock Rose left. Bobby finished the sack he was working on and went to get his money. "Twelve sacks today young man, that's three quid".

Bobby cycled home feeling rich and happy. This is what being in love must be like he thought.

The next day, Wednesday, he was back at the field at seven o'clock again and as yesterday Rose and her group arrived shortly after. She came over to his part of the field and they picked again from either side of the row. As lunchtime approached Bobby started to think about what had happened yesterday as hoped that he would not embarrass himself again. When they stopped Rose went with him to a corner of the field away from her group. They ate their sandwiches and when she had finished Rose lay on the ground. "Do you like my tits"? she said. Bobby was astounded, he had heard the word tits before from the older boys but never from a girl.

"They're gorgeous" he said before he could help himself.

"Why don't you touch them then? said Rose.

Bobby felt as though he was dreaming. He leant across and put his hand on her t-shirt. She quickly took his hand off and placed it under her t-shirt directly onto the breast. Bobby felt his willie grow enormous.

Rose looked him, "he's getting playful again" said rose touching the bulge in his jeans.

Before he could answer she had undone the button and slid down the zip of his flies. She put her hand inside his underpants directly upon his willie. He felt sort of dizzy and came immediately in her hand. He had never experienced anything in his life like this.

"Well that didn't last long " said Rose as she sat up and wiped her hand on the grass." You need a bit more experience". She smiled at him, pulled her t-shirt down and got up to go back to work.

"Sorry" said Bobby as he got back to join her.

"Stop apologizing. Its natural what happened. You must have led a sheltered life. You ever had a girl?"

"No, not yet, too busy working".

"You should never be too busy for a girl. If you had a regular girl, work would be more fun".

The end of the day came and Rose left. Bobby had earn't another three pounds. Bobby rode home, ate his dinner, went to bed and tonight couldn't sleep. His mind was full of what had happened. He had read about sex and had heard some of the older boys talk about it but he never thought that it would like this. Her breasts were lovely and he really enjoyed touching them. What surprised him was that she seemed to like it too. He really was confused. Is this what his mother had meant all that time ago when he had caught her in bed with Mr. Constantine?

He eventually went to sleep and it seemed almost straight away that the alarm went off and he was up and out again.

He was back at work again by seven o'clock and as before the van with Rose's group arrived soon afterwards. Rose came over to work with him again, "Hi are you ok today?"

"Great, you?"

"I'm really good" she said with a big smile. Bobby thought that she was the most beautiful woman he had ever seen. She was wearing similar clothes as previous days, a short cotton skirt and a v-neck t-shirt with no bra. She was gorgeous.

Lunchtime came and they went to the corner of the field and eat their sandwiches. As soon as they had finished Rose said "now lie down and relax". Bobby did as he was told. She undid his jeans and slipped his already erect penis out of his underpants. She gripped it gently and started to move her hand up and down. "Just relax and enjoy it" she said. On about the sixth stroke he came, shooting warm semen over her hand.

"That's better. Lasted a bit longer that time" she said as she got up and wiped her hand on the grass again. Bobby had never felt so happy in his life.

They worked all afternoon and as on previous days Rose left at six. "See you tomorrow" she said over her shoulder as she left the row.

Another twelve sacks another three pounds, Bobby thought life was very good. Back home, dinner, bed and thoughts of Rose. He must be in love.

The next morning, Friday, Bobby was back picking again by seven o'clock and as usual Rose arrived shortly after. While they were working that morning Bobby plucked up the courage to say "would you like maybe to go out somewhere with me sometime?"

Rose stopped and looked at him, "like where?"

"I don't know the pictures? I saw a James Bond film at Easter".

She smiled at him" You really are lovely but I don't know where Seven Kings is and you don't know where Deptford is, so I think that it is a bit unlikely, don't you? But I think that it's very nice that you have asked".

Bobby didn't know what else to say so just carried on picking in silence. Lunchtime arrived and they went to the corner of the field and ate their sandwiches. Bobby hurried his, deep down he hoped that Rose would make him come again. She finished hers and said "undo your jeans., Bobby did it in a flash. "Now slip them and your pants down over your hips. Bobby did so and couldn't believe how hard he was and how big his willie had got, or how quickly. Rose lay back on the ground and lifted up her skirt, she had nothing on underneath it.

"I think that you are ready for this" she said with a husky voice as she put her arms around him and pulled him on top of her. He slid between her legs and his hard-on slipped inside her. It was the best thing that he had ever experienced. She held him tight and he moved up and down a couple of times and then he came into her. It seemed to Bobby that it would never stop, he just kept on getting these overwhelming sensations. He thought that he was going to pass out at one time. He collapsed on top of her. She rolled over and they came apart and Bobby lay on the ground exhausted. She leant over him and kissed him on the lips.

"There, now you're a real man" she said as she got up smoothing her skirt down. "One day you are going to break girls' hearts". She smiled at him and went back to picking peas. Bobby didn't know what she meant by that but did not feel he could ask her.

Again six o'clock came and Rose went with her group. "Bye" she said, waving as she made her way to the van.

"Bye" said Bobby, "see you Monday". Bobby finished his sack and went to collect his money. He had only managed nine sacks today, still that was still over two pounds.

CHAPTER 20

Bobby went to bed early on Friday. He couldn't sleep thinking about Rose and what had happened at lunchtime. He was surprised how easy it was. His penis had just slipped in without any trouble or problems. It must be that Rose and he were completely physically compatible. He couldn't wait for Monday and hoped that they would do it again. Next time he would try and make it last longer.

The weekend was routine. He got up on Saturday morning and went swimming, then went to see his father, then went home, did some reading, listened to the radio and went to bed. Sunday it was mass, Sunday lunch and then went round to see Nick and his Mum and tea with them. He told them what he had been doing pea picking but left out any reference to Rose and what had happened with her. Back home on Sunday evening Bobby went to bed early hoping that it would make the morning come faster.

He was up at six and picking again seven o'clock on Monday morning. Time was going fast and there was no sign of Roses' group. Bobby thought that they may have had an accident or something. He kept on looking up but all he could see was the foreman in the shed and two other elderly pickers on the other side of the field. There seemed fewer peas that last Monday and it took Bobby much longer to fill his sack. When it was full he took it to the foreman and as casually as he could, said "where is the group from Deptford then? They are usually here much earlier than this".

"Oh, they won't be back until next year now. Probably gone to Kent for the hops. One week of good picking, followed by the pick-your-own weekend. There's not a lot left now, not enough money to make it worth them gypoes' while. They'll be back next year, they always come".

Bobby was shattered. He picked slower and slower. When the farmer came at four o'clock he had only picked four sacks so he decided to call it a day. "Not much left now is here son" said the farmer as he gave him his one pound. "We'll have another public pick-your-own day next weekend then I'll get it ploughed up and some new spuds put in for the spring".

Bobby cycled home feeling miserable. Once he had eaten his dinner he went to his room to read. He couldn't concentrate so he lay on his bed and thought of Rose. He would meet her again one day and was going to marry her he decided. He was nearly fifteen and was already a man, Rose had said so.

CHAPTER 21

Nick was away for the next two weeks, on holiday with his Mother. Bobby was surprised how much he missed his friend. His relationship with his sister had deteriorated to such an extent that it was not until she arrived home one day with her new school uniform that Bobby realised that she had not passed her 11 – plus and was going to Canon Palmers school, the secondary modern. Bobby wanted to tell her how pleased he was that he wouldn't have to see her on the train coming home but as he hadn't spoken to her for several months he felt that it would be better to say nothing. While thinking about it he realised that his mother had completely accepted the situation between them.

On the Saturday he spent the afternoon with his father as usual. He told him about the pea picking although not saying anything about Rose and what had happened. He talked to his father about computers and what he was reading. "They were talking about getting one of those as the council before I left" he said. "It seems that all of the councils are looking at them. They can store huge amounts of information and it can be accessed very quickly, much quicker than the index cards that they use now. I think that you are very sensible looking to do something with computers, I agree with teacher, they are the future".

Nick returned in the middle of August and told Bobby all about his holiday on the Isle of Wight. It had been hot and sunny and Nick had enjoyed himself although he did say he was pleased to be home. Bobby and Nick had been invited to two parties during the holidays on two Saturday evenings. Bobby had felt a bit bad about not spending those Saturday evenings with his Dad but Robert told him that he should go and enjoy himself.

On the first Saturday Bobby took his new trousers, shirt and shoes he had brought to his Dads, changed there and then went to Nicks. He was staying the night at Nicks so he left his changed clothes there and Nick and Bobby walked to the party in Ley Street, near the station. Neither had been to this sort of party before, girls in their best dresses, boys trying to look smart, some of the older boys drinking beer and the older girls drinking port and lemon or whisky mac's. The party was being held by one of the girls that they met regularly on the train and her brother who was eighteen years old so the guests were from fourteen to nineteen years of age. The music was loud, The Beetles were playing when they arrived and there was also music from the Stones and the new Motown groups. Bobby particularly liked these. He was particularly a fan of the Temptations, Marvin Gaye and Smokey Robinson.

Nick and Bobby both grabbed a glass of Coke and went to chat with some of the other boys and girls that they knew. Some of the older people starting dancing so after a while some of the younger ones did too. Both Bobby and Nick decided not to. After standing in the kitchen talking for a while with a group of girls who went to Coburn School in Mile End and whom Bobby and Nick both knew, one of them said "I will be an old lady if I wait for you to ask me to dance

Nick". She took hold of his hand and led him into the lounge to dance. Bobby hoped desperately that nobody would take his hand and do the same. Fortunately they didn't.

It had been an experience for both of them, their first 'adult' party and both said that they had enjoyed it when Nicks mother asked them about it at breakfast the following morning. The two friends met in the library in Ilford on the following day. They discussed the party and Nick said how much he had enjoyed dancing so close to the girls. Bobby would have liked to tell him about Rose but decided not to. They planned their week which included playing some tennis. In the fourth year at school they had an option for sports activities. In the winter they could play rugby instead of football and tennis instead of cricket. Bobby's dislike of cricket was well known. When they had talked about it Nick had mentioned that he played tennis at his previous school and been quite good at it. They decided they would give it a try during the holidays. They ended up playing three times over the next two weeks. Bobby found it far more difficult than it looked but he was impressed by how well and accurately Nick hit the ball.

Two weeks after the first Saturday evening party there was another only this time there were no older brothers and sisters, all the guests were of a similar age. The party was being held by one the boys who went to St Bonaventure's and met Bobby and Nick on the train but also Bobby had known him at St Peter and Paul's. When Bobby and Nick arrived somebody said "here are the terrible twins". Bobby wanted to know why "terrible". It turned out that there was no reason for this other than it sounded good but because they looked so similar and often were found together, they had earned the nickname of being twins.

They had only been in the house for about ten minutes and both of them were grabbed by the hand and taken into a lounge to dance to the Rolling Stones. It seemed that both Bobby and Nick were popular with the girls so as the evening wore on both had danced with a number of them. As it was getting later the music of the Rolling Stones and the Beatles gave way to slower music the couples got closer together. Bobby was dancing very slowly with a girl called Brenda and he moved his hand from behind her back and slid it over her breast. She held his hand and removed it to her waist. After a few minutes he tried again and this time she allowed him to leave it there. After another few minutes he moved his hand down to touch between her legs. At this she broke away from him and said softly, "no Bobby, that's out of bounds". He decided that he didn't understand women.

CHAPTER 22

The holidays were over all too quickly and they were back at school. Bobby was to study not only math's but also applied math's and he had dropped French. Nick seemed to have an aptitude for languages so was not only to study French but also German. Both were studying physics and both joined the after school computer club along with four other students. Bobby was a bit disappointed with only six people but Mr. Rosen seemed happy with it. During October Mr. Rosen arranged for the group to visit the Computer Technology department at Queens Mary College, part of London University, just along the road at Mile End. Bobby was fascinated. He hadn't understood that the language of computer was basically a 0 and 1. He was able to actually able to produce his own basic programme and punch the cards to run it.

Christmas arrived quickly. As last year Bobby had Christmas dinner with his Mum and Jane, although he didn't speak to her, and Gran who had come to stay for a couple of days. Not for the first time Bobby thought that his Gran was looking older and she also moved slower and was generally ageing. Bobby thought that they should all make an effort and see Gran a bit more. After lunch he went to his father's house and spent the afternoon and evening with him. Nick and his mother went to one of his relations for Christmas and when they returned Bobby went to see his friend and gave him a present of a new tennis racquet. Nick was really pleased, it had turned out that tennis was Nicks favorite sport.

The two friends spent most of the Christmas holidays together, swimming, playing tennis, visiting the cinema and occasionally the library to study, Bobby about computers and Nick mainly geography.

The new term started. Bobby had decided that he needed to find some way of earning money now that he was no longer cleaning cars. He had been talking to one of the boys that he met on the train who worked early on a Saturday. Following up on the information Bobby cycled to Forest Gate early on Saturday morning. He went to Prices Bakery, near Princess Alice and found a job immediately helping the driver on a wholesale bread delivery round. He started at 4.30am and loaded the lorry. At 5.00am the lorry left and his driver round was the Islington, Highbury, Stamford Hill area. It involved delivering to the shops and small supermarkets in the area and also some restaurants and canteens such as the sorting office at Mount Pleasant. Bobby's driver used to call off at a small bakers in Islington and load up with 250 of their rolls to sell as well, he made extra money in that way.

"Always look for an angle" he would say. The deliveries would be finished by about 8.30am so Bobby and his driver had breakfast in a cab stop café just off of Upper Street. At 9.00am they revisited the shops to collect the money due for the deliveries that week. They arrived back in the depot by 11.30am so Bobby could be back to Ilford and his father's by the time his father got up at lunchtime. He earn't one pound ten shillings for the mornings work. He could start building up his savings again. The only problem with the new job was that Bobby could no longer go swimming on a Saturday and this affected his performance at the East London Schools Gala in April. Bobby did win the 100 metre freestyle and helped the team win the relay but was beaten in the other two races he entered.

His school mates were very disappointed for him but strangely Bobby did not feel too upset. While he was talking to Nick about it a few days later they decided that they both had so much going on in their lives that something would have to go. Bobby's priorities were school, his father and earning some money in that order. Nick's had just found a job working on Saturdays at the Wimpy Bar in Cranbrook Road. This paid only one pound fifteen shillings for the whole day but he did keep the tips.

During the summer term the friends played tennis instead of cricket. Nick was the best tennis player in the school. He represented the school and regularly won inter school matches. At first Bobby partnered Nick in the doubles games but soon realized that he was not up to his standard. Bobby told his friend what he thought and that to succeed in the doubles he needed a different partner. Nick teamed up with a fifth year called Melvin Cohen and was immediately successful. The "terrible twins" as they were referred to more and more, both were the school heroes in their respective sport fields. Bobby was very happy for his friends success. Term ended and as last year Nick went away on holiday with his mother. The second week of the holiday arrived and Bobby couldn't wait to get to the farm on the Eastern Avenue to pick peas and see Rose again.

On the Monday Bobby arrived at seven o'clock and shortly after the same old Bedford van that came last year, rumbles into the field in a cloud of smoke. Out got the women out got the children, but no Rose. Bobby was so disappointed; he hadn't fully realized how much he had been looking forward to seeing her again.

He picked peas all morning with only part of his mind on the work. At lunchtime he plucked up the courage to go and talk to the group from Deptford.

"Hi" he said "You were here last year weren't you?"

"Yeah, we remember you, you're the posh one who always went to the other side, the one our Rosie spoke to a lot". They seemed pleasant enough.

"That's right. Where is Rose? Is coming again this year?"

"No luv. She's just got married. She's having a baby in January". Bobby was devastated. He had thought that he would marry Rose. He got through the week and managed to pick enough peas to earn himself twelve pounds. He didn't talk to the Deptford group at all, as he felt that if he talked to anybody about Rose he would blurt out the whole story. He also wondered if the baby could be his as they had had sex but remembered that it took nine month for a baby to develop and if it was him who was the father she would have had it by now. He was very disappointed that she had had sex with somebody else; he thought that she loved him.

Nick came back from his holiday and there were parties arranged for three Saturday nights before school started again. At the first one, in a house in Quebec Road, at the back of Valentines Park, Bobby and Nick decided that after something to drink they would dance with some of the girls and see how hard they could press up against them. Bobby had told Nick about last year's party when he had put his hand on one of the girls breasts and Nick wanted to do that as well. Walking back to Nick's house after the party they both considered that they had had a great time. Both had snogged, both had pressed very hard up against the girl they were snogging and both had got a hard on as a result. Both had had a feel of a breast, through a blouse, and both had groped their partners bum, through their skirts, and pushed it harder into themselves. Both couldn't wait for next week's party. It seemed that girls liked the physical contact as much as they did. They had also arranged with many at the party to go swimming at Valentines Park Lido on the Tuesday. Tuesday was a hot sunny day and they arrived about eleven o'clock. Both Bobby and Nick were almost six feet tall. Bobby had broad shoulders, muscled arms and legs, and a trim waist. Nick was not as broad as Bobby but he too was filling out due to the amount of tennis he was playing. They were both very attractive to the girls at the pool. Of course Bobby was also an excellent swimmer so when he dived in and started to swim he was an impressive sight. Because he was so well developed and looked older than he was, now almost sixteen, many of the older girls at the pool noticed him too.

Bobby and Nick were a popular pair and both the girls and the other boys. Many of those at the Lido were going to the party on the next Saturday which was in Lynn Road, near to Ilford football ground. The party was being held by Mick and his brother Brian who was three years older than him. Saturday arrived. Bobby was up at a quarter to four as usual and cycled to Forest Gate to work. He arrived at his father house in Ilford at about twelve thirty and they had lunch together. They had a chat about school and about Roberts's job at the garage. He was a bit bored with it and told Bobby that within the next year or so he would be looking for something else and that may mean leaving Ilford and starting somewhere afresh. Bobby was a bit concerned about this but Robert assured him that he would do nothing as long as Bobby was still in school and after that he said, who knows where Bobby may go. Bobby left his father early, about 4 o'clock, so that he could go home and have a rest before he got ready for the party. He felt refreshed when he got out of the bath at seven o'clock.

Lynn Road was half way between Nick's house in Ilford and Bobby's in Seven Kings so they decided to meet there. Some of the older boys, friends of Brian's had brought beer to the party. Large cans of bitter, Pipkins Party Seven's, were left on the kitchen worktop for the boys to help themselves. Mick, whose party it was came into the kitchen just after Bobby had arrived.

"Help yourself to beer Bobby. If it's a bit strong put some lemonade in it" This sounded like a good idea so Bobby made himself a shandy. Just as he was doing this Nick arrived so Bobby made one for his friend as well. The party took off immediately mainly helped by the older guests, friends of Bryan. They started dancing and smooching to Hermans Hermits and the Supremes and so the younger ones, thinking that it was sophisticated, joined in. Soon Bobby and Nick were both dancing with attractive girls in short skirts and both could feel themselves aroused. They would have a smooch and a grope, go to the kitchen for a top up drink and then return to find another partner to dance with and try out. Often in the breaks they would discuss the person who they had just danced with. "When I squeezed her bum she pressed right up against me" Nick said of one of his partners. "She must fancy you Nick, she didn't do that to me when I danced with her two dances ago. But Norma, who I just had, boy she pushed her tits into me hard and she felt my bum too", the evening progressed this way for a couple of hours.

Bobby was on his own in the kitchen pouring another drink, Nick had been pulled onto the floor by another admirer.

"Hi there Bobby."

"Hi" said Bobby looking at the girl who had just walked into the kitchen.

"You do remember me don't you? At the lido this week".

"Of course" said Bobby trying to place her. "I met so many people, it was so crowded, that I had to think for a minute". As he looked at her he wondered why he hadn't remembered her. She was tall, with red hair down to her shoulders. She was wearing a low necked black blouse, a short black skirt and black stockings with high heeled black shoes. She was not fat by any means but had large breasts and big hips. Bobby tried to imagine what she would look like in a swimming costume but could still not remember her.

"My names Celia, people call me Ceel. I'm a friend Brian's. We went to the same school but of course we have left now."

"Where do you work? asked Bobby.

"I work for a shipping company in London, near Cannon Street". Bobby couldn't think of anything else to say. He didn't know what a shipping company was or where Cannon Street was and did not want to appear stupid to this obviously attractive girl.

"Oh, that's interesting, would you like a drink?" was all he could think of.

"I'd rather have a dance". So they went into the lounge just as the Temptations 'My Girl' started to play. Ceel moved in very close to Bobby as soon as they started to dance. He thought her body even better to feel close to his than it was to look at. It seemed that he could put his hands anywhere and she didn't mind. When the Temptations finish The Stones 19th Nervous Breakdown came on so they moved apart to dance. Before it had finished Ceel said "I fancy a cigarette, do you smoke?"

"No" said Bobby.

" Fancy coming outside with me while I have one".

Bobby followed her through the kitchen and out into the

garden. "It's better to have a fag out here rather than in there. If somebody knocks into you, you can drop it and burn the carpet". They sat down on the garden bench behind the shed. "This is a nice place, we can't be seen from the house here" said Ceel. She lit up her cigarette. She took a drag, exhaled and then turned to Bobby and kissed him. He responded and soon they were in a tight embrace. He moved his hand inside her blouse and put his hand over her breast, she moved away slightly, still kissing him, and reached behind her and undid her bra. Bobby could then feel her breasts properly instead of through a bra, he was very excited. As if Ceel knew this she put her hand onto his trousers and felt his erection. She sighed while still kissing him hard. He moved his hand from her breast and put it up her skirt and felt how wet she was.

"My fanny wants you" she whispered as she moved away from him. She stood up threw her cigarette away and slipped her knickers down over her suspenders and stepped out of them. She then undid Bobby trousers and his pants, freeing his willie which by now was huge and throbbing and very erect. She then sat astride him putting her arms around his neck and her lips firmly on his mouth. He slipped into her wet opening and she started to move up and down. He put his hands, one on each breast and fondled them while he too was pushing against her. It seemed as though they came together and collapsed against each other when it was finished. She climbed off of him, put her knickers in her handbag and said "I'd better go to the bathroom and get dried. See you in a couple of minutes".

Bobby pulled up his underpants and trousers and sat there for a few minutes. He felt great, sex was the greatest thing in the world as far as he was concerned. It seemed to him that girls liked it too and they liked it with him. He went back into the house soon after and met up with Nick in the kitchen. The two friends smiled at each other. Obviously

Nick knew that Bobby had been in the garden with a girl but Bobby didn't think that Nick would suspect what had actually happened, that he and Ceel had actually had sex.

They danced some more, had a few more shandy's and about midnight people began to leave. Ceel came up to Bobby, "are you going to walk me home then. I live about fifteen minutes away"?

"Of course" said Bobby, "Lets go". He turned to Nick "you OK with that Nick"?

"Me? Of course I'm fine with it". Then he whispered to Bobby "and bloody good luck mate". When they got outside of the house Ceel put her arm through Bobby's and gave him a kiss. They strolled to her house kissing and cuddling all the way. Bobby felt himself starting to get aroused again. When they got to her front gate she put her finger to her lips and said "Ssh, my mum and dad will be asleep. Do you want to come in for a few minutes?"

"OK, fine" said Bobby. Ceel opened the front door quietly and ushered Bobby inside and into the front room. She closed the door behind them. "Do you want a coffee or something?" she said.

"A glass of water would be good" he replied.

"Good idea, I'll have one as well". She disappeared and was back with the water in about two minutes. Bobby was sitting on the settee when Ceel returned. It was a large three seater settee that stretched along almost the whole of the lounge wall. They had not switched any lights on but there was a street light outside of the window and with the curtains open the room was well lit. Ceel gave Bobby his glass of water which he drunk down quickly. With all the shandy he had that evening he was surprised how thirsty he was. Ceel was standing in front of him.

"Feel up for it again Bobby" she said. Bobby, not quite sure what she meant just looked at her and smiled. Ceel pulled her blouse over her head. She then undid her skirt, let it fall to the floor and stepped out of it. She reached behind her and undid her bra, that too fell to the floor. She undid her stockings and slowly slid them down her legs and over her feet. Bobby now had another huge erection in his trousers. Ceel undid her suspender and pulled her knickers down and stepped out of those. She stood in front of Bobby completely naked. Bobby had never actually seen a naked girl before. She was gorgeous, lovely round boobs and a fanny that glistened.

"Don't just sit there, get yer clothes off" she said with a smile. Bobby stood up, there was nothing slow and sensual in the way he undressed. Soon they were both naked and Ceel lay him on his back on the settee and climbed on top of him. He was already hard and ready and she was already wet and her fanny was very welcoming as he slipped inside. She moved up and down on him and very soon they both came again. Bobby let out a small moan but Ceel put her hand over his mouth so that her parents, who were in the room above asleep, would not hear. Both spent. they lay there for several minutes until Ceel got off and Bobby sat up and started to dress. Ceel put on her knickers and blouse and they cuddled and kissed a bit more. "You had better go now, I need to go to bed".

Bobby walked home. He was in a bit of a daze. He couldn't wait until next week's party to see who he could have sex with there. That's what party's were for as far as he was concerned.

CHAPTER 23

During the following week Bobby spent two days cleaning cars for Mr. Constantine. Malcolm was away on holiday so Mr. Constantine was working at the lot in Seven Kings. Malcolm would normally clean the cars when he was not with customers but Mr. Constantine would not do that sort of thing.

Mr. Constantine would sometimes come and chat to Bobby. How was his Dad, how was school, did he know what he wanted to do when he left school? When Bobby told him he wanted to do something with computers Mr. Constantine said to him "you are one of the brightest kids I know so I thought you would do something clever". Bobby thought that that was a nice thing for Mr. Constantine to say.

Saturday came and it followed the same plan as the week previous. Up before dawn, working on the round at Prices Bakery, lunch with Dad, home for rest and then to the party. This weeks, which was entitled "bad news - almost back to school party" by the host was near South Park in Ilford. It was in a bungalow. Bobby had never been in a bungalow before but it was only like the flat he had lived in at Kingston Road but it didn't have a floor above it. Bobby had cycled to Nicks house and then he and Nick had invested in a taxi to get to the party. Working as he was Bobby was feeling quite wealthy so offered to pay for a taxi both ways. The pals went to the kitchen as usual but as George, whose party it was, had no older brothers and sisters, there was no beer, only soft drinks. Both Nick and Bobby had enjoyed their shandy the previous week so were a bit disappointed but that soon lifted when other people that they knew and liked starting arriving and coming into the kitchen and chatting.

Bobby suddenly realized that Ceel was not one of Mick's friends, the boy whose party he had meet her at, but a friend of his brother Bryan. Maybe she wouldn't be here tonight. He suddenly realized how much he had been looking forward to seeing her. When Mick came into the kitchen Bobby said, trying to sound casual, "You know that Ceel that was at your party last week?"

"The one you couldn't keep your hands off you mean?"

"What do you mean by that" said Bobby.

"You couldn't help missing you two groping whenever you were on the dance floor" replied Mick.

Relieved that was all Mick meant Bobby said "yeah well I was wondering if I was going to get a repeat performance tonight".

"Wouldn't think so mate" said Mick "firstly she is three years older than you so wouldn't really be interested and secondly her regular boyfriend came home from his holidays last Sunday so I would think that she is out with him tonight". Bobby was gob-smacked. She had a regular boyfriend and they had fucked, really fucked, twice, the day before he was due back from holidays. For some reason Bobby felt very let down about this and although he danced with four or five girls during the evening, he was not really concentrating. Well before midnight he was bored and decided he wanted to go home.

As he was staying with Nick he looked around for him

but couldn't see him anywhere. Bobby smiled to himself, Nick must have scored he thought. He decided that he couldn't begrudge his friend some female pleasure so went back to the kitchen for another drink. After about half an hour Nick walked in with a large smile.

"What have you been up to then"? said Bobby grinning at his friend.

"I'll tell you later" he said returning the smile.

They both had a Coke and then Nick telephoned for a taxi. When the taxi arrived they got in the back seat and as soon as it pulled away Bobby said "come on then, what happened".

"Not here, wait 'till we get home".

As soon as they got back to Nicks house they went into the kitchen and Bobby said "well?

"Have you ever had your cocked sucked"? said Nick. Bobby just looked him open mouthed. "Its bloody brilliant" continued Nick. "I was snogging that Mary from the Convent, you know the fat one with the big tits, and she let me put my hand right in her knickers and grope around. She was so wet Bobby that after a bit I decided that I needed to go and wash my hand. I went upstairs to the bathroom and she followed me right in and locked the door. As I went to the sink she came up to me, went down on her knees, opened my zip, took my cock out and put it in her mouth. She started moving backwards and forwards on it and, well, I just exploded. It was bloody brilliant".

Bobby was lost for words but then said "good for you mate". Nick was so happy about it Bobby decided not to tell him of his experience with Ceel and why he had felt so down that evening. He was genuinely delighted for Nick.

CHAPTER 24

A couple of days before the start of school it was Bobby's birthday. He went to see his father that afternoon before he went to work and was surprised and really pleased that his Dad had brought him a cake and put sixteen candles on it.

"I missed too many of your birthdays" he said, "maybe I can start making up for that now".

"My birthdays have never been that important Dad" said Bobby. "I've had cards and presents and that but we've never had a fuss. I leave that to Jane and her poncey party's."

Sometimes Bobby did think about his life at home. He wasn't actually unhappy but he knew that his total blanking of his sister wasn't normal and he also knew that he was moving apart from his mother emotionally. He knew that this too was not natural and neither was it that he didn't seem to care. They were still civil and she still cleaned his clothes and cooked for him when he was there.

"I do wish that you and Jane got on better", his father's voice brought him back from his brief muse.

"Ain't gonna happen Dad, so don't hold your breath. You know she still tells everybody that you are dead?"

"I know. It was her way of dealing 'with the problem

at the time and now she can't get out of the problem" said Robert sadly.

"That's rubbish, she could still come and see you". The conversation ceased for a while until Robert lit the candles and Bobby blew them out.

"Did you make a wish?" said Robert.

"Sure did" was the reply.

All too soon Bobby was on his way home and Robert was going to work.

The school year started and this term there was more pressure at school and more homework than ever. Bobby and Nick were in 5S, Mr. Smiths form. He taught German so Bobby didn't have him for any lessons although Nick did. With the additional homework Bobby decided that the swimming club had to be put on hold which meant that for the first time in years he was not swimming at all. The after school swimming lesson was on the same night as the computer club, Saturday was now work time, so swimming didn't fit in anywhere.

With the extra work the time flew. It seemed that every week was the same, school, homework, Saturday job, visit his Dad, go home for more study and Sunday was mass and more study. During the study periods at school Bobby was keeping up with his reading about computers and still sent to the after school computer club which Mr. Rosen still held. There were now only three boys attending, the others including Nick had dropped out. Mr. Rosen didn't seem to mind though.

One day Nick saw an article in the Financial Times about The Legal and General Assurance Society. It was a report on their investment in an update of their IBM computer at their head office in London. They also had a large office in Kingswood in Surrey which also had a very large computer system housed in it. At the next computer club Bobby mentioned this to Mr. Rosen. He told him that his brother worked for a large insurance company, not Legal and General but another, so he would ask him what he knew about it. "They all talk to each other and all seem to know what the other is doing" he said, "I am sure he will be able to give me some information".

A week later Mr. Rosen had a reply. "You were right Bobby, Legal and General have invested heavily in computers and they do have large machines at both the London and Surrey offices. My Brother says that his company and other large insurance companies and bank are all investing in similar equipment. He says that you are right to pursue this interest and there will be many opportunities opening up in this sector".

"Then I'm going to work for Legal and General" he said.

CHAPTER 25

Christmas came, same old routine. There were no party's for Bobby, only time with his parents, both his father and his mother and Gran came and stayed for five days this year. Bobby was worried about Gran; she looked frail to him and coughed a lot more than before. She also seemed to be smoking more. The two friends discussed school just after Christmas sitting in Nicks kitchen. This was their last term of study and very soon when they went back after the Easter break it would be exam time. Bobby felt good about his studies and felt he would do well. His teachers thought so too. Nick was also doing well. It seemed that he had a flair for languages and was talking about staying on in the 6th form and not only doing French and German at A level but also studying Spanish at O level. Bobby wanted to get out to work and was going to apply for a proper job as soon as possible.

It was back to school on January 5th. Bobby and Nick both thought that it was an unusual atmosphere, all of the fifth formers seemed a bit quiet and withdrawn. It was not only at school but also on the train going home. All of the fifth years from Davenant, Coburn, Bonaventure's and both the convents in Forest Gate and Ilford, all seemed a bit tense and occupied. They were all focused on the forthcoming exam's, being told by teachers and parents that they would affect the rest of their lives.

Easter came. Bobby still worked at his Saturday job at Prices Bakery and still visited his father afterwards, sometimes staying the night at his house but he did not do any car cleaning for Mr. Constantine as he had done in previous holiday breaks, he used his time to study and revise.

Easter over and back to school. Exams started during May. During exam time the boys only had to go to school when it was an exam day, there were no more lessons. There were voluntary study groups in the school and the careers master was there to help the boys who had decided to leave school and start work.

CHAPTER 26

Bobby applied for several positions at insurance companies and banks who Mr. Rosen had told him would all have computers. He wrote a special letter to The Legal and General with the help of Mr. Rosen and Mr. Rosen suggested that Bobby might like to offer his name as a reference, which he did. Two weeks after applying Bobby received a letter offering him an interview at Temple Court. The day arrived and Bobby went to the office in Queen Victoria Street. He had bought himself a new shirt and suit from his savings and cleaned his black school shoes especially. He was pleased that it was not far from the Bank Station so if he got a job there it would be an easy journey.

He was interviewed by a man called Mr. Hythe who explained he was from the personnel department. Bobby had felt fine on the journey up to London but as he waited for the interview he became nervous. As soon as Bobby started to talk to Mr. Hythe he forgot all about his nerves. He asked Bobby why he wanted to work for the L&G. Bobby started to explain about the articles he had read about the new computers and that he thought the Legal and General were at the forefront of computer technology. After a very short time Mr. Hythe asked Bobby to wait and he left the room.

He returned shortly and explained to Bobby the normal procedure for employing school leavers. "We assess their overall potential and if its satisfactory we make them an offer. When they start we allocate them a position within a department but that could be anywhere in the organization. It seems to me that you want to apply only for a position within the computer section, is that correct?"

"Yes" said Bobby "I want to work with computers".

Mr. Hythe explained "that is outside of my field of competence. I have just telephoned the manager of the computer section and he is interested in seeing you but I am afraid that will mean another interview next week".

"That's fine" said Bobby, and it was arranged for the following Tuesday at 10.30am. Bobby returned to school and told Mr. Rosen what had happened. Mr. Rosen thought that it looked the fact that they had offered a second interview looked promising.

CHAPTER 27

On Tuesday morning Bobby was back at Temple Court. This time he was taken to an office in the computer section. To get there he had to pass bank after bank of computer processors with what looked like large tape recorder spools going backwards and forwards. Bobby kept stopping and looking, eventually they reached the office of Dr Schulz who was the head of computers. There were two other men as well as the Doctor in the room and they welcomed Bobby and introduced themselves. Dr Schulz started by asking Bobby why he wanted to work with computers. He explained his interest and his various readings. They asked him if he understood binary and he said that he did and then explained it to them. They then asked if he knew what Cobol was. He again said that he did and told them about his visits to the London University College in Mile End and the fact that he had already written some programmes in Cobol. They seemed impressed. After what seemed like no time at all to Bobby, but was in fact about an hour, the interview finished.

Dr Schulz said "Well Mr. Parsons normally we only recruit graduates for positions in the department but you made a very good point in your initial interview, that this is such a fast developing technology that the best way of learning is in the workplace. You certainly seem to have gained a lot of knowledge through your own efforts and you certainly have the enthusiasm we need here. We will take up your references, which usually is only a formality, and I feel confident that we will be able to offer you a position here and look forward to working with you. I see that you are predicted to get A's and B's in almost all of your subjects, that would be satisfactory. Bobby was ecstatic. The three men stood up and each shook his hand and then Dr Schulz himself led him out of the office towards the lifts.

"When do you finish your GCE's "asked Dr Schulz?

"I have three exams left, two next week and one the following Monday"

"When would you want to start work with us? Are you having a holiday"?

"As soon as possible, I have not planned any holiday so I could start in two weeks time if that would be OK".

"That would be good. Well as it seems that you will soon be a member of our little select team I think it may be a good idea if I take you around and introduce you to the other's here." Dr Schulz took Bobby into the office's of the computer section and as he introduced him he told everybody that he would be joining in three weeks time. Bobby chatted to the others as he went around and some were surprised about his level of knowledge and the questions that he asked.

"It's been a pleasure to meet you and I will see you soon" said Dr Schulz as Bobby got into the lift. Bobby went back to school and told Mr. Rosen what had happened. Nick had a French exam so Bobby waited for him to finish and travelled back to Ilford with him telling all of the details about his morning. Nick was genuinely pleased for his friend, he had rarely seen him as happy as this. Bobby got off the train at Ilford and went and told his father about his morning and his Dad too was really happy for him. In fact everybody that he told seemed pleased for him and they all could see how happy he was. He told George, the driver who he worked with at Prices on Saturday's that next week would be his last, George said he was sorry to lose him but how pleased he was that Bobby was moving on and up. His mother was pleased for him too and to celebrate she invited Gran to tea on Sunday. Even she commented that she had never seen him so happy about anything. Jane had gone out to have tea with one of her friends.

On Monday Bobby went to the library to study and on the Tuesday he went to school to sit the applied math's exam. Mr. Rosen sought him out before the exam. "Mr. Parsons, although it is very good news about the position with Legal and General it is still important that you focus on the examinations".

"I am" said Bobby, "I spent all of yesterday in the library revising. I do realise how important it is to get the predicted grades".

Bobby finished the paper just before the allotted time and left the exam room with the sixteen other boys sitting it. He spent Wednesday in the library revising for the English Literature exam which was on Thursday afternoon. Bobby got up on Thursday morning a bit later than usual. He was in no hurry. He planned to get to school at about 1 o'clock for the exam at 2pm. Jane had gone to school and his mother had gone out to work, she was working at Fords at Warley on a three month contract. He was eating some toast for breakfast when the post was delivered. He ambled to the front door to pick it up and there was a letter addressed to him from the Legal and General Assurance Society. He quickly opened it and read…..

> *Dear Mr. Parsons*
> *We refer to you recent application for*

a position with our Company and regret to inform you that you were unsuccessful and we will not be making you an offer.

We would like to wish to every success in your search for a career.

Yours sincerely

P Smith
Personnel Department

Bobby was both confused and devastated. He had thought that he had been guaranteed a job with the computer department. He thought that here must be some mistake and that he had been sent the wrong letter. He decided to telephone Mr. P Smith. He got through almost immediately. Mr. Smith knew who he was too. "I am very sorry Mr. Parsons but there is no mistake. I know what Dr Schulz said to you but I am sure that he explained that it was subject to references and I am afraid that following this a decision was made not to offer you a position. I am afraid that I cannot go into any more detail".

Bobby hung up the phone stunned. What had happened? It obviously wasn't a mistake as Mr. Smith knew the details of his meeting with Dr Schultz. He was at a loss. Almost on remote control Bobby got ready for school and went to take his examination that afternoon. He arrived at school just as lunchtime was starting. For the students there for the examinations it was always tense but today they all noticed that something was not right with Bobby. Many asked him what the matter was and to each the reply was the same, "nothing, I'm fine". But obviously it wasn't. While they were waiting in the hall for the start time a group of teachers entered. Among them was Mr. Rosen. He noticed that something was not right and walked up to Bobby and said "is everything alright Mr. Parsons, you look a bit pale today?"

Bobby looked at Mr. Rosen, pulled the letter out of his pocket and gave it to him without saying anything. Mr. Rosen read the letter. "There must be a mistake" he said. "They must have confused you with another applicant and sent you this letter in error".

"There's no mistake. I telephoned this Mr. Smith and he knew all about my interview with Dr Schulz and all about what had been said. There's no mistake".

"Will you let me keep the letter for a while? I will contact my brother and see if he can find anything out for you. Come to the staff room after the examination and we can talk about it then". Bobby just nodded, it was time to go to the exam room. He completed the paper, Shakespeare and Dickens, not his favorites, and then went to find Mr. Rosen.

"I have telephoned my brother, you may remember I told you that he works for an insurance company. He actually works for Sun Life of Canada but knows a number of people at L&G. He has offered to make some enquiries because neither he nor I understand what has happened here. We feel that even if they could not offer a position in the computer department they would have offered somebody of your calibre a position somewhere in the organization. He says that you should apply to Sun Life, they are always on the lookout for people as bright as you".

"Thank you very much Mr. Rosen, that's very kind".

"You are here next Tuesday for your final examination are you not? Come and see me after you have finished and I should have some news for you" Mr. Rosen said as he handed Bobby back the letter.

Bobby slunk out of school and started his journey home. He got off the train at Ilford and walked to Nick's house. Although he knew that Nick would be revising he felt that he needed to talk to somebody about the problem. As soon as Nick opened the door he knew that something was wrong.

"Come in, what on earth is the matter?" Bobby gave him the letter to read.

"Well there must be some mistake" he said.

"There's no mistake" said Bobby. "That's what I thought when I got it but I telephoned and believe me there is no mistake. I've fucked up somewhere". Bobby rarely used that sort of language and Nick realized the depth of his disappointment.

"Come on mate, there must be an answer to this, it doesn't make sense" Bobby then told Nick about his conversation with Mr. Rosen and that his brother was investigating.

"There we are" said Nick "you have got the right people on your side and if you don't get an offer from this lot, well go and work for Sun Life. Rosen's a good old stick, his brother is likely to be the same. Now cheer up. You know that a lot of the people have finished exams this week, my last one is tomorrow, and that there are parties almost every Saturday for the next three months: girls, beer, lots of fun".

"Not this weekend Nick, I need to revise for next Tuesday. By the way can you keep this quiet, only you and Rosen know about it and I would like to keep it that way until I know more, if I ever do".

"What about telling your Mum and Dad?"

"Not yet, don't want to worry them" said Bobby. "Thanks for listening; I'll leave you to get on with your revision".

"Bobby, I'll come and see you tomorrow when I have finished my exam. Maybe I can persuade you to come to the party on Saturday".

"I'll see you" said Bobby as he walked down the path waving to Nick but not looking back. Instead of going back to the station Bobby decided to walk home, down Ley Street and Aldborough Road. It took him three quarters of an hour.

CHAPTER 28

Everybody noticed that Bobby was very quiet during that weekend. Both of his parents asked if there was a problem and he told them that it was the strain of the exams. Both asked if he had heard from the Legal and General about the job and he told then both that he hadn't and added when his father asked, that he was rethinking his options anyway. George the bakery driver brought him a black rolled umbrella as a going away present. "They use stuff like that at those posh London offices" he said. "Good luck son, although I don't think you'll need it". If only he knew, thought Bobby.

Nick came to see him on Friday but could not persuade him to go out on Saturday. He came again on Sunday and told Bobby that it had been a great party. There was another one next Saturday at a house in Norfolk Road, not far from where Bobby lived. Ralph, whose party it was, had promised to lay on plenty of beer for the boys and Babycham for the girls. His older brother was getting it for him. "You know what those convent girls are like after a bit of alcohol "said Nick trying to cheer his mate up.

"I'll let you know" said Bobby. Monday he revised, Tuesday he went to school to sit his final exam. Mr. Rosen was waiting for him at the hall entrance. "I saw you coming in. I have some news from my brother about your problem. Come and see me in the staff room after your examination".

"Can't you tell me now?"

"Its complicated, better after the examination".

As usual Bobby finished the paper before the allotted time, checked it and was satisfied that he had done the best he could. He then went to find Mr. Rosen. He knocked on the staff room door and Mr. Rosen opened it. "I think that 5W's form room should be empty, lets go along there". Bobby followed Mr. Rosen along the corridor and they went into the empty classroom and Mr. Rosen closed the door behind them. "Sit down please Bobby" he said. It was the first time ever he had called him by his first name. "My brother Solly knows a few people at Legal and General and one of them works in the computer section. In fact he was one of the people on your interview panel. They were very impressed with you and all three of them wanted to offer you a position. It went to the personal department for ratification and while taking up references they discovered that your Father has been in prison. Not only that but that he was in prison for financial fraud. For this reason personal would not confirm your appointment".

"But I was eight years old when that happened, it was nothing to do with me and anyway he was framed".

"Nevertheless he has this record and that is what they considered. I find it incredible that in this day and age, 1966, something like this could be held against you but my brother says that all insurance companies and banks would have the same policy. It's not you but they assume that your family may have criminal connections and that pressure may be put on you. I know that it seems very unfair but my brother says that they would consider somebody with your talents and knowledge of computers could probably find a way of programming them to divert money from the company.

Sadly Bobby it seems that you will need to look elsewhere for a career".

Bobby felt tears welling up in his eyes. "Thank you Mr. Rosen, for everything. You've been great support for me. Thanks for trying".

"You could always come back here in the 6th form you know, continue your education. You are one of the brightest physics pupils that I have taught in 20 years and your math's reports are excellent".

"What for Mr. Rosen? To become more qualified to work in Woolworths? Thanks for everything, I'll be alright". Bobby shook his hand and walked out of the classroom, out of the school, along the road towards Stepney Green Station and home for a new life. He stopped off at Ilford on the way and went to see Nick. He told him of his conversation with Mr. Rosen.

"What are you going to do now?" said Nick, "you've got to tell your mum and dad".

"I'll tell mum but not dad. He may blame himself and it's not his fault. I'll have to come up with something else for him".

That evening Bobby told his mother all that had happened. She was as angry as he had ever seen her.

"That stupid bugger has ruined all our lives. Wait 'till I next see him".

"No mum" said Bobby, "he mustn't know. He may have been naive but it wasn't really his fault. I don't want him blaming himself for this. The fault is with that Wilkinson bloke who set him up and the stupid outdated system that the City of London has, where the father's sins are laid upon the sons".

With that both of them lapsed into silence, reflecting on the inequalities of life.

CHAPTER 29

The next day Bobby spent in bed. In the afternoon he read a book, a Harold Robbins book called The Betsy. It was about American big business and the car industry. Bobby decided that he needed to get into business somehow and would start looking first thing in the morning.

The next day he was up early and cycled to the labour exchange on the corner of New Road. He went to the enquiry desk and was pointed in the direction of the boards at the end of the floor which displayed positions for junior staff and school leavers. He looked at the cards and saw one for a 'Junior Assistant for a busy office of a Timber Importers in River Road Barking. Must be good at Math's'. He took the card to an enquiry desk and asked how he went about applying for the job. The clerk asked him to fill out a form giving details of his name, address, date of birth, school attended etc and when he had done that the clerk then made a phone call to the company advertising. He gave Bobby's details to person on the other end of the line and after a few minutes he covered the mouthpiece and said "ten o clock tomorrow morning OK with you for an interview?"

"Yes" said Bobby. After a few more words the phone was

put down. "There we are then, ten o'clock tomorrow, this is the address, you are to ask for a Mr. Allen. Understand?"

"I understand" said Bobby, what's not to understand he thought.

The next day he went for the interview at Hobday and Sons, Timber Importers, in River Road, Barking. They explained that it was a small but busy office. His main job would be to keep stock records up to date but he may be asked to do more duties from time to time. Mr. Allen gave him some additions and subtractions to do all of which he did quickly and correctly. "That's great" said Mr. Allen "it's important that the stock figures are calculated correctly. I think that you could do the job very well. The hours are nine in the morning to five thirty in the afternoon, there is one hour for lunch, three weeks holiday and we would pay you five hundred pounds per year salary. Would you like the job?"

"Yes, fine, thanks" Bobby was surprised at the speed of offer. "Do you want references" he asked.

"Why?" said Mr. Allen. "Either you can do the job or you can't. If you can do then well, if not your out on your ear. When can you start?"

"As soon as possible. My exams are over so I left school this week".

"Lets say Monday then shall we? Nine a.m. bright and early. With that Mr. Allen stood up and shook Bobby's hand. He led him out of the office and showed him to the door. "Bye Bobby, see you Monday" He said as he turned away.

Cycling home Bobby thought 'five hundred pounds a year', that's nearly ten pounds a week, every week. That's pretty good'. His spirits lifted a bit, He went to see Nick to tell him the news. Nick was very happy for him, he could see that the gloom of recent days was lifted. "Coming to Ralph's party on Saturday then"? said Nick.

"You bet. Girls watch out, the terrible twins are on the prowl". They both laughed again at the thought of being thought of as the terrible twins. Nick thought that it was like old times.

Bobby told his mother about his interview and job offer and she told him how pleased she was for him. She could see that he was much happier than he had been for a while but she felt that the disappointment of not doing what he really wanted to do, work with computers would eventually make him unhappy.

Nick saw his father on Saturday afternoon and told him about his new job. "What happened to the job at the Legal and General and the computers?" he asked, surprised at the turn of events. Bobby had been waiting for this question.

"Dad, I've been traveling on the train to London for five years now. I went for my interviews and thought did I want to do this journey for the rest of my life? The answer was no. So I have got a job that is local. If it doesn't work out then I will think about going up to London but I want to try a short journey". His father seemed satisfied with this explanation.

He went to the party with Nick. They both had a great time. They both had a few shandy's and were a bit lightheaded. A lot of the girls also were lightheaded so they snogged with four or five girls each and had good gropes with every snog. Bobby got as far as getting his hand inside one of the girls knickers when she stopped him. "Come with me" she said, leading him upstairs into one of the bedrooms. "We are not going to have sex because I want to be a virgin when I get married, but I will relieve you if you like".

"Yes please" said Bobby, undoing his trousers. He had never been wanked by a girl before but knew all about it. He pulled his trousers down and lay on the bed. She knelt between his legs, gripped his willie and started to move it up and down. He soon came. She went to the toilet and came back with some toilet tissue. "Feel better?" she said.

"Much" said Bobby. "Do you want to do it again?"

She laughed "You couldn't. Men!"

Bobby went back downstairs. When he next saw Nick he told him what a happened. "You lucky bugger" he said, "all I've got is few handfuls of tits". They were standing in the kitchen talking and laughing when the girl who Bobby had been with walked in for fresh drink.

"This is my friend Nick" Bobby said. He walked over to her and whispered in her ear.

"Really" she said in a surprised voice, "is that true".

"Cross my heart" said Bobby.

"Better do something about it then hadn't we? Come on Nick, come with me". She took Nick's arm and led him out of the kitchen and upstairs to a vacant bedroom.

About an hour later the two friends were walking back to Bobby's house where Nick was staying the night.

"That was OK wasn't it" said Nick.

"What, the party or the wank?" said Bobby.

"Both, by the way who was she? I thought I recognized her but couldn't remember her name".

"I think she goes to Canon Palmers but I don't know her name either. I'll ask her next week if she's there, useful to know her name for future reference". The two friends laughed.

"Don't forget though that next week is the World Cup Final, it should be England, at least it will be if they leave Martin Peters and Geoff Hurst in the team" said Bobby. "I'm watching that before any old party". Nick noticed how happy and relaxed Bobby was compared to the last couple of weeks.

CHAPTER 30

Bobby started work on the Monday. He cycled to River Road in Barking and arrived at twenty to nine. Mr. Allen was already in the office.

"I try and be here by eight normally" he said. "That's the time the yard starts and if there isn't anybody about they spend the first hour of the day drinking tea. The others will be here soon so take a seat, that's your desk". He pointed to a desk at the back of the rather small office. It contained five desks in total, Mr. Allen's faced the others backing onto a large window which looked out onto a yard with many piles of timber of all sorts of types and sizes. There was another two, facing each other on the left of the office and three against the right hand wall facing his desk. The back one of these was Bobby's.

After about five minutes two men walked in the office talking and laughing. The older one, a man of about 50 looked at Bobby and said "hello son, you must be Bobby Parsons. I'm Mac and this useless git is Phil. How do you do?"

"Hello" said Bobby.

Mr. Allen said "OK, yes this is Bobby, Bobby this is Mac and Phil, they are two of the inside salesmen here. We have three reps, Jeff, Leo and Brian and all of them have a sales support person here in the office. You'll pick it up fairly quickly. Phil, can you show Bobby the ropes, take him round and introduce him and then show him what he has to do".

"Right Guv" said Phil, just as the door opened and another person walked through it.

"Hi peasants" said the newcomer, a man of about thirty, rather overweight, with his shirt open at the waist and his suit very creased. Although it wasn't that hot he was already sweating.

"This is Joe" said Phil. "Joe, this is Bobby, he starts today"

"Hello young lad, welcome to hell" said Joe, but with a smile on his face. "Let me give you some advice, don't get married, don't have kids" he said as he sat down at the desk in front of Bobby's. Bobby noticed he had a photo on his desk with a very plump woman and two plump children in it, both of which looked like Joe. "These two both arrive in cars, looking fully refreshed, me? I'm on a push bike. My wife needs the car to take the kids here or there or somewhere".

"Don't pay any attention to him" said Phil, "he loves them dearly. Come on I'll show you around. They went out of a side door and up some stairs. The room at the top was the accounts office. Bobby was introduced to Mr. Elgin and his assistant Robbie. Phil then went along the corridor, at the first door he pointed and said "men's toilets" at the second, "ladies toilets", at the third "kitchen" and at the end of the corridor he stopped and knocked.

"This is Mr. Hobday's office. He's the managing director, the boss".

"Come in" said a voice.

Phil walked into the room with Bobby following, "Good morning Mr. Hobday. Can I introduce Bobby Parsons, he's the young lad that's starting today"

Mr. Hobday was about sixty, with a wisp of grey hair.

"Hello Bobby, welcome, I hope you will be happy here. There not a bad bunch downstairs, just don't believe all that they tell you. Whenever somebody new starts they always try and pull their leg. They can be a bunch of jokers".

"Thank you sir" said Bobby, he couldn't think of anything else to say.

Back downstairs, just next to the sales office was the switchboard room. Phil introduced Bobby to Terri. " Terri is our switchboard operator, she also does the filing, types any letters that we need done, makes the tea and generally looks after us, don't you my love? This is Bobby, he starts today".

"Hi Bobby", said Terri. "You can always come in here when you need a bit of sanity from that lot" she said. She smiled at Phil and he and Bobby returned to the sales office. Phil then explained the system that they worked and Bobby's job to him. Each of the salesmen had order pad set's that had four carbon copies for each order. The customer would phone the company and place the order. The customer's name and address would be put on the form and the type, dimension and volume of the timber that they wanted. The bottom copy of the set would go into the yard for the measurers to select the timber as close as they could to the required specification. They would mark on their copy what they had selected. This would always be the type and dimension of the actual order but could vary slightly in volume. As Phil explained, "a customer may ask for 20 pieces 6 feet long. We may have only 10 pieces 6 feet, 8 at 7 feet and the remaining 2 at 8 feet. Therefore although the customer has ordered a total of 120 lineal feet, we need to charge for 132 feet, because that is what we are supplying. This is also where you come in Bobby, because you will be responsible for the stock record so you will have to write off 132 feet". He continued "the bottom copy then comes back in here to us and we amend the three copies that we have on our desks. The top two go onto

Nigel's desk, that's his there" pointing to the empty desk, "he usually comes in at about 10 o'clock because he works 'till the yard closes".

Bobby was a bit confused. "Who is Nigel?" he asked.

"Nigel is the works and transport manager. As he does the transport, he has the copies and sorts out what goes on which lorry. The third and fourth copies will come to you".

Phil then continued to explain to Bobby that he would need to take each yard copy and on the day the order was picked, he would need to select the stock card and deduct the quantity picked from it. The cards were in drawers, these were removable in what was referred to as the Scandex file case. The drawers were arranged in the order of the thickness of the timber, so the top drawer was half inch and five-eights, the second three-quarters, and so on. When he had finished a pile he would take the third copy upstairs for invoicing and the fourth copy went to Terry for filing.

"Any problems just let me know" said Phil. Here are some that were picked after we went home last night, lets see how you get on". Phil put a pile of about 20 orders on Bobby's desk. Bobby picked them up and walked to the Scandex file and selected the' 1 inch' tray, for the first note. He soon got the hang of it and by the time he had completed the pile from yesterday there was another small pile that had been picked that morning.

Just after ten fifteen Nigel arrived, said hello and put on an old donkey jacket and went out to the yard. At ten thirty Terri came in and asked Bobby if he would like tea or coffee. "Coffee please, one sugar" he said as she smiled at him.

"You're in there son" said Mac, "she doesn't normally smile on a Monday". Bobby just smiled back at Mac. Bobby found the work very easy. As soon as the notes came in from the yard he went to the Scandex, and adjusted the stock. He had understood the stock card system within hours. At twelve thirty it was lunchtime and Phil and Mac went out. Joe sat at his desk with his newspaper and ate some sandwiches that he had brought from home. Bobby cycled to a small shop in Ripple Road and brought himself a pork pie and a bottle of coke. He hadn't thought to bring a sandwich for lunch.

Phil arrived back just before one thirty and Mac came in almost two O'clock. Bobby couldn't help notice that he smelt of beer or something like it. As if reading his thoughts Mac said "liquid lunch at The Volunteer, best type of food my lad. I'll take you with me Friday if you like, they have strippers up there Friday lunchtimes". Again Bobby just smiled. Five o'clock came and they all tidied their desks to go home.

Mr. Allen came up to Bobby just as he was about to leave. "You've done very well lad. I thought that you were doing it a bit too quick but I've been checking your figures and your spot on, I haven't found any mistakes.

"Mistakes?" said Bobby surprised, "its only simple subtraction".

"I know but well done anyway. See you tomorrow". Bobby cycled home. As he was going up the hill by Upney Station he decided that he did not want to do this ride every day and as soon as he got his first months money he would buy himself a second hand scooter. The next day at lunchtime he cycled to the local post office and completed the form for a driving licence, brought the postal order for the fee and sent it off.

By the end of the week Bobby's enthusiasm had waned. The job was simple and boring. It took him far less time to do that Mr. Allen said other people took so he was spending long periods of time doing nothing. He met with Nick on Friday and told him. Nick suggested that he should ask Mr. Allen if there was anything else he could do but Bobby said that Mr. Allen knew the position, he was sitting and looking at him doing nothing.

CHAPTER 31

O n Saturday they all meet at Aiden Givens house, he had the biggest television and his parents were on holiday in Spain. England were playing West Germany in the world cup final at Wembley. Aiden had managed to get several bottles of cider from somewhere so the nine lads there started to drink it about 1 o'clock, two hours before kickoff. By 3 o'clock they were all very happy. The game was terrific and very close and tense. Bobby Moore particularly was brilliant but the Germans equalized with almost the last kick of the game. Into extra time and Geoff Hurst scored the third goal for England; "of course it's over the line" they all shouted and cheered the ref when he gave it. Just at the end the Germans attacked again. 'Oh no' they thought 'not another equaliser' but it was alright Bobby Moore had won the ball again. He passed it pin point down the field to Geoff Hurst who hit it high into the net past the German keeper. "Goal, four two", England had won the world cup but as far as Bobby was concerned it was West Ham that had won it.

None of the boys there went out that evening. They spent it at Aiden's house drinking cider and saying "they think its all over, it is now" and laughing.

The following Monday morning Bobby was back at work.

As he got quicker at the stock adjustments he got more bored because he had more time on his hands.

On Tuesday it was pouring with rain. He arrived at work soaking wet. While he was drying his hair on the roller towel in the toilet Bobby decided to buy himself a scooter as soon as possible and not wait for payday. After all he had one hundred and twenty pounds in his post office account so why wait.

On Wednesday he asked Mr. Allen if there was anything else he could do. "I've noticed how quickly you do the job, it's much faster than anybody has done it before. You are very accurate as well but I have given up checking your figures. One of the things that I do is put the stock on the cards, maybe you could try that". Mr. Allen explained how this was done from the goods inwards notes and gave Bobby three deliveries to enter. This involved a calculation at the stock cards showed lineal measure while the goods inwards document was in cubic feet. "Its only simple multiplication" thought Bobby, no big deal, but he did not say anything as he didn't want anybody to think that he was big headed.

On Thursday he bought the Ilford Recorder on his way home. He looked in the classified section and found an advert for a 1959 Vespa 125cc scooter. It was £55 ono and included a crash helmet and the three months unexpired tax. He telephoned the number and arranged to see it that evening. As luck would have it the owner lived in Pembroke Road, which was only a few roads from where he lived. He borrowed ten pounds from his mother and went to the address he had been given. The scooter was not much to look at, it had been hand painted in gold paint and the helmet had been painted to match. But it started first time on the kick start and the engine sounded OK. All of the lights worked and so did the scooter. Bobby offered fifty pounds which was accepted. He left the ten pounds as deposit and said that he would be back the next evening with the balance.

The following lunchtime he went to the post office and withdrew seventy pounds. His mother had offered to arrange the insurance with her Prudential agent who was at Bobby's house when he arrived home that evening. The insurance was fourteen a year which Bobby paid to the agent in return for the cover note. He then walked to Pembroke Road to collect the scooter. He realised that he needed some L plates so he rode the scooter to the Esso garage in Seven Kings High Road and brought some. He was now completely legal.

He rode home to show his Mum and then to Nicks to show him. He took Nick for a short ride on the pillion although he knew that it was not legal.

On Saturday morning he rode to the Army and Navy store in Manor Park and brought himself an ex army combat jacket. It was waterproof and had a blanket lining, just what he needed to ride to and from work in the winter. He then went to see his father to show him his new transport. His dad was very pleased for him but told him to be careful and make sure that he wore his helmet at all times.

That evening he and Nick decided to stay in and watch television. Nicks mother was out at a function at the local Methodist church, there was a party they had been invited to but they thought that the person whose party it was, was boring. They sat in and talked. They talked about Bobby's problem with L&G and his father, how bored he was at work and how long he felt he could put up with it. They talked about Nick going back to school to do language A Levels and how he would tell his mother that he wanted to join the army afterwards. He knew she would be very unhappy as she was a pacifist and also he was an only child and she would think he would be in danger. They talked about what Nick could do to earn money for the next two years, he didn't feel that he could get up at 3.30 on a Saturday morning like Bobby had done to work at Prices but he was going to try pea picking. They also talked about girls and sex and what had happened to them although Bobby still did not tell him about Rose. Bobby really enjoyed the evening, being relaxed and just chatting to his best friend.

Bobby arrived at work on Monday on his new scooter. Joe made a comment about Nick being a lucky sod and he wished he could afford but the others just said that it was good idea for him to travel on it to and from work.

Over the next week Bobby chatted more to Terri when he took the filing into her room. She tried to explain to him how the switchboard worked with all of the leads and the plugs that went into the board which in turn put the call on the correct extension. Bobby liked chatting to Terri, she was easy to talk to and very friendly. She was rather plain and a bit plump with dull shoulder length mousy hair, not a looker Bobby thought, but nice and friendly.

He found out that Terri was eighteen, almost nineteen. She had been working there for just over a year and her sister Sandra had done the job before her. Sandra, who was twenty, had got married almost a year ago and moved to Shenfield. Sandra's husband was twenty and had just been taken into hospital with a kidney problem and they were all a bit worried. Terri had been working in London where she had been trained to operate a switchboard and when Sandra said she was going to leave Terri applied for the job so that she could work locally. She lived on the 8th floor of a high-rise block just the other side of the A13 main road. She had a fifteen year old sister, Karen and a thirteen year old brother Kevin.

She also knew all about the other people in the company. Nobody seemed to know how long Mr. Allen had worked there but his father had worked there before him and was with old Mr. Hobday when he started the company in 1919. Joe was 31, married with two children and despite his moaning Terri said that his wife was his childhood sweetheart, they had been together since they were 14 years old, and he thought the world of her and the children.

Phil was 35 and married with two children too but he kept himself to himself and never discussed his family. Everybody thought that Phil was being trained to take over from Mr Allen when he retired. Mac was about 55, he was divorced and lived in a small flat over the post office in Katherine Road in East Ham. He had a problem with drink and would often come in on a Monday with a hangover and was often back late from lunch when he always went to the pub. Terri thought that they put up with him because he had been with the company a long time and actually everybody liked him.

She didn't really know the reps very well. When they came into the office for a sales meeting they would go upstairs to Mr. Hobday's office with Mr. Allen and nobody would really see them. Bobby had only been at the company for a few weeks but was already bored. He thought that if he didn't chat to Terri he would go mad.

CHAPTER 32

The following Saturday evening Bobby arrived at Nick's house. The results of the CCE exams had arrived the day before and Nick was anxious to see how Bobby had got on and also to tell Bobby how well he had done.

"I got an A in French, English and Math's and a B in German, Physics and Geography and C in Biology and Chemistry, I'm well satisfied. What about you?"

I got an A in Math's and applied Math's, Physics, History and English Literature and a B Geography, Biology and Chemistry".

"What did your Mum and Dad think?" said Nick.

"I haven't told either of them. It makes no difference now to me what results I got so why tell them".

They decided to go out for a ride on the scooter so they rode out along the A12 to Margareting and had a celebratory drink in a pub called the George and Dragon. When they got back to Nick's house Bobby decided that he had better apply for a scooter driving test so that when he carried Nick it was legal.

Nick had started to play tennis again during the day at the courts in Valentines Park and Bobby noticed how fit he was beginning to look. He felt that he was getting a bit flabby. He had not swum for many months and now he was not even cycling any more. He decided that he needed to start swimming again.

"Good idea" said Nick when he told him. "You'll never pull the birds looking like Michelin Man".

Nick got a summer job working in Sainsbury's at Barkingside, loading shelves and filling the vegetable racks. They told him that after the holidays he could work there on a Friday evening and 8.00am to 4.30pm on a Saturday doing the same thing. Nick was pleased about this as it gave him an income for the next two years while he was at school. Because of his job he didn't go away with his mother for their usual summer holiday but stayed home. He asked Bobby if he wanted to move in for the two weeks. Bobby thought it a great idea. He was becoming more remote at home. He never spoke to Jane and since starting work he seemed to have less and less to say to his mother.

On the middle weekend of his stay the two friends went to a party. This one was unusual as it was in a record shop at Gants Hill called Guy Norris's. One of the boys they sometimes met on the train home from school had a Saturday job there and the shop was celebrating its 5th birthday. Mr. Norris the owner had invited all of the staff and told them that they could all bring some friends if they liked. The boy, Deano, invited 5 mates including Bobby and Nick. When they arrived Deano took them around and introduced them to the other staff. He took them and introduced two girls, Lizzie and Pauline.

"What do you think then" Deano said to the girls, "didn't I say I had some tasty mates?"

"You were right Deano, hello boys" said Pauline, "come and have a drink with us". They had a drink and a couple of dances and then Nick left them to find the toilets. On his way back he found Deano.

"What's going on there with them Deano?"

"Oh they kept on about how boring all the boys here are and I mentioned that I had a couple of really tasty mates so they said if that's the case bring them to the party so here we are."

"Well thanks for the compliment but why did you think that they would think that we are tasty?"

"Don't be silly Nick, all of the girls fancy you and Bobby. The blokes reckon that those two are a couple of slags but they are not bad looking, you should really score tonight". The evening wore on and Bobby and Nick stayed with two girls. At about 11.00pm people started to leave.

"Where are we going now then?" said Lizzie.

"Well, we were going home" said Bobby.

"That sounds good" said Pauline "got anything to drink there?" Bobby looked at Nick to see what he thought. "We've got some beer but we can stop off at the off licence if you want something else". They left the shop, the girls hailed a taxi, Nick gave the driver his address and they stopped off and bought some 'blue Nun' wine on the way.

Once at Nick's house he put on the latest Marvin Gaye record and poured the drinks. They started dancing slowly, Nick with Lizzie and Bobby with Pauline. Soon they were snogging followed by the boy's hand exploring breasts and groping bottoms. Lizzie moved apart from Nick, took his hand and led him upstairs.

"What's good for them must be good for us" said Pauline as she took Bobby hand and followed the other two up the stairs. Nick had gone into his bedroom and Bobby went into the spare room where he had been sleeping for the week.

Both the boys shed their clothes as soon as they were in the rooms and the girls followed soon after. Neither of them noticed the moans and groans that came from the other room. After about two hours all four of them fell asleep.

The next morning at about seven, Bobby stirred. At first he couldn't think where he was but almost immediately the previous night came back to him. He looked a Pauline lying beside him as she opened her eyes and smiled. "Hello" was all she said.

"Hello" was all Bobby could think of saying.

She reached out and put her arms around his shoulders and pulled him close. "Fancy a quick one before we go?"

He was immediately hard again. "You don't take much asking" she said, rolling on her back and pulling him into her.

The girls left after a cup of tea and a piece of toast. Lizzie knew the number of a taxi company and they were picked up at about half past eight. Bobby and Nick sat in silence for a long time after they had gone, it occurred to Bobby that it was probably the first time that Nick had had actual sex.

"We had better change both the beds" said Nick. "I know Mum's not due back for a week but she has some sort of second sense about things and I certainly would not want her finding out about last night."

"Bloody brilliant though, wasn't it" said Bobby beginning to laugh.

"Bloody brilliant" said Nick also beginning to laugh.

CHAPTER 33

Bobby and Nick spent the morning changing the beds, doing the washing and cleaning the house. Mrs. Mead was very house-proud and her home was always spotless. It appeared that Nick often helped her so surprisingly he knew how to work the washing machine and Hoover. They went to the Valentine pub for lunch and spent the afternoon relaxing and watching television.

On Tuesday Bobby went to the swimming club for the first time in months and was pleased that he had not lost much of his speed. While he was out Pauline phoned Nicks house and arranged with him that the four of them would go out for a drink on Wednesday. Nick was beaming from ear to ear when he told Bobby as soon as he arrived home.

Wednesday evening arrived and they met the two girls at the Black Horse in Ilford Broadway. They had a couple of drinks each and at 9.30pm walked back to Nick's house. As soon as they walked in the girls headed for the bedrooms, the boys followed and spent the next hour or so in sexual bliss. At half past ten the girls phoned for a cab home and as soon as they had gone Nick and Bobby changed the beds again and put the dirty bedding into the washing machine, "just in case Mum comes home early" said Nick.

On Saturday Bobby got up for an early morning swim. The two friends had cleaned the house again the previous evening as well as changing the beds yet again. Nick left for work at Sainsbury's on the bus. After his swim it was too early for Bobby to go and see his dad so he went to the Wimpey Bar in Cranbrook Road and had a bender, egg and chips. While he was eating it occurred to Bobby that he had had no contact with his mother for the two weeks that he had been at Nicks. He arrived at his father's house just after eleven which was when he usually got up. Bobby let himself in quietly and was surprised to see his father in the kitchen making a cup of tea.

"Hi" said Bobby, "you're up early".

"Yes" was the reply.

Bobby was a bit surprised. His father was usually really pleased to see him.

"Everything alright? Said Bobby.

"Not Really".

"What's the matter"? said Bobby.

"Why didn't you tell me truth about the Legal and General job?"

Bobby was stunned. He had only told two people, his mother and Nick. He had never wanted his father to find out.

"I wouldn't expect you to lie to me about something like that" his father said when Bobby didn't reply.

"I didn't actually lie" said Bobby trying hard to get his thoughts organized.

"What do you call telling me something that is not true, like you didn't take the job there because you wanted to work locally, and not telling me the reason that they had rejected you. That's not a lie?"

"I didn't tell you all of the facts because I knew it would upset you. Also there was no point, there is nothing that you or anybody can do about it". The rest of the day passed very slowly. Robert's mood did not improve and instead of waiting until tea time to leave Bobby made an excuse and left around three o'clock. Traveling home his mind was going round and round. How had his father found out? He had only told his Mum and Nick. By the time he arrived home he knew that the source could not have been Nick.

He walked in the front door. His Mother was in the kitchen. "Hello sweetheart" she said "its good to have you back. What would you like for your tea?"

"How did Dad find out about what happened with L&G?"

His Mother turned around to look at him "I'm really sorry Bobby, it just came out".

"What do you mean it just came out, how?"

"Look, I can see that you are angry. Sit down and I will explain. You father has not been working on Wednesday night for the last couple of months so most Wednesday evenings either I go around to his house or we go out for a meal or a drink. Last Wednesday I went to see him and , well he asked me something and didn't agree with what I said. It was silly but we started to argue and then, well then it just sort of came out in the argument. I'm sorry".

"Sorry? You're bloody sorry"? Bobby was becoming more furious and frustrated. "Do you realise what its done to him? He thinks that its his fault".

"Well in a way it is Bobby".

"No its bloody not, he was duped, you know that".

"He was silly and that is why he got involved and anyway please don't swear at me Bobby, I am your mother".

"Mother or not you're bloody irresponsible, that's what you are" said Bobby as he turned, walked out of the kitchen and up to his bedroom, "irresponsible and selfish" he shouted as he went up the stairs.

That evening Bobby and Nick went to The Avenue Hotel in Newbury Park for a drink and Bobby told Nick what had happened. Bobby was still very uptight about the whole situation. "I may not be seventeen for another week or so" said Bobby "but I have got to find somewhere else to live away from Mum and Jane."

Nick was a good listener and by the time they got back to Nicks, where Bobby was to spend the night, Bobby had calmed down a bit. They were not late back and Mrs. Mead was still up. She had had a lovely holiday and thanked Bobby for leaving he house so clean and all of the washing done. She was sure that Nick wouldn't have left it so clean if it was left to him.

The next Sunday was Bobby's Birthday so his father had a cake for him when he arrived on Saturday morning. He seemed much more like his old self. "Sorry about last week Bobby" he said. "It was such a shock when I heard it. I'm really sorry about what happened".

"Don't worry Dad, everybody tells me that I'm clever so I will sort something out".

"Don't be angry with your Mother Nick, she is very upset that she let it slip. The argument was as much my fault as hers"

"Why didn't you tell me that you now had Wednesdays off as well as Saturday?"

"I was going to but your Mum said let's keep it quiet, it can be our time, so I did".

"Then good for you" said Bobby smiling. "Any chance of you two getting back together maybe?"

"No chance at all I'm afraid Bobby. In fact that is what the argument was about. Nuff said, lets drop it eh?" Bobby spent a nice afternoon with his father. Bobby suggested that they could go and watch the Hammers during this season. They should do well now that they had won the world cup for England they joked. As he was leaving Robert gave Bobby an envelope with 'happy birthday' written on it. "Not to be opened until tomorrow" he said, "but happy birthday anyway". He hugged Bobby at the doorstep and told him to be careful and that he loved him. Bobby thought that he was being a bit over the top, but assumed it was because of the job problem.

That night Nick had organized a birthday party for Bobby in the Valentine Pub. He had told the barmen that it was an 18th because if they knew he was only 17 they would not have allowed it. Both Bobby and Nick were 6 feet tall, both were well developed because of playing sport for many years, not gangly like many 16 and 17 year olds, and both looked much older than they were. Nobody asked their age.

Both Bobby and Nick had developed a taste for Directors Bitter so they enjoyed sitting drinking for the evening. There were people in the pub who Bobby did not know who came up and said happy birthday. Some of the girls were making suggestive remarks to both Bobby and Nick but they both decided that they just wanted a nice drink and be sociable. "Anyway its raining" said Nick, we would get soaked having a shag in the car park". Both of the boys had begun to realise how attractive they were to the opposite sex.

The evening ended and he boys walked home to Nicks house. It was almost always that Bobby spent Saturday night in the spare room in Nicks house. In the morning Nicks mum made them breakfast. She gave Bobby a birthday card and Nick gave him a present of a pair of leather gloves to wear on his scooter. "It'll be winter soon, you'll need to keep your hands warm". They both laughed at the innuendo. Bobby opened the envelope his father had given to him. Bobby was amazed to see that it contained £120. He knew that his father could not afford this. His job would only pay little more than Bobby's. There was a large card, especially made

'For My Son' and inside was written 'remember that I will love you for always'. Bobby felt uneasy about his. He would try and give it back to his father next week and suggest that he used it to buy himself a scooter to save cycling to and from work in future.

CHAPTER 34

The following week was routine. Bobby working in Barking and Nick spending the last days of his holiday at Sainsbury's before going back to school to study languages. They went out for a drink on Friday night and on Saturday morning Bobby went to the early morning swim session at the baths. He went into a café behind the town hall for some breakfast and then went to see his father. He arrived at the house, put his key in the lock but it wouldn't turn. He tried again but the key did not fit. He knocked on the door but there was no answer. He kept on knocking and banging on the front window for about twenty minutes but got no response. So he decided to go home.

His mother was surprised to see him. "What are you doing home, what about your dads"?

"I can't get in. The key won't work and he doesn't answer the door".

"Did you try knocking?"

"Of course, for about twenty minutes, there was no answer. When did you last see him?"

"Wednesday".

"How was he"?

"Fine, He was very relaxed and we had a very nice evening".

"What time did you leave?"

"About 1.00am" said Bobby's mother blushing.

"There's nothing to be ashamed about if you went to bed with him for God's sake. I just want to know that he is alright". Bobby's mother, now blushing even more as Bobby realized what they had been doing said "I am sure that there is a good reason for it. He has probably put the catch on the front door and overslept. He puts it on when I am there". She blushed again.

"I'll have a sandwich and go back there after lunch and see if he's up."

Bobby returned to his father's home at two o'clock and the result was the same. He returned home again but as he rode towards his house he noticed Mr. Constantine's car parked outside. As he walked through the front door his mother shouted from the kitchen "still no answer then?"

"No" said Bobby as he walked into the lounge. "Hello Mr. Constantine, what are you doing here?"

"I phoned him" said his mother. "I just wanted to check that your father hadn't moved or something and Mr. Constantine hadn't changed the lock. He hasn't but he tells me that your father hasn't been into work since Tuesday. Wednesday was his night off but he didn't go in on Thursday and Friday either".

"Something's wrong" said Bobby, "we need to break into the house".

"I agree" said Mr. Constantine "come in the car Bobby and we will both go in".

They left the house immediately and got to Kingston Road in 15 minutes. They tried the key again and knocking on the door. No answer. Mr. Constantine then went and knocked at the house next door. He spoke briefly to the man who opened the door and then called, "come on Bobby, through this house, over the fence and in the back door". Bobby thought Mr. Constantine was surprisingly light on his feet as both of them climbed over the fence. Mr. Constantine picked up a large stone from the garden and broke a glass pane in the back door. Fortunately the key was in the lock so he was able to reach through and unlock the door. Bobby rushed in calling for his father as he did. Mr. Constantine followed and went into the lounge to look for Robert. Bobby went into the bedroom. There was his father in bed. He seemed asleep but as Bobby touched him he was cold. Mr. Constantine walked into the bedroom carrying two envelopes. "These were on the mantelpiece. One is addressed to you, the other to your mother". Bobby took them. His eyes were full of tears but he was trying hard not to cry.

"Go home Bobby, I'll deal with this" said Mr. Constantine softly.

"He's my Dad, I will deal with it." Even Mr. Constantine was surprised at the force with which the boy had said it.

"OK. Do you want me to stay with you for a while?"

"No thanks. I will call the police as see what they say. Maybe you could go and tell Mum what has happened and, here, take her the letter". He took the letter and left the house just as Bobby dialed 999. The police said that they would send a car. Bobby went back into the bedroom, sat on the bed and opened the letter.

> Dear Bobby
> Of all of the things that I have done in my life it is you that I am most proud of.
> I am so sorry that by being stupid I have not only messed my life up but it seems yours as well. If I am dead then you will not have

to enter anything when they ask for fathers details, you can just put deceased.

Its better this way, I have had my chance at life you have not. You deserve so much and I am only going to hold you back.

You will never realise how much your support since I have been out of jail has meant to me.

Don't give up Bobby, don't accept a dead end job, you are much too good for that. Get a goal and go for it, you can achieve anything that you want. I hope that I will be looking out for you from heaven; I know you will make me proud.

Don't be too hard on your mother. I love her and in her own way she loves me too.

Good luck for the rest of your life. I have always loved you and always will.

All my love
Dad.

There was a knock on the door and when he opened it there were two policemen there. He told them what had happened, omitting that Mr. Constantine had been with him, and they called an ambulance and made a cup of tea while they waited for it to arrive. They were concerned about Bobby especially when he told them that he was only seventeen but he explained that his parents were divorced but that he had got a message to his mother. The ambulance arrived and took away the body. The police explained that although it looked like suicide there would still need to be a post mortem to find out exactly what happened. When they left Bobby went back into the bedroom, sat on the bed and read the letter again. Then he cried.

At about 6 o'clock he telephoned Nick and told him what had happened. Nick said that he would be round straight away but Bobby told him that he would rather be on his own this evening but would see him tomorrow. After several hours of sitting in the dark on his father's bed, Bobby lay down and fell asleep. He was emotionally exhausted.

CHAPTER 35

The autopsy confirmed suicide. His father had taken a whole bottle of sleeping pills washed down with a bottle of whisky. The body was released to the funeral directors. Bobby and his mother went to make the arrangements. Mr. Constantine had driven his mother there.

"You don't need to worry Bobby, I have told your mother that I will take care of the cost" he said.

"No you won't" said Bobby, "he's my father, I'm paying". Once again there was a tone in his voice that even Mr. Constantine did not argue with.

The funeral was held at St Peter and Paul's church and then the body was taken to the City of London Cemetery in Manor Park to be cremated. Bobby arranged for the ashes to be buried and placed in the Garden of Remembrance and a rose bush planted next to it. Only his Mother, Gran, Nick and Mr. Constantine attended the funeral. "Not many people for a lifetime" thought Bobby, "and where was Jane? Couldn't she even attend her own fathers funeral".

They returned to the house in Seven Kings where they had some sandwiches and cups of tea. As Mr. Constantine was leaving he said to Bobby "Like your dad said, don't be too hard on your mother, it is not really her fault".

"No, I know. It's that bastard Wilkinson's fault. If ever I see him I would like to really hurt him, to pay him back just a bit for what he has done. I'd like to really make him suffer and let him know that I was causing him the pain". For the third time in just over a week Mr. Constantine was surprised at the coldness of Bobby and the steel in his voice. It was the same emotion that he had sometimes heard during the war, when he had fought for the partisans in Greece against the Germans. It was the same sentiment that some of his fighters had when their families had been killed in German reprisals.

"Maybe one day you will" He said as he walked to his car.

CHAPTER 36

During the next weeks the boys got into a routine. In the week Nick was at school, Bobby at work. On Saturdays Nick would work at Sainsbury's and Bobby would go swimming. He would then have a large breakfast in a café behind Ilford Town Hall and then he would go and spend a few hours in the library reading a wide variety of books. If West Ham were at home he would sometimes go and watch them and, on occasions he even persuaded Mac to go with him. He would leave his scooter outside of the Post Office above which Mac lived and they would walk to Upton Park. In the evening Bobby and Nick would usually go to the pictures, either the Regal in Ilford or the Odeon at Gants Hill. They preferred the Odeon as they could go The Valentine for a drink before the film. Although neither of them was eighteen they were becoming regulars in there.

In October Bobby got a date for his scooter test. He asked Mr. Allen for a few hours off. Mr. Allen reminded him that he was entitled to three weeks annual holiday so starting when he did he should take eight days off before Christmas. So Bobby took the day of his test as holiday. Mr. Allen had advised him to take the test route carefully. "They will fail you for going 31 mph but nobody has ever failed for doing

25" he said. Bobby took his advice and passed his test. He celebrated by riding to his old school and collecting Nick to bring him home as he said he would if he passed. When Nick came out he said "Mr. Rosen would like a word with you Bobby, if you have time".

Bobby got off the scooter and followed Nick inside. Mr. Rosen seemed genuinely pleased to see Bobby. "How are you young man? He said with a broad smile on his face, shaking Bobby by the hand. "Silly question, young Nick has been keeping me up to date, I am very sorry about your father".

"Thank you" said Bobby.

"Anyway" said Mr. Rosen, "that isn't why I asked to see you. Bobby, you are very talented. You achieved excellent results at O'Level and you shouldn't waste them. I know of all of the problems but I have been looking at your options. You live near to East Ham. There is a technical college there where, with your qualifications you could go to evening classes and take an accountancy course. If you went for three years you could qualify as an accountant. That would open up a whole new world for you".

Bobby was very appreciative of Mr. Rosens efforts and said that he would look into it.

Bobby thought about what he had said and the next Saturday he went to the library and checked the courses available. What Mr. Rosen had said was correct, East Ham Tech ran evening courses in accountancy. One of the courses was a three year course, two evenings a week, which if all exams and course work was passed, would result in a qualification of chartered accountant.

After work on Monday he rode to the Technical College in High Street South and enrolled for the course. It had started three weeks earlier but the enrollment officer thought that with Bobby's school record and obvious ability at Math's, he would soon catch up.

On Tuesday evening he went to his first class. He was surprised at how much he enjoyed it. He told Nick about it on Saturday and asked him to tell Mr. Rosen and thank him for his advice. Nick was surprised when Bobby told him that his Mother didn't know anything about it.

"But you're not getting home until after ten, doesn't she ask where you have been?" Bobby explained that although they were always polite to each other it was rather like he lived in a B&B rather than a real home. Nobody was interested in what he did or where he went.

CHAPTER 37

At work the following Monday Terri asked all of the sales office if they would like to come to a party she was having the following Saturday. Mac said he would come if she could lay on a fifty something nymphomaniac, Phil said he had other plans, Mr. Allen said he didn't think it was his thing and Joe said he would love to come if his wife could get a baby sitter. Bobby said he would see what he could do but he had arranged to go out with Nick. Terri said to bring Nick too. Terri said that she knew that none of the others would come but would really like Nick to. Both Phil and Joe were making comments saying things like there really was no party she just wanted to get him on his own; Bobby had already decided not to go but told Terri that he would talk to Nick and see what he said.

On Wednesday evening Nick phoned Bobby, it was most unusual for him to phone during the week.

"Hi Bobby, look mate I've got a bit of a problem. There's this girl at Sainsbury's who been chatting me up a bit. Well she phoned me yesterday evening, its her sisters 21st next Saturday and she wants me to go with her. I don't know why but I just sort of agreed to go. If it's a problem I will pull out…………"

"Don't be silly Nick, you go, that's great. Good on you. As a matter of fact the girl in the office, Terri is having a party on Saturday so I'll go there".

"Thanks Bobby" said Nick sounding relieved, "you're a real mate. Come round on Sunday and tell me all about it. I'll get Mum to sort you out Sunday Lunch".

Bobby told Terri that he would defiantly be at her party. She jumped up and kissed him on the cheek she was so pleased.

Saturday arrived, Bobby went swimming, breakfast, library and then home for some course work before going out. He arrived at Terri's at about eight thirty and the party was already in full swing. There were lots of her old friends there, some from her schooldays but there was also her Mum and Dad and some of their friends. It was an old fashioned family party, the flat was bulging and everybody seemed to be having a great time. Terri introduced him to her Mum and Dad and her friends. As usual the drinks were in the kitchen so she told Bobby to go and help himself. Bobby was introduced to Terri's old school friends and danced with six of them. He never had considered himself a snob but he was not impressed with them at all and thought how much better Terri had done for herself than her school friends there. The final clincher to this view was Cherry. He was dancing with her when she told him that she was three months pregnant and getting married in two weeks time to Spike, her baby's father. He lived in a flat in the same block as Terri, two floors below her. Spike was not at the party although he may come later. He was in his flat with six of his mates "getting rat-arsed pissed" as Cherry said it. Having told him all of this as the dance ended she asked him if he fancied going up to the landing above and having "a quickie knee trembler". Bobby did not consider himself a prude, and he certainly enjoyed sex, but he was taken aback at this offer. He retired to the kitchen and the sanctuary of the beer. He looked at his watch and it was only nine thirty, he thought that it should be later. It certainly seemed like it. He looked at his watch about every five minutes, time was dragging so much. He wondered how Nick was getting on at his party. He certainly hoped that he was having a better time than he was.

He looked at his watch again, it was ten o'clock. He thought how soon he could leave without it seeming rude and upsetting Terri. He sensed somebody come into the kitchen, looked up and saw the most beautiful woman that he had ever seen. She was average height, although she looked taller due to her high heeled shoes. She had shoulder length blonde hair, a beautiful slim body, piercing blue-green eyes, long legs and a wonderful broad smile. He realised he was standing staring at her.

"Hello you must be Bobby" she said in the most lovely voice he had ever heard.

"Yes" was all he could say.

"I'm Sandra, Terri's sister" she said holding out her hand. Bobby took it and shook it and reluctantly let it go.

"You don't look anything like her" he said without thinking and then regretting it.

"It wonderful what a bit of hair colouring, makeup and stress can do".

"Stress?"

"My husband is in hospital. He has been in there for months and they can't find out what the problem is. The worry and the visiting every day and generally chasing around has made me lose over a stone".

"Well it certainly suits you" said Bobby, again wishing he hadn't said it as soon as the words came out of his mouth.

Sandra didn't seem offended "thank you" she said.

Bobby couldn't think of anything else to say. He just stood and looked.

"Well, I'll get my own drink then" she said.

"Oh sorry, sorry. Please let me get you a drink. What would you like?" Bobby was flustered. It was a new sensation for him and it made him feel a bit foolish. "A gin and tonic would be nice please".They stood in the kitchen talking until Terri walked in and said "why aren't you two dancing? Get out there".

"She's only just arrived" said Bobby laughing.

"That was an hour ago" said Terri. Bobby looked at his watch. It was just past eleven pm, it seemed like only five minutes had passed, not an hour. They danced and chatted until well after midnight, Bobby was feeling more relaxed and had stopped staring he was pleased to realise. He felt that he had regained his self control.

People were starting to leave the party. "I'd better go" said Sandra "cabs get a bit scarce after about one o'clock".

"Where have you got to go to"? said Bobby.

"Shenfield, I live in flat above the shops on the main road opposite the station. Do you know it?

"Never been there, but I can take you home if you don't mind riding on the back of a scooter".

"That would be really nice of you, thanks" she said.

So they left the party and Bobby rode through Barking to Ilford, to Gants Hill, along the Eastern Avenue to Gallows Corner, to Brentwood and then turned right in Brentwood and on to Shenfield. He took it very carefully, he was in no hurry, aware all of the time that he had the most wonderful girl he had ever met clinging to him with her arms around his waist. They arrived at her flat at almost one o'clock. "Do you want to come up for a coffee?" she asked. Bobby of course agreed, he didn't want the evening to end. Sandra put the kettle on and made two cups of coffee. She sat down next to Bobby on the settee and kicked off her shoes. Bobby couldn't remember how but it seemed that the next second they were in each others arms kissing. Bobby knew that she was special, not like any of the other girls that he had known, so he didn't want to push things too far. He started slowly moving his hand over her breasts. She didn't resist. He then moved down and fondled her bum, again she just kissed him harder. He slipped his hand up inside her skirt, no resistance. She was wearing stockings so it was easy to reach inside her knickers. She moaned slightly and held him tighter. He was feeling her and rubbing with his finger and she was getting wetter and wetter. Suddenly she moved one of her hands from around his neck and took his hand. He thought that she was going to take it away but instead she moved it very slightly. She whispered in his ear "rub there, right on my clit". Bobby could feel a slightly raised bit so he caressed it gently. She started to sway slightly and softly moaned, suddenly she arched backwards and let out a long loud sigh. She stopped moving, looked into Bobby's face and smiled a huge smile. "Bloody hell I needed that" she said. She then just cuddled up to Bobby and held him tightly. He removed his hand from her crotch and although it was very wet he just put it around her and held her tightly too.

They sat like this for what seemed ages. Eventually Sandra said that she needed to go to bed, it was almost three o'clock. Bobby asked her if she would like to go out sometime and to his amazement she agreed. They arranged to go out for a meal on the following Saturday evening, Bobby to meet her outside of Oldchurch Hospital at 8.00pm after visiting. Sandra asked Bobby not to say anything to Terri as she felt that it was better kept a secret. Bobby rode home on auto-pilot, he was so happy.

The next day he went to see Nick and told him all about his evening and about Sandra. Nick was happy for him but advised caution. "Bobby, just remember that she is married. You could be asking for a lot of trouble there, however much you like her". Bobby knew his friend was right but at the moment it didn't seem to matter.

Nick too had had a good evening. Nick's dates name was Jennifer. She had a nice family who lived in a house in a road off the Barkingside Road, not far from the Odeon. Jennifer was nice and had asked if they could go out together sometime.

"Well I'm with Sandra on Saturday evening so why don't you go out then?" said Bobby, pleased that his mate would have some company on Saturday evening. Bobby stayed at Nicks for lunch but went home for the afternoon to change his clothes as they had decided to go out for a quick drink that evening. They went to the Black Horse at Ilford Broadway where they had live music on a Sunday evening. It was a jazzy-pop type group playing, rather like The Peddlers. They both liked the music.

CHAPTER 38

B obby couldn't wait for Saturday, the week seemed to drag. Terri asked him what he thought about her sister. He tried to be casual about it "she seemed nice, what a shame about her husband, being in hospital for so long " he said trying to move the subject on.

Saturday eventually came. At a few minutes past eight she walked out of the gate up to his scooter and kissed him. "Hello, I've been looking forward to this evening" she said, "where are you taking me?" They decided that it may be too risky to stay locally so they rode to Grays and had a meal in a Chinese Restaurant near the town centre. It was a lovely evening. Sandra told Bobby about herself, she had gone to the local secondary modern school where she was in the top group. Most of the pupils were studying for CSE's but they had decided that she could do a couple of O'levels and she passed Math's and English. She got a job locally so that she could go to night school and study but before she could she met Frankie, her husband and that was that. He was a television engineer for Radio Rentals and she now worked for an insurance agent in Romford and was going to start an insurance course in the New Year. It was quite expensive but her company were sponsoring her.

The time flew for both of them and before they realised it, it was past eleven O'clock. They went back to Shenfield and Bobby followed her into the flat. The front door was hardly closed before they were in each other arms. They collapsed onto the settee with their mouths clasped together. Bobby put his hand up her skirt and this time found her spot without being guided. She starting to breathe rapidly and moan softly and then went rigid and let out a loud sigh. She relaxed and smiled at him. "God that was lovely" she said and held him tight. After a while she got up and went to make some coffee. When she came back with the two mugs of coffee she said "do you want to stay the night?"

Did he? What a stupid question, but all he said was "yes please". They drank their coffee and Sandra went into the bathroom to clean her teeth. "There's a spare toothbrush in there if you want to use it" she said as she came out. When Bobby had cleaned his teeth he went into the bedroom where she was already in bed. He took off his clothes and slid in next to her. Their arms met and they lay there on their sides cuddling. They moved slightly so that Bobby was on his back and Sandra laid her head on his chest. As they lay there her breathing deepened, she fell asleep in that position. Bobby lay there gently kissing the top of her head. This was like nothing he had experienced before. They hadn't had sex but he felt wonderful and so content. Eventually he fell asleep with his arms around her.

They awoke just before six o'clock. "You had better leave Bobby, I don't want the neighbours seeing you." They kissed at the front door. "Can I see you next week?" he said.

"Saturday? Outside the hospital, same time?" Bobby pushed his scooter a couple of hundred yards along the road before he bump started it and went home.

He saw Nick that afternoon and told him about his evening. "What, you made her come and she didn't do anything for you?" said Nick when Bobby told him. Nick thought that was a bit peculiar.

"It didn't matter" said Bobby, "funny isn't it but as long as she enjoys it that all that counts". Bobby felt that Nick couldn't understand this especially as he told Bobby that he had come in Jennifer's hand. That evening they went to the Black Horse again, had a couple of pints of beer and listened to the music.

CHAPTER 39

Saturday arrived at last, and again Bobby was outside of Oldchurch Hospital at eight. This time they went to a Beefeater in Basildon and both had steaks. They were chatting about work and Sandra's family and Bobby said again how unlike Terri and her sister Sandra was. "We may have different Fathers" she said. "Very few people know that and you must never tell Terri". Sandra explained that when Frankie became ill the hospital asked all of his family to have blood tests in case it may help in future. Sandra had volunteered although she obviously was not a blood relative and when she asked her mother if she and her father would do the same her mother had said that she would not and then explained why. Basically she was worried that if results of blood tests had been known and it showed that Sandra was not her father's daughter there would be so much trouble. It transpired that her parents got engaged while her father was in the army and the war was still on. When it finished he was posted in Germany for a further year so did not get out of the army until 1947. Sandra's mum had become friendly with an American airman who left England at almost the same time as her father returned. They got married straight away and she found out that she was pregnant almost immediately.

Sandra's Dad thought he had done the business on their honeymoon but less than two weeks before her mother had spent a 'goodbye night' with her American. Sandra had only known this for a few months and had not told anybody else.

Bobby then told her about his father, his prison sentence and suicide, the problem he had with his job and how he had no real relationship with his mother or sister. Sharing such intimate secrets made them seem closer together. They arrived back at the flat at about eleven o'clock and instead of kissing him as soon as they were inside Sandra said "do you want to stay the night again?"

"That would be great" said Bobby.

"Go and clean your teeth then and get into bed. I'll bring us both a cup of coffee" she said as she disappeared into the kitchen.

Bobby was sitting up in bed when she came in, put the mugs on the bedside table, kissed him on the lips and then went to the bathroom. When she returned she was naked and climbed into bed next to him. She came into his arms and they kissed passionately. They touched each other all over their bodies, both of them becoming more and more aroused. He felt that Sandra was so wet and she whispered to him, "come lie on me".

He moved on top of her and slid into her, they moved together and came together. Afterwards she lay with her head on his chest and fell asleep. Bobby lay there listening to her breathing. He could never remember being so happy in his life. He had had sex before but this was different. He understood why it was referred to as making love, that is what they had done tonight.

He left the following morning at six and this time they arranged to meet on Wednesday evening just to go for a drink. On Wednesday he drove her home and although he went in for a coffee he did not stay the night but left after about one hour.

For the next few weeks they met every Wednesday for a drink and every Saturday when they went for a meal, talked a lot and then went back to the flat and made love. Bobby saw Nick every Sunday. Most Sunday's he would have lunch at Nicks house and then they would go for a drink in the evening. Nick seemed to be getting on well with Jennifer which Bobby was pleased about. At least that way he did not feel as though he was letting his best friend down on a Saturday night. They too seemed to have got into a routine. She was eighteen so could go into pubs and have a drink, so they would go to The Valentine for a drink and then go to the pictures. They would then go back to her house for a while until it was time for Nick to go home. As he was busy studying during the week and working Friday evenings, Saturday was the only evening that they spent together.

Bobby decided that he needed to learn to drive a car and then he would give Nick his scooter so that when he dated he didn't need to walk everywhere. He booked himself some lessons on a Saturday morning and hoped to take his test and pass before February. Nick's birthday was in February so the scooter would make a great present.

CHAPTER 40

It was the middle of December1966. Bobby and Sandra were having a meal at an Italian Restaurant in Ingatestone. It was only about ten days before Christmas. Bobby had been thinking about Christmas and decided that the only person he wanted to spend it with was Sandra. He knew it would be difficult but he wanted to take her away to a hotel for the holidays. His company only closed on Christmas Day and Boxing Day but as he had had very little holiday all year he plenty of days in hand and had booked from Christmas Eve until the new year off. Bobby knew that it would be difficult, he was sure her family would want to see her and so would her husband but he thought that maybe they could go away on Boxing Day for a few days. He felt he needed to pick the right moment to talk to her about it. He felt that she was a bit less talkative than normal and thought that maybe she too was thinking about Christmas.

Back at the flat they went to bed and Bobby felt that their love making was better than ever. It was slow and sensuous and satisfying. It was making love and not just having sex. Afterwards they lay in silence, she resting her head on his chest and he with both arms around her holding her tight. "Sandra, I would like to talk to you about Christmas".

She moved her head up and rested it in her hands, putting her elbows on his chest. She looked into his eyes and Bobby noticed that they were moist. "Bobby, Frankie's being discharged on Wednesday, he's coming home."

"Coming home? What, home here?" He realized how stupid that sounded as soon as he had said it.

"Of course home here" she said gently, "this is his home, it's the only home that he has". She explained that they had not cured him but the progression had stopped, controlled by drugs, and there had been a small improvement lately. There was nothing else that they could do in hospital for him so were sending him home in time for Christmas in the hope that with the drugs he would gradually get better.

"What about us?" said Bobby.

"There can't be an us Bobby" she said with tears in her eyes.

"But I love you Sandra, I really love you".

"I know you do Bobby, and I think that I love you too. But I am a married woman. I have had less than a year with my husband at home. I loved him when I married him and actually, whatever I feel for you now I do still love him too. I need to give my marriage a good try and I know that I cannot do that if I am having an affair with you. You would always be between us. The only way it will work is if, when you leave here tomorrow I don't see you again. If you love me you would do that for me".

Bobby didn't know what to say, so he said nothing. Sandra laid her head on his chest and he felt her tears roll down his side. He too felt his eyes water up. Sometime later she fell asleep; Bobby was awake all night but could think of nothing to offer as a solution to the problem.

The following morning at six o'clock they clung to each other in the small hall before Bobby left. Bobby had been thinking all night about what he was going to say.

"I do love you Sandra and because of that I will do what you want, no phone calls, nothing. But I know that I will never love anybody like I love you. If it doesn't work out with Frankie this year, next year or in five or ten yours time, contact me. I will be there for you". Tears rolled down her cheek as she kissed him for the final time and he left the flat to ride home.

Later that day he told Nick about it. "You're not going to want to hear this mate but you have only known her a few weeks, she's a married woman, she's three or four years older than you, it didn't really stand much of a chance did it?" Bobby agreed with what Nick said, it would seem that way but he knew that it had been different.

"How's Jennifer?" he asked wanting to change the subject.

"She's nice girl and she fairly good looking. She gives great hand job, but she's so boring".

Bobby laughed at the way Nick stretched out the 'boring'.

"She has no interest in anything except Sainsbury's, her family, getting married and having four kids and what she is wearing. I would just like some conversation sometimes".

Bobby laughed again. "Maybe the marriage and kids talk is aimed at you".

"I've thought about that. I even told her that I was still at school and that things like that were years off. I had decided to end it anyway but now after your news I can do it gently. I will tell her that you have had your heart broken and need me to help you though such difficult times".

They both laughed and relaxed for the afternoon. As usual they went for a drink that evening. Bobby was determined not to appear miserable for Nick's sake but that night when he got into bed he felt that a huge hole had appeared in his life. He felt that it was just as bad as when his dad had died.

CHAPTER 41

Christmas arrived, his mother had told Bobby that his Gran was not well enough to spend Christmas with them this year so on Christmas morning he rode over to Forest Gate to see her. She was surprised to see him but seemed genuinely pleased. She still had her dressing gown on at eleven o'clock and Bobby thought how frail and old she looked. He gave her his present and spent about an hour with her before heading home for Christmas dinner. There was only him, his mother and Jane. It was eaten in almost complete silence and he decided that this was the last Christmas that he would spend at home. By next year he would be eighteen and that, he thought was old enough to have somewhere to live of his own.

He spent Christmas evening with Nick and his mother. On Boxing Day they both went to Upton Park to see West Ham beat Spurs 4-2, Budgie Byrne scoring two goals. The rest of the Christmas period Bobby spent at the library and with Nick but he had also managed to book an additional six driving lessons between Christmas and the New Year.

Bobby was pleased when it was the New Year. The last year had been horrible and he hoped that 1967 would be better. When he went back to work in January he applied for his driving test and got a date at the beginning of March. He had some money saved, enough to buy a car, but he needed to save a bit more for the tax and insurance.

The two friends soon got back into their old routine, pictures and a drink on Saturday evenings and the Black Horse on Sunday evening to listen to the music and have a couple of pints of Directors. Bobby swam on Monday evenings and Saturday mornings, went to college on Tuesday and Thursday, driving lessons on Wednesday evening and Saturday mornings. He thought of Sandra every day and wondered how she was, but he was determined to keep his promise and not contact her. Nick was at school all week, worked Friday evening and Saturday and studied when he got home each night.

CHAPTER 42

It was a Monday evening late in January when the phone rang. Bobby had just returned from the swimming club. "It's for you" his mother called. He knew that it was Sandra. He rushed to the phone, his heart skipping. "Hello Bobby, Ari Constantine here" a voice said. "I want to talk to you. Can we meet for a drink?"

"What about?" said Bobby.

"I'd rather discuss it face to face. How about this Wednesday, The Seven Kings Hotel, say about eight, after your driving lesson". Bobby agreed to meet him. As he hung up the phone it crossed his mind how did Mr. Constantine know about his arrangements for Wednesday evenings.

Mr. Constantine was waiting for him when he arrived. He bought Bobby a beer and sat down. "Bobby, do you remember at your Dad's funeral you said that you would like to hurt Mr. Wilkinson for what he had done? Do you still feel the same?"

Bobby felt again the sorrow he had felt for what had happened to his father and his hatred for the man he blamed.

"Yes, I think that I do. Why?"

"He's been released from prison. He still owes me money

so I want him to be reminded of it. Normally I would send Stavros and his brother to give him a reminder but if you would like to do it, well, I can arrange it".

"How would that work?" asked Bobby.

"I would arrange for him to be put in a taxi and taken to a property I own. It would be up to you then how much you want to hurt him and how".

Bobby didn't take long to think about it. "OK let's do it" he said.

"Good, I'll sort something and let you know when are where". They finished their drinks and went on their separate ways, Bobby on his scooter and Mr. Constantine in his brand new BMW. Although Bobby told Nick everything he decided not to mention this latest development. The following Monday evening Mr. Constantine phoned again. It was arranged for the next evening at a factory unit that Mr. Constantine owned in Ferry Lane, Rainham. Bobby would have to miss college for the evening.

Bobby arrived at eight o'clock as arranged. He saw Mr. Constantine's car outside, another car and a transit van. He walked through the small side door and saw Stavros and another man talking to Mr. Constantine. It was a huge building. It was a mixture of a warehouse, there were a few boxes piled on pallets, and a factory, although it was difficult to see what it manufactured. It was not very well lit and smelt a bit damp and was very cold. Bobby felt a bit apprehensive now that he was inside the building. He wondered what was expected of him. Just inside the door, to the left was a small kitchen and the three of them were standing by the door, Mr. Constantine with a mug of tea or coffee in his hand.

"Hello Bobby. Stavros you know, this is his brother Demi. Wilkinson is over there", he said pointing to the far side of the warehouse. Bobby saw the man, he was tied to a chair which was itself tied on a pallet which was on the floor but on the forks of a forklift truck. He was very overweight despite his years on prison food. His complexion was pasty and his suit and shirt were crumpled and neither fitted him properly. He was almost bald and was sweating profusely. He had two bright spotlights shining on him so that he could see nothing of what was happening behind them. Bobby looked around the building. There was a workbench along the wall on the right. Beyond the kitchen on the left there were a couple of offices that were empty. There were some large boxes and crates piled up along the far wall beyond where Wilkinson was, but mainly it was empty.

"Over to you son. You can make any amount of noise, there is nobody within a mile or so and the sound doesn't go far outside the factory walls anyway". Bobby walked up close to Wilkinson, walking beyond the spotlights. He looked at the man and all of his hate for him came to the surface. He felt somehow possessed. A sort of inner passion seemed to come over him. He wanted to pummel this man with his fists but he knew from books that he had read that it could be far more menacing to be cool and calm and deliberate.

"Who are you, what's going on?" said Wilkinson.

"Couple of things" said Bobby sounding very cool, feeling almost detached at what was going on, "first thing is that you owe Mr. Constantine some money and he would like paying".

Despite being bound to a chair, Wilkinson laughed. "They sent some kid to frighten me, can't he do better than that? Tell him I'll get his money, its only about £300".

"It was £300 pounds before you went to prison, with interest it's now just over £5000" said Bobby, still very calmly.

"Piss off kid", said Wilkinson. Bobby turned around and walked away. He walked back to where the other men were. Bobby had read somewhere that a man will feel more vulnerable without clothes on. "Can you take his clothes off, I'd like him naked". Mr. Constantine nodded and Stavros and Yuri went forward to strip the victim. A few minutes later Bobby went back to see Wilkinson. He was still tied to the chair but completely naked. "Don't tell me to piss off again, I don't like it" said Bobby. Wilkinson was not as confident as he had been previously.

"So" said Bobby, "the money. You will make every effort to pay back Mr. Constantine the money you owe him soon will you?"

"OK, OK" said Wilkinson showing a bit of anxiety. "Let me go now and we will forget about this, OK?"

"Not really. There is the second thing I want to talk to you about, Robert Parsons".

"That fucking idiot" said Wilkinson. "It's his fault that I ended up in prison. If he had done what I told him to properly, nobody would have discovered it. What's he to you anyway, the blokes a loser".

"He was my father" said Bobby calmly as he watched Wilkinson go pale.

"Look, I didn't actually mean that he was a loser and an idiot, its just that I have been in prison for long time…….."

Bobby didn't hear the end of the sentence he had walked away again. He had noticed a large club hammer on the workbench. He picked it up and walked back to Wilkinson. He stood in front of him swinging the hammer. "Now, you are going to clear his name, you are going to find some way of convincing the authorities that he was working under your instructions, knew nothing about what was going on and was not guilty of the conspiracy charge that was made against him".

"Impossible" said Wilkinson. As soon as he had said it, Bobby brought the club hammer down, with all of the strength that he could muster, onto the big toe of the right foot. Blood, flesh and bone sprayed out from the hammer. Wilkinson let out a piercing scream. His toe was flattened. Bobby walked away and back to where the others were. Mr. Constantine was now sitting behind the spotlight watching. He just smiled as Bobby walked passed him and went to the kitchen to put the kettle on.

A few minutes later he was back. Wilkinson had stopped moaning but was obviously very scared of Bobby standing before him with the hammer in his hand. Bobby thought that he could actually smell the blood that was seeping across the floor. Certainly he could smell Wilkinson's sweat.

"Look, how about your dad and me get together and discuss a way out of this. We could go and see a solicitor maybe and I could sign an affidavit or something. How about that?"

"There's only one problem with that, my father committed suicide because of what you had done to him". As he finished saying it Bobby brought the hammer down on the other big toe, on the left foot. Wilkinson screamed again. Both his big toes were completely crushed. Again Bobby walked away leaving him moaning.

He walked into the kitchen and selected a mug from the draining board by the sink. "Coffee and tea are in the cupboard" said Stavros.

"I don't want them" said Bobby, pouring the boiling water into the mug. He then put four tablespoons of sugar in the water. Bobby had read that if somebody spilt tea over themselves, the more sugar that it had in it the more it burnt. It was something to do with the sugar causing the liquid the stick to the skin and make the pain worse. He carried the mug back to where Wilkinson sat. He was now just moaning quietly. "So let's get back to the matter in hand" said Bobby. "You are going to find some way of clearing my dad's name. If you don't I will see you again in a couple of months time and then, instead of making a couple of toes useless, it will be a couple of limbs. Do you understand?"

"I understand what you want but I don't know how to go about it" he whined.

"Well think of something" said Bobby, as he started to pour the boiling water slowly over the top of Wilkinsons sweating, bald head. Wilkinson screamed again and Bobby could see the blisters forming on his scalp as he poured. It seemed to work, the water with that much sugar in, didn't run off as it would have done if it was just water.

"Lets hope that we never meet again" said Bobby as he stopped pouring and walked away. He walked back to where Mr. Constantine and Stavros stood.

"Well you are a surprise" said Mr. Constantine. "I certainly think that he got the message. Here", he said, handing Bobby a brown envelope. Bobby put it in his pocket and walked out of the door. As he was riding home he realised that what he had done had been disgusting and cruel and yet he didn't feel any remorse. It was as though somebody else had gone into the factory this evening and Bobby had just watched.

When he arrived home he went to his room and looked in the envelope that he had been given. Inside was £250 cash.

The next day he left messages for Mr. Constantine to phone him at the car sales showrooms in Manor Park and Seven Kings. Mr. Constantine phoned that evening and told him to keep the money. He said that Bobby had helped him and he always paid the people that helped him. Why not Bobby thought, he could obviously afford it. Bobby took the money and paid it into the bank. It would be useful when he and Sandra got together.

CHAPTER 43

Work was becoming even more boring. Bobby found that he could complete all of his work in about two hours a day. To fill some time he was doing the filing for Terri. He desperately wanted to ask her about Sandra, how she was, was she happy, but didn't want to risk it as, as far as Terri was concerned he had only met her once, at Terri's party. The others in the office pulled his leg about spending time in Terri's office and how they could tell she fancied him. He just smiled, he couldn't tell them that he was saving himself for Sandra. He sometimes felt that it was only his swimming and his time spent studying and reading that kept him from going mad.

In February Mac and Phil both went down with the flu. The office was short staffed. On the first day that they were away Mr. Allen and Joe were both very busy on the phones. After a while Mr. Allen signaled to Bobby to answer a phone that had been ringing for a while. He moved to Phil's desk and answered. He took an order and completed the order form. Immediately he hung up the phone rang again. He picked it up and dealt with that enquiry. Mr. Allen finished his call and said "you seemed to manage those OK, you had better stay on the phones for the day".

On the third call Bobby took the order and then asked if there was anything else the customer was looking for. He took another order for something that the customer didn't think that they stocked. Mr. Allen had listened and complimented Bobby on his initiative. They normally only took orders and never asked the customer any questions about other requirements. From that morning the sales office practice changed. For the next week Bobby was on the phones. His stock keeping was done when he first arrived in the morning for the orders taken the day before and then he was on a sales desk. It was a very successful arrangement.

Bobby was promoted. They installed a phone on his desk and he was to take sales calls. He got a £50 a year salary increase.

Towards the end of February he received another phone call from Mr. Constantine. Again he wanted to meet Bobby for a drink and a chat and again they arranged to meet at the Seven Kings Hotel. Bobby arrived and Mr. Constantine was already there with a large scotch on table in front of him and a pint of bitter for Bobby.

"I was very impressed with your performance last month Bobby. I would like you to persuade another of my acquaintances to part with some money that he owes. How about it?"

"Sorry Mr. Constantine" said Bobby, "that was a one-off. It only worked because I hate the bastard for what he did to my dad and the effect that he has had on my family".

"I realise that Bobby. Look, I can get Stavros and his brother to give guys a good smack, but it doesn't work with some people. This guy that I'm talking about has had a visit from them twice. He has plenty of cash, he is just taking the piss. I need something more than a couple of heavies here."

"I don't think that I could do it to a stranger Mr Constantine".

"If it helps this guys a shit bag. He specialises in prostitution of young girls. If you help me out here its worth five hundred pounds to you".

Five hundred pounds was what Bobby earned in a year. It was a fortune, think of what that would do when Sandra wanted them to get a flat together. "I'll think about it", he said "can you let me have a phone number that I can contact you on"? They parted company with Bobby agreeing to contact him within a week. Bobby thought about the money and then about how interesting it would be to try some psychology. He went to the library on his way home the following evening and withdrew a book on the subject. The following day he phoned Mr. Constantine and asked what the person was frightened of. Sometime later Mr. Constantine phoned him back and said that he was not really frightened of anything except rats, apparently he had once been bitten by one and now it was the only thing that frightened him. Apparently he was a bit of a hard case.

Bobby was back in the library on Saturday morning and after more than two hours of searching he found what he was looking for. He phoned Mr. Constantine that afternoon. He had noticed when he was in the Ferry Lane factory the previous month, that there was some welding equipment in the work bay area. He asked for two saucepans to be welded together, base against base, with a leather belt caught in between them. He also wanted two rats. Mr. Constantine said he would get Stavros to get the rats but that Bobby should go to the factory during his lunch hour on Monday and see the welder whose name was Jock, and tell him what he wanted. The appointment with the victim was arranged for the following Monday evening at the factory.

CHAPTER 44

B obby arrived at the factory at 8pm. He was carrying a two pint bottle of meths. As before Mr. Constantine, Stavros and his brother were there already. They greeted Bobby as he walked in. He saw that there was another man with them. He was tall and very well dressed. He looked at Bobby but said nothing.

"He's over there" said Stavros, nodding towards the far side of the factory. The forklift forks were raised. The man was naked with his wrists bound, one attached to each of the forks. They were raised to a height so that the mans feet just touched the floor.

"Can you put a pallet on the forks and tie him to it, lying down. Then raise the forks so that they are about three feet in the air". Stavros and Yuri went to do as asked, on this occasion without waiting for Mr. Constantine to agree. They did what Bobby had asked and then walked back to where Bobby and Mr. Constantine stood. Bobby picked up the two saucepans, welded together as he had shown Jock and walked towards the man. As before the spotlights didn't allow him to see what was behind them.

"I don't know who the fuck you are but your dead meat" he said when he saw Bobby. Bobby ignored him.

"Are you listening to me you little shit? Fucking untie me or you will regret it for the rest of your short miserable life". Bobby acted as though he hadn't heard him. He placed the saucepans, the bottom one face down, onto the mans stomach and strapped the belt around his waist securing it with the buckle on the side.

"What the fucks this? You going to do some cooking?" said the man. Bobby said nothing.

Bobby walked away behind the spotlights. "Come here you little bastard" the man yelled as Bobby disappeared from his view. The two rats were in a box. Bobby put on a pair of leather welders gloves and carried the box and the bottle of meths over to the forklift truck.

"Are you fucking dumb or something, or just fucking stupid? "said the man.

"Neither" said Bobby, in a quiet calm voice. It helped that he didn't like this victim at all.

"What's this about then? the man said.

"This is a message from Mr. Constantine. Apparently you own him a considerable amount of money and are refusing to pay. He has sent his representatives to see you and you have ignored their requests".

"You mean tweedle dum and tweedle dee, the Greek dummies. So they failed and you are going to succeed? Fuck off". He was almost laughing at Bobby but his demeanor suddenly changed when Bobby opened box and pulled out a rat.

"OK, jokes over, take it away, let's talk about the money" he said in staccato words. Bobby ignored him, he levered up the bottom saucepan and placed the rat underneath so that it was trapped within the saucepan on the mans stomach. He visibly winced, before he could say anything Bobby had picked up the second rat and put that under the saucepan too.

The man could now feel both of the rats crawling around on his stomach, he was now sweating profusely.

"Get them off, get them off" he shouted. "You win. I will get him his money this week, just take them away". The victim was on the verge of hysteria. Bobby ignored him. He took the two pints of meths and poured it into the other saucepan which was face up. He reached into his pockets and pulled out a box of matches and lit the meths.

"Now, let me explain what is going to happen here" he said. "Rats are frightened of heat. If they feel it, they try to escape. The top pan will get hot from the meths and being metal, will transfer some of that heat to the bottom pan. When the bottom pan starts to heat the rats will panic and they will try to dig their way out. They won't go upwards because that is where the heat is coming from. They can't go sideways because that is the metal sides of the saucepan. The only way they can go is downwards, digging and gnawing through your stomach. It's a very ancient technique devised by the Chinese three centuries ago for getting information from traitors". Bobby smiled at him.

The man was now staring at the saucepans with his eyes wide open. He then started to scream. Bobby didn't know whether that was fear or whether the rats had started to dig.

"So then" said Bobby, "you are going to reconsider your comments about me being dead meat aren't you?"

"Yes, yes, just get rid of them", he managed to get the words out just before he screamed.

"And you are going to pay the money that you owe to Mr. Constantine as well aren't you?" At this point the mans bowels gave way and Bobby could smell a mixture of sweat and shit.

"Yes, please do something." He was now close to panic and screamed again, this time much louder and longer. Bobby noticed blood seeping from the bottom of the saucepan. The rats had started to gnaw their way through his stomach. He undid the belt and lifted both of the rats off and returned them to the box. He threw the saucepans aside and walked away from the man who was both sobbing and screaming at the same time. He walked calmly back to where Mr. Constantine and his friend stood, put the box of rats on the floor, took off the leather gloves and said "that should do the trick".

"It should indeed" said Mr. Constantine with a grin on his face. He took and envelope out of his coat pocket and gave it to Bobby. Bobby left by the side door and rode home. In his bedroom he opened the envelope. As promised it contained £500. In bed that night Bobby thought about what he had done. He felt that he should feel some remorse but he didn't. As with Wilkinson, it was as though it had been someone else doing what he had done. It was as though he was an actor in a film, it wasn't really him.

CHAPTER 45

Bobby passed his driving test. That evening he phoned Mr. Constantine as asked him if he had a suitable car. He didn't want something big or expensive, just something to get around in that was a little more stylish than he Morris 1000 that he had learnt in.

"You may be in luck. I have just got in a nice little Triumph Herald, good condition, nice little car. It's worth about £300 but I took it as payment for a debt of £180 so you can have it for that".

This seemed just what he wanted so he told Mr. Constantine that he would pick it up on Saturday morning. "Don't bother to get the money out of the bank Bobby, I know that you are good for it. Anyway I want to have a chat that may be worthwhile for you".

On Saturday Bobby arrived at the car lot in Manor Park about ten o'clock. Mr. Constantine was there. The car was parked in the road; it was two tone, light mauve and pink. It had no rust on it and looked very smart. Bobby went to the office and Mr. Constantine gave him the ignition key and log book.

"You know last month when we went to the factory a friend of mine was there. Well he has a little problem similar to the one that I had and he would like to use your special talents". Bobby was surprised at this development. "I don't want to make this my job. I did the first one because it was Wilkinson and the other one as a favour to you".

"You also did it for £500 and you also did it because you get some power from it. What I am saying is that it seems to work, I got my money within two days. You are very good at it and you could get very wealthy as a result. This job would be worth another £500 cash to you and I will throw in the car as a bonus".

Bobby heard himself agreeing before he really thought about it. It was although it was somebody else controlling him. He asked Mr. Constantine to find out some things about the victim and left in his new car.

That evening he rode to Nicks as usual on a Saturday. Nicks Birthday had been the month before and Bobby had told Nick that he had a birthday treat for him but couldn't give it to him yet. Nick had been intrigued but had not pushed it further. Bobby parked the scooter outside the house and when he went in he reminded Nick about what he had said. "Happy belated Birthday" said Bobby handing Nick his crash helmet with the log book and steering lock key inside it".

"What's this?" said Nick.

"Its your Birthday present, the scooter. Now you can ride to work instead of waiting for bus and it will be a great aid for pulling the birds". He told Nick about passing his driving test and his new car, omitting the details about how he was paying for it. Nick was overjoyed. He ran out and drove up and down the road. They then rode to Gants Hill to go to the cinema.

CHAPTER 46

Easter came and went. The week after Bobby was chatting to Terri when she mentioned that Sandra and her husband had been over to visit on Easter Monday. Bobby, trying to sound very casual said "Oh yes, I remember her from your party. Wasn't her husband ill or something? How are they?"

"He was in hospital but he came out just before Christmas. He's not right but is improving. I think Sandra is finding it a bit tough. She doesn't seem like her old self". Bobby felt overjoyed, this quickly changed to guilt at feeling so happy about the person he loved being unhappy. But it did mean that she may contact him soon if the marriage wasn't working.

April moved into May, May to June, June to July. Work was better but Bobby knew that he had to try to move on. He was now doing a 'favour' for Mr. Constantine or one of his friends almost every month. He had almost £3000 in his bank account. He was studying tax accountancy in his course when it suddenly struck him, if the tax authorities found out about the money he had, how could he explain such a large bank balance with a salary of £550 a year. A couple of days later he had thought of a plan. The next time he got a call from Mr. Constantine he would have a proposal for him.

The expected phone call came in the middle of July. Bobby agreed to meet at the offices at the car lot in Manor Park one evening.

"This one is for a friend of mine but it's a bit different". So far all of the 'persuading' had taken place at the factory in Rainham but this one was to take place at the victims house in Chigwell.

Bobby was a bit concerned about this. "What about any noise? I don't want the neighbours to start getting worried and phone the police".

"This guy has so much land around his house that nobody will hear. Anyway, if you're not happy all you have to do is leave. This one is worth £1200".

Bobby said "if it's worth that much the answer is no".

"What do you mean?" said a surprised Mr. Constantine.

"I have a money problem" said Bobby, who then explained his dilemma and concern about the tax authorities.

"Quite a clever little bugger aren't you" said Mr. Constantine smiling. "Don't tell me, you have a solution I suppose".

"Yes actually I do. The lots at Seven Kings were all individual a few years ago. The last one that you acquired, the one nearest the Seven Kings Hotel, has eight cars on it. Their retail value is £2290 as of yesterday. Given your usual markup that would mean that the trade price would be about £1500. The land is worth about £3000, total value £4200. I will buy it from you for £3000 cash, you can lend me £1500 for three months interest free for payment of the balance. That way I have a vehicle to lose any cash payments. What do you think? Will you sell it to me?"

"I have a counter proposal" said Mr. Constantine. "Seven

Kings lots are only pieces of land with portakabin offices. Here at Manor Park the lots were originally shops with flats above. I have just bought Smart Cars, the three shop units on the opposite side towards the Three Rabbits. There are twelve cars on the lot, worth about £2200 trade. The units are worth about £10000. For £3000 cash and the £1200 you will earn from his job I will sell you a 50% share. You will run it any way that you want but I will get to see monthly accounts and 50% of the profit paid quarterly. You also have the benefit of the accommodation above. It's used as offices and storage at the moment but it would be easy to turn one of the units into a very nice two bedroom, self contained flat and it would be effectively rent free. That's a good offer Bobby, what do you think?"

"51% and you have a deal" Mr. Constantine smiled and held out his hand for Bobby to shake on it. "I always said you were a smart kid. I have the partnership documents drawn up tomorrow. You can sign whenever you like. So that's a yes on the Chigwell job then".

Bobby nodded, "thank you Mr. Constantine" he said "we have a deal".

"You had better call me Ari if we are going to be partners" he said.

Bobby drove home felling very satisfied. A new job and a new home, that was better than he had expected. He hadn't thought of the accommodation issue. What a result. He told Nick that evening although not giving him all of the details. He couldn't explain to Nick how he could have over £4000 having worked for a year, most of which was at a salary of £500 per annum. Nick congratulated him but Bobby thought that he was less enthusiastic than he had expected.

The following week he signed the partnership documents with Ari and took possession of the lot and flats. He resigned from his job and although a bit surprised, all of the staff were very nice about it, wished him the best of luck and said that they felt he would be a great success selling cars. He had had some business cards printed and gave them each one in case they ever wanted to buy a car. Terri was a bit tearful and said that she would miss him. He said that she could pop in to the lot anytime she wanted.

Despite not being close to his mother any more, he was disappointed with her easy acceptance when he told her he was moving out and going to live in a flat over a car lot. She said that she wasn't surprised that he was leaving home and wished him luck. He brought a sleeping bag and moved into the middle of the three flats the following weekend. Business was not busy on the Saturday and the lot was closed on the Sunday so Bobby cleared out all of the old papers, car spares and other rubbish that was in it so the is was ready for decorating. He brought a kettle, a toaster, a fridge and a television and apart from his sleeping bag, made do for a while. He put his Triumph Herald on the lot and took a Vauxhall Victor as his new car. It was four years old, silver and maroon, and he thought that it was right for his new position, a nice car but not too flashy.

CHAPTER 47

Two weeks elapsed before he headed for Chigwell. Because this one was different than previous jobs he had gone into more detail and planned the operation. Because of the potential difficulty he had asked for more money and was surprised when the fee had been increased to £2000 without any resistance. He was with Stavros driving in a Ford Zephyr to meet two of the men employed by Ari's friend at the Maypole pub in Hainault. Upon meeting the two men Bobby was a bit concerned. He had asked for particular skills but these looked like two heavies. The victim was the right hand man to their boss. He had helped run the illegal bookie operation and also the distribution of marijuana and LSD drugs to pubs and clubs in North London. It had been discovered that he was skimming the betting money, mixing the drugs with other materials so that he could sell more and keep the money for the excess and was also running his own protection racket without the consent of his boss. Not only was he to be taught a lesson but it was believed that there were records he kept that needed to be retrieved. His weakness was that he was scared of the dark and always slept with a light on. Also he was proud of his sexual prowess, boasting that he could do it three times a night every night. Bobby was planning on using both of these factors.

They arrived outside the house. It had large gates that were locked as expected. One of the men got out of the car and had the lock undone in about three seconds. Bobby thought that he had misjudged them. This was one of the skills he had asked for. They left the cars parked in the road and walked quietly across the lawn to the front door. This lock took the same man about ten seconds to open. There were lights on in the house and a car parked in the drive but the entered the hall silently and stood and listened. Bobby heard a female giggle upstairs. That was the only sound that he could hear. He signaled for the two men to go with him upstairs and for Stavros to stay in the hall in case somebody else was in the house. They crept up the stairs and heard the giggling again, coming from one of the bedrooms. The door of the room was slightly ajar and Bobby could see a young woman lying on the bed wearing only a pair of very flimsy panties. Kneeling next to her was a man with a pair of boxer shorts on and a shirt which was unbuttoned. One of the men, the other one to the lock picker, took a small bottle and a cloth from his pocket. He soaked the cloth in the liquid from the bottle, chloroform. Bobby and the two men then entered the room quickly. Just as the man on the bed turned, the cloth was clamped over his mouth and nose and after about five seconds of being held he went limp. Bobby said to the girl "don't make a sound" and she just looked at him, wide eyed and scared, but silent. The two men picked up the unconscious victim and carried him downstairs. Bobby said to the girl "You, downstairs in the lounge now". She immediately got off the bed and ran downstairs into the lounge and sat on the settee with her arms folded trying to cover her naked breasts.

The two men had placed a dinning chair in the middle

of the room and were tying the victim to it binding his hand behind his back. Bobby took two small discs of black plastic from his pocket. They had been cut to the size and shape of eye sockets. He then took two tubes and spread a line from each onto the table. He then mixed the two lines together. The tubes contained Araldite adhesive. By mixing the two tubes together the setting was achieved by a chemical reaction and not by drying as with normal glues, this meant that the glue set very quickly. He placed the two black discs over the eyes of the victim and glued them there with the Araldite glue. It would set in about ten minutes. He then removed the man boxer shorts and tied a piece of thin cords around the back of his penis and testicles and pulled it tight, restricting the blood flow. He then sat on the settee to wait for the victim to regain consciousness.

In a soft voice the girl, who was sitting next to Bobby said "if you are going to fuck me, can you do it quickly, I need to get home".

"Nobody is going to fuck you and you're not going anywhere" said Bobby. "Where are your clothes"?

"In the bedroom" she said. Bobby signaled for Stavros to go and get them. He brought them in to the room and she quickly put her dress on, not bothering with her bra or tights. "I really need to go home" she said again.

"Sit down, shut up, you go when I've finished" said Bobby.

The victim stirred. Bobby stood up. "Back with us then are you?" he said.

"What is this"? said the victim, and then realising his situation he said "what's happening, I can't see, what have you done". He was starting to panic.

"Bobby moved close to him and said quietly, "you have been bit naughty. Your boss wants the money that you have skimmed from him and the details of the scams that you have been operating. Now, your blindness can be dealt with if you cooperate and so can the fact that we have cut off the blood supply to your balls. If that is left for very long then the cell walls in your prick will collapse and you will not be able to get it up, so time is important".

The victim was silent. "Also we have your girlfriend here and of course she may suffer too if we don't get the information we need".

"You can do what you like to her, she's only a little tramp".

The girl was visibly upset by this comment. "You bastard" she said, "you told me you loved me".

She sat back on the settee. Bobby tightened the cord around the victims testicles. "Look, I don't really know what you are talking about" said the victim. "I admit that I have been taking a bit of commission and also that I have been blending the grass, but its very small money and I don't have any records. Do what you like to the girl but let me talk to the boss before you do anything else, I can explain everything".

"Sorry, you give me the information or you go permanently blind and you prick falls off". The victim suddenly, unpredictably panicked. He started to sob. The tears had no way of escaping from his eyes which resulted very quickly in a buildup of pressure on his eyes which confirmed in his own mind that he was going blind. He started to moan and sway on the chair.

"Why don't you just tell me where the records are" said Bobby calmly.

"There's a wardrobe in the spare bedroom with a false bottom. I've seen him put stuff in there" said the girl.

"Go with Stavros and show him where" said Bobby. He returned a few minutes later with two holdalls. The victim was now incoherent and still just rocking backwards and forwards. Bobby had been reading books on psychology and thought that the victim was having a nervous breakdown.

Bobby opened the first bag. It contained bunches of banknotes, Bobby estimated that there were many thousands of pounds in it. The second bag contained books, records. They listed names, amounts and dates. Bobby didn't study them, just put them back into the bag. Stavros picked them both up and left the room. The two men followed him into the hall and out of the front door to the cars. Bobby nodded to the girl, "you can go now, but forget you were here tonight and everything that happened. Those men kill little girls for fun". She quickly got off the settee and ran for the front door and into night without saying a word. Bobby cut the rope that was binding the victim and left him sitting rocking and moaning. He got in the car with Stavros who drove him home to Manor Park. As had often happened previously, Bobby wondered how he could feel such a different person when he carried out these contracts, it was almost as though it was somebody else doing the work. He forgot about the victim immediately. He didn't care that he had left him naked and thinking that he was blind.

"My friend is very happy with the outcome the other night" said Mr. Constantine when he visited Bobby a few days later. He is a big face in North London and has said that he may like to use you again. Is that alright with you? Its good money from him".

"It's fine as long as he pays" said Bobby. Bobby realised that he had accepted that this type of thing was part of his life, at least for now. He still often thought of Sandra and still hoped that he could make a life for the two of them. He managed to persuade himself that he was doing these things to earn money for their future life together.

CHAPTER 48

Nick broke up for the holidays. He spent some time at Bobby's supervising the builder that Bobby had employed to put in a new bathroom and kitchen and decorate. Other times he worked at Sainsbury's. Bobby bought some new furniture and curtains and by the end of August the flat was finished and Bobby was very pleased with it. They had been invited to a few parties during the holidays so decided to have one themselves in the flat. Most of the people that came were from his schooldays. He had phoned Hobdays and invited Terri but apart from her, everybody that was coming had been invited by Nick. It dawned on Bobby that he had no friends except Nick. For a short time this worried him but he pushed it to the back of his mind as the day of the party drew near.

The party was a huge success. Nick had shut himself in one of the bedrooms for an hour with the biggest breasted girl there and eventually came out with a huge grin on his face. Bobby had been propositioned by at least three of the girls including Terri. He had told them all that he was very flattered but he was saving himself until he was married. This impressed them all.

The holidays were soon over, Nick was back at school for

his final year. Bobby's 18th Birthday came and went. He got a card from his mother but no phone call. He did get one from Gran though and promised to go and see her soon. Sales in the car lot had improved. Bobby had painted the façade and the whole premises had been painted and given a face lift. He got a phone call from Ari late in September, another contract, another £1000. He also went with him to visit what Ari called a miscreant. They only talked about the problem Ari had with the man and the matter was resolved without any further action. Bobby was paid £500.

In November business was slow so Bobby cleared out all of the old paper and bits of cars from the other two flats and employed the builder to put in new bathrooms and toilets and to decorate those too. He discussed with Ari letting them out. Ari agreed that it was a good idea if Bobby was OK with it so it was decided to do it in the New Year.

Bobby spent Christmas with Nick after visiting Gran on Christmas morning. He had brought her a hamper from Selfridges, she was really pleased. He had bought the same present for Nicks mum as she too was very pleased with the luxury cake, biscuits and chocolates. He didn't see or speak to his mother over the Christmas period.

The New Year arrived with a lot of snow and some very cold weather. Nobody wanted to buy cars but he did let both of the flats for £30 per month each. Both tenants were negro families who had trouble renting good accommodation in the area. As long as they paid the rent on time Bobby didn't care what colour they were. He studied his accountancy books and made some plans for the future. It had occurred to him that he still had too much money going into his bank account. Since he brought into the car lot he had earned another five thousand pounds. He decided that he was going to take Ari's route and invest some money in property. He found a house for sale in Elgin Road, in Seven Kings. It was a large, double fronted house. Bobby decided that he would buy it and turn it into two flats. He would live upstairs and he would let the downstairs flat. With this property being all his, he would not have to share the rent with Ari. He paid cash for the house and had enough money left over to do the alterations that were needed.

Two days after he bought the house Ari came to see him at the car lot. He knew all about Bobby's purchase, which surprised Bobby, but he wished him the best of luck and said it was the right thing to do, Bobby should be investing his money. Bobby showed the house to Nick that weekend and told him that he could afford the mortgage because the sales had been so good. He had a feeling that Nick was dubious about this but he didn't ask any questions.

CHAPTER 49

The summer months passed quickly. Bobby now saw his Gran almost every two weeks as he had said he would at Christmas. She told him that his Mum and Jane were both fine and that Jane had a job working in Bodgers Department Store in Ilford. Bobby listened and he was pleased that his Gran didn't push the fact that he had no contact with his mother or sister.

His car sales were going very well, he moved into Elgin Road and let both the flat above the car showroom and the ground floor flat in Elgin Road. His accountancy course was going well and he was expected to get good results at this year's exams.

He thought about Sandra less than he used to but still he often wondered how she was. He changed his Vauxhall Victor for a new Ford Zodiac and as he was working for Ari or his friends on a regular basis he had an additional income so far this year of over £8000. He was actually 'persuading' less and less. It seemed that Ari and his friends just wanted him to be with them mostly when they discussed problems with the transgressors.

Nick sat his A levels in June and was then finished at school. Bobby gave him a job washing cars and working in the office while he waited for his results and decided what he was going to do next. One Sunday evening in late July they were sitting in The Joker at Seven Kings, having a drink, when Nick said "I'm going to join the Army".

"The Army? What an earth for. What good are all the A levels if you are going to march up and down a square or be shot at"?

"Its not like that" said Nick, and then he explained what he intended. The army had offered to sponsor him through university to study modern languages. He would start at Bath University in October if his grades were as predicted. He would be as any other student during term time but in the holidays he would be in the army, training to be a soldier. He would get only two weeks holiday twice a year but apart from all of fees being paid and the books being bought for him, he would also be paid while at university. He would earn the salary of a First Lieutenant. It would mean that he would have to go to Sandhurst before he went to Bath but he said that actually he was looking forward to it.

Bobby found this choice amazing but he could see how enthusiastic Nick was about it and knew that he had long ago wanted to go into the army so he congratulated his friend and told him how happy he was for him. "What did your mum say"? said Bobby.

"I haven't told her yet. I was hoping that you would come back with me and we could tell her together. If she sees how happy you are Bobby then maybe she will be OK".

"When are you leaving?" said Bobby.

"Monday week, just over a week's time" replied Nick. They finished their drinks and then left to go and break the news to Mrs. Mead. She was sad that her Nick was leaving home and shed a few tears but she too could see how happy he was about this opportunity so she hugged him and just told him to be careful.

A little over a week later, on the first Sunday in August, Bobby drove Nick and his Mum to Sandhurst in Berkshire, to the army officers training college. They left Nick in his dormitory with his new colleagues, to start their training the next day. Nick said he would be home for the weekend before he went to Bath and would see them both then. Bobby and Mrs. Mead then took the long journey back to Ilford almost all the way in silence. "Don't worry Mrs. Mead, he will be fine" said Bobby, adding "If there is anything you need while he is away you must let me know".

"Thank you Bobby, I will. You're a good boy and have been a good friend to Nick" she said as she patted his hand.

Back in his flat Bobby looked around. His flat was very nice, comfortably furnished, with the latest television, music centre, kitchen appliances' and fittings. He had lots of money in the bank, property and his own business. He was not yet even nineteen years old but he suddenly felt lonely. He thought of Sandra again. He would love to know how she was, how was she doing, was she still married? Should he contact her?

Nick returned for a weekend in October before going to Bath. He told Bobby that he wanted to make up for lost time having been incarcerated for two months at Sandhurst. He had a very short haircut and looked very fit after the two months of training. They went out on the Friday night to the pub, and Bobby had a party in his flat for him on Saturday. He invited everybody that he knew who also knew Nick and told them to invite anybody that he didn't know who would know him. Over seventy people arrived, the flat, although quite big, was bulging. If Nick judged the success of the weekend by the number of girls he had sex with, two on Friday and at least three on Saturday, it was a great success. On Sunday Bobby drove him and his mother to Bath. He had accommodation on campus so they settled him in, met the other guys on the floor he was on and then left him with his new friends for the long drive back. It took three hours and Mrs. Mead hardly said a word, lost in her thoughts. Bobby agreed to go to lunch with her on the following Sunday.

In early November Bobby received a phone call from his mother, the first time she had phoned him. His Gran had died. The funeral was at St Anthony's church in Forest Gate. He picked up his mother on the morning of the funeral and took her to Forest Gate. There were about twenty other people there, all elderly, none of whom Bobby recognized. They all came and offered their condolences to his mother after the service. Bobby didn't ask his mother why Jane was not there. He had decided that as far as he was concerned she had ceased to exist. There was nowhere to go afterwards for the traditional tea, sandwiches and cake. They could have gone to Gran's flat opposite the church but his mother hadn't organized anything so he just drove her home and dropped her off at her house, he didn't go in.

CHAPTER 50

July 1980

Delroy Campbell was twenty years old. He lived with his mother in the Guinness Trust flats in the Old Kent Road, behind the World Turned Upside Down pub. He had two older sisters, Charmaine and Blossom, both of whom were married and lived elsewhere. His mother had come to London from Jamaica in 1954. She had brought her two daughters with her. She told everybody that her husband had been killed in the war fighting in the British Army and that was why she was now in England. Delroy was twelve years old when Blossom had told him the truth, that her husband was a drunk who had left her for a prostitute in Kingston who could earn the money to buy him his rum.

Delroy didn't know who his father was. He suspected that he was the result of a one-night-stand when his mother had had one too many stouts on a Saturday night and had been careless. He may have been unplanned but his sisters and is mother loved him dearly. He was a happy baby and an even happier child and gave none of them any problems.

It wasn't until he left school at fifteen that Delroy realised that a black boy in South London, in the 1970's had problems. You either were talented at music, very talented at football, went into crime or took menial jobs that the white men didn't want to do. There were some black businessmen but they often treated the black boys worse than the white men did.

Delroy left school and got a job working in a hostel in Stockwell. It was a stop off house for immigrants just arrived from the Caribbean. It wasn't a very good job. He cleaned, stripped the beds, cleared up the plates after the meals and generally did all of the mundane tasks. But he did them as he did everything else, with a smile on his face and a pleasant and polite manner. He met some of the other black boys from Stockwell and Brixton and although he was too young to get into the pubs with them, he did go to the private clubs and listen to the music and the conversations.

He had been working at the hostel for about six months when he was approached by a man who had arrived the day before.

"Do you know where I can lay this off man?" he said. Delroy didn't know what he was talking about and it must have shown in his face.

"Grass man, I need money for the grass I have".

"Oh pot" said Delroy realising what he was talking about. "How much do you want?"

"Its worth at least ten pounds" said the man, pulling a package out of his bag and showing Delroy. Delroy didn't know much about drugs but he knew that they were sold at many of the clubs and he had seen them sold openly inside them. The police would never come in the places where he went. He also had a feeling that in small quantities it was worth more than £10.

"I'll get you £10 for it in an hour" he said. The man seemed satisfied. Delroy went to see the manager and asked for an advance of £10 on his weeks wages. Delroy had always been a good willing worker, he hadn't had time off ill or even had a holiday so, although he didn't normally do so, he got out his wallet and gave Delroy the £10 advance.

That evening Delroy went down to the clubs and sold his grass £60. Two days later another resident recently arrived approached Delroy. "You buy grass?" he said. Another £10 purchase yielded another £55 that evening. It seemed that everybody coming from Jamaica or Barbados, Trinidad or Tobago, was bringing in pot, very high quality pot so Delroy asked them when they first arrived if they had any and if they did he offered to buy it from them.

One evening about three months after his first sale he was sitting in one of his favourite clubs in Brixton. He was approached by a large man in his twenty's with a smart suit and gold teeth. He sat down at Delroy's table. He explained to Delroy that he was the local dealer and Delroy was taking his trade. Delroy was suddenly scared. He was sensible enough not to want to cross this man. However he seemed to be friendly and complimented Delroy on his success. He told him that he was impressed with his entrepreneurial attitude and he was impressed with Delroy's sources. They agreed that Delroy would supply him wholesale and that he would not retail in the Brixton and Stockwell area, this could be Delroys own patch. Delroy was happy with this, although it meant a reduced margin he had less work to do, buy the grass and make one delivery.

Throughout the next few months other pushers approached him to source them too. Delroy was worried that he couldn't meet the demand but he was surprised that he had soon developed a reputation. Many immigrants coming from the Caribbean sought him out. He had got a name for being nice to deal with, fair on the price and always paying cash.

About ten months after he started his dealing he was

in the Ram Jam Club one evening when he was confronted by a large man that he did not recognise. He knew all of the local faces and this one certainly wasn't one of them. Delroy noticed that all of a sudden the space around him was empty apart from the man and two large minders standing six feet behind him.

"Delroy Campbell I assume, pleased to meet you". Delroy smiled his best smile. "Pleased to meet you too, I hope" he laughed.

"You will be pleased to meet me. I have a business proposition for you. You have a reputation for being a reliable trader. I have some merchandise which I want to shift. I sell it to you in bulk, you break it down and sell it on. You make money, I make money. Win win".

"What is the merchandise?" asked Delroy.

"Heroin, white gold" said the man. He explained to Delroy that the Columbian drug barons were having problems getting their production into the United States through Florida or California so were shipping it into Jamaica for onward shipment to Europe. The man was the London end of the organization. They got young girls to swallow condoms filled with heroin, board a plane to London and when here, pass the condoms and recover the heroin. The man wanted three or four trusted partners in London to meet the 'mules' as the girls were called, recover the powder and pay the organization. It was a big jump up the league for Delroy but he agreed to give it a trail run. The man said that he would need to set up somewhere where the mules could go when they arrived at Heathrow, and stay until they had passed the condoms. Delroy knew a place and said he would organise it. They shook hands, the first shipment was to arrive in three weeks.

Delroy had a friend who owned a cab company in Coldharbour Lane. He brought it from him paying well over the real value but it gave him the flat above the cab company for the girls to stay in for a few hours and he could use the cabs to collect them from the airport. He phoned the man and told him of the arrangements and he seemed very satisfied. He also found that the girls were coming over from the West Indies with little money and nowhere to go once they had delivered the powder. Delroy had an idea. He had generated a lot of cash that he needed to invest. Some of the girls were very attractive. So brought a large house in Fentiman Road in Vauxhall, had it decorated to a very high standard. He installed two of the girls in the house after first trying them out. As he expected they were experienced sexually and knew how to please a man. Back home they would have been used by men since their early teens and passed around, so that they would appreciate a variety of male tastes. He brought them nice underwear and dresses and they entertained clients. Delroy gave them 50% of whatever they earn't and they kept all of their tips so they were happy and so was he. He gave the same interview to other girls, they had to be attractive, clean, drug free and be able satisfy him. He eventually had four working from the Fentiman Road house and another four in a house in Catford. He decided that this was something to invest more in for the future.

He was generating so much cash that he decided to buy some others houses and let them out to people who came over from Jamaica. He still had his job at the hostel and still lived with his mum in the Old Kent Road, but this was just a front.

By the time he was twenty years old he owned seven houses and had thousands of pounds in the bank.

CHAPTER 51

In 1980 Bobby could look back at the last ten years and know that they had been good years for him and Nick. Nick had graduated with an honours degree in modern languages. He could speak French, German and Spanish and the army had sent him on courses to learn Arabic, Mandarin and Urdu. He was now a major and was on secondment to NATO in Germany. He had only been in a war zone once, for a six month tour of Belfast. This pleased his mother who Bobby kept in touch with and who he knew worried about him while he was in Ireland.

Bobby now owned seven car showrooms, four of them more upmarket than the Manor Park lot. One of them was an official BMW dealership. As part of one of his purchases he had also acquired a rundown breakers yard in Chadwell Heath.

He lived in a large detached house in Vicarage Lane, Chigwell and had eleven other properties which were let out, the three he had in partnership with Ari and eight of his own. He was a millionaire. He still did work 'helping' Ari and his friends. Many times though it seemed that only his presence was required to achieve the desired effect. His fee now varied from £5000 to £12000 per job and the people that employed him didn't seem to have a problem with that. He always delivered the goods. He no longer swam regularly but was a member of the local golf club and squash club and this kept him fit and trim.

Ari Constantine had got married. Although he was in his forties he hadn't been married before. His bride was twenty three and a daughter of an old friend in Greece. Bobby was flattered to be invited to the wedding. His wife was rather plain but very nice, friendly and caring. Bobby referred to her as Mrs. C which, for some reason she found funny. Stavros had told Bobby that Ari wanted a family and an heir and that she came from good breeding stock, she had seven brothers and sisters. Bobby thought it a funny reason to get married. However his wife duly obliged and Ari now had a six year old daughter and a four year old son, both of whom he thought the world of.

Nick had completely lost touch with his mother and sister but he did not think of this. He visited Mrs. Mead about once a month for Sunday lunch and she told him of the letters she had received from Nick. Bobby didn't tell her that Nick wrote almost identical letters to him. When Nick came home on leave he would spend most of the time with Bobby. The second bedroom in Bobby's house was Nicks. When he was on tour all of the clothes and possessions were left there rather than at his mothers.

Bobby was very popular at the golf club. He was a good golfer so was often chosen to play in competitions. He was good company so was popular with the male members. He was thirty years old, unmarried, wealthy, had a BMW 635, dressed well, and was meticulously clean and smart, so he was very also sought as company by the female members some of whom were of a similar age and divorced. They agreed Bobby would be a good catch. He did date some and one or two had managed to spend the night with him and maybe even the weekend , but he was not interested in a long term relationship.

When Nick was with him they were doubly popular, similar age, similar looks and Nick too was a good golfer. As Nick did not have much female company when on tour he always managed to spent at least one night with one of the divorcees when at home and sometimes had a mid-week treat with one of the married women whose husbands spent the week away on business. Bobby often reflected on how happy Nick was with his life, he loved the army and what he did in it and he loved the time he spent at home with Bobby.

Bobby had appointed managers for all of his businesses. He was very popular with his staff as he paid them a good wage and generous commission or bonuses on top. That way he expected and got, staff loyalty. It meant that although he tried to visit all of the companies every week, when Nick was at home he could spend as much time with him as they wanted.

CHAPTER 52

It was the evening after Bobby's birthday in September when the phone rang at his house. "I need you to sort some little black bugger out" said Ari as soon as Bobby had picked up the receiver.

"When?" said Bobby.

"Now" replied the caller.

"We don't work like that Ari", Bobby said. "We investigate the victim, find his weaknesses and then plan".

"There's no time for that, The boys picked him up five minutes ago and he will be at the Rainham factory in an hour".

"Lets talk about this first Ari" said Bobby, "I'm not……………….."

"Right, the Loughton House in 15 minutes, then we go together to Rainham". Ari put the phone down when he had finished, not giving Bobby any chance of a response.

Bobby was concerned. The Loughton House was only about 10 minutes from his home so he could get there in the time Ari had said, but he was not happy about the situation. He had never done a job without planning it. Also Ari seemed more annoyed on the phone than Bobby could remember. He had less to do with him these days but he had defiantly mellowed since his marriage.

Bobby arrived at the house and parked his car in the drive next to Ari's Bentley. The Loughton House was Ari's latest business venture and it seemed very profitable. He had formed an exclusive member's only club. Subscription was expensive so the members were all wealthy men. It was a large six bedroom house on the outskirts of Loughton, standing in a large plot. Ari had extended the house at the rear, installed a swimming pool in the large garden and altered the interior layout. As you walked into the large entrance hall, to the right was the old lounge and dining room. This was now one room with a number of blackjack tables in it. Beyond it was the extension with a large roulette table in the centre of the room. To the left of the hall was a lounge bar, All drinks were served by waiters in dinner suits and black ties or attractive women in evening gowns. Behind the bar area was a small office for Ari and his manager. The décor was opulent and the whole place oozed class. In the hall, discretely placed was a small hook board with six keys on it. Each key was for one of the six bedrooms. These were furnished to the same high standard as the rest of the house and were for the use of the members to entertain their female guests. The member would take a key, use the room for a maximum of one hour, leave the key in the lock when they left, at which point the staff would enter the room, change the bed-linen and the towels in the en-suite shower rooms, and when completed return the key to the hook board for the next guest. The rooms were free, they were covered by the membership fees. As its reputation had grown the club had attracted business and community leaders who wanted to entertain and impress mistresses.

Bobby walked in and was greeted by the staff, most of whom knew him as a colleague of Mr. Constantine's. He walked through to the back office. Ari was about to explode, "some little nigger bastard from south of the river is muscling in on my turf and pushing his black shit drugs. He even had the fucking cheek to try and push some in my own fucking club in Shorditch. I want you to gently, slowly, cut his fucking balls off and make the little bastard eat them".

Bobby was stunned. Ari rarely swore. Bobby had never seen him so angry. "Lets think about this Ari, nobody in the know is going to push on your turf let alone in your own club. This sounds like someone with a death wish or no brain. Lets find out more before we have every black from Brixton coming over to avenge a brother".

"Too late". A couple of caretakers from the club put him in a car and are taking him to the factory. I've sent Stavros over to open it up. Come on, we're due there now". Ari got up, swept past Bobby and headed for the door. Bobby followed and got into the Bentley as Ari started the engine and pulled out of the drive. They were at the Rainham factory twenty minutes later.

Bobby walked into the warehouse with Ari. Little had changed since he first walked in there fourteen years ago. The spotlights shone a young black man, about twenty years old, tied to a chair naked, on the pallet held by the forks of the forklift truck. "Déjà vous", Bobby thought.

He took Stavros's knife and approached the man. He could see immediately how frightened he was and how he was sweating profusely.

"Well you have been a very naughty boy" Bobby said to the victim.

"Hey man I don't know what you are talking about. I was just having a drink in a club with my girl and these two big honky's picked me up, put me in a van and dumped me here".

"Well you weren't just having a drink were you? You were pushing dope. And…..its not the first time. Today it was he club in Shoreditch but last week it was a pub in Hackney and before that in Bethnal Green. The pubs pushers are supplied exclusively by Mr. Constantine and the club is actually owned by him. He is the supplier for East London and all the pushers buy from him or…………they don't push".

"Hey man, I was just getting a bit of extra to impress my girl. I didn't think it would do any harm".

"What's your name?" said Bobby.

"Winston."

"Where are you from" said Bobby.

"Battersea man", said the victim.

"So lets just get this right Winston. You expect me to believe that you come north from Battersea, you have a girl in East London and you come over here with a pocket full of hash to earn a bit of extra cash to buy her a drink? You think I believe that". Bobby took Stavros's knife from his pocket and inserted the tip into the scrotum of the victim. Winston screamed hysterically. Bobby knew that it was not due to the pain, he had only nicked the skin, but the thought of what was going to happen next.

"Who supplies you with the drugs?" Bobby asked. "Delroy, Delroy Campbell", he blurted. Bobby knew that the victim would now answer any question truthfully but just for certain he pushed the knife into the scrotum again. Winston let out another yell and then urinated over the chair. He had lost all control.

"So" said Bobby calmly, "this Delroy character sends you over the river to deal drugs on a new turf".

"No man, he know nothing about it. I deal for him in Battersea and Wandsworth. I'm here for my girl. She lives in Cricklewood but all the pubs there are paddy pubs and they don't like us coloureds so we go east where we get no trouble, that's all".

Bobby looked at the man and lifted the knife again. Winston tried to pull back. Bobby turned and walked away.

He went back to where Ari was standing. He seemed to have calmed down a bit."I think that we should let him go without any further damage" said Bobby.

"Lets the black fucker go?" said Ari, not believing what Bobby was saying. "You going soft on me or something. Cut his fucking balls off".

"Look Ari, this guy is small fry. I think he is telling the truth and he is just stupid. If we do him any harm it may have repercussions. How many of your customers are black? What do you think they would do if it got out that you had cut up one of their brothers. What would happen if the South London coons paired up with Mad Paddy for example. That could be big trouble. Why not just send him on his way with a message?" Ari was quiet for a few seconds. Then he smiled at Bobby. "You are smart sometimes, that's why I like you as a partner, you actually think. OK let him go with a warning".

Bobby went back to where Winston was sitting. He could see the fear in his eyes. "This is your lucky day Winston. Mr. Constantine has decided that he would rather be at home in the arms of his beautiful wife than piss around with a stupid black bastard like you. Just to show you that there is no hard feelings Mr. Constantine has asked me to tell you that you are welcome to visit any of his pubs or clubs and have a drink at any time, but if you deal drugs in any of them, he will have your balls cut off and feed them to his dog. Is that clear".

"Yes man clear as clear, thanks man". Bobby walked away as Stavros moved forward to cut he victim free. Bobby and Ari climbed into the Bentley and went back to the Loughton House for Bobby to collect his car. Ari was in a much better mood. "I don't have a dog to feed his balls to" he said with a smile.

"You won't need one, he won't be back" said Bobby.

CHAPTER 53

Ari Constantine was sitting in the office of one of the car lots in Manor Park. He had moved on in life since he brought this lot almost thirty years ago but he still felt comfortable in this dingy office with its old furniture. He was smoking a cigar looking at some figures for car sales last month when the phone rang. "Yeah?" It was his customary response on the phone.

"Is that Ari Constantine? said the caller.

"Who's asking?"

"My name is Delroy Campbell. You detained one of my soldiers the other evening".

"He was returned unharmed. He was a silly boy and got off light, so piss off and don't cause me any grief".

"I know, I'm ringing to tell you I agree, he shouldn't have done it and I have given him a bit of a telling off as well".

"That's alright then, goodbye" said Ari.

"No wait" said Delroy "I have a business proposition for you".

"What possible business would I want with some nigger from Brixton or somewhere"?

"I can supply you with more drugs, cheaper, more reliably and of a better quality than you are buying now" said Delroy.

There was a silence on the other end of the phone, Delroy knew that he had caught his interest. "Why don't me meet and discuss it"?

Ari thought about it. "I'm not coming to South London. You come here and we'll meet".

"How about neutral ground" suggested Delroy. "The Tower Hotel". They arranged to meet in the Tower Hotel near Tower Bridge the following Thursday at 11 o'clock. "How will I recognize you?" asked Ari.

"I'll be the only black man not in a cleaners overalls" laughed Delroy. They met as arranged. Ari was impressed with how well informed Delroy Campbell was. He told Ari that he knew that all of the main North London wholesalers, Ari, the Cohen Brothers, the Turners and Vlasov's, all sourced from Mad Paddy O'Rourke. He ran West London from a pub in Kilburn and let the rest run their areas. Delroy told him that Mad Paddy sourced from Liverpool where had originally come from. Drugs were imported through the docks there, coming in on lorries from Ireland.

"We all know that Mad Paddy looks after his own area first and sometimes that means that the rest of you don't get enough to go around. He mixes his stuff, he put grass from the parks in his grass and any old powder, usually baking powder in his white stuff. You never know what you are buying or how strong it is. What I am offering you is however much you want. A weekly delivery against a weekly cash payment. All of my stuff is guaranteed pure so you can bulk it and cut it yourself and offer whatever quality you want not, what your given by Mad Paddy". An arrangement was made that Delroy would arrange for a weekly delivery to be made to Ari. He would phone first to get a delivery address and the goods would be delivered later that day. Five days after the delivery Ari would arrange for cash to be taken to Delroy, the same arrangement of phoning would apply. That way the delivery and meeting places would never be the same two weeks running. It was the first time in his life that Ari had shaken hands with a black man.

The following week the first delivery was made to a car lot in Seven Kings. Five days later Stavros drove to Brixton and gave a carrier bag of cash to Delroy. Their business relationship had started and it worked well for both of them. Delroy was surprised at the amount of heroin that Ari could shift, Ari was surprised at how reliable Delroy's supplies were.

CHAPTER 54

Nick was involved in a project in Germany at the end of 1980 and decided that as he was only to get leave for Christmas Day and Boxing Day, that he would not come home. At his suggestion Bobby agreed to visit him and spend Christmas in Germany. It was the first time that he had been out of England. He had had to go to Petty France in London and queue for a passport because he needed one quickly and couldn't rely on the post. Nick was staying on an RAF base near a town called Padderburn in Northern Germany. Nick had booked him into a small but nice hotel there. Bobby arrived on Christmas Eve and Nick met him at the hotel at seven o'clock. The two friends hit the town. It was full of young Germans celebrating the season. Nick moved comfortably between them, chatting and smiling as he went. Bobby did not speak one word of the language and felt somewhat uncomfortable about that. They moved from bar to bar and in fifth one they visited there were some British RAF man and women. Although he was in civilian dress they recognized Nick, stood to attention and saluted. "At ease" said Nick, and they all relaxed and went back to their beers.

"What's that about?" said Bobby.

"Senior Officer, they have to do it even off duty. British Service protocol old boy", said Nick laughing. Bobby and Nick together were an irresistible force and soon there was a large group of people around their table. As usual one of the first questions was were they brothers. When they said that they weren't they were asked how long they had known each other and so he evening went on. Bobby noticed that unusually none of the females were coming on to Nick although they were coming on to him. They happened to meet in the toilet and Bobby pointed this out to Nick. Nick explained that it was against regulations to have a relationship with a junior rank. If he had sex with anybody but a major he could be court -marshaled. "Regrettably" he said, "there are no female majors on the base."

Bobby found one of the women particularly attractive, a sergeant communications officer who had come from Bradford originally. Bobby thought that she spoke funny, but she had a nice smile and a great body. When the bars closed at midnight she went back to his hotel with him and stayed the night. In the morning Bobby realised that he had not had a woman in his bed for almost a year.

Christmas Day was very quiet. Bobby and Nick had lunch in the hotel and then got drunk. Nick stayed the night sleeping on the floor in Bobby's room. The next day Nick had borrowed a car and took Bobby out to see some of the countryside. They chatted as they always had about this and that, and about Nicks mum, and about Bobby's mum and the total breakdown of that relationship. Nick pointed out that Jane may be married with children and that Bobby may be an uncle, but he really didn't care. He told Nick that when he had thought about it, as he used to do years ago, he decided that something in his brain had programmed him not to have a relationship with anybody. Nick pointed out that they had a great relationship that had lasted almost twenty years.

On 27th December Nick was back at work and Bobby caught the train to Frankfurt to catch the flight home.

On New Years Day 1981 Bobby played golf in the New Year Texas Scramble completion at his club and won. To celebrate his win he brought drinks for everyone in the bar, had dinner in the club restaurant with one of the female members and then went back to his house with her, where she stayed the night. After sex she had fallen asleep. Bobby lay awake listening to her breathing. He quite liked having somebody with him. He reflected that he enjoyed the sex both with her and the sergeant on Christmas Eve, but he felt that there was something missing. For the first time in a long time he thought of Sandra.

CHAPTER 55

As January moved on all thoughts of Sandra and relationships faded. His businesses were getting busier especially the higher class car showrooms and the higher quality flats that he owned. People seemed more prosperous under the new Thatcher Government and wanted to spend their money. Even his breakers yard in Chadwell Heath was making money. He had put a new manager in there who had extended the business beyond just cars to encompass all metals of scrap value. He also stripped the more recent models that had been in a crash and made a good profit on selling the second hand spares. Wheels and tyres particularly brought a good price.

In February he received a phone call from Ari. A friend of his needed Bobby's special skills. Bobby obliged, and similarly in March. In April the phone call came again. "I want you to do me a favour" said Ari.

"What is it this time and what has he done?"

"Nothing like that" said Ari. "Stavros's uncle who lives in Greece has died. Stavros and Demi have had to go back to sort things out. They will probably be away for three weeks. Every week Stavros makes a delivery of cash to South London for me. I need someone that I can trust with a lot a money. Will you deliver it for me, please".

Ari explained the procedure. Bobby was very surprised that Ari was doing business with Delroy Campbell. The last he heard was when his man had been caught in one of Ari's clubs and that was many months ago. When Bobby went to meet Ari two days later to collect the cash he told Ari how surprised he was. "Business is business son. We can't always choose who we deal with. I didn't tell you anything about it as I know that you don't want to be involved with drugs, but I do owe you a thank you. If we hadn't done what you said on that night at the factory, and if we had cut his balls off, I don't think that I would be doing this business now and it's very lucrative".

Bobby drove to the address in Coldharbour Lane that he had been given. He walked inside the dingy taxi office. A huge bearded black man, wearing a red and green and yellow knitted hat, looked up, saw Bobby and without speaking, indicated with a nod of his head to a door at the rear of the shop area. Bobby walked through it. It led to a yard and a flight of stairs. Bobby went up the stairs and stood on the small landing looking at three doors. A voice with a Caribbean accent called out from one of the rooms "well if it isn't a real white honky visiting us poor black folk in the southern slums."

Bobby walked through the door of the room where the voice was coming from. "I'm looking for Delroy Campbell".

"You sure found him white boy" the man replied.

"I don't think so" said Bobby. "I'm sure that Delroy Campbell wouldn't talk like a refugee from Uncle Tom's Cabin".

Delroy laughed and said, with no trace of an accent other than South London "never read Uncle Tom's Cabin but I'll see the film when they make it. So you're the famous Bobby

Parsons? Pleased to meet you" he said as he stood up and held out his hand. Bobby had been certain he would not like Delroy Campbell but in spite of himself he found that he was shaking his hand and relaxing as the man smiled his disarming smile.

"I wouldn't say famous" said Bobby as he took his hand away from the others firm handshake.

"Don't be modest. You have a big reputation that has even spread down here to the badlands". Everything he said, Delroy said with a smile.

"Well here's the money. Do you want me to wait while you count it?" he said.

"That's ok" said Delroy, "its never been short yet". Bobby nodded and turned to leave. "See you next week" said Delroy.

"Seems so. Maybe you can pick somewhere better than this shit hole to meet" said Bobby, who turned to look at Delroy as he spoke and showed that he too could give a broad disarming smile. "I'll need to send my suit to the cleaners after being in here".

The venue the following week was better. Delroy had phoned Ari that morning and arranged the meet at the Selsdon Park Hotel, room 236. Bobby had driven over Tower Bridge wondering what sort of dump he was going to but his fears were proved unfounded as he pulled into the entrance gate of the hotel and parked in the car park. Even his BMW didn't look out of place here.

He went into the hotel, found room 236 and knocked on the door. It was opened by Delroy, smiling broadly as usual. "Come in white boy" he said with the characteristic laugh in his voice. Bobby entered the room. Lying on the bed were two very attractive black women. Both wore only underwear, very sexy underwear, but not cheap. One wore a white bra, briefs and suspender belt, which set of well against her almost ebony skin, the other was in the same style underwear but red in colour.

"Nice eh?" said Delroy. "I'm interviewing them for a new house I've bought in a posh area. You can help me out if you like. There are two of them and only one of me so pick one and see what she's like. They 'd like a handsome white boy like you, wouldn't you girls?" Both of the girls laughed and nodded.

"No thanks, I'll pass" said Bobby.

"Coffee then?" said Delroy.

"Actually that would be nice thanks" said Bobby.

Delroy rang room service and ordered a coffee and a bottle of champagne. While they waited Delroy told Bobby about his new house. It was in Dulwich Village, which apparently was a very expensive area. He told Bobby that he was modeling it on the Loughton House of Ari's but instead of taking your bedroom playmate to the house with you, at Delroy's house they would be provided. As with Ari's, Delroy was aiming for the exclusive clientele. Bobby was surprised that Delroy knew about Ari's Loughton House and especially as he gave the impression that he had been there.

"It's amazing how many straight, middle class white dudes want to bang a black chick" he said. Delroy told the girls to go into the bathroom when the drinks arrived and the three of them then drank the champagne while Bobby drank his coffee.

The following week the drop was in the house in Fentiman Road in Vauxhall. They exchanged the money and then went to the pub, The Fentiman Arms, for lunch. After lunch Delroy again offered Bobby 'an hour of pleasure' with one of the girls and again Bobby said thanks but no.

"Stavros should be back next week" said Delroy as Bobby was leaving. "I can go back to meeting in shit holes again". Both Bobby and he laughed.

"I'll send you an invitation to the opening of my Dulwich House" he said as Bobby got into his car.

"You do that. Who knows, I might just come" he said as he drove off. Despite himself Bobby was starting to like this pleasant, happy black man from South London.

CHAPTER 56

Nick had been stationed in Germany for almost a year. His tour was coming to an end and he had two weeks leave due in June before he went to Aldershot for training and reallocation. He wanted to go on holiday where there would be plenty of sun. He suggested to Bobby that they holiday in Spain. Bobby was all for it. Even some of his employees went to Spain for their summer holidays and they all came back with great tans. Nick took care of the arrangements and he booked 14 days at a 4 star hotel in a place called Sitges. They arrived in the early hours of the morning and went straight to bed in their twin bedded room. They awoke in the morning, had the buffet breakfast and then took their towels to the pool. As they walked along the poolside both of them were aware of female eyes following them from behind sunglasses. There were no sun loungers left unoccupied so they lay their towels down by the side of the pool and just lay on them. Already the sun was hot. It took Bobby only half an hour before he wanted to cool off in the pool and although he hadn't swum for a few years, he was very fit from his golf and squash and still had the technique. He cut through the water like the record breaker that he had been. They lazed by the pool all morning and in the middle of the afternoon went for a walk on the beach. As they strolled they noticed again that they were being watched by a number of young females.

They had dinner and then at about ten o'clock went out clubbing. In England they would have been too old for the types of clubs in Sitges but there were all ages on the floor from twelve to sixty. Although it was the 1980's, the music was that of the 1970's. It was disco music that everybody knew, The Stylistics, The Tames and Boney M. The flashing lights too were a replica of English disco's of the 1970's. Bobby and Nick had barely got themselves a drink, started moving to an Archie Bell and the Drells song, Soul City Walkin', when they were being chatted up by women. Two unattached, good looking men were a major attraction to the predatory women.

The first night there they ended up in bed with two of the women from the club and this was repeated every night of their holiday. On one occasion they went back to the hotel room of two sisters from Croydon. They had one each, slept with them, then swapped sisters in the morning before going back to their own hotel to shower, change and breakfast. Nick called it therapy, after being closeted with the krauts and frogs for a year, as he put it. They arrived back in England after fourteen days both refreshed and exhausted. Two days later Bobby drove Nick to Brize Norton for his next duty. That evening he took a phone call from Ari.

"Where the hell have you been? I needed to contact you a week ago and nobody knew where you were."

"I was on holiday, the first one that I have had for years".

"I know that, your people all knew that you were on holiday but they didn't know where or how to contact you". Bobby felt himself start to get angry. "Do you tell your staff how they can contact you when you go on holiday to Greece?

Anyway I didn't want to be contacted, I was on holiday. Nothing was that urgent that it wouldn't wait".

Ari sensed that Bobby was getting uptight about this conversation so he softened his attitude. "One of my friends, a very powerful friend, wanted to employ your talents. He couldn't understand why I couldn't get hold of you, that's all".

"Tell him to find somebody else. I want out of this, no more jobs". Suddenly Ari was panicking, he was not prepared for this turn of events. "Don't say things like that, you're upset. Let's have lunch tomorrow and we can talk about it. Sensing that it would be better to finish the conversation now, Ari said "got to go Bobby, one of the kids is calling. I'll meet you tomorrow, twelve thirty at the Dick Turpin". He put the phone down.

The following lunchtime Bobby and Ari met in the Dick Turpin restaurant in Hainault for lunch. Ari decided to get in first and try and defuse the situation. "Maybe I was a bit short on the phone last night, but if you could just let me know when you are going on holiday and when you are coming back I can deal with any requests that come up when you are away".

"It doesn't matter Ari. I don't want any more requests as you put it. I've finished with that. Contrary to what people may think I don't enjoy what I do, terrorizing people. While I am doing it its fine, it's as though I'm on some sort of remote control or it's someone else carrying it out. I switch off. But when its over and I'm at home I wonder why I do it. Well, no more. I don't need the money, Christ I earn more money than I can spend".

Ari looked at him with a mixture of sadness and fear in his face. "Its not that easy son" said Ari softly, "You have done work for some of the most important faces in London. They all appreciate you as a unique specialist. You always get what they want, you always deliver. They will not let you just retire because you are fed up".

"What can they do?"

"Don't ask Bobby. Just to prove a point they would have your legs broken but if you did not co-operate eventually you would disappear. Some of these people are bad Bobby, they can't afford to lose face. If you go up against them they will make you pay one way or another. Believe me you cannot get out".

Bobby considered what Ari had said. Unfortunately it made sense to him. "I'll think about it" said Bobby.

"Think hard Bobby, and then think the right thing, there's no way for you to get out Bobby other than to die". Bobby was at home that evening drinking a glass of wine. Deep down he knew what Ari had said was probably true. The fact that he couldn't get out depressed him. The phone rang. He picked it up and a West Indian voice on the other end said "is dat ma white brother from de nort dare on de telephone?"

His depression suddenly lifted, Bobby smiled. "Tell me Delroy, how does a nig nog like you have a name the same as a Scottish soup company?"

"Dat is da fault of de old slave massa who use all a de girls and when they have little kids they call dem after shit soup".

Bobby laughed. "Its actually good to hear from you" he said.

"It gets better "said Delroy, now speaking without an accent. "I am inviting you to the party of the century my man. I told you about the Dulwich House. Its official opening is Saturday, there's a party and you are invited. Before you say no there are going to be some other white folk there".

"I don't know" said Bobby.

"Good, then that's a yes then white brother", said Delroy,

"see you about nine o'clock, black tie". He had hung up before Bobby could say anything more. Bobby arrived at the house shortly after nine on Saturday evening. Delroy had been telling the truth, it was in a very up-market area, not far from Dulwich College. It was in a road of large detached houses. It must have cost Delroy a fortune. He parked his car and walked towards the front door. There were two large bouncers standing by it but he was obviously expected as one of them opened the door as he approached and said "good evening Mr. Parsons".

As he walked through the door Delroy spotted him and came over. Big smile as usual, hand held out. He grabbed Bobby's hand and shook it and said "welcome white brother, welcome to Delroy's Dulwich Palace". As they were shaking hands a tall, attractive black woman with a tray of drinks approached. "You remember Cherry" said Delroy, just loud enough that the all of the guests could hear. "The last time you saw her she was lying on her back on a bed in a hotel room. You may not recognize her because she's wearing clothes now".

Bobby couldn't help but smile. He took a glass of champagne from her tray. "Thank you" he said. "That's a very nice dress you're wearing".

"You should see what she's got on underneath it" said Delroy in a whisper. "Catch up with you soon and show you around" he said as he moved towards another guest who had just arrived.

Bobby looked around. The house was indeed plush and very large. As with the Loughton house there was a card room and a roulette area. But there was also a small but comfortable restaurant and bar area. At the rear there was a very large conservatory with a sound system installed in it and the large floor area was obviously designed for dancing. Tonight drinks were being served by six black girls, all dressed in what looked like expensive evening dresses and all very attractive. Behind the bar there were two men, neither of whom had a lot to do. The guests numbered about 30, almost all male, all in dinner jackets and black ties. It was about a 50/50 split black and white. All seemed fairly well to do although nobody was gambling yet and there was nobody behind the tables. Bobby finished his champagne and went to the bar." Lime and lemonade" he said. He had a feeling that this would be a long evening.

At ten o'clock Delroy called for silence. He welcomed everybody and thanked them for coming, he toasted his new 'members only' club and welcomed again those present who had already become members. As the girls moved round the room the trays now had piles of gambling chips on them instead of drinks. Delroy invited everybody to take one pile, each worth £100, and gamble at the tables with his compliments. All of the guests then took a pile of chips and moved to the tables were the dealers and croupiers had appeared.

Bobby was still at the bar, Delroy wandered over." You not gambling man?" he said.

"Never gamble" said Bobby, "even with somebody else's money".

Delroy looked at him and smiled, "very wise man, you never see a poor bookie. Come on I'll show you around". They started downstairs. Delroy told him again how he had based it on Ari's Loughton House but with some adjustments. One was the restaurant. He had employed a chef who would cook a limited but high quality menu. Delroy believed that the accountant, bankers, traders, barristers etc who he hoped would make up his members list, would come more frequently if there was a good meal available. He also hoped that they would bring clients, nice surroundings, good food and a beautiful woman as dessert. The women were the other main difference, they were provided. The six who had been dispensing the drinks lived in the house, one in each of the sox bedrooms. They would be dressed smartly, available to talk to, drink or dine with, dance with and take to bed if wanted. Their time was billed to the member, appearing in the monthly account as restaurant and bar bill. Delroy laughed as he said that by billing as this is was seen as a legitimate business expense and was therefore tax deductible. The girls lived free, in safety, in comfort and were happy with the arrangement. He then told Bobby that included in the guest list that evening was a local detective inspector, the chairman of the local council, the chairman of the planning committee of the local council and other important dignitaries. They had all been given complementary membership. "Same for you white brother, free membership, come anytime you want. It's all free for you tonight but free membership still means you pay for the services after tonight". Delroy was still smiling. "Come on, I'll show you the rest". Delroy showed Bobby through the kitchen, it was spotless. Behind the kitchen, hidden away was a large room which was a new extension. This was Delroy's office. It contained a huge desk with one chair behind it and two in front, two large settees facing each other with a coffee table in between them. On stands against two of the walls on either side of the room where two huge twenty-six inch televisions. On a sideboard on the wall opposite Delroys desk was a sideboard with a Bang and Olufson sound system on it. Bobby walked round the room admiring the fittings. He stood at Delroys desk and noticed that fitted into it were eight small television screens. "What are these?" he asked.

"Security" said Delroy. He opened a drawer and flicked a switch and one of the screens came to life. There was a picture of the entrance area at the front of the house." Latest technology" said Delroy. "I can sit here and keep an eye on things".

They then went upstairs. There were eight rooms, two not yet used except for storage and six which were the girls rooms. They had all been decorated the same, king size beds, rich colours in the décor but good quality finishes, designed with a lot of taste. Delroy could see that Bobby was impressed. "Not bad for a black kid from the Old Kent Road is it?"

"Not bad at all" agreed Bobby. Back downstairs the party was in full swing. A DJ had arrived and some of the men were dancing with the girls. Some were still gambling, the winners staking it all on the next hand of cards or the next spin of the wheel, the losers using their own money to buy more chips. Bobby thought how clever Delroy had been to give away free chips. He counted on the punters getting the bug and spending their own money too. As the night wore on Bobby realised that although he had been slowly drinking glasses of wine he was now on his fourth. He should have something to eat. He ordered a burger and when it arrived he found that it was delicious. He danced with Cherry who he found to be very nice and then danced with Crystal who was also a very nice girl. Both of them made it clear to him that they would welcome him in their bed that night. About one o'clock the party started to break up. People seemed to be leaving all at once. Many of them seemed to know each other and were saying their goodbyes. Bobby sat down on one of the settees in the bar area. Delroy bought him another glass of wine and sat down next to him. "Did you enjoy yourself white brother?" he said.

"I did, its been a nice evening, thank you, I needed a break, a bit of light entertainment".

"You got troubles white brother?" said Delroy, for once not smiling.

"We all got troubles Delroy, I will sort mine somehow. But thanks for a nice evening".

"Anytime, anytime white brother" he said as he got up to say goodbye to another guest who was leaving. Bobby sat back and closed his eyes. The next thing he knew he woke up, it was daylight, he was laying on the settee with a blanket over him. Somebody had covered him up and taken off his tie and shoes. He lay there for a while and then got up, took off his jacket which he was still wearing and wandered into the kitchen. Nobody was around. He put some freshly ground coffee into the percolator and switched it on. He found some bread in the fridge and put two slices in the toaster, He looked at his watch, it was almost eight o'clock. He couldn't believe how late it was.

"I smell coffee" said Delroy walking in, obviously he spent the night on a settee in his office. He too had no shoes or tie on.

"Be ready shortly" said Bobby, "Toast?"

"Sounds good, you want to work as my breakfast chef?" said Delroy, "good rates of pay and great fringe benefits". They both laughed.

"Did somebody tuck you up as well?" said Bobby.

"No I have to look after myself. Cherry tucked you up but I think she would have preferred to have you in her bed rather than down here. Just because she does it most nights for money doesn't mean that they don't want to do it for pleasure sometimes, and for some reason they seem to find your skinny white body attractive".

"Coffees ready" said Bobby laughing again.

As he poured the coffee, Cherry and one of the other girls appeared.

"HI" said Bobby. "Would you like some coffee"?

"Yes please" they said together.

"Toast?" said Bobby.

"Great" said Cherry. "Can we have him here every morning cooking breakfast for us Delroy?"

"What am I, your mother" he said smiling as he always did. Bobby took his toast out of the toaster and took it in for the girls with a mug of coffee each.

"Nice girls" said Bobby to Delroy as he walked into the kitchen.

"Yes they are" said Delroy quietly. "They have had shit thrown at them at home for years but they have come through it mainly unharmed, mentally I mean. Yeah, they may be whores but they are still good girls".

"We're all whores Delroy, one way or another. We may not lie on our backs and open our legs but we are no lesser whores".

Delroy looked at Bobby "you are right man, but you seem to have a heap of trouble on your shoulders. If you want somebody to listen, I am here".

"Thanks Delroy, I appreciate that". Bobby changed the subject and went into the bar area to chat with the girls. As he was leaving Delroy followed him to his car. "Don't forget man, you are a member here, don't be a stranger". They shook hands warmly and Bobby drove home.

CHAPTER 57

Bobby visited his businesses as usual during the week. When he visited his BMW dealer he was told that they had just taken a five year old Mercedes 500SL in part exchange for a new 5 Series. He saw it, a bright red car with a cream interior. He decided that he would buy it as fun car. He had it valeted and delivered to his house. The following weekend he took it to the golf club and it got many admiring glances. It was a good talking point in the bar.

A few weeks later Nick phoned. He was being posted to Saudi as a NATO consultant for their army. He had been given two weeks pre-posting leave. "Six bloody months in the sand and heat and shit with no booze and women in masks. I've got two weeks to squash in six months living".

"You wanted sun, sand, sea and sex a few months ago. Now us taxpayers are giving you two out of four free and you're moaning. Never satisfied you squady's" Nick arrived a few days later. Bobby had told him to use the Merc whenever he wanted. He thought it was a lovely car so was thrilled at the being able to drive it around. "Should be able to pull in this" he said.

The next afternoon Bobby and Nick played a round of golf. Nick wanted to take the Merc so they went in that instead of the BMW. Nick didn't play golf very often but he was a natural at it and although Bobby beat him it was until the 16th hole that it was secure. They stayed at the club for a drink and some dinner. As usual a group of people chatted with Bobby and Nick. Nick was getting on very well with a woman called Emily. Her husband was away in the Far East on a business trip. Bobby decided to go home at about nine o'clock, he had a meeting with an estate agent the following morning. Nick was obviously not ready to leave so Bobby said his farewells and got a cab home. Nick and Emily arrived about an hour later. They were still in bed when Bobby left the next morning.

Bobby hardly saw Nick during the week that followed. He spent all of his time with Emily. After a week she stopped as her husband was due back from his trip in a couple of days. Nick and Bobby spent the rest of his leave together apart from the day that Nick spent with his mother. Bobby took Nick to Aldershot. "I probably won't see you for six months. I will write though as I will be bored stiff stuck in the desert".

"I look forward to your epistles. When do you actually go?"

"About a week. Got to have a medical check and then get some new desert kit and then I'm off". Bobby and Nick said their goodbyes and Bobby drove back to Chigwell. The following week he received a phone call from Ari Constantine, he had a friend who needed Bobby's help. Ari said that this was only a case of Bobby accompanying the client, they thought that this would be enough. Bobby arrived at the venue and was surprised to see Ari there. It was routine and the victim caved in almost immediately. As Bobby was driving home he wondered if Ari was there to check on him. He hadn't attended this type of meeting for many years so

Bobby concluded that this could be the only reason for him being there. Again he decided that he had to find a way out.

The estate agent that Bobby had met over the previous weeks had been offering a plot of land in Hornchurch. It was offered with planning permission for five detached executive houses. Bobby completed the purchase of the land about a month after Nick had left. He didn't want to build executive houses, he wanted to build starter flats. He had decided that he wanted to do something different. Rather than buy houses and let them out he wanted to actually build them. He thought that with the increased employment opportunities in the City as a result of "The Thatcher Revolution", there would be a demand for small flats, two bedrooms, affordable to first time buyers, with a good specification of fixtures and fittings. An additional bonus of this plot was its proximity to an underground station which offered easy access into London. Bobby employed an architect and started the process of getting the planning permission changed.

The weeks dragged on. The planning permission was taking ages to reach the committee, his businesses almost ran themselves and even Ari had not phoned for nearly eight weeks, which Bobby wasn't unhappy about.

Bobby had played a lot of squash and golf during the summer. The squash had kept him fit and trim and amount of golf he played had resulted in his handicap getting into single figures. Unfortunately it was the end of October and it had been wet. Bobby was bored. He was sitting in the office in his house one Wednesday afternoon and on an impulse phoned Delroy. He had two numbers for him, the taxi shop in Coldharbour Lane and the house in Dulwich. He was at neither. Bobby left a message at both that he had phoned. He returned the calls twenty minutes later. "Hi white brother, you up man?"

"Hi Delroy". I'm fine but a bit bored so I thought I

would accept your invitation to visit the Dulwich House on Saturday. I don't want a girl, as lovely as they are. Just a drink and a burger. Will you be around?"

" If you are comin' I'll be there man. No burgers, I'll get the chef to put in a couple of prime steaks. See you about nine". Bobby hung up. He found that that had lifted his spirits. On Saturday he arrived at the Dulwich House and Delroy was at the door as he approached it. As usual he had a smile which seemed to cover about half of his face. Just looking at him made Bobby smile and relax. "You're looking a bit tired honkey" said Delroy, "come on In and have a drink. I've actually got some decent Shiraz on the bar for you".

They went into the bar area where Delroy poured out two large glasses of wine. "You even got me drinking this poofter drink now" he said as he handed Bobby the drink. "Cheers". Bobby was surprised at how empty the club was. There were only three men at the roulette table and apart from Bobby and Delroy in the bar area there was only two of Delroys girls sitting there too.

"Its always like this on Saturdays and Sundays" explained Delroy when Bobby asked him. It is not something that I thought of when I opened it but it is a club for businessmen. During the week we are very successful but at the weekend we are dead. My other houses are at the busiest on Friday and Saturdays but here, ...its different. Those three guys will be gone by ten, two of the girls are upstairs with two members, they'll be gone within an hour and then we may as well close".

"You only have four girls now?" asked Bobby.

"There's only four tonight. Normally we would still have six during the week but two have gone to one of the other houses to earn money. You know the rules in this game, get laid to get paid. These two here will earn nothing tonight, the two that are in Battersea at the other house will take between six or eight punters if they are lucky". Delroy introduced the two girls as Rosie and Janice but told them that Bobby was not a punter as soon as they started to push their boobs out towards him. Delroy went into the kitchen to tell the chef to cook the steaks and then close up and go home. While they ate they chatted about business. Delroy was a pimp, brothel keeper and drug dealer, all things that Bobby hated. But somehow apart from liking him as a man, he respected his peculiar honesty. He didn't pretend to be anything that he wasn't and he actually cared about all of the people that worked for him. All of the girls were looked after and well paid and had little pressure put on them. He had even held a party a few weeks previous for one of his girls who was going back to Jamaica. She had enough money to buy a house and live comfortably for a few years.

The steaks were delicious and so was the cheesecake that had been left for dessert. Bobby had told Delroy about his plans to build flats and the delay in obtaining the necessary permission. "We have had to modify and modify again. My architect thinks that it will not be allowed as the people in the area don't want flats".

"What colour is the council man, and I don't mean black or white?" he said laughing.

"Blue, they're Conservative"

"What are you doin' on Tuesday evening?" asked Delroy.

"Nothing, why?"

"Be here at about ten o'clock. Maybe we can help this along". Bobby was intrigued but Delroy would say no more.

Bobby left about midnight, he thanked Delroy for a very pleasant evening and said he would be back on Tuesday.

Tuesday arrived and Bobby was at Dulwich by ten o'clock. Delroy welcomed his as always. Bobby followed him straight into his office. "The chairman of the local council here is a big noise. He runs this council, whatever he says happens. He also is a friend of the local MP and gives a lot of money to the Conservative party. He sits on national forums and knows all of the leaders of all the Conservative Councils in Southern England. After every council meeting he comes here to relax, that's how I knew he would be in here tonight. Come and have a look here".

Bobby walked around Delroys large desk. Delroy had switched on the security monitors. One of them showed the entrance area, one the bar area and two the gaming area. Bobby had already seen these. What he hadn't seen before was the six others, one for each of the bedrooms.

"Each bedroom has two hidden cameras. Each monitor is connected to a video machine so any of the action can be filmed. This is our council leader....". Delroy flicked another switch and both of the big televisions in the office showed a middle aged man, lying on his back while a beautiful naked black girl sat astride him bouncing up and down and faking an orgasm."

"Christ Delroy" said Bobby who was both amazed and shocked. "Is this a blackmail scam"?

"No" said Delroy. "As soon as I do that they will know about the cameras. Even the girls don't know about them. But you never know, if ever I need to, what a lever I have. My solicitor is a barrister, a partner in a large practice in Lincolns Inn Fields. He has a son as a day boy at Dulwich College, I won't tell you what that costs. He is on the PTA, he's a member of the local Conservative party, the local golf club, the Masons, and the lions and the slob is even a lay preacher at the local C of E church. He's married with three children and his father-in -law is a high court judge. Once a week he visits here. His particular favourite pastime is having one of the girls sit on him with their back to him, sucking his cock, and he licks their fanny as he comes in their mouth. What do you think would happen if that got out to his chambers, or clubs or lodge, not to mention his wife and father- in- law. What would the masons think? It would probably be OK for him to be unfaithful to his wife, even with a hooker, but tonguing a black bird?"

Bobby was lost for words. "Look Bobby, we all know what happens in the bedrooms. The fact that they know that I know is enough, without cameras, without videos. We ask our leader to invite your leader down here. He goes upstairs, gets fucked, comes down to the bar and you introduce yourself. Not nice but effective".

"Let me give it some thought" said Bobby.

"You're too straight you are" said Delroy. "Look, I'm going to set it up. I'll let you know when. If you come you come. If not he'll just have a bloody good shag on the house and you won't build your flats".

Bobby woke up in his own bed the next morning and thought about what Delroy had said. "Why not" he thought, and left a message for Delroy that he was up for it.

CHAPTER 58

It was arranged for the first Friday evening in December. In the couple of weeks that had elapsed since Delroy had told him of the idea, the thought of it had begun to actually excite Bobby. He arrived at the club early but Delroy was there before him, smiling as always. The club was busier than normal for a Friday, not as busy as a weekday night but Delroy thought that some of the members were making the most of it before having to spend Christmas with their wives. About eight o'clock the targets arrived. Bobby sat in the bar area in a corner. Delroy welcomed them both and took them to the bar for a drink. He gave them both a complimentary £20 chip and they straight away went to the blackjack table with two of Delroys beautiful girls. An hour later they were each in a bedroom. Bobby was watching on the television screens in Delroys office. He had never met the leader of the Hornchurch Council. He was a very fat man, with unhealthy looking pink skin. While he was pumping away he was wheezing. Bobby had a funny thought. "You ever had anybody have a heart attack while they've been shagging any of your girls?" he laughed.

Delroy laughed too but said "no, but don't even joke about it". Both men finished having sex, and as they got dressed

Bobby moved to a stool at the bar. The men came down and stood next to Bobby as they ordered a drink for themselves. Delroy arrived and asked for a word with his council leader. It was obviously planned, Bobby was calling in a favour.

"Hi" said Bobby to the Hornchurch man. "You local"?

"No, I live in Brentwood".

"Long way to come here isn't it? You obviously think its worth the journey for what you get upstairs" said Bobby in a humorous and casual way.

"It's a bit special" said the man. "Never had a black bird before. God they love it, don't they?".

Bobby forced a laugh. "Do you work locally?" asked Bobby.

"No. I don't really work, well not any more. Investments, you know". Bobby nodded knowingly, playing the game.

"Actually I spend most of my time on council business, I'm the council leader for a large council in Essex"

"Would that council include Hornchurch?" said Bobby.

"Yes actually it would. Why?"

Bingo thought Bobby. "I'm having a bit of a problem getting some planning permission through, some flats on a site near the station, you probably know it. I could do with some help, fellow club members and all that".

Bobby then held the man with his eyes and the man knew that he had been set up. "I'll see what I can do", he said as he carried his drink away from the bar and from Bobby.

An hour later the two councilors were leaving. As they got to the door Bobby called out, "bye, I'll give you call next week".

CHAPTER 59

Nick did not come home for Christmas. As he was stationed in Saudi his tour of duty finished on 7th January, the Islamic holiday of Ashura. Bobby spent Christmas Day with Mrs. Mead so the hopefully she would not miss Nick too much. It was a pleasant and relaxed day and it surprised them both when, while chatting they realised that they had known each other for almost twenty years. Nick phoned during the afternoon to speak to his mother. He had a chat with Bobby too. They arranged for Bobby to collect him from Brize Norton where he was flying into. He would be home for two weeks and was then going back to Saudi. He hadn't wanted to but it was orders and it helped by the fact that he was to be promoted to Lieutenant-Colonel. "I hope that I can borrow that nice little Merc again and maybe you could let that Emily know that I will be around. Very hot she was."

"I would be pleased to let her know Nick" said Bobby with a smile on his face. I saw her last week at the golf club. She's six months pregnant and looks like a hippo".

"I'll pass on that then" said Nick. Then as an afterthought he said "did you say six months pregnant?".

Bobby knew that he had realised the significance of that. "Yeah six months. You might be a Daddy".

"Don't even joke about that" said Nick. "Gotta go, see you on 8th". On the morning of 8th January the post arrived just as Bobby was leaving to drive to Brize Norton. He had got his planning permission. He phoned Delroy from his new car phone and told him. Delroy seemed genuinely happy for him.

Nick arrived home. He was pleased to be back. The desert had been boring, he said but he was happy to go back as it had meant promotion. He now had his sights set on being a full colonel by the time he was thirty five. The evening that they arrived back in Chigwell they went out for a quiet meal in a Chinese restaurant. This was Nicks choice, he liked Chinese food and had not had any since he was last in England. Bobby had booked a round of golf for the Friday despite the weather forecast suggesting rain. In fact they played only nine holes before giving up. Drenched they retreated to the clubhouse where both of them were greeted by the four ladies that had playing in front of them and had also given up at the ninth. Bobby described Nick as having his tongue hanging out. "What would you be like if you hadn't seen a pair of legs or a shape of a women for six months" was his reply.

On Saturday evening there was a quiz night and Nick said that they were going. He arranged to meet one of the ladies group there. They went, came second in the quiz competition and predictably Nick ended up bringing the woman home for the night. It seemed very effortless and Bobby remembered what it had been like for him some years ago. Nick told him that it was still the same, he just had to open his eyes and look, all of the women fancied him. Bobby just wasn't interested. It sometimes occurred to him that there may be something wrong with him.

Bobby left Nick to his own devices for a couple of days

during the next week. Nick had the little SL500 and could come and go as he pleased, but they always spent the evening together. Bobby met with his architect about appointing a contractor for the building of the flats. He also decided that he was going to computerise his company's. He had read that it was possible now to have computer terminals in each of his showrooms and premises and all of the trading records and accounts activities could be relayed to a central computer down a phone line, He was planning to have the central computer installed at his home office so that he could see the activity of any company at any time. Bobby had found a company that could install this and had a meeting with them as well.

Nick had lunch at the golf club on Wednesday and got an invitation for him and Bobby to a party on the Saturday. It was one of the members fortieth and it seemed that lots of people that they knew from the club would be there. It was snowing when they left the house and the roads were getting slippery. Bobby drove slowly, fortunately it wasn't far. Nick seemed to anxious to get there. He was right about the numbers. It was a large house in the centre of Chigwell and it was bulging. The music was loud and the bar was help yourself. It was situated in the kitchen, which was huge. It took Bobby back to his teen years when he spent a lot of time in kitchens at party's. Nick was dancing and Bobby in the kitchen when Emily and her husband arrived. They both greeted Bobby, Emily got herself an orange juice, her husband a beer. Emily looked huge. Bobby asked how she was, she said was fine but had only just stopped being sick.

During the evening Bobby noticed Nick talking to Emily while dancing with her. Shortly after Nick came into the kitchen with two women. "Come on Bobby, dancing time, this is Fiona" he said leading one of them to Bobby, "and this is her friend Carla. Carla's parents are Spanish. She speaks it fluently so we can talk and nobody knows what we are saying". Nick was having fun. It was his last weekend. Fiona was a member of the golf club. Nick hadn't spoken to her before but he had seen her a few times. Carla was her friend from school who she had brought along to the party. Fiona was divorced and Carla's husband worked on the oil rigs in the North Sea and spend a month away and a month home. He was apparently a control freak according to Fiona, and it was doing Carla's head in. He had gone away only four days ago after being home for four weeks and always when he went away Carla let her hair down. After a couple of dances it was apparent that Fiona assumed that Carla would spend the night with Nick and that she was available to Bobby. "What the hell" he thought. It had been a long time. The four left just after midnight for the slow drive home through the snow in Bobby's car. Both of the girls didn't leave until after lunch on Sunday. Just as she was going Bobby found himself agreeing to go out to dinner with Fiona on the following Thursday.

"Good on you" said Nick as they sat down in the lounge. "its about time you actually went out with somebody, You are in serious danger of ending up a lonely old man Bobby Parsons".

"As opposed to you I suppose. All you do is shag them not date them, and most of them seem married. By the way how was your conversation with the very pregnant Emily?"

"Umm, she doesn't know whose it is. Apparently we had sex about ten times in the week we had together but in the same month she had sex with her husband twice, so it could be either of ours. Fortunately we are both dark haired and similar skin colour so he won't be able to tell if its mine or not. I told her keep quiet and just go along with her husband. If he found out and kicked her out she wouldn't like life in a service house at Aldershot while I was away wherever".

On Wednesday Bobby got a call from Ari. "I've heard that you got your planning permission for the flats, well done. You'll have to tell me how you did that. I was told a few weeks ago that you had no chance". Bobby wondered where Ari got his information from. Whenever Bobby went into any business deal Ari seemed to know about it before Bobby told him. Bobby was surprised when Ari got to the purpose of the call. He had been married ten years soon and he was having a party, Bobby was invited, and a partner if he wanted to bring one. Bobby thanked him and said that he would be pleased to come. Ari had hired the function room at Ye Olde Kings Head at Chigwell. He was arranging outside caterers and a disco. That was so near to where Bobby lived that he could walk there.

Bobby had dinner with Fiona on Thursday evening as arranged. He was worried all afternoon about what he should do at the end of the evening. It was like dating at sixteen again. For some reason that he couldn't understand, he didn't want her staying the night again. He enjoyed the meal and found that he enjoyed her company. He was saved from his dilemma of uncertainty when they got into the car at the restaurant. "I'm sorry Bobby but its that time of the month. No hanky panky tonight I'm afraid. I'm a bit tired so I would really appreciate it if you just took me home and dropped me".

Bobby found that he was relieved, "that's fine, you just have a good nights sleep".

"You are a nice guy" she said, thinking that his tone was understanding and concern rather than the relief he felt.

He drove her to her house, they kissed goodnight in the car and then Bobby drove home. "Pull yourself together, you're not a teenager for Christ's sake and neither is she" he said to himself, annoyed at his own uncertainty. Maybe what Nick had said had struck a chord. Apart from Nick he had no real friends, no family and no relationships. Fiona was a nice girl, quite pretty, and he had enjoyed her body on Saturday, she was certainly good in bed. She was good company and he liked her, maybe he should make an effort with her. He went out with her three more times over the next two weeks and on the third time she stayed at Bobbys for the weekend. Sex with her was good and she was easy to be with, but Bobby knew that he didn't love her. Thoughts of Sandra came back to him and he remembered how he felt when he was with her and how much he wanted to be with her. After many years he wondered how her life had turned out.

When the time came for Ari's party, he decided to go on his own. Fiona was put out that Bobby was going out on a Saturday to a wedding anniversary party and not taking her. He had been totally honest about where he was going and the occasion. He tried to explain that it was business but she thought that she should still be included especially as Bobby had admitted that Ari had invited him and a partner. Bobby ended any further discussion on the subject by saying firmly "I have always kept business and personal completely separate. This is business, you are personal." Fiona seemed to get the message that Bobby's mind was made up and it was not worth arguing about further.

CHAPTER 60

The venue for Ari party was a nice place, and inside the function room it was laid out beautifully. The DJ was playing lots of old Motown and Stones records which suited Bobby. As he walked in Ari and his wife came to greet him. Bobby liked Stella, Ari's wife. She wasn't a beauty but she was a very nice person. Bobby thought she had put on a lot of weight since he had last seen her which was probably about six months previous. She had a big smile and was very proud of her husband and children and was a great Mum.

Bobby went to the bar and looked around. He knew hardly anybody there. To Bobby's critical eye some of them looked like real villains and some as though they didn't belong in this company. As he stood there people were coming up the bar and introducing themselves to him. They all seemed to know who he was. Stavros suddenly appeared with his wife. It had never occurred to Bobby that Stavros was married. She told Bobby that they had been childhood sweethearts in Greece. When the Germans came they forced her to work in the villa that was the local SS headquarters. Stavros said that she never spoke of what happened there. Stavros had joined the resistance where he had meet Ari and as the Allies advanced and the Germans were preparing to withdraw, the group that Ari ran with Stavros as his lieutenant, entered the villa, and rescued all of the occupants who were about to be executed. Stavros had cut out the heart of the German commander while he was still alive and held it up in front of his face so that he could see Stavros cut through the aorta. Bobby shivered slightly at the thought of that.

"Who are all of these people?" he asked Stavros. "I recognise a couple from his car lots but most of them............. who are they?"

"They are mostly business contacts. He has not had the time for real friends although some of the people here are Mrs C's friends".

Just then a large man came up to Bobby. "The famous Bobby Parsons, good to meet you at last. I have a job that needs to be done by you. I'll have a word the Ari about it next week, tonight's not the time". He walked away.

"Who was that"? Bobby asked Stavros. He didn't say his name.

"A very nasty person, one of Mr C's main customers of H. You're better off not knowing his name believe me". Stavros led his wife by the arm to meet another guest. Bobby stood by the bar and had another drink, he was bored already. Maybe he should have brought Fiona.

Time dragged. Bobby was drinking too much. It was as well that he had walked and didn't have a car. As he stood there a woman made her way to where he was standing. She was stunning. She had long red hair, green eyes, the most unblemished pale skin that Bobby had ever seen and a brilliant smile. Bobby guessed that she was about twenty or twenty-one. "Hi", she said, "you've been standing over here for ages, you look lonely. Do you want to dance?

Bobby was on the dance floor before she had time to blink. She was one of the most sexy girls he had ever met. The Four Tops were singing Walk Away Renee as they went onto the dance floor but then played Barry White's Just the Way You Are. She and Bobby were now dancing up close. She had obviously done this before and he felt an erection in his trousers like he used to when he was in his teens. As the music finished and they moved apart Ari suddenly appeared. "We need to talk" he said.

"Not now" said Bobby.

"Yes right now" said Ari.

"I'll be right back" said Bobby over his shoulder following Ari of the dance floor.

Ari took him to a corner. "A word of warning, stay away from her. She's Mad Paddy's daughter and she's a nympho. She'll have you outside for a screw and if her old man finds out he'll hurt you. The last person he found out had fucked her, he cut off his prick, without an anesthetic, and posted it in a jiffy bag the guys wife. He thinks that she's as clear and white as the driven snow and that the guys are taking advantage of her. Nobody has the guts to tell him that she's a tramp".

"Thanks for the warning Ari. Actually I don't feel so good so if its OK with you I think that I'll duck out the side door and head home for an early night."

"Very wise son. We'll talk next week".

Ari thought that it was his chat that had decided Bobby to leave early but Bobby was relieved that he had the excuse. He was walking home when a car pulled up beside him. It was Fiona. She said that she had been at a friends for the evening and was just on her way home when she had seen him. Bobby didn't want to remind her that she lived in the opposite direction to the way she was traveling.

She drove him home and stayed the night. They got into the bedroom and took their clothes off. Bobby threw her onto the bed and drove into her, taking her harshly. He was annoyed with her, annoyed with himself and annoyed with life, and was taking it out on her. Fiona mistook it for passion. "My god Bobby, you needed that" was all she said. Bobby got off her and had a shower. Climbed back into bed and went to sleep leaving Fiona waiting to be satisfied. Just as he was falling asleep he felt her masturbating. The following morning Bobby was quiet. He was angry with himself but was not going to admit that to Fiona. She left just after breakfast and Bobby knew that it was over as far as he was concerned. There was no future with her for him.

CHAPTER 61

The expected phone call came from Ari later that week. "My friend needs your talents but this is a bit special". Ari explained that his friend was his biggest customer of drugs. Bobby was amazed when Ari told him that Delroy's stuff was so pure that it could be cut into larger than normal numbers. The victim had worked for Ari's friend for a number of years. He was recutting some of the packages and mixing with other powder. He was then skimming the excess. His boss had been investigating this for several months and the excess had not found its way onto the market, at least not locally. This meant that either there was a stockpile of gear somewhere, worth about a million pounds, which his boss wanted to know where it was stored, or it was being sold on for distribution outside of London, in which case his boss wanted to know to whom. Ari, knowing the sort of question that Bobby would ask said that the victim had a morbid fear of water. Apparently he had almost drowned when he was younger. It was so important to Ari's friend that a successful outcome would be worth £50,000 to Bobby. Bobby felt that it was better not to remind Ari that the money was not important. He knew that he had to do the job. Bobby said that he would get back to him in the next few days with a plan.

Two days later Delroy phoned. "Hi white brother. How are you? You haven't been back to my club." Bobby knew Delroy would be smiling and this made him smile too.

"It's the strain of resisting all of you lovely ladies".

"Well don't resist man, go with the flow, they will take you to heaven".

"I don't want to be a porn video star thanks" said Bobby.

"For you white brother, I would turn off the machine. Anyway I have a business proposition for you".

"I don't do drugs Delroy, you know that".

"This is not drugs, its cars and it legit. How about you meet me next Tuesday and we will go and see and talk to a man". Bobby agreed to meet at the Fentiman Road house the following Tuesday morning.

Before leaving home to meet Delroy, Bobby phoned Ari with his plan for the latest job for his friend. He then drove to South London, over Tower Bridge, through the Elephant and Castle, and towards the Oval. He turned right into Fentiman Road. The house was on the left, almost opposite the pub. As he pulled up Delroy left the house and joined him in his car. "Hello white brother" he said with his usual smile, "to Streatham my man".

They chatted as they drove south and as they arrived in Streatham Hill, Delroy told Bobby take a right and then left down an alley behind some shops. They pulled up at three units that were a car repair business. As Delroy got out of the car a big West Indian with untidy grey curly hair walked out of the middle unit and shook hands with Delroy. Bobby followed Delroy. "Goat, this is my white brother Bobby Parsons, Bobby this here is Goat". Bobby held out his hand and shook Goats. Goat pointed to a Ford Cortina parked in front of Bobby's car. "There's the wheels" he said. Bobby looked at it, it was a couple of years old, looked in good condition but he could see that it had been recently resprayed.

"What's that worth?" said Delroy to Bobby.

"I don't know without looking at it closely but I would say a couple of thou".

"Eleven hundred to you" said Delroy.

"I don't deal in hot cars Delroy, you should know that".

"No, this is strictly legal Bobby. Goat here is a craftsman. This is two cars. One car had a head on, front caved in, the other was shunted up the arse, back gone. They are insurance company write-offs. The insurance company sells them as scrap. Goat cuts them in half and welds the two halves together. You have the means to sell them on. But more important you have a breakers yard, Goat has supply problems. You register with the insurance company's and buy the scrapped wrecks, let Goat have them to work on and then buy them back from him and sell on a legit car. You know that the car is legal and not nicked 'cause you've supplied it. A good idea?" Bobby went and had a closer look at the car. Under the head lining he could feel the weld line and also he could see it underneath, but the car on the surface looked fine.

"We put the plates on that are the front car so that the engine number matches and all the documents match" said Goat.

"OK" said Bobby, we'll give it a go. I'll take this one and put it on the lot and see what interest I get and if the public pick anything up and I'll register the yard as you suggest. I'll have to see about getting the car over".

"The price is delivered" said Delroy. "You forget I own a taxi firm, it's easy for me to sort brother" Bobby shook hands with Goat on the deal. Goat gave him his phone number for when he had set up the supply side of the deal and Bobby and Delroy left. They went back to Fentiman Road and had lunch in the Fentiman Arms before Bobby headed back home.

CHAPTER 62

The following day was phoned by Ari who said he had managed to make the arrangements that Bobby had wanted for the next job.

On Wednesday evening of the following week, Bobby found himself driving to Burnham on Crouch. As the victim was afraid of water Bobby suggested that he would be most likely to talk if he were on a boat, on the side, looking at water. It was cold and dark when Bobby found the marina and located the boat. It belonged to another friend of Ari's who was providing two men to crew the boat. There were another two men on board who were obviously heavies from the client. As he climbed on board one of the heavies, a huge man, said "Parsons?".

"Yes. Is our man on board?"

"'e's downstairs still out from the chloroform. We were told you liked them naked so we took 'is clothes off".

As Bobby had climbed aboard, the cruiser had cast off and was now moving down the River Crouch towards the mouth. It was colder now than it had been on land. Bobby had an overcoat and gloves on and so did the two heavies.

"Let's hope that he doesn't freeze before he gives us the

information then" said Bobby. "Lets get on with it, bring him up".

The two men went below and came back with the victim. He was naked except for heavy chains around his feet and ankles and handcuffs on his wrists. He was still groggy from the chlorophyll but soon came round when he came into the cold air. He was placed on a chair which was usually used for fishing but tonight had been placed as close as possible to the small rear tender deck which over looked the water. In seconds he realised his predicament and started to shiver.

Bobby approached. "Lets cut the bullshit, get this over and go home to warm beds . I'm told that you have been creaming off drugs from your employer for about two years. Where are they? Simple, you tell me, we look, then we go home. You don't tell, you go for a swim with the chains around your feet. Tomorrows fish food. What's it to be?"

The victim capitulated immediately. He told Bobby three locations where there were drugs hidden and also the identity of the person to whom he had sold some. This information was sent by the boats radio to a land base. The land base then relayed it by car phone to some teams standing by to check if the victim was telling the truth. Bobby instructed the two heavies to move the man from his precarious perch while the information was being verified. It could take a couple of hours. The victim huddled up in a corner on deck. Bobby gave him a blanket to keep warm. If the information proved correct the victim would be safe. If not Bobby felt that he would need to be more persuasive as he was getting tired and cold out here on this boat. The crew made some tea for the heavies and Bobby but didn't give the victim any. It was about two hours later when the call came through on the radio. The victim had been telling the truth and the stash of drugs had been recovered. The victim was safe. The boat was just about at the mouth of the river so started to turn around to go back to the marina.

"OK" said Bobby, "you can take the chains off now and give him his clothes back. We've finished for tonight".

The two heavies walked to the victim, picked him up and threw him overboard. His scream lasted about a second before he disappeared under the water. Bobby jumped up. "What the fuck are you doing? We got the information"

The larger of the two heavies looked at Bobby and said "orders" and then both of the men went to the cabin. The two crew members just stared forward and said nothing. Bobby spent the long journey to the moorings on deck, in the cold. He was the first off when the boat docked. He walked quickly to his car, started the engine and phoned Ari from his car phone. It was past two o'clock in the morning and all he got was the answerphone machine. "Pick up fuck you" he yelled at it, but there was no response. He arrived home at about three and sat in his lounge in darkness with a glass of brandy, something he normally only kept in his cupboard for guests. He felt as though he was in a state of shock.

At six he tried Ari again and still his phone diverted to his answerphone. He got showed and changed and tried again, still the answerphone. "If you don't pick this fucking phone up now I'm coming round to your house and I will sit in your fucking drive with my hand on my hooter until you fucking talk to me."

There was no answer so Bobby left the house and drove to Ari's. He pulled into the drive and as he did so Ari opened the front door and walked out in his dressing gown. "Calm down Bobby. This is not the place to have this conversation".

Bobby was as uptight as Ari had ever seen him. "Not the fucking place. They threw the guy over the side tied in chains Ari, where is the fucking place to talk about that"?.

"I know, I heard. Look, this is nothing to do with my

family and I don't want them to hear, do you understand". Bobby detected menace in Ari's voice. Of course he would want to protect his family.

"What about the family of that poor shmuck last night?"

"There's nothing we can do about that now. Go home, have some breakfast and meet me at the Loughton House office in three hours".

Bobby turned and left. Three hours later he was at the Loughton house. He went straight into Ari's office. He was sitting at his desk.

"What the fucks going on Ari? They chucked the bloke overboard. We had all the information and they had the goods. The big goon said it was orders, whose fucking orders".

"I know. I heard what happened. It's a pity you had to see it".

"Bollocks about 'it's a pity'. Why do it?"

"It happens Bobby, it goes on all the time, if you didn't think so you are naive. You just haven't come across it before that's all".

"Naive? Bloody hell Ari, this was murder. I've never been a party to killing people". Ari could tell Bobby was very upset and that his voice was getting higher in pitch. He decided to go on the attack.

"No Bobby, you just fucking hurt them. Not just physically but you fuck with their minds too. You are involved in the business whether you like it or not. Look at yourself. A rich, successful businessman. You have property's and money in the bank. You drive an expensive car, belong to the best golf club in the area, wear designer clothes and where did the money come from? Where did it all start? You got paid to hurt people. You had a wad of cash that bought the partnership, the partnership bought the house, that bought others houses, other businesses. It started with the money from hurting people so don't get all fucking high principled now, now that you don't need it anymore. You're in it for life and if some stupid shmuck gets dissed along the way, well tough fucking luck".

Bobby stared at Ari, he had never heard him talk like that before. He turned and left the house without saying another word. He felt that this was a world that he wanted nothing to do with but that he was involved whether he liked it or not. He realized that had drifted into it many years ago and should have not agreed to go further than the man who he blamed for his father's predicament. Ari was right, he was a wealthy man and he was so because of what he did to his victims, people that he never knew. Once again he decided that it had to end, he had to get off this wheel.

CHAPTER 63

B obby phoned Delroy the following week. He had a letter
from two of the five insurance companies he had written
to saying that they would put him on the list for scrapped
car disposal. He told Delroy that he hoped to hear from all
five but would keep Goat informed about what cars were
coming in.

"Hear that you had a bit of trouble last week white
brother".

"What did you hear?"

"'bout a man went to his maker by way of a wet grave".

Bobby was shocked that it was common knowledge.
"How the hell do you know about it?"

"Ears to the ground my man, ears to the ground. Word
is you were close to following him".

"What do you mean?" Bobby was surprised.

"You fronted Eddy the Elephant, asked him what the fuck
he was doing. People don't do that and survive usually".

"It was a reaction, I didn't think about it".

"You sound down white brother. How about lunch on
Sunday? Meet me at Fentiman Road about twelve".

"I am a bit pissed off. I was thinking of coming to Dulwich
on Saturday".

"That's good. I will be there. Bring a change of clothes for Sunday and stay the night. Before you say anything I mean in a room on your own. Two of the girls are working away so there are two rooms spare. We can talk if you like in private". Bobby went to Dulwich on Saturday. He had dinner with Delroy and they talked about what had happened. "That man of yours knows some tough, mean bastards. He has got himself locked in because of you and that means that you are locked in too".

Bobby knew that Delroy was right but it didn't help his mood. After dinner they sat in the bar and talked some more, about cars, football, business, mainly small talk. As before the club was not busy on Saturday. Only one of the girls was upstairs with a member, two others were in the bar, Cherry, who he had first met at the hotel what seemed like many years ago, and a new girl called Iris. Cherry was soon going back to Jamaica, she had enough money to set herself up in business. She was buying a hotel for tourists with her brother. She was making sure that Iris was settled before she left. They joined in sometimes with funny comments about some of the punters. "I'll miss Cherry" said Delroy. "She's been like my manager for the girls, been very helpful". Cherry smiled at the compliment. Bobby was struck again at how content the girls seemed to be given what they did for a living.

Delroy had put him in a room in the house that was one of the girls who was at another of Delroys houses for the Saturday. She would be back at about eleven on the Sunday so Delroy arranged to pick Bobby up at that time. Delroy went home and Bobby finished his wine and went upstairs to bed. He showered and slipped between the satin sheets. He had been in bed about ten minutes and was just dropping off to sleep when the door opened. He looked up and saw Cherry come into the room. She closed the door and walked towards Bobby. She slipped a robe from her shoulders, she was naked underneath. Bobby had to admit she had a terrific body. She slipped into bed next to him. "Don't worry, all of the camera's are off".

"I didn't think any of you girls knew about them" said Bobby.

"Only me. I have to switch them on sometimes if Delroy is not here. I think you have problems Bobby, you are all tense so lay back and let me de-stress you". She kissed Bobby's chest and then worked down his body. He lay back. She was very good at what she did. She made him forget all of his troubles for a night. In the morning when he awoke she was gone.

Delroy was there at eleven. They got into Bobby's car.

"Where are we going then?" asked Bobby "you haven't said".

"Wait and find out" Delroy smiled at him. "Just head back to London man, I'll tell you where to go".

They went back on the South Circular and then cut up towards the Elephant and Castle. They were traveling along The Old Kent Road when Delroy said "stop, park there. Its dinner with my Mum today". Delroys mum had lived in her flat for just over twenty five years. It contained a lot of oversize furniture, most of which looked as though it was many years old. It was very cluttered with nick-knacks and photos of Delroy and his sisters and it smelled of the lunch cooking. Bobby loved it. It was so relaxed and homely. Delroys mum welcomed him like a long lost relation. She obviously loved Delroy and Delroy loved her. Bobby sat in the lounge while Delroy helped his mum in the kitchen. He looked around him and thought that he had never had a home like this, it was rather like a womb, protective, warm and secure. Bobby thought about Delroy the pimp, but how he looked after his girls and wondered if it was the caring upbringing that he would have had living here that had conditioned that caring side. They had a chicken casserole that was slightly spiced, dumplings and sweet potatoes for lunch and a dessert of homemade apple pie and custard. It was delicious. Bobby couldn't remember when he had last had a real home cooked meal. Bobby almost envied Delroy his mother.

The afternoon was over too quickly. Delroys mother had told Bobby that he was welcome at any time and she had scolded Delroy saying that he didn't bring enough of his friends home. As he drove home across Tower Bridge and along Commercial Road he realised that he did not know where Delroy lived. Did he live with his mother in the flat? He suspected not.

CHAPTER 64

B obby threw himself into the development of the flats. He had employed and architect and the ground works had been completed but Bobby project managed the build. He was on site every day and the was pleased to note that the project was on time and on budget. The business with Goat seemed to be going well. Bobby was supplying wrecks and about two weeks later getting back whole cars at forty percent below normal trade rates. He decided to keep these cars isolated so he put them all in a lot he owned at Chadwell Heath. That way he felt that he could monitor them.

In April he received a call from Ari who had a job for him. Bobby said "no thanks" and put the phone down. The next day Ari arrived at the site in Hornchurch. "Look Bobby, we've had this conversation, you can't say no. You're in and that's that. Anyway this is a simple one, you just need to be there, no heavy stuff, no violence". Bobby agreed to go.

Spring turned to summer Bobby was playing golf again but noticed that the women, although polite, didn't come on to him in the same way as before. He was actually pleased about this.

Nick came home on leave at the end of June and it was just as though he had never been away. This time he was home for a month. As usual he stayed with Bobby and spent his time mainly playing golf and pulling women. Every weekend Nick had a female guest to stay and sometimes during the week too. He visited the Hornchurch site with Bobby a few times and was impressed with what Bobby was achieving. He had already sold seven of the eighteen flats off plan. Nick said that maybe he should invest in a property, Bobby offered to do him a special deal, a fifty percent discount. Nick said that he would look at it. He had not been advised of his next posting yet and thought that they may want him to stay in London for a while. If he did he said that he would take Bobby up on his offer.

Nick wanted to go somewhere warm on holiday as they had the previous year. Bobby was reluctant to leave the site for two weeks but said he would go for one. Nick booked a break in Benidorm for the end of August, one week with Bobby and a second week for himself alone.

The week before they were due to leave Ari phoned Bobby. He needed him to do another job. Ari had phoned a lot less since the episode on the boat so Bobby assumed that he was being selective about what he asked Bobby to do. Given that their relationship had become somewhat strained as a result of that night, Bobby appreciated this. He told Ari that he was going on holiday and agreed to meet him the week that he came back.

They arrived in Benidorm. It was just what Nick wanted although Bobby's initial reaction was that it was a bit bigger and noisier than he would have liked. Bobby would have preferred a restful holiday in the sun but it seemed to him that Nick wanted to party and pull women. Bobby put it down to being a reaction to his military life, being on camps for six months at a time. That evening they went out to the clubs which are numerous in Benidorm town. Bobby was surprised again at how predatory the English girls are when on holiday. As soon as they arrived in a bar or a club, the two friends were immediately approached by women. Having danced all evening Bobby decided to call it a day around midnight. He waved to Nick to signal that he was leaving and then went back to his hotel room, showered and fell asleep. He awoke in the morning and realized that Nick had not been back all night. He got up and showered and was dressing when Nick arrived.

"You missed a great night. Twins, I couldn't tell them apart. I had one and then they went into the bathroom and came out and said it was the other one's turn. I had to tell them which one that was, the one that I hadn't just had. I didn't know, so they said in that case I would have to have them both again. I'm knackered. They saw us and thought that we were brothers. They thought it would be interesting the two of them and the two of us so I've agreed to meet them tonight. Hope that's OK".

Bobby agreed. Nick got showered, they went to breakfast and spent the rest of the day lazing by the pool. That evening they met the twins, spent the evening visiting various bars and clubs and returned to the hotel in the early hours of the morning. Nick had been right, the girls were really up for sex and they led the way. They had them and then swapped. The girls then discussed their performances in a humorous way. They eventually fell asleep. It was Nick who woke up and started again. Bobby enjoyed sex but with Nick it seemed to be a necessity.

The following night Bobby again went back before Nick. He had been in bed about two hours when Nick came in. He pretended to be asleep as Nick had sex with his partner. She left after about an hour. Nick was aware that Bobby had been awake and thanked him. "We couldn't go back to her place, her husband was pissed and went back there to sober up. We couldn't risk him waking up while I'm shafting his wife in the bed next to him", he laughed.

Bobby returned home at the end of the week leaving Nick there. The day after he got home he telephoned Ari and arranged to meet him to discuss the job. "I never understand these pratts" said Ari. "This is another one where the idiot has been skimming and shafting his boss. They all earn good money but get greedy and think that they won't get caught. This one's running a protection racket using his bosses name as a sales aid and his minders as enforcers. Apparently though he is a hard case and the initial feedback was that he wasn't afraid of anything. With a bit more pushing we found that he was scared of snakes, so let me know what you want set up."

"OK I'll be in touch in a few days. One thing though Ari, and I mean this whoever is involved, if one of those goons from the boat show up, not just here but at any gig, I walk away immediately. So you tell whoever you need to tell because I mean that one hundred percent". Ari nodded.

Bobby left Ari to go to the Hornchurch site and to think about the job he had just been given. He enjoyed being on site and seeing the flats nearing completion. Another two had been sold while he had been on holiday. He had decided that when this project was finished he would find another site and do it again.

Nick came home at the end of the week full of himself. He had had a great time in Spain. He told Bobby that he needed to spend the next couple of days resting to recover, he had had little sleep since Bobby had come home. A letter had come for him while he had been away. It was from the Ministry of Defence. It instructed him to contact an office in London as soon as possible. He telephoned them and was told to report the following day for a meeting. This he did and was told that he was to be stationed in Norway for the next three month where he would be on a total immersion course in Russian. They expected that he would be fluent in it by the end of the three month training period. "Bloody Norway, how bloody boring will that be. Locked in a house in the middle of nowhere with a couple of Russian defectors for three months. Thank goodness I've had my three month quota of shags during the last two weeks."

"Maybe that's why you are a Lieutenant Colonel, it's because you spent so much time in these glamorous places".

Bobby had phoned Delroy and asked if he knew anybody who could supply snakes. Delroy had said that he could but Bobby would have to visit the person and discuss his requirements.

Nick needed to return to Aldershot the following Wednesday so Bobby arranged to visit Delroy after he had taken Nick there.

CHAPTER 65

Bobby met Delroy at the cab offices. It was the same as it had been when he first met Delroy. "Why don't you clean this place up? A coat of paint wouldn't be a bad thing".

"If we make it smart the people down here will be thinking that we make too much money and use another cab company. This way we get the sympathy and the customers". Bobby laughed at Delroys business logic. They went down Railton Road and turned right to a house in Milton Road. Delroy greeted the man and introduced him to Bobby as Pete. Pete was very chatty.

"I come from Haiti man. There we have voodoo. There's voodoo all over the Caribbean but it's big in Haiti. They use snakes to frighten people. That's what you do ain't it. So do you want a snake to frighten somebody or kill them?"

"Only frighten them" said Bobby, "I don't want them to come to any real harm".

"I knows what you need then" said Pete. They went upstairs and into a converted area in his loft space. It was full of glass tanks, all with a snake in them. He pulled one out of a tank. He held it just behind its neck. It hissed as he pointed it at Bobby. "This is a black mamba. It's a favourite with the practitioners". He pulled a piece of thick card from his pocket and held it towards the snake's mouth. It lunged forward and bit the card leaving two small puncture marks on it."This baby is the very poisonous. If it bites a human he would normally die an agonising death in four to five hours. Right now he is harmless. He has just ejected his venom into the card, it takes about five hours for him to regenerate enough to kill a man. After about an hour he will have enough to make an arm go numb for an hour or two. After two hours it could do some permanent cell damage to the bitten area and maybe a bad headache. After three hours it could cause some irregular heartbeats and if the person had a bad heart it could kill them. After four hours it could be dangerous and after five, death unless the person has the antidote fairly quickly. The voodoo mans use one that has been cleaned about an hour ago. It bites a victim who then starts to go numb. The victim thinks that they are dying and the voodoo man makes a spell and then the victim gets better. The people think that it is magic".

Bobby said that he would come for the snake in about a week. He would let Delroy know when. Bobby contacted Ari and told him that the arrangements were made. He would need to know the venue and two days notice of the meeting.

It was set for the following Wednesday evening. Bobby arranged to meet Delroy and his snake man in The Bricklayers Arms. As they were leaving they went to a taxi that Delroy had waiting in the car park. The snake was in the boot. He watched as the keeper took it out of a vented box and held it so that it bit the card. "That gives you an hour, one and a half at the most, to guarantee no lasting problems". Bobby knew little about snakes and was a bit uncomfortable having this creature in his car. He also knew that it would be killed at the end of the evening by Stavros or one of his men. Although Bobby hurt people he had sympathy for animals that were mistreated. They didn't ask to be involved with humans after all.

Bobby then put it in his boot and drove across the river to a factory unit in Haringey where the meeting was to be held. Stavros met him at the door. He took him into the factory and Bobby saw that he already had the scene set up, a man, naked, tied to a chair. There were two other men in the unit, Bobby had never seen them before.

Bobby walked up to the victim carrying the box. He put the box on the floor and put his face close to the victim.

"Hi, I'm Bobby. I hear that you have been a bit silly and that's upset your very powerful boss".

"Fuck off" said the victim.

"That's not very friendly"

"Look, I know what this is about. So just give me a kicking and get on with it because I ain't gonna give you the details of something that has taken years to build up. Its my pension see?"

"But if you don't give me the information you may not live to spend a pension, thought of that?"

"They don't kill people for this. Kill me and there's no lists".

"They may not, but I am not they". Bobby picked up the box and took out the snake. The victims demeanor changed immediately. "OK, put it away. Lets talk about this".

Bobby looked at his watch. It was one hour and five minutes since he had collected the snake. He held it near the victim. The snake hissed, the victim tried to move away but couldn't. Bobby moved the snake nearer the victim who was now sweating a great deal. The snake lunged forward and bit the victims arm. The victim screamed. Bobby put the snake back into the box. He pulled a hypodermic syringe from his pocket. It contained water and a small amount of tea to give it colour.

"Now, the poison is in your body heading for your heart. Here is the antidote. You tell me the information that I need and I will inject this in. You don't and your body will be found on waste ground tomorrow morning".

"How do I know that you will"?

"You don't, but you don't have an option. Is your arm going numb yet?"

"Why?" said the victim.

"That's the first sign. It's the arm, then the chest, then it's too late".

"Yes it is going numb" said the victim. His voice had got noticeably higher and quicker. "OK, OK. I'll tell you". He started to give all of the information, clients, helpers, amounts, Stavros stood and wrote down the information. When he has finished, Bobby gave the victim the injection of the tea solution. He indicated to the two men to cut the victim loose. They did this as Bobby and Stavros left by the same side door as they had entered. As they drove away, he victim started to get out of the chair as the numbness in his arm started to get less. He was almost standing when another man walked across the floor behind him. He had been watching in the dark from an upstairs office. He walked up to the victim from behind, pulled his hair to force his head back and ran the blade of a sharp knife across his throat, cutting through his jugular. The victim fell to the floor clutching his neck and writhing and, for the next two minutes, bled to death.

CHAPTER 66

Bobby finished the flats in Hornchurch. They all sold and he made a profit overall of two hundred and eighty thousand pounds. He started looking for another plot of building land. His car businesses were all doing well and the business with the stitched cars in Chadwell Heath were doing well too. Bobby had changed his car for a new BMW 730.

Nick came home reporting that he was now fluent in Russian. He was to be given a new posting in January. He didn't know what it was yet but suspected that it would be somewhere cold where they spoke Russian. Nick and Bobby spent Christmas Day with Nicks mum. On New Years Eve they went to Trafalgar Square to see in the New Year. It was nineteen eighty three.

Bobby took Nick back to Aldershot at the end of January. As usual Nick had spent many nights with a number of women during his time at home with Bobby. Nick had a job to do for Ari the following week. It was completed without any problems. He found a plot of land in Woodford, employed the same architect to draw up the plans and act on his behalf. This time there was no problems with planning. He set about building twenty two, two bedroom flats.

Nick phoned him towards the end of February. He was coming home for a long weekend. He had received his posting. It was not somewhere cold, he was going to Virginia to work with the US forces. He could not tell Bobby any of the details but it was something to do with monitoring Russian naval vessels from the Arctic down to Cuba. He would be gone for a year. They didn't go to the golf club that weekend, just chatted and went for a meal on Saturday evening. Nick seemed a bit quiet, Bobby thought it must be because of the prospect of being away for a year.

Nineteen eighty three was a very routine year for Bobby Parsons. He completed his Woodford development which made him a lot of money. He brought two new car lots, one in Benfleet and one in Chalkwell. The one in Benfleet he turned into another outlet for the stitched cars. He did four jobs for Ari, less than he had done previously. He was a regular at the Dulwich House on a Saturday evening although he never took advantage of the women on offer. His friendship with Delroy developed and he had Sunday lunch at Delroys mothers on a number of occasions. He spoke to Nick by phone almost every fortnight, Nick sounded about as bored as Bobby was. He told Bobby that he was 'let out' as he put it, every third weekend for four days. The only consolation as far as he was concerned was that his English accent was as 'bird magnet', his words, and he never slept alone during these weekend breaks. Bobby couldn't help but smile when Nick told him this. As the year moved on Bobby became more wealthy and more bored. He played golf every other day during the summer. He was popular with both the male and female members but the females had definitely stopped coming onto him and he was never included in any of their activities outside of the golf club. He was healthy, wealthy and successful. He knew that he was good looking and was good company. He was educated and well read and he was unhappy. He desperately wanted to change his life. Occasionally he would mention this to Delroy who always said the same thing, that he was stuck with it and should just relax and enjoy the benefits he had.

CHAPTER 67

Nick wasn't home for Christmas. His term was extended a few weeks because of a specific project that he was involved in. He came home at the beginning of March 1984. He was home for a month and started where he left off, at the golf club chatting up the women. He seemed to be most attracted to the married ones and they were attracted to him. Very often during the month Bobby would be woken up in the early hours of the morning with moans of ecstasy emitting from a female that Nick had brought home and was now seducing.

On the third Sunday of Nicks leave they played golf in the morning and decided to have the carvery lunch in the bar. As they were eating Bobby looked up and saw Emily walking towards the table. "Hello Nick, Bobby" she said.

"Hi Emily. How are you?" asked Bobby. "Still playing lots of golf? Haven't seen you down here recently".

"Hi Emily. You look great" said Nick.

"Thank you I feel great. No, I'm not playing much golf at the moment. It's difficult with a toddler. They're a full time job, but worth it, he's just lovely". Just then a small boy walked over to her. "Mummy" he said holding out both arms. Emily bent down and scooped him up. He looked just like a small, young version of Nick, same shaped face, same shaped nose and the same very dark hair.

"Well bye, good to see you both". Emily walked away. Bobby and Nick looked at each other and Bobby knew that Nick had seen the same as Bobby had. Nick was quiet in the car on the way home. He didn't say anything until they pulled into the drive. "I wonder if there are any more. Could be couldn't there. I've screwed around, never once used a condom. I could have kids all over the place".

Bobby said nothing. Although he hadn't had as many women as Nick, the same could apply to him. As quickly as this thought came to him it was dismissed, he was sure that he would have been approached, for maintenance if nothing else.

Nick returned to Aldershot early in April. He was due to be there for retraining for a few months before being reassigned. They had lunch in a pub in Camberley before Nick reported. They were just chatting about small things and it occurred to Bobby how comfortable Nick was with his life in the army. He seemed happy and content.

Bobby returned to work. He always let it slip a bit while Nick was around. His tour of his companies reinforced his belief that they almost ran themselves. He had checked their trading positions periodically on the computer link and all was well. Trading was good. The building project was slightly behind schedule but nothing serious. Bobby realised that he needed to find another piece of land so that he could move on to a new project when this one was finished. The building projects not only made him money but also occupied his time.

CHAPTER 68

Ari had another job for him in early June. He met with Ari in the Loughton house. This one was a bit different. It was for somebody who Ari didn't actually know but was a friend of a friend. "Your fame is obviously spreading. You could be working regularly outside of London soon if you play your cards right", Ari said it as though it was a good thing. It was the last thing that Bobby wanted to hear. Ari passed him a file on the victim. "This one is different. You need to read this and decide what you want to do. If he dies when you finish it would be good for humanity".

"There's never an excuse for killing somebody" said Bobby as he picked up the file and left Ari sitting behind his desk.

Bobby started to read the file when he got home. He was disgusted by the time he had finished reading it. The victim lived in Colchester. There were areas of Colchester where there were social problems, unemployment, alcohol and drug dependency, dysfunctional families. He groomed young children mostly from theses areas, boys and girls, for sex, often allowing them to be raped by the people who paid him money to supply them. The victim himself used them sometimes. His particular favourite was to be sucked by young boys. As an added bonus he took pictures of the acts taking place with a Polaroid camera and then sold the photos to pedophiles. He had made a mistake with one of his targets. She was thirteen, underdeveloped physically for her age and had slight learning difficulties. She had a pale, blemish free complexion and straight blond hair, she looked about ten. She was the niece of a local drug dealer, his only sister's only child. He had found out that the victim had got her hooked on heroin and because she had no money to pay for more, she would visit his house on the way home from school where he would have one of his clients waiting, who liked young virgins in school uniforms. Once she had had sex with client she would get her fix. It only came to light when one of the clients, having her doggy fashion, scratched her back when he climaxed. Her mother saw the scratches, got the story from her and phoned her brother. He said he would kill the man, who he knew, as he supplied him his drugs, but held back when his niece had told him about the pictures. He wanted them first. Killing the man could still result in them getting out to the nonces on the area. The uncle contacted his wholesaler and asked for his help, he contacted Ari and ergo, Bobby was involved.

He was considered the answer firstly because the victim would not know him and secondly Bobby would use his expertise to find out where the pictures were. He realised that when he had this information the uncle would kill the man but Bobby found that in this instance he didn't care. He read the detailed file with the numbers of children involved and decided that the man was evil. The only thing missing was the key to the mans fear. Bobby would have to improvise.

The venue was a disused farm building in a village near Marks Tey. As usual Stavros was again involved in the preparation and when Bobby arrived the victim was naked and tied to a chair by his ankles and wrists.

Bobby approached him. "Now I don't care how much I hurt you because you are scum so if you want to draw this out, fine, I can hurt you a lot. I will also make sure that I keep you conscious so that you feel the pain and you would know all about that because I would use amphetamines to do so. I want to know where you keep all of your filthy pictures of the children that you have raped. You can tell me now or you can suffer. Your choice".

The victim looked at him. Bobby took out of a bag a long, thin tube. He put on rubber kitchen gloves and spread vaseline onto the tube. He then inserted it into the tip of the mans penis, pushing it in about six inches. The victim watched, wide eyed, in fascination. Bobby then took a small funnel and pushed it over the top of the tube, securing it with tape so that it wouldn't leak. He then picked up a plastic container with liquid in it. It was only when he opened the container that the victim realised that it contained petrol. Bobby poured the petrol into the funnel and down the tube into the victims bladder. He then struck a match.

"OK stop, please. I'll tell you"....he was pleading, Bobby ignored him and lit the petrol. The flame spread up the tube, the victim watched wide eyed in horror. It reached his penis and continued to burn inside the tube, inside his penis. As it burnt, the tube melted with the heat. The pain must have been almost unbearable as the flame would have burnt inside the victim until it went out because of the lack of oxygen. The victim passed out. Stavros revived him by throwing a bucket of water over him.

"Now where are the filthy pictures you take" said Bobby, picking up another length of tubing. The victim couldn't talk quickly enough. He gave two addresses in Colchester where he had photo's stored. Stavros made notes and when he had them he went to use his car phone to pass the details on.

Bobby returned to the victim. He took a small plastic bag, the type that was used to put sandwiches in. He placed it over the victims penis and testicles and taped it in place. He cut a small hole in the top and poured in some petrol. The victim looked at him horrified. "I've told you all you want" he said. He was near to hysteria.

"Just making arrangements in case you are not telling me the truth". It was over an hour later that two men arrived at the unit, each with a suitcase. They were filled with disgusting pictures. Bobby tipped the photos into one case. He poured petrol over them. He then put the case at the feet of the victim and placed his feet in the case. He then took the last of the petrol and poured it over the victims thighs and groin. He then lit the petrol soaked photo's. The flames caught and ran up the victims legs and into his groin. He was screaming as he burnt. Bobby waited until he was satisfied that the pictures had all been destroyed and turned and left. He knew that the pain had been too much for the victim, he had died in agony. The two men who had brought the cases in watched with eyes as big as dinner plates.

Bobby drove to Marks Tey, turned onto the A12 and headed towards London. He could not stop his mind replying what had happened, what he had done. He knew that he had crossed the line tonight. He had actually killed somebody. He had sat in judgment on that man and carried out his sentence. He had considered what he had done and the way he had treated vulnerable children, found him guilty and executed him in the most painful way that he could think of. What worried him most of all though, was that he didn't care.

Ari phoned him the next day to ask if he was alright. He had obviously had a report back from Stavros. He also said that the client was very happy with the result as had asked Ari to thank Bobby for his actions.

The following Saturday evening Bobby had dinner with Delroy, he told him what had happened. "I ain't never killed nobody Bobby, and probably never will. But people who shit with kids is different. If anybody messed with my nieces or nephew, I would happily slit their throats personally. But you be careful now brother, you don't want to get sucked in to a new level. You make sure that the Greek bastard who runs you don't up the anti".

"He doesn't run me Delroy and I am not a killer. This was different".

Delroy looked at him and let it go. He changed the subject. They had a drink after dinner with a couple of the girls who had nothing to do and Bobby spent the night in an empty bedroom.

Bobby bought a big, very dilapidated house in Wanstead in September. He obtained permission to demolish it and build a four story block of flats on the land, two two bedroomed ones on the first three floors and two one bedroom ones on the top floor. His architect advised a steel structure for something as high as this. Bobby went along with this, it was another thing for him to spend his time with and try and forget the episode at Marks Tey.

During the second half of 1984 he did three other jobs for Ari but they were all ones that just required him to accompany Stavros. It was easy money but also disturbing to Bobby as he realized that he was effective because of his reputation. He didn't want to be that well known.

There was a demand for flats in 1984 and by Christmas he had sold three of his new project off plan. It seemed to Bobby that everything that he was doing at the moment was making him money. He wished that he could just stick with his legitimate businesses.

He had Christmas lunch with Nicks mother but otherwise spent it on his own at home. Nicks mum seemed pleased to have him there. She had insisted on cooking a full Christmas dinner and fussed around him as if he were her son, not her son's friend. Maybe that was it; he was her surrogate son and she was his surrogate mother.

CHAPTER 69

Nick came home at the end of March 1985. The day before Bobby was due to pick him up from Heathrow he sold the last of the Wanstead flats. He now needed another project to work on when Nick went away.

Nick was so enthusiastic about America. He had loved his time there and hoped that he would be going back. His job in Virginia was finished but the US Army people that he has worked with were now moving to Phoenix on a new project and he hoped that he would be appointed the UK liaison officer. He told Bobby that when he left the army he would like to go and live there. He talked about the things that he had done and the people he had met, for hours on end. Bobby had never heard him so verbal about anything before. Even when they visited the golf club he was more intent on talking to people about his time stateside as he put it, than trying to chat up the women.

The three weeks with Nick passed quicker than ever. It was time for him to report back to camp and be briefed for his next posting. Bobby took him back to Aldershot. Nick had bored him stiff about America but he knew that he would miss him. He had grown to realise that he was more relaxed and content when Nick was around.

Ari had his ear to the ground. He never phoned Bobby when Nick was home but the day after Nick had left Ari phoned Bobby with another job. It was a straightforward one so Bobby left the arrangements to Ari to sort out.

Bobby spent his time looking for land. He found a large area between Chadwell Heath and Dagenham. It was an old plant nursery, it covered over eight acres and was covered with now empty greenhouses. He could build more than one hundred houses on it. He contacted his architect who contacted the local authority who confirmed that a planning application would be looked on favourably. Bobby bought the land. He was very excited. This was something new and different, much bigger than anything he had done before. He even set up a new, separate company to deal with it. He called it 'Roberts Developments' after his father.

It was a warm, clear evening in May. He had been on the new site with the architect and arrived home late. He pulled into his drive and his senses told him something was wrong. He turned off the car engine, got out of the car and stood and looked and listened. It was dusk. He could see that there was a light on somewhere in the house. He knew he had not left one on when he left home that morning. He walked quietly up to the front door. It was closed and showed no sign of having been forced. He walked as quietly as he could around the side of the house. The French windows were locked and so was the back door into the kitchen. There were no signs of anybody having broken in. He went back to the front door. It had two locks, a Chubb mortise lock and a Yale. He put his key into the Chubb to unlock it. It was already unlocked. He was positive that he had locked it that morning. He turned the Yale and stepped into the hall. He stood in the hall and listened. He heard nothing. The upstairs landing light was on, he was sure that he had turned it off before leaving that morning. He heard a slight sound of movement from upstairs. He stood still and listened, then he heard it again. There was somebody upstairs in a bedroom. Bobby crossed the hall silently, opened the hall cupboard where he kept his golf clubs and took out his driver, his biggest club. He could hit a golf ball over 200 yards with this club, it would certainly put a dent in this intruders skull. He crept up the stairs. As he reached the landing one of the floorboards gave a slight creak. He raised the club in case the intruder had heard him. "Is that you Bobby?" Nick called out.

"What the bloody hell……..?"

Nick appeared on the landing from his bedroom. "What are you doing with that golf club?"

"Bloody hell Nick, you scared me shitless. I thought that somebody had broken in. What are you doing here? You always phone and let me know when you are coming home. How long are you back for? Why didn't you let me know? Shouldn't you be somewhere glamorous by now anyway?"

"I've been kicked out of the army". Bobby was speechless. He just stood and stared at Nick.

"Lets go downstairs and have a drink and I'll tell you what's happened". They went into the lounge and Bobby opened a bottle of brandy and poured two large glasses. He gave one to Nick. "Come on then, tell me. What have you done, fucked the Brigadiers wife".

"I've not actually been kicked out. I'm to be invalided out. I had a medical as I always do before an assignment. They found some sort of irregularity so they did some tests. It seems that I have got the same liver problem that killed my father. It seems that there is about a 50% chance that it can be passed from generation to generation. There is no cure, I'm dying."

"This is ridiculous. We will get another opinion. I'll sort something out tomorrow with a specialist".

"Bobby, the British army doctors are some of the best

in the world, they are not going to be wrong, especially not with this, the same thing that my father died of. Anyway they have offered to lump sum my pension rights so I will get a good amount of money. I need to sort buying somewhere live with it".

"Why? Stay here. There's plenty of room for Christ's sake. How long are they saying that you've got"?

"Eight to nine months. The next three or four I will have no pain, then the pain sets in but can be controlled by drugs for about the next two, then it gets serious for the last two or three. I remember my Mum with my dad. He was a total invalid. I will need to go into a hospice or somewhere, I will need nursing care and spend most of the time drugged up so that the pain is tolerable".

"That's decided then, you are most definitely staying here".

"No Bobby I couldn't have you nursing me"?

"Maybe not, but I can employ a nurse. There must be agency's that can arrange twenty four hour nursing care. You're my best friend, my only real friend, I'm not having you on your own or in some institution. You're staying here. What about your Mum, when are you going to tell her?"

"When I get ill. No point in upsetting her before that. She's been through it twenty years ago with my dad". They talked into the night about what had happened and what Nick was going to do now. Nick did finally agree to stay living with Bobby in Chigwell. He would take his army pension as a lump sum and leave it for his mother.

The next day Bobby located a liver specialist in Harley Street and made an appointment for Nick to visit. The specialist confirmed the diagnosis. He did offer to supply some different drugs. They were not available on the national health. They were American and expensive but they would prolong Nicks life by a few months, maybe give him a year, and they would also delay the worst of the effects of the condition so that the really severe period would be reduced from about three months to one month. The cost would be £3000 pounds a month. Nicks was horrified and said he didn't have that sort of money. Bobby wrote a cheque for £30,000 and gave it to the doctor. "Lets just make one thing clear, money is not an issue here" He told Nick as they got into the taxi outside of the consultants. Nick was about to say something when Bobby said "Nick, I make loads of money, I am a millionaire many times over. I have nothing to spend my money on. Let me spend some on you making the rest of your life as good as it could be".

The next day they went into a travel agents in Chigwell and booked a two month holiday in America. They were to fly to New York, take the train across the country to Seattle. Fly to San Francisco, visit the Grand Canyon, Las Vegas, Los Angeles and then across the country again to Texas. Bobby phoned Ari and told him what was happening and why saying that he couldn't be contacted while he was away. He told his architect that he was selling the site and would he look for something else more in line with what they had done in the past. He would deal with all the details while he was away by fax. He visited all of his businesses and explained that he was taking a holiday and that he would be contacting them by phone from time to time while he was away.

He had everything sorted before he and Nick left for their holiday.

CHAPTER 70

They arrived home at the end of July. They had both had a wonderful time. Nick was so enthusiastic about America and Bobby had to agree that it was a spectacular country. Nick's health was still fine. Because of the drugs he was still having no effects from his condition.

Bobby's architect had sold the site to a housing developer. As the site was now clear and had planning permission for houses it was worth a lot more than he had paid for it. The architect sold it showing Bobby a £1.8 million pounds profit. He had found three options for new sites, at Bobby's instructions he had arranged the purchase of two of them. The first one was in a place called Little Heath, near Goodmayes. He had already applied for planning permission for eight houses. The other was in Romford and he had drawn up plans for two small blocks of flats, each one with nine flats per block. Nick had said that he would like to be involved in something, he couldn't just sit around the house. So far there was no sign of any effects of the problem. Bobby gave him the flats development as his project. He threw himself into it with enthusiasm. He and the architect seemed to hit it off straight away. Bobby bought him a Land Rover Discovery so that he looked and felt the part.

In November they had a long weekend away. Nick had talked about how much he had enjoyed learning to ski when he was in Norway. Bobby booked a ski holiday. Spring would have been better but Bobby did not want to risk waiting that long. So far Nick had shown no signs of any problems but spring was getting to close to the time predicted for problems. They were to go to a small select French resort close to the Swiss border. They would fly into Geneva and then drive over the border. Bobby had some business to do first so he booked the first night in a hotel in the city. He had briefed Nick and took him with him in case he needed a fluent French speaker. They had an appointment with a manager of Le Premier Banc De Geneve. Bobby arranged to open a numbered Swiss bank account. He passed over one thousand pounds in cash to open the account and said that further substantial funds would follow. He was shown to the vaults and he set his personal security number.

They then drove to the resort and checked in just in time for a drink and dinner. The resort was not packed as it would have been in a month or so's time, but it was still fairly busy. The snow was higher than the resort so they were bussing people up to the slopes. After dinner they went to a popular bar. Most of the people there were French. Nick was very relaxed speaking to everybody, Bobby knew about five words. Bobby excused himself and went to bed at eleven. He awoke at about six the next morning as smiled as he noticed that Nicks bed had not been slept in. Nick arrived about an hour later with a big grin on his face. "Bloody hell, its ages since I've had a shag. Forgotten how good it was".

They went up the mountain to ski. Nick took to it very easily and was soon off of the nursery slope. Bobby decided it was not for him after four hours of falling over and getting bruised. He got the bus down to the hotel and had a leisurely late lunch.

That evening Nick was at it again. They alighted on two attractive young ladies. Nick was charming to them both. Their English was about as good as Bobby's French so he found the evening dragged. Again at eleven o'clock he excused himself and went to bed. He woke up in the morning and was not surprised when he saw that Nick had not come back to the room. Predictably he arrived about an hour later. He had spent the night with both of the girls.

When they arrived home Nick was once again all business and worked hard on site all day making sure that the work was being done properly and on time. Bobby started preparatory work on the Little Heath site. He had transferred two million pounds to his numbered Swiss account.

Ari phoned Bobby. His client had another job for Bobby. He was so impressed with the Marks Tey job that he wanted somebody else burnt. Bobby went ballistic at Ari. "I'm not a fucking killer. That was emotional. Different." Bobby told him to get one of the two men watching to do it, or Stavros, but rule him out. He slammed the phone down. Ari phoned him back the following day. "I've told him that you are nursing your best friend and can't do it this time but Bobby, you let Pandora out of the box, you can't walk away now for ever". Bobby said again to himself, he had to get out of this somehow. He realized that he had made a mistake by killing the peedo. The word was now out that he would kill.

They invited Nicks mum for Christmas. Bobby thought that Nick's mum enjoyed Christmas 1985 more than she had enjoyed Christmas for many years. She didn't know the true situation. As far as she was concerned Nick was still in the army and he was home on leave. It was Christmas afternoon when the first pain came. Bobby already had the painkillers stocked so Nick got through the day without showing any effects.

During January he deteriorated slightly but during

February the situation got very much worse. As planned, Bobby engaged an agency to supply twenty four hour, seven day nursing care at home. Nick was spending more time in bed with strong painkillers to mask the pain. By March he was having to be fed intravenously and was bleeding internally, the blood leaking from his anus. His mother had been told in January and had moved into the house to with Nick during March. Nick had spoken to her and told her that he had appointed Bobby as his executor. His only asset was the money he had from the army and some in a savings, all of which he passed to his mother. In April Nick was going in and out of a coma. He died on April 23rd 1986 at four twenty in the morning.

CHAPTER 71

Nick was buried on 30th April after a service at his
mothers church. Bobby, his mother and two officers
representing his regiment were all that attended. As he was
no longer a serving officer he was not entitled to a guard of
honour. Nick's mother had returned home the day after he
died. She thanked Bobby for looking after Nick and making
the last year of his life so enjoyable.

Bobby went home after the funeral. He needed to sort
through what little stuff Nick had and put his affairs in order.
He was sitting on the bed in his room, with all of the paper
work spread out on the bed. His bank statement showed
that he had a balance of £27.15p. The rest he had already
transferred to his mother. There was his army demobilisation
papers, birth certificate, passport, driving license, national
insurance and tax documents and other bits of irrelevant
clutter. He would need the documents to register his death.
As executor it was his job to do it.

He was sitting looking at the passport when it struck
him, his way out. For years everybody had said how alike they
were, they looked like brothers. Now Bobby looked at the
passport. They were almost the same age, same height, same
colouring, same build. And they did look alike. He hadn't

registered the death yet so Nick wasn't officially dead. He would become Nick Mead.

As soon as the idea occurred to him he became energised. He realised that he needed to act quickly. He had to register a presence for Nick. First there needed to be a house. He considered where to buy one. It couldn't be anywhere in North or West London, Ari had too many contacts, he would be spotted. It couldn't be Essex, he knew after both the Colchester and Burnham jobs that Ari had contacts there too. He didn't want to go South of the river. Although he trusted Delroy, his visits over there had exposed him to a number of Delroys people and he would not want to risk that if Ari did offer some sort of reward for information. On the other hand it could not be too far away because for the time being he would need to have easy access to East London and Essex as Bobby Parsons. He decided to look in the area between Watford and Hemel Hempsted.

The next day he had his haircut shorter, to look more likes Nicks military style, and he spent some time practicing Nicks signature. Two days later he drove to Watford. He parked his car in the Asda car park at the junction of the A41 and the St Albans Road and went inside. He purchased a local paper and local map and sat down in the café with a coffee and looked at the small add's . He found the section for 'rooms to let' and made some calls on his new mobile phone. His story was that he had just left the army and was looking for somewhere to buy in the area. He was looking for a temporary place to live while he searched. He would also be traveling a lot during the week so would not be there very much. He anticipated a three month let. Some of the landlords wanted a longer term tenant but eventually he found something that sounded suitable just outside of Watford in Maple Cross. He arranged to view that evening.

It was a double room at the back of a three bedroom

house just of off the Rickmansworth Road. It was basic but clean. It had in it a double bed, single wardrobe and small chest of drawers. It was convenient for the M25 and the M1. Bobby could be on the North Circular Road in twenty five minutes outside of rush hour periods. The house was owned by a divorcee who was about fifty years old. She was rather short, a little over five feet tall and rather plump. Her daughter who was twenty two and looked exactly like her mother, also lived there having recently returned home after a break up of her relationship. Locally there were a couple of restaurants that also did take away and a small supermarket. Bobby agreed an initial three month tenancy and paid the landlady, Mrs. Stephens, three months rent in cash. He moved in on the Saturday morning. When he viewed the house he had parked his car around the corner out of sight. Now he needed to be more mobile, he parked his car in the car park at Luton Airport and hired a Ford Escort from Avis to use around Watford. He got his key and then went into Watford, to the Harlequin Centre, and equipped himself with some towels, sheets and a duvet, a small television, an electric kettle and some toiletries.

He returned to his new home to get settled in. As he was making his bed he laughed at himself. He was so happy and relaxed about what he was doing. Many years ago when he was reading a lot more than he did now, he read an article about schizophrenia. He wondered then if he was a schizophrenic as he often felt like somebody else was doing the things he did to his victims. With this dual life he now felt that he truly was. He slept there Saturday night after watching television in the lounge with Mrs. Stephens. He found out that she had been divorced for ten years and that the house had been her divorce settlement and that to keep it she had to agree that she would make no claim on her ex husband for maintenance either for her or her daughter. As a result she had taken in lodgers and also gone back to work. She still had the same job, she worked in the office of a local engineering company.

On Saturday Bobby visited the local estate agents. He had decided that he would buy a flat so that he did not have to bother with the garden and also it would be more secure than a house if he was away for long periods. He would prefer two bedrooms so he had somewhere to store things if he needed and he wanted somewhere modern and low maintenance. He was given a number of options, all of which he drove around and looked at but nothing really interested him.

He drove back home to Chigwell on Sunday evening having told Mrs. Stephens that he was travelling to Yorkshire on business. His story was that he had been an accountant in the army and although now a civilian he had been given a contract to audit various NAFFI's and other civilian - military operations. This would account for his periods of absence.

On the Monday he transferred £57,430 into Nick's bank account at Barclays Bank Ilford, this being the exact amount he had received from his army pension that he had given to his mother. He also sent Nicks driving license to the DVLA advising them of his new address in Maple Cross and he also informed the Inland Revenue of the same detail. If there was to be a problem with this identity theft, he would soon know.

He resumed his normal routine, visiting his businesses and the building sites which by now were both nearing completion.

On Wednesday he traveled to the Watford area, again via Luton Airport. He went to the Ford dealers in Watford and purchased a Ford Granada GL, which they had in stock. He agreed to pay the full list price provided they had it ready for his collection on Saturday, fully registered and plated. They would normally expect a buyer to haggle for a discount so being offered the full price they agreed to push the registration through. He filled in the documents in the name of Nick Mead and gave them a cheque for the full amount drawn on Nick's account.

In the local paper he had found an advert offering a lockup garage. It was in an area south of Watford, South Oxhey. He visited it early on Wednesday evening. It was in a large block of garages off Gosforth Lane. It was not overlooked by houses, Bobby rented it. Again he paid three month rental in advance.

On Friday evening he drove to Gosforth Road. He parked his BMW in the lock up garage, walked through the local shopping centre and took a cab to Maple Cross and stayed the night in his new home. On Saturday morning he went to the Ford dealers to collect his new car. It was not ready. They had not managed to register it in time. They offered Bobby the loan of a Ford Escort which they normally used as a courtesy car for service customers. They told him that his new car would be ready on Tuesday. Bobby took the Escort and drove into the Town Centre. He purchased a new mobile phone in the name of Nick Mead. He then visited the town centre branch of Barclays Bank and arranged to have the back account moved to there from Ilford. The presentation of Nicks passport and driving licence were accepted as proof of identity. He had passed his first real test.

He then visited some other estate agents and got more details of flats in the area, now looking as far away as Boreham Wood to the East, Rickmansworth to the West, and Bovingdon to the North. He would not look further South. He drove around to look at them and found three that he wanted to view. He arranged with the agents to see all three the following day.

On the Sunday he got up, made himself some toast in the

kitchen and chatted to Mrs. Stephens. His first appointment was at eleven o'clock and the agent accompanied him on the viewing. The flat was in Croxley Green. It was about ten years old and although it was in fairly good condition Bobby did not feel that he could live there. The other two too did not come up to the standard that he was looking for. He did not consider himself fussy but he anticipated that the flat would be his home for at least a year while he created his new identity and then found a way of getting away from his present life.

On Sunday evening he drove to South Oxhey, changed over the cars in the garage and drove his BMW home to Chigwell.

Bobby went to the Ford dealers on Wednesday after transferring cars at South Oxhey. This time his car was ready and he drove it out of the showroom, back to Oxhey where he swapped cars again and returned to Chigwell. That evening he went to Dulwich in the hope that he would see Delroy. He was at the house. "Hey brother long time no see. Sorry about your friend, very sad, but welcome back to the cultured lands of the south, the land of pleasure". Bobby hadn't said anything to Delroy about Nick but somehow he knew all about it. It had been several months since Bobby had been to Delroys club, he hadn't realised how long it had been until Delroy pointed it out to him. It seemed though that Delroy understood. They sat at the bar chatting as though they had last met only a few weeks ago. Delroy told him how pleased Goat was with the deal on the stitched cars, he had taken on new premises and two new welders because business was so good. Bobby also told him that Ari's drug sales had increased threefold over the last eighteen months, he must have some new dealers. Bobby was interested in this, Ari never discussed his drugs business with Bobby. Delroy told Bobby of his plans to set up a company making pornographic films. They would not be the videos from the hidden cameras, all of the participants would be aware of what they were doing and he would sell them in the clubs in South London. Delroy asked Bobby if he would be interesting in starring in one, but Bobby did realise that Delroy was joking. Bobby felt good to be back with Delroy, relaxed in one of his places again. He would need to be careful not to alert Delroy about his other life until he was ready.

He arrived back at the Maple Cross house on Friday evening. He had post. There was his new driving licence, a letter from the Inland Revenue thanking him for advising him of his change of address and a bank statement, all in the name of Nick Mead. That weekend he again spent in the Watford area looking at flats. He was disappointed that he could still not find one that he really liked despite viewing five of them. On Saturday evening he stayed in and watched television with Mrs. Stephens. Her daughter came in at about ten o'clock and joined them. In the hour or so that they were together she made it very obvious to Bobby that she was available to him. Bobby did not find her attractive in any way.

CHAPTER 72

On the Tuesday afternoon, Bobby got a phone call from Ari, another job. This was the same old thing, the victim creaming from his boss and the boss wanting the information. Bobby arranged with Ari to set up the Rainham factory for the following week. He was to liaise with Stavros for what he wanted.

Late on the Thursday afternoon the mobile phone that Bobby had bought in Nick's name rang. This was the first time anybody had phoned it so it was a surprise for Bobby.

"Mr. Mead?" said the voice.

"Yes, this is Nick Mead".

The voice introduced himself as from one of the agents that Bobby had been dealing with in Watford. He informed him that a sale he was arranging had just fallen through. It was for a new two bedroom flat in a small development just off of Gammons Lane in North Watford. The development was of eighteen houses and a small block of eight flats. It was almost finished and the only unit left was the show flat. The prospective buyers had a problem with their mortgage and had pulled out. The builders wanted a quick sale, Bobby had told the agent he was a cash buyer. He arranged to visit the flat the following afternoon. The agent met him at the flat. Bobby already liked the location, good access to both the motorway and the Town Centre. The flat was not large but not small either. It had a small but well fitted kitchen, a good size lounge, one double bedroom and a single one. It was on the ground floor and the lounge had sliding patio doors that led out on to a private lawn. It was just what Bobby was looking for. As it had been the show flat it was still fully furnished, including the carpets and curtains. Bobby agreed to purchase it and asked the agent if he could negotiate with the builders to leave all of the furniture and fittings. Bobby also asked the agent if he could recommend a local solicitor to act on his behalf, which he did. As soon as they left the flat Bobby went to the solicitors that was along the St Albans Road. He introduced himself to the legal executive that met him as the actual solicitor was with a client. Bobby gave her all the information she needed along with a cheque for the ten percent deposit.

Bobby then drove to his room in Croxley Green for the weekend. The following day the agent phoned him and told him that the builders would accept fifteen hundred pounds for the entire contents provided he complete within twenty eight days. Bobby confirmed that he too would like a quick completion and confirmed that he had engaged the solicitors and left the ten per cent deposit with them.

CHAPTER 73

The following Tuesday he was at the factory in Rainham with Stavros. This victim too was scared of water but after his last experience Bobby decided to stay away from boats and rivers.

Bobby had arranged with Stavros to have a large bath placed in the factory, with the plug hole sealed up. The victim was naked, hands tied behind his back. His ankles were also tied together but these were raised and secured on the top of the bath by tying the ankles ropes through the holes that the taps would normally be fixed in. This meant that it was extremely difficult for the victim to lift his head very far.

Bobby walked up to him. "I'm sure you know why we are here and what we want so I'm going to cut the crap and you just tell me what I want to know whenever you are ready". Bobby turned and walked away. There were two other men in the factory watching Bobby. He walked over to the side wall where there was a water tap. Stavros had connected a hose to it. Bobby picked up the hose and turned on the water. He splashed himself slightly and realised that the water was very cold. He walked over and started filling the bath. The victim started to struggle. Bobby just continued to fill it.

The victim started to strain to raise his head. "What do you want? he screamed.

"I think you know, what have you been doing behind your bosses back?"

"Nothing, honest, nothing".

"Wrong answer" said Bobby.

The water was now going into the victims mouth, he was staining to raise his head and spit it out. He still hadn't said anything. Bobby wondered if there was a mistake here and that in fact he was not involved as he claimed. Suddenly he started to choke, "alright, she set it up, she made all the plans…………."

Bobby stopped filling the bath and pulled the mans head clear of the water level by his hair. He couldn't wait to tell his story which was a lot more than Bobby expected. The victim had been having sex with his bosses wife for more than two years. He claimed that it was she who had come up with the plan to skim her husband and she kept the money. The victim had given her the cash every time, she was looking after it so that when they had enough they could go away together.

This was enough for Bobby, he had done his job. With the help of Stavros he pulled the man from the bath. "Untie him and let him go Stavros, I would suggest that you tell him to go far away, skimming from your boss is one thing, bonking his wife, something else".

Bobby turned to the man, "I've finished with you, piss off now."

Exactly three weeks later, on a Friday afternoon, Bobby moved into his new flat. He had already registered himself as Nick Mead with the council for the rates, and the gas and electricity suppliers for power. During the following week he changed the address on his driving license, bank account and all of the Inland Revenue and DHSS documents too. He was now established as Nick Mead and so far there had been no problems. He had said his goodbyes to Mrs. Stephens and her daughter. The daughter had come on to Bobby fully the previous evening saying that if ever he wanted someone to warm his bed and get his blood pumping she was available. It had been necessary to move quickly but Bobby was not sorry to be back on his own.

He now needed to start a social life. It seemed the best place would be a golf club. The solicitor had mentioned that he was a member of Moor Park so he went there. He was told that there was a waiting list for membership. There was also a joining fee which seemed a lot of money to Bobby. It was suggested that he may like to try the club on the other side of Watford, off of Bushey Hall Lane. They obviously didn't want him to join. Nevertheless he filled in the form to go onto the waiting list.

He then went to the other club suggested and they had membership available and he joined there. He decided that he needed to play regularly, even if it was to get known in the area. He had met a few of the neighbours but it seemed that all of the flats and many of the houses were lived in by people who worked all day during the week and were out most of Saturday, so he didn't meet many of them.

The weekend after moving in Bobby went to the club in Dulwich. He was totally accepted there and felt very comfortable and relaxed. As usual Delroy was there. "I hear that you got an interesting result in Rainham recently" he said.

"How do you know?"

"Keeps my ears to the ground brother, never knows what you hear. The man you met has disappeared, there's a price on his head. His partner in crime, the lovely wife, apparently took an overdose of painkillers and was found dead in bed by a grieving husband when he returned from a card game. Nice people". They had a good meal always and shared a bottle of very nice claret. They discussed their businesses, all of which seemed to be doing well and as he often did, Bobby stayed the night in one of the empty bedrooms.

Back in Chigwell the next day, Bobby decided that he needed a plan to become Nick and make him credible. Bobby was a qualified accountant, Nick wasn't, so Bobby had to be careful with the story about him being an accountant. He also needed Nick to have a real income stream to build up his legitimate earnings. He decided to investigate if there was a quick way to get Nick qualified as an accountant, after all he had the knowledge.

He had read an article in the business press about a couple of men who had copied an idea from America of letting space, small units, some only the size of a big cupboard, to members of the public to store personal belongings. It had been very successful and they had expanded quickly over the past couple of years. This seemed like a good idea. As Bobby had lots of spare cash which sometimes he needed to make legitimate, he thought that even if the units were empty he could ghost rent them and pay Nick rent. .

He stayed in Watford on Monday night and on Tuesday he visited the library in the town centre. He found a business college called "The Distance Learning Centre". It offered a large variety of business courses and were obviously aimed at adult students who were already working and wanted to obtain a qualification in their spare time. They were allied to Thames Valley University based in Slough where they held Saturday workshops and where the examinations were held. Bobby took their details and decided to phone and find out more.

He also spent some time trying to locate a warehouse suitable for his plans. He found one surprisingly easily. It was in a small estate just off of Tolpits Lane in West Watford. It was rather run down but structurally sound. He had a surveyor calculate the cost of installing two mezzanine floors and putting up partition walls and doors on the rooms on each of the three floors. When he had all of the figures he went to see the bank manager at Barclays Bank. Although Bobby could easily have afforded to fund it himself he needed to keep his own funds out of the transaction. He was cautious about making sure that there would be no way of being able to trace money back to him.

The manager was more difficult than Bobby had anticipated. Nick had no cash assets and the bank were concerned about their exposure with somebody with no real business experience. At the end of a meeting that lasted over an hour, the manager agreed a stage loan, the first amount to cover the purchase price, the balance released in amounts to fund the work that needed to be done as it was done. He had to offer the flat as security. It was difficult for Bobby as he had many times the loan amount sitting in bank accounts but it was not Nick's money.

It took a few weeks for the details to be tied up. He used the same solicitor as he had used to buy the flat but as this was a substantial business investment he took more of an interest. He and Bobby met on a number of occasions during the purchase process. In casual conversation Bobby mentioned that he played golf. The solicitor said that he played too and that they should have a game soon. On the day that it was finalised they shook hands. The solicitor wished him luck and said that if he ever needed his services again please contact him. He then asked him if he fancied a round of golf at his club, Moor Park. He was the vice- captain. Bobby said he would be delighted. They arranged a game the following week.

Bobby went back to Chigwell that night and spent the following day visiting some of his car lots. He had decided that he needed to keep a high profile in his life as Bobby and also keep in touch with Delroy as well as balancing his life as Nick. He planned out the space in the warehouse and employed the surveyor that had done the original survey to oversee the work. He organized three quotes and Bobby selected the one that he considered best and the builder was appointed. Incorporated within the accommodation were some offices. On the ground floor, immediately inside the doors was an admin and security office. There was another office to be located next to this one in case the requirement for administration was larger than expected. On the top floor, over the entrance was the only room with a window. This was to be Nicks office. It was to be a base for whatever projects he may get involved in. Bobby had confidence in the surveyor and left him to get on with the project.

He met Charles, the solicitor, at Moor Park Golf Club. It was early August and the weather was delightfully warm and sunny. Bobby had been playing at his club in Chigwell so he was well practiced. He played above his normal standard and went round on what was a difficult course in eight over par. Charles was eighteen over. Charles was obviously impressed and suggested that Nick should join. Bobby then told him of his application and how he had been told that there were no vacancies.

"There's always a way round things. I will sponsor you, I am to become club captain next month, you can be my nominee".

So Nick Mead joined Moor Park Golf Club.

He got into a routine of going to see Delroy every second Saturday, the other Saturdays he was at Watford, usually at the golf club. The weeks he was at Delroy's he went to Watford for the Wednesday evening and stayed until Saturday afternoon. On the other weeks he went to Watford on a Friday and returned to Chigwell on the Monday. During the weeks he played golf at Chigwell, visited his businesses, did the occasional job in the evening for one of Ari's friends and once in a while he went to Delroys club in Dulwich, he did enjoy the hamburgers that the chef made. It was a strategy to try and ensure that nobody missed Bobby when he was Nick, or Nick when he was Bobby. The development of the mobile phone had helped. He had the two, one in each name, so he was always contactable.

He had purchased a set of golf clubs for Watford exactly the same as those that he had in Chigwell. He bought duplicate sets of clothes, especially his underwear, socks and shirts, so that he was not transporting anything between houses. This way when he switched cars at the garages in South Oxhey he did not need to take time moving cases or bags. He did not want to attract any unwanted attention.

Moor Park Golf Club had a number of what Bobby thought were snooty members, old school, old money. But many of the members were there for the golf like him. He played regularly and played in the club competitions. His handicap was down to six so he was winning things and therefore was popular. He had the occasional lesson with pro and always purchased his balls, tees and gloves from the pro shop so was a popular member with them too.

CHAPTER 74

It wasn't until November that the warehouse was finished, it had taken longer than anticipated. Nevertheless Bobby was happy with the final result. It had thirty-four rental units on the ground floor, forty-six on the first and forty-four on the second. They varied in size from two metres wide to twelve metres wide and were all six metres deep. He had advertised in the local paper, sent mail shots to the local businesses and put cards in newsagents windows. At the end of November he had let only sixteen of the units. He wasn't worried. He ghost let another sixty. They were fictitiously let, it was a devise to bring money into the company that was owned by Nick. Bobby now had more than £3 million in his Swiss bank account and he was transferring the money to pay the rental on these unlet units. His breakeven point was a fifty percent occupancy, so he could now show a profit. He started immediately to pay off the bank loan.

He had started the accountancy course in October. He was sending in his monthly assignments and obviously getting good marks. He was doing the work at a pace of graduating in one year.

Bobby spent Christmas day with Delroy. His mother had insisted that Bobby should come to Christmas dinner.

Before going to the Elephant, Bobby stopped off at Mrs. Mead's house. He had kept in touch with her since Nick had died. She looked well but Bobby could tell that she still missed Nick, she wasn't celebrating Christmas. Bobby spent just over an hour with her, chatting about what he was doing with the car lots. She asked him about his mother. It was a bit of a shock to Bobby, he realised that he hadn't even thought about her for probably years. Mrs Mead had turned more to her church. She had already been to the early service and was going again to one later in the morning. Bobby felt a bit guilty leaving her after such a short visit, he didn't see her very often any more, in fact not at all since Nick's funeral. Still as he left she was getting ready to go back to church.

Bobby arrived at Mrs. Campbell's flat with a bottle of champagne and a large bunch of flowers. Christmas dinner was delicious, turkey with stuffing, roast potatoes, carrots, brussels and roast parsnips. For dessert they had Christmas pudding, very traditional but beautifully cooked. Mrs. Campbell obviously loved cooking and especially cooking for Delroy.

They left the flat at about four o'clock and headed for Dulwich. The club was closed today but the girls were celebrating Christmas, not only the girls from the club but also from the Fentiman Road, Battersea and Catford houses. The club was packed, there were twenty two girls in it and eight men. The men, Delroy explained were trusted employees of his who didn't have any other family. Delroy said his hello's and Bobby got a hug from the girls at the club that he knew. At around seven somebody put some music on the DJ deck and they started dancing. Bobby was still very fit but he hadn't danced for almost twenty years. With there being many more women than men Bobby was a popular partner. He was exhausted by nine o'clock. He and Delroy sat and had a drink.

"Look white brother, I think that you may have a problem" said Delroy.

"Only one? Said Bobby laughing.

"Seriously man. You know the three flats you have with Constantine in Manor Park?"

"Yeah. That's the first deal that I did with him. What about them?"

"How tight are you about who's in them?"

"Not at all, I leave all that up to agents. They let them and send me the money every month minus their commission."

"I hear on the bush man, that one cat has them all and is putting women in them. If it's true you own brothels man. I know what you think about pimping but I don't think that King Ari would be happy either, his property being used as competition".

"You're right, thanks for the tip, I'll look into it".

Bobby left about midnight. The conversation had worried him. He didn't like cheap brothel's, he knew that the women who worked in them were usually pressured into prostitution. He also knew that Ari would not be happy. He was not familiar with Ari's business interests but he felt sure that he would be running women in one way or another.

Three days later Bobby visited the car lot in Manor Park. He asked his manager if he knew who lived upstairs but he said that he had never met them. Bobby went around the back of the lot to the entrance doors of the flat. He noticed that the normal door bell that had been there had been changed for an entry phone system. He rang the bell. There was no answer. He rang it again, twice more. A sleepy sounding female voice answered, "were closed, come back later". Bobby was not happy. Bobby then went to see the agent. He said that he had let them to three brothers, one flat each, who had paid the rental six months in advance. He had taken up references and they seemed alright.

Bobby decided that he would tell Ari. He phoned him and Ari invited him to his house for a drink to see the New Year in. On New Years Eve 1986,Bobby told Ari of his suspicions.

"Lets talk on 2nd at the Loughton house, say eleven o'clock" Ari said. When they met Ari took the news very calmly. "Lets go see then shall we?" Later that day Ari made two phone calls. At ten o'clock in the evening Ari and Bobby went to Manor Park. As they pulled up in front of the car lot, two other cars and a van were parked there and as stopped a number of men started to get out of them. Ari rang the door bell. A voice answered. Ari said "'allo darling, can we come up for a bit of company?" He sounded like a slightly drunk cockney. The door release buzzed. Ari, Bobby, Stavros and three other men from the cars went in the door and up the stairs. There were two men at the top of the stairs, they tried to bar the way. Both of them were put out of action by Ari's heavy's. A couple of the girls started to scream, Ari told them to shut up in such a way that they were immediately quiet. About six men, in various states of undress ran out of the rooms and headed towards the stairs, most of them carrying their clothes. Bobby noted that the layout of the flats had been altered since he lived there. Doorways had recently been knocked in dividing walls so now all three flats could be accessed from one front door. The double bedroom of each flat had a partition wall dividing it and so did two of the lounges. This meant that there were now thirteen bedrooms in the small space which had originally been three flats. There was a rigged up lighting system to light the rooms with looked like a single 25 watt bulb. The whole place looked dirty and dingy. Ari came up to his shoulder. "I know what you're thinking, this is a cheap knocking shop. Get a client in and out in twenty minutes. It has to be dark like this because if you could actually see the tarts you wouldn't get a hard on".

The man that Ari's men had disabled was talking without any persuasion. They were two brothers but their elder brother was the ring leader. He was at another massage parlour in East Ham. With a knife at his throat one of the men phoned the other address, spoke to his brother and told him that there was a problem. He was on his way. Half an hour later there was a sound outside the door. Ari went downstairs followed by Bobby. There was a man, very much like the two upstairs but a bit bigger, he was being held by four other men who had arrived in the van. Ari looked at him, he spat in Ari's face. Stavros kicked him in the groin and he doubled up in pain. "Put him in the van, and the other two as well" said Ari. Stavros went back upstairs with two of the men and brought the other two brothers down. Both of them had their hand ties behind their backs.

"You stay here Stavros and look after things. I will be back in a couple of hours".

Ari then turned to Bobby, "you can go home now if you like. You did the right thing telling me. I'll sort it out and phone you tomorrow". Bobby left and drove home. He didn't want to think what the men's fate would be, but he found that he didn't really care.

It was two days later Ari phoned and invited him to lunch. They met at the restaurant at Ye Olde Kings Head in Chigwell. "Well Bobby, those flats' are a right mess. They've knocked down walls and put up other walls, the wiring for the lights is a potential fire risk. Tell you what. I'll buy back your half share of the flat's and the car lot".

Bobby smiled at him. "You want to run it don't you?"

Ari returned the smile. "I know better than to ask you if you want to come in with me. Your're too much of a puritan. Well, will you sell? I'll give you a good price?" The price was a good one and Bobby agreed to sell to Ari. Actually he was pleased about it. It was one less connection they had when he could manage to make the break.

The following Saturday he spent in Dulwich. Delroy already knew about what had happened at Manor Park although he didn't know about the sale. "Thanks for the tip off Delroy" said Bobby. "I don't know where you get your information from but it was right on. I just hope that those guys don't come back with some hired muscle and try and take it back".

Delroy laughed. "For a bright honkey you sure are dim sometimes. Those three guys don't exist any more. They will be at the bottom of a gravel pit somewhere in Essex by now. Constantine will take over the East Ham parlour and he will probably try and buy you out and run the one in Manor Park too. He already has five or six and they make him good money. My girls are artists, and they are well paid and looked after. His have to take anything up to twenty punters a night, it's the bottom end, ten pound a blow, twenty for a full shag. Fifteen minutes in and out, next one please. The girls get a pittance, about thirty percent of their take, but it's all they can do short of going on the streets." Bobby reflected, he knew that Delroy was right. He was glad he was out of it.

CHAPTER 75

B obby needed a project. He was bored. He had the money from Ari for Manor Park and he wanted to invest it. But he also wanted to do something as Nick. He decided to run two projects in tandem. He put agents on alert in both the Romford and Watford areas that he wanted development land. Within two weeks they both had come up with interesting proposals.

The Romford agent had a plot of undeveloped land that had planning permission for industrial building. It would accommodate six units of about one thousand five hundred sq metres each. Bobby decided to buy it.

The Watford agent had found a small estate at the end of an industrial estate road, Olds Approach. It was a ramshackle collection of buildings, some empty, some occupied. It would be a real challenge. Bobby decided to buy that too.

The Romford site was easy. He employed the same architect he had used before and asked for him to design six small starter units of approximately 600 sq metres each and get full planning permission for the revision.

The Watford site was more difficult. Again he employed the architect who had designed and managed the warehouse. He suggested the demolition of the main building and a rebuild. There were some small units on the edge of the development that were occupied. These were structurally sound. There were four of them, let to three tenants. All were involved in the motor trade and were concerned about what was happening. Most new estates didn't want the motor trade, they wanted high tech. Having seen the plans for the development and being happy with them Bobby arranged to meet the tenants. He assured them that their premises would remain intact. He would improve the access for them and he would also make any repairs that were necessary.

The Romford site was approved and work started. It was a simple construction, a steel frame, clad with steel cladding and block walls dividing the structure into six units. Bobby hoped to sell these.

Watford was more complicated. When obtaining quotes for demolition it was discovered that there was asbestos in the building. There was also an old fuel tank buried under the hardstanding. Both had to be disposed of by specialists. Bobby architect took it in hand and although it caused a delay and an extra expense the work on the new site was going ahead.

Bobby's office in Watford was less than a mile from the site and less than two miles from the golf club. This meant that he was spending more time there. He would often play nine holes with a group who would go onto play the whole eighteen. Bobby would pop in for lunch as well, even if he was not playing. If he was staying at his Watford flat, which he was now doing for a night during the week as well as weekends, he would also go in for dinner. As the light evenings got longer he found that he could go there at about six thirty and get in fourteen or fifteen holes. Bobby was a regular and he was popular. He would always buy his round, as good a golfer as he was he would play with anybody and try and help those not as good as him. As had happened in the past some of the women came onto him, he was after all a wealthy, fit, ex army, bachelor. On all these occasions he politely resisted the advances. He did not want to get involved and he did not want to make any of the husbands jealous and cause problems with them.

In July it was the Captains Cup followed by the club dinner and charity auction. Bobby had become very friendly with Charles, the captain for this year, and offered to support his charity. He asked Charles what he would like Bobby to give as an auction prize. It was decided that he would donate a weekend for two golfing in France.

Bobby played in the championship. As had happened at Chigwell he was one of the first tee times due to his low handicap. He teed off at seven fifty-four. He was back in the clubhouse before midday having gone round in thirteen over, not good with his handicap. The competition for 'closest to the hole' was on the par three, eighth. Bobby did get within about 20 centimetres with his drive, he would have to wait until the end before he knew if he had won. He decided that he would stay for the afternoon and chat to his fellow golfers as they arrived at the clubhouse. It was very relaxed and he found that he enjoyed himself just chatting with the others.

He went home at five to shower and change and was back at seven for the dinner at seven thirty. There were ten tables set in the restaurant. Nine were set for members with wives or husbands and at the tenth were seated the 'singles'. Bobby of course was on this table. There were twelve on a table, on Bobby's there were five men and seven women. Most of the women had made passes at Bobby previously. Next to Bobby was Victoria, Vicky to her friends. She was a wealthy divorcee. She was known to the men as Barbie as she had made herself look like a Barbie doll. She had long blonde hair, long false eyelashes, large boobs thanks to plastic surgery, wore coloured contact lenses which made her eyes look unnaturally blue and wore copious amounts of makeup. She was wearing a low cut dress that was very short and very high heeled shoes. Bobby suspected that he was probably the only one around the table who she had not seduced.

"Well Nick, this is good isn't It" she said kissing him on the cheek as she sat down. "I've been waiting to have dinner with you for ages and you always have an excuse. Now here you are at last".

"Everything comes to those who wait" Bobby replied.

"What's on the menu, I'm starving" she said as she picked up the menu card in front of her. "Pea and mint soup, steak dianne, and lemon cheesecake. Do you like lemon cheesecake Nick, because I can think of a much better desert for you tonight, much tastier".

"Actually I like lemon cheesecake" said Bobby with a smile.

"One day Nicholas Mead, either you will accept an invitation from me or you will be destined to live a life never knowing what you have missed". She smiled as she said it but then turned to speak to the man on her other side.

The waitresses were starting to serve the soup. Bobby turned to his right. "Hi, I'm Nick Mead" he said to the woman sitting there.

"Hello, I'm Frances Baker, my friends call me Fran", she held out her hand to shake Bobby's. "You'll upset our Vicky, keep turning her down, she's not used to that" she said softly but with a big grin.

"I'm sure that she will find somebody else to amuse her" he said. Fran was almost the exact opposite to Vicky. She had dark brown shoulder length hair, dark brown eyes, she was quite petite but well proportioned. She wore makeup but it was very discreet. She had on a fashionable and nicely cut black trouser suit and white blouse.

They started eating the soup course. "I've seen you around

the club Nick but we've never actually met. I understand that you are a very good golfer. Why don't you ever play in any of the inter-club matches? I'm the fixtures secretary and we could always use a member with your handicap playing for us".

Bobby explained that he traveled a lot and would find it difficult to commit a few weeks ahead. He told her that he had had the same conversation with Charles and explained it to him too. He could look a week ahead but no more than that. Bobby was still using his story of being a travelling accountant to explain why he was not there sometimes for all week. "We have a match next week and need a male, how about it? she asked.

"I'll let you know" he replied. They settled down to eat. They chatted all through the meal. She was thirty three years old and divorced. She had worked as a personnel assistant at a large American pharmaceutical company in Brentford. Her husband had been working for the parent company in the USA and was appointed Financial Director of the UK Company. They met and fell in love and married two years after he came to the UK. They had three happy years married before he got posted back to the US. Obviously she went back with him. His new position required a lot of traveling, not only within the US but also to the Far East and Australia, sometimes he was away for weeks on end. To start with they traveled in the US. They stayed for three months in one city and three months in another. This lasted a year and a half. Then they settled down in one place. They lived in a small town about thirty miles from Cleveland in Ohio. She found that the locals, although friendly, didn't include her in any social arrangement. She did not go to the local church, did not have a child at the local school and her husband was away a lot. She had made some good friends while traveling, some of whom she was still in touch with, but in Ohio she found that difficult. Her Husband said it was small town mentality. She became very lonely. Eventually the marriage broke down and she returned to England. The divorce was amicable, she got a generous settlement and was still friends with her ex husband. They would meet once a year for dinner and discus how their lives were going. He still worked for the same company and now lived in Texas. Neither had got involved with anybody else.

She asked Bobby about himself. He told her his version of Nick, how his father had died when he was young, how he had gone into the army, how he had qualified as an accountant and traveled the world auditing army units. How his mother had died and his best friend too. How he had come out of the army after many years and was now building a life in civvy street. They touched on relationships when Fran surprised Bobby by telling him that the women in the club thought that he was gay.

"Why, how do they reach that conclusion" he said incredulously.

"Because they've come onto you and you haven't responded of course, and also because you haven't come onto them. Look at them, they are so lovely that the only explanation there can be is that you're gay". She was grinning at Bobby as she looked around the room.

"Just because I haven't slept with any of them they think I'm gay?" Bobby was a bit shocked.

"Of course. There are men here who chase anything female, most of them are married. You are not married and don't chase, ergo, gay. Don't worry, I'm a lesbian". She was still smiling as she said it.

"How can you be if you were happily married for years?"

"I'm joking you twerp. Of course I'm not. But the men say that I am because that's the only reason that they can think of that I haven't given in to their enormous charms and slept with any of them". Bobby realised that she was probably telling the truth but considered it a joke, he laughed too.

The prize giving for the day took place after dinner. Bobby won twenty-four Titlist golf balls for being nearest the pin.

The auction was held and his donation went for £400, to Fran's best friend Emma, and her husband Jack. Charles had taken Bobby's pledge and organised two nights at Le Manoir Hotel in Le Touquet and two rounds of golf, one of each of their courses.

At the end of the evening all of the guests were saying their goodbyes. Fran said "what about Tuesday then, you said you would think about it".

Bobby didn't know what she meant at first. "Tuesday? What about it?"

"The golf match, we are playing Redborn Golf Club and we are a man short. Will you fill in? I need a partner".

"OK you're on. What time?"

"We meet here around eight, have a bacon sandwich and coffee and then go off together". When Bobby arrived home he was thinking that he had to be careful not to get sucked into life in Watford too quickly. If this was going to work he needed not to arouse suspicion in London with Ari and his colleagues and when the break came to just disappear and never go back. He stood in his kitchen with a cup of coffee and considered the situation. Life in Watford was what he wanted life to be, he had a modest but comfortable home, he had an income that was almost legitimate, he had a social life and he had friends, Charles in particular.

He went back to Chigwell on Sunday, on Monday he visited as many of his car lots as he could and on Monday night traveled back to Watford to be at the golf club for eight o'clock. He and Fran played together and were by far the best pair playing. They won their match and helped the club win the competition. They all went back to the club house for a drink. Fran suggested to Bobby that they play a game the following Sunday. Bobby had decided that he would go to Dulwich Saturday evening so he told her that he couldn't make it.

"I'm not trying to pull you" she said, "it's only a game of golf". She appeared a bit off with him.

"It's not that, I am leaving on Saturday to go up North. I have a job to do in Cumbria on Monday so I won't be around on Sunday".

She seemed pleased with that explanation. Then, to placate her Bobby said, "How about Friday, or even Saturday morning?"

"That would be great" she said, "Friday it is. I will book a tee time at about ten and then we can have a snack lunch afterwards. See you Friday", she smiled and walked away.

Bobby was back in Chigwell on Wednesday. He went to the factory site in Romford on Thursday. It had been a flat site with good access but he was still pleased with the progress. The architect who had now worked with him on all of his developments in Essex, was pushing the plan along so that it was on schedule. It wouldn't be long, maybe a month or so, and he would be able to start marketing the units.

He went to Watford on Thursday evening and was at the golf club when Fran arrived on the Friday morning. They played their round, again both played well but Bobby dropped a couple of shots so on handicap Fran beat him. She was a good player and she was very easy to be with. He decided a bit of distance was needed. He bought her lunch and spent a few hours with her before leaving and driving back to Chigwell. As usual he swapped cars at the South Oxhey lock-up. It was a good arrangement but Bobby was finding it tedious.

CHAPTER 76

He slept in the Chigwell house on Friday evening. Early on Saturday morning his home phone rang, it was Ari.

"Bobby, when did you last see your Mother?"

Bobby had almost forgotten that he had a mother. He hadn't even thought of her for ages apart from briefly at Christmas when Mrs Mead had mentioned her. He snapped back "I don't have a mother". Ari responded angrily. "Don't be fucking daft son. Saying that is a fucking insult to those of us who don't have mothers. I don't have a mother because she was raped by god knows how many Germans and then they shot her in the head. You have a fucking mother even if you have chosen to be a prick son and ignore her for years. Anyway I'm phoning to tell you that she's very ill. She has terminal cancer and is in King Georges Hospital. She is not expected to last much longer so I thought that you might like to make your peace while you still can".

Bobby felt a bit humbled. "OK Ari, thanks for that. I'll give it some thought. I haven't seen her for about fifteen years so I want to think about it first".

"OK son, well I've let you know, the rest is up to you".

On Saturday morning Bobby phoned Ari and got the

ward name and where her bed was on the ward. She was in a small geriatric side ward with four beds in it. He went to the hospital and found the ward. He got to the door of the room and looked in. There was his mother, he wouldn't have recognized her. Her face was almost all skin and bone and she had just had wisp's of grey hair where once she had thick brown, long hair. In a chair next to her was a woman, he assumed Jane, his sister. She looked a lot like his mother had looked when she was younger. Bobby turned around and walked away.

He got into his car, turned left onto the A12 towards Goodmayes and Romford. He didn't want to go home. He couldn't think straight. There was his mother dying, a woman that had been dead to him for years, a woman that he hadn't even thought of for years, so why was he so uptight. He drove along the A12, past Gallows Corner, onto the A127 and took the slip road onto the M25. He headed south and pulled off the motorway at the services at Thurrock. He went and used the toilets and realised that he had had nothing to eat that day. He went into the restaurant and had steak pie, chips and peas and a coffee. The chips were limp and cold, the peas were tasteless and cold and the pie had soft cold pastry on the outside and tepid fatty, grisly meat inside. The coffee was at least reasonably hot but was bitter and stewed. Bobby thought it was the worst meal that he had ever eaten.

He left the services and headed over the Dartford Bridge. He drove around the motorway until he reached the M23 and then turned towards London. He stopped off at a Little Chef on the Purley Way and had another coffee. He was killing time. At least this cup of coffee was decent. He arrived at the Dulwich house before it was open for the evening. As the girls knew him they let him in and told him to help himself from the bar. One of them must have phoned Delroy because he arrived half an hour later, about three hours earlier than he would normally have done.

"Hi white bro, you got a problem then?"

Bobby looked at him. "Dunno what I got" said Bobby. He then told him about Ari's phone call, the visit to the hospital, how he saw his mother and sister and left. He also told him about his family history, about how his dad was in prison and how Jane had denied he was alive and what had happened when he came out, and that was the main reason he had lost contact with his mother.

"I knew most of that Bobby, but it's good that you told me yourself. Look my friend, I cannot really help you other than listen. I have not been in your position. First, I never had a father, second I love my mum and she loves me and I see her almost every day. I have two sisters who I love and they both have kids who I love, so I cannot get where you are man. My life was very happy, I was looked after by my Mum and my sisters and it wasn't until I had to go out and earn a living that I realised that the world could be a hard place and was sometimes unfair. But one thing I will say, you are a loner, you had a good friend and he died, who do you have now? Me? Ari? And Ari's no friend to you believe me. Who else? I would bet nobody. That ain't healthy man. Your mum's your mum. You should think maybe about her problems when your dad got put away, how it shook up her life. You should see her and make your peace, when she goes you will need closure man, you ain't gonna get it by running away and from what you say it will soon be too late".

They had another drink and then an early dinner. The chef cooked a chicken breast, wrapped in bacon, stuffed with cheese and sautéed potatoes and sweetcorn, it was delicious. "At least you always get fabulous food here" said Bobby when he had finished. For the first time ever he considered taking one of the girls upstairs, just to relieve the tension that he felt.

He remembered the video cameras and although he trusted Delroy, he decided that he didn't trust him that much.

He decided to head home and have an early night so he left the house just before eight and was home by nine. He had an early night but didn't sleep well. He kept on thinking about what Delroy had said. He was right about one thing, Bobby had not really thought how it affected his mother when his father, her husband was put in prison. Bobby had been ostracised, she probably was as well. He tossed and turned and eventually got up and had a beer. He went back to bed and as he lay there he decided that he would visit in the morning and make his peace with her and maybe with Jane as well. He looked at the clock, it was twenty past three. He turned over and having made his decision he fell asleep and slept soundly.

He awoke just before eight, showered and dressed in a smart pair of Ralph Lauren chino's, a YSL shirt and YSL v-necked jumper. He decided that he wanted to look good for his mother. He stopped off at a garage on the way and bought a bunch of flowers. Visiting time started at ten o'clock, he drove into the car park at three minutes to ten. He felt good about seeing his mother again. He went up to the first floor where her ward was, along the corridor and into the side ward. He went towards the bed, it was empty. There was a nurse at another bed, he asked her where his mother was. She told him that she had died at twenty past three this morning. He put the flowers on the bed and left.

As he was walking across the car park to his car, his phone rang, it was Ari.

"Your mother died last night" he said.

"I know, I'm at the hospital now".

"Did you see her yesterday?"

"Yes, I didn't recognize her".

"No. I hadn't seen her for a long time and her appearance

surprised me when I saw her about three weeks ago when Jane first told me about the illness. Do you know when the funeral is?"

"No" said Bobby." I don't even know whose organizing it".

"Jane will, I'll let you have the date when she tells me. I'm glad you went yesterday". He hung up. Bobby decided not to tell him that he got to the door and then left.

He went home. He felt very confused. He felt that he should be sad about his mother's death but he wasn't. He supposed that he felt this way because he hadn't seen her for so long, she was a stranger. He sat for hours thinking about his life. He decided that it was a heap of shit. No family, no friends, at least no real friends. He had money, lots of it but no real life. His time in Watford seemed to make it worse, the life that he had there was normal, or almost, with normal nice people. Why had his life turned out like this? After sitting on his own for hours he felt that he was in danger of developing a serious depression. For the first time in years he decided to go to the pictures. He decided to relive his Saturday nights with Nick, first a drink in the Valentine and then whatever is on at the Odeon Gants Hill. The film was Police Academy 11. It was a comedy and all in the cinema laughed, except Bobby.

He got up late on Sunday morning and drove to Watford. He went straight to the golf club and had the carvery lunch. Some members were there and said hello but none of those that he knew well. He sat and ate lunch on his own. The course was not busy that afternoon so he went to his flat picked up his clubs and returned to the club and played a round on his own. On his way home he looked in to the Watford site. It was many weeks behind the Romford one, he would have to start chasing the contractors.

Ari phoned him on Tuesday, his mother's funeral was set

for Friday. There would be a mass at ten o'clock at St Cedds church in Goodmayes and then a short service in the chapel at the cemetery in Manor Park before she was cremated. Jane has arranged for the ashes to be buried in the memorial garden under a rose bush. Bobby wondered if Jane knew that this was what he had done for their father.

Bobby tried to keep to his normal routine during the week. He had gone to the Watford site on Monday, stayed in Watford Monday evening, Tuesday he left Watford and visited some of his car lots. On Wednesday he visited the Romford site and on Thursday he visited other car sales sites, finishing at his BMW dealership.

Friday arrived. Bobby went to Goodmayes. He parked in the High Road and watched the funeral party go into the church. There were not many people. After they had all gone in he walked across the road and snuck in at the back of the church. Jane was there, with a man who Bobby assumed was her husband. There was his aunt Mavis and her husband who Bobby recognized, although he had not seen them since he had stayed with them in Woodbridge all those years ago. There were ten other people who Bobby thought must be friends. He was surprised that Ari was not there. The mass finished, Bobby moved to a corner of the church and watched as the coffin and the party left the church. When he was sure that they would be gone he left and drove to the cemetery. He went to the chapel just as the service started. Again he crept in and sat at the back but as the chapel was so small he was noticed. All of those there turned round and looked. Ari had come to the chapel but most of the friends had not. As the casket was placed on the platform to be burnt Bobby left and went outside. He stood opposite the chapel and watched as the party came out a few minutes later. They walked over to where the wreaths had been laid. Bobby stayed where he was. His sister looked up and saw him, looked at him for a few, long seconds and then looked away. The look was uncannily like one he remembered as his mothers. Vague memories of his mother came back to him but few of them made him feel happy. His sister stayed there for about ten minutes and then left, to return to their cars in the car park. Ari walked over towards him.

"Its good you came Son. Jane told me that she saw you at the church too. Are you coming back for a drink and a snack? There are sandwiches at Jane's house. Her and her husband live in Chafford Way, Little Heath, number eleven. You know that you'd be welcome".

"No thanks Ari, I think that that would make things awkward. Tell her if she needs money to let you know and I'll get her some". Ari nodded, said nothing and walked to his car. Bobby waited a few minutes and then walked to his car and drove to Watford. On the way he reflected again on his mother. He felt guilty about not being more sad. His memories of his early life with his mother and father in Forest Gate were happy ones, but he realised that once they moved to Ilford he was never content. Although not exactly unhappy he was always looking for something, he thought.

CHAPTER 77

Bobby played golf with Charles on Saturday morning. He played badly, his mind wasn't on his game. He couldn't tell anybody about his mother because as Nick, he had said that both of his parents were dead.

Fran and some of her friends were in the clubhouse when he and Charles had finished their round. When Bobby told them that he had played so badly the normal comments were said, offers to soothe his brow, massage his shoulders, suggestions about how he could be helped to relax and de-stress. Fran stood by the bar quietly and smiled. They spent a couple of hours chatting to members coming and going until Charles said that he had to leave as his wife was cooking dinner for six o'clock and he needed to get home. Bobby went to leave when Fran said "what are you doing for a meal this evening?"

"Don't know really, haven't thought about it", he replied.

"There's a really good Chinese in the St Albans Road in Watford if you fancy it" she said.

"I don't know" Bobby hesitated.

"I'm asking you for a meal, in public, travelling in our own cars. I not trying to seduce you" she said.

Bobby smiled, he realised he was being stupid, Fran was just being a good friend. "Sounds great" he said, "lead on McDuff". They both smiled and left for the car park.

Bobby hadn't had Chinese food for ages and he enjoyed it. He not only liked Chinese food anyway but Fran had been right, it was a very good restaurant. Bobby had a pleasant relaxed evening, just what he wanted after the week he had had. During the evening they had discussed where they lived. Fran lived near the Golf Club on the Moor Park Estate. This was an estate of very exclusive houses with security at both of its entrances. Her house backed onto the playing fields of Merchant Taylor's School. Bobby told her that he lived very close to the restaurant, in a flat that he had brought only recently.

When the bill came she insisted that they split it 50/50. As they left the restaurant Bobby thanked her for the evening, he had enjoyed himself. "As you live so near you can invite me back for a coffee."

Bobby obviously looked alarmed. Fran laughed. "Just coffee, and the chance for me to see where you live, you are a bit of an enigma you know. I promise I won't come on to you and I have no ulterior motive".

Bobby smiled, "OK then, come on. We just turn into Leavesdon Road, along Gammons Lane and turn left just after the park and the school. The flats are on the left, mine's ground floor, number 1". She followed him and they arrived together. Bobby led the way, opened the front door and turned the lights on. He ushered Fran into the lounge. "I'll make the coffee, I assume that you would like some?"

"Yes please, white with two sugars. Can I look around?"

"Help yourself. If you get lost just call me, I'll send out a search party". Bobby made the coffee while Fran walked around the flat. They met back in the lounge.

"Very nice" said Fran.

"What do you really think"? said Bobby.

Fran smiled, "its very masculine. It's a house not a home. There are no photo's, no nick knacks, no ornaments. You have the best of everything, nice furniture, nice curtains, nice carpets, all very well put together, you obviously have an eye for style. You have expensive things in the kitchen, the kettle toaster and coffee machine. Apart from that the only things that are personal are your records. You obviously like Motown music. There may be soul in the music but there is no soul in the home, it's a single mans house".

"Phew, that puts pay to the rumour that I'm gay then, that's a relief". They laughed.

"I shouldn't have said all of that should I"? she said. "It was a bit rude".

"No, I'd rather have the truth, only thing is, my taste may be crap too, because this was the show house and I bought all of the furniture that was in it, including the carpets and curtains. The kitchen stuff is mine though. I guess I'm not a homely person".

They drank their coffee and then Fran got up to leave. Bobby showed her to the front door. Fran turned and gave him a kiss on the cheek. She smiled at him, "there, that's as passionate as I'm going to get, your honour is safe", and she walked to her car and drove off.

Bobby went to bed and slept soundly for the first time in days. He was strangely content.

CHAPTER 78

Bobby spent the next weeks alternating between the Romford site and the Watford one. The Romford site was going well and the units were put on the market for sale off plan. The Watford site was slower so he held back on offering that. Rentals at the storage warehouse had increased. He now had almost a forty percent occupancy so with his ghost rentals the books were showing a ninety percent occupancy rate through the books. He hadn't heard from Ari or Jane so assumed that she did not wish to make contact. He wasn't surprised and wasn't upset either. Bobby made a point of keeping in touch with Delroy although his visits to Dulwich had dropped from every two weeks to every three. He hardly played golf at Chigwell any more, preferring the company at Moor Park.

In early October Bobby sat the accountancy exams. He had crammed three years of work into one. There were three exams and they were held at Thames Valley University in Slough. He passed, Nick Mead was now a qualified accountant.

He played with Fran in a match against a team from a club in St Albans, played at Moor Park which they won again. He also spent time visiting his car sales company's in

East London and Essex. At the end of October the last match of the year was against Stokes Poges golf club, a rather posh club in Berkshire. Moor Park had a team of eight, four men and four women. Moor Park won, by a total of only three holes. Bobby and Fran won their match by four so it was they who were responsible for the win. They went out to dinner at the Harvester at Gerrards Cross after the match. Bobby realised that he enjoyed Fran's company, she was very easy to be with. He was always aware of not wanting to get involved, his track record with women that he cared about was not good. His mind went back frequently to Rose and Sandra. He had long ago realised that Rose was only an infatuation because it was she who had taken his virginity but Sandra had been different and he had thought about her often for many years after their brief relationship.

As the year moved into Autumn there was less opportunity to play golf and with shorter evenings he could spend less time on the sites. Romford was finished and the units were all on the market. By the middle of November three of them had sold and the agent had interest in all of the others.

It was the second weekend in December when Bobby finished his round of golf, most of which had been played in pouring rain. He walked into the bar having dried himself as best he could. The bar was fairly full. Fran and some of her friends were in there, also wet. She smiled at him and waved. He went over to her and asked if she wanted a drink. "I keep meaning to ask you, what are you doing for Christmas"?

"Oh, I don't know yet, this and that".

"That means you have no plans then, just Christmas on your own, in your bachelors flat. Come to lunch at my house. Before you think up a reason to say no, my sister and her husband are coming and their children. You would be doing me a favour. You can talk to them while I'm getting lunch, keep them occupied".

Bobby thought he should say no but somehow his brain did not connect to his mouth and he heard himself saying "thanks, that would be nice, I accept".

The week before Christmas Ari asked him to do a favour for a friend. It was the first time for many weeks that he had been in touch and it was only a case of going along with Stavros and another man to 'chat' to the victim. Even for jobs of his type Bobby was being paid three thousand pounds.

On Christmas Day 1987 Bobby went to Fran's for lunch. It was the first time that he had been there. The estate was impressive. She had said that they were nice houses and they certainly were. Her house had a large drive in front of the garage in which he parked his car. There was no other car in the drive so he assumed he was first there. Fran had heard him coming and was waiting at the front door. She kissed him on the cheek and he gave her the wine that he had bought.

"I haven't brought you a present, actually I didn't know what to buy".

"That's perfectly alright, I invited you for you, not for any present" she smiled at him. "Come on have a drink". They chatted for a while and then her sister, Clare and family arrived. She had two sons, Edward and James. Her husband was also Edward but they called him Ted. He was a GP in Bletchley. They had met when he was working in a hospital and Fran's sister had been a nurse there. She was a bit older than Fran, they were very alike in looks and personality. Nick was introduced to them, as a friend from the golf club, just a friend, but Clare kept on referring to him as 'the boyfriend', and every time she said it she smiled in the same way that Fran did. Bobby poured Ted a scotch and the boys a coke. Clare helped Fran in the kitchen. Initially the boys were exited as Bobby told them he had been in the army but less so when he explained that he was an accountant who only ever worked in an office an had never killed anybody.

They spent the afternoon playing games, trivial pursuit, careers and card games. Bobby easily won the trivial pursuit but was hopeless at cards. They all stayed to tea and then sat down and watched television. Bobby and Ted both fell asleep on the settee. Without really thinking they had been drinking steadily all afternoon and had both got through at least a bottle of wine each apart from the scotch.

Clare shook her husband awake. As she did so Bobby stirred too. It was almost ten o'clock.

"Time to go. The kids are tired too. Give me the car keys, you've had too much to drink to drive us home". Ted got up off of the settee, reached for his jacket and gave Clare the car key.

"Bye Nick, good to meet you" he said as he held out his hand and shook Bobby's. "Bye Fran. Thanks for a great day and a lovely lunch. You two will have to come over to ours soon and Clare can cook for us". He kissed Fran on the cheek and headed for the door.

"Yes thanks for a lovely day" said Clare to Fran "and it was a pleasure to meet you Nick. You look after my little sister now because she's precious to me. I don't see her enough so Ted's right, you will have to bring her over and have dinner with us." She kissed Bobby on the check and followed Ted and the children out of the door.

Bobby and Fran waved them goodbye as they pulled away from the drive. "I'd better be going too" said Bobby.

"Don't be silly Nick, do you know how much you've had to drink? You can stay here the night and before you say anything I mean in the spare room which has a bed already made up".

She smiled at him and he smiled at her. "That would be nice, thanks".

Fran made them both a cup of hot chocolate. Bobby had never had this before, he considered it for old people, but he didn't want to upset Fran so he accepted it. He was surprised how much he enjoyed it.

They went to bed just after eleven. Fran had put a towel on Bobby's bed. Her bedroom had an en-suite shower so the bathroom was his. He showered, and putting the towel around is middle knocked on her bedroom door.

"Yes"? she called out.

"Do you have a spare toothbrush?"

"Yes, I have a box of them, specially for all of the men I invite to stay the night here". As she said it she opened her bedroom door. She was wearing a full length, thick toweling dressing gown. She was also wearing a wide smile. "Of course I don't have a spare toothbrush, do you at your house? Use mine, wait there and I'll put some toothpaste on it". She turned, disappeared into her shower room and returned with a loaded toothbrush. "Leave it in the bathroom when you have finished and I'll pick it up tomorrow morning. Night, sleep well".

Bobby finished in the bathroom, got into bed. He had enjoyed today and was very relaxed, he put his head on the pillow, thought about how much Fran smiled and what a nice smile it was and then fell into a deep sleep. The following day, Boxing Day, Fran woke him at nine o'clock. He decided to go straight home and shower there so that he had clean clothes to put on but he returned after about an hour and they went out to lunch together.

On the 28th, Bobby went back to Chigwell for two days and did a quick tour of the car lots to check that everything was alright but mostly to be seen in the area. His profile must be one of a bored, lonely single person, looking for something to do.

There was a New Years Eve dinner and disco at the golf

club that they both went to and at midnight they kissed as they wished each other happy new year. It was the first time that they had kissed on the lips and an observer may have thought it was a slightly longer kiss than would pass between just friends.

CHAPTER 79

Bobby was very busy during the early part of 1988. The Romford factory units sold quickly. The economic situation was good. Britain had emerged from the worst of the Thatcher years, the inflation, the recession, the long miners strike and the high levels of unemployment, to become prosperous. Business confidence was high and the high street was recording record levels of sales. Property prices were escalating month by month so the selling price of the units was higher than he had originally projected. He made a profit of over half a million pounds on the project.

It wasn't just commercial property's that were increasing in price, houses were too. Bobby had a large portfolio of houses and flats and he considered selling some or all of them. He realised that eventually he would need to be rid of them if he was to fully exchange Bobby for Nick. However he thought that this may not be the time. He did not want to tip off Ari of what he planned and if he did start to sell properties, however careful he was, Ari would find out.

In February the development in Watford was finally completed. The agent found a tenant quickly, an electrical wholesalers who needed dry, secure storage for their white goods. Bobby had improved the access, not only to the new unit but to the existing ones as well so those tenants were happy too.

He had been spending more time with Fran. They played golf at least once a week, usually with another couple, they went out to dinner at least once a week. They spent Saturday evenings together although Bobby always went home at the end of the evening. Only on one Saturday evening since Christmas had Bobby been to Dulwich and on that occasion he had told Fran that he was going up North and stayed in Chigwell until the Wednesday.

He was becoming concerned about managing the split between his two lives. He was spending more time in Watford than he had intended and also he had become very fond of Fran and that, he decided was a complication that he could do without. It was a platonic relationship but he very much enjoyed her company and always looked forward to seeing her.

Towards the end of February, one Friday evening, he drove from Chigwell to Watford, went to his flat, changed his clothes and then went to the golf club. There was a group of people sitting around a table, Charles and his wife, the couple who had won the auction for the golf in France prize that Bobby had donated, Fran, one of her close friends and her partner, and another couple who Bobby knew vaguely.

"Its Nick, just the person we've been waiting for" said Charles as Bobby walked over to him. "We've been talking about organizing a club weekend break. You know Jack here won the auction for the golf trip you donated. He and Emma had a brilliant time and said that Le Touquet is geared up for golf trips. Not only that but there are some great restaurants there, so we thought that we would organize a trip around the end of April. How about it, you in?"

"Sounds great" said Bobby, "let me know when. But I'm

a bit busy at the moment with work so I won't be much help in organising anything."

"That's OK" said Jack "Em and me will do all of that. We've got the details of the hotel we stayed at so we can phone them and make the bookings. Its just a case of knowing the numbers at the moment. They will book tee times and make that arrangement for us that end. Then there's the ferry booking, but we can do that too. We'll put your name down then, that's good".

They all sat around for a while and had a drink and then people began to drift off home. Neither Fran or Bobby had eaten so they went to a small restaurant in Gerrards Cross that Fran had had recommended to her. It was called Sunborns and had a live jazz group on a Friday and Saturday evening. The meal was excellent and the music was also very good. Bobby had forgotten how much he enjoyed live music all those years ago on Sunday evenings in Ilford. "I've got a favour to ask" said Fran as they were driving back to the golf club to collect her car. "My sister has asked if we could go to dinner there a couple of times since Christmas and I've fobbed her off. She had some friends due to go tomorrow and one of them has come down with something and can't make it. She phoned just before I came out tonight and asked if we could make up the numbers. She has planned the meal and brought the food and ...."

"OK, that's fine with me".

"It would mean a lot to her if we................OK? You don't mind? I thought that you would not be at all keen".

"Look, I thought they were nice people. You want to go, so that's fine with me".

Fran clapped her hand and leant across and kissed his cheek. Bobby gave her his mobile phone. "Here, ring her now and tell her we'll be there". There's that smile again, he thought.

On Saturday evening Bobby picked up Fran from her house. She seemed both tense and happy during the drive to her sister's house. She explained to Bobby that this was the first time that she had been to dinner since she had left for America, many years ago. Clare and Ted welcomed them. Clare was obviously very pleased to see Fran. "You must be a good influence on her" she said to Bobby. "This is the first time for years she has accepted one of my invitations to dinner".

There were two other couples already there. "This is my sister Fran and her boyfriend Nick" she said. Fran was very quick to correct her, "Nick is my friend and he is male, but he is not my boyfriend in the accepted sense of the word".

Clare whispered in Bobby's ear "I can't believe that you haven't had sex yet Nick, if what she tells me is true of course". Clare had the same impish sense of humour that Fran had. The evening was very pleasant. Bobby was careful what he had to drink as usual. Losing his licence would be a major problem given his lifestyle but Fran and Clare both had good amounts of wine, and although neither was drunk, both were relaxed and became very uninhibited. They were obviously very good friends as well as sisters and told stories about each other that had the guests laughing.

The dinner party broke up around midnight. As they drove home Fran chatted happily. She was slightly tipsy but had had a very nice evening. She thanked Bobby for being such good company and being so friendly towards her sister's friends. She then started singing Spandau Ballet songs. They arrived at Fran's house and she got out of the car, Bobby followed. They walked into the kitchen and Bobby put the kettle on and started to make some coffee.

"A nice strong coffee is what you want" he said to Fran.

"Coffee is not all I want" she said as she put her arms around Bobby's neck and kissed him. Without thinking he reacted, pulled her to him, held her tight and kissed her back. "Just so that you know, I'm not drunk, so you are not taking advantage me, I am fully in control of my senses and am fully aware of what I am doing, or hope to do" she said with that smile again.

She took his hand and led him to her bedroom. They slowly took each other clothes off and still kissing got into bed. They caressed each other and kissed. When eventually they made love they did it with a frantic passion that came from neither of them having had sex for a long time. After they had finished they lay together holding one another tightly.

Fran lay thinking that she thought she may be falling in love again. Bobby lay thinking that this was a problem that he could do without.

CHAPTER 80

By the time the trip to play golf in France took place at the end of April, it was considered that Bobby and Fran were a couple. Bobby had all but moved into Fran's house. He had his own key and kept clothes and personal belongings there. He only rarely slept at his flat. For Bobby it was an extremely difficult balancing act. He still had to be around Chigwell and his businesses in East London and Essex. He still had to be available for the odd small job for Ari and he still had to keep contact with Delroy without anybody suspecting that he had an alternative life in Watford. Despite the difficulties Bobby enjoyed his time with Fran. Whenever he was with her he felt happy and content. They made love frequently but it was not just the sex that he enjoyed, he just liked being with her and it seemed she felt exactly the same.

There were eight couples that went on the trip to Le Touquet. Some of them had decided to share cars but Bobby and Fran were in Bobby's car on their own. They drove to Dover and took the ferry to Calais and then drove to the town. Bobby was slightly apprehensive about his passport, it being Nicks, but the examination was only cursory so there was no problem. They had hoped to stay in Le Manoir Hotel but it could not accommodate all sixteen people so instead they, and two other couples stayed at the Holiday Inn. They arrived late Thursday afternoon, checked in and decided that they would eat in the hotel that evening as some of the drivers felt a bit weary after the journey. Bobby enjoyed the meal, although it was not very French, and he also enjoyed being in company as part of a couple. After dinner Bobby and Fran decided to head for the town and have a look at the beach. They walked along the promenade looking out into the channel across the magnificent wide, sandy beach. They walked slowly, arm in arm saying nothing. It occurred to Bobby that maybe he was falling in love, it was not something that they had discussed. He was both thrilled and terrified at the thought. He pushed it to the back of his mind as they finished their walk, drove back to the hotel and went to bed.

The five days sped by. They played three rounds of golf, two on the courses at Le Touquet, La Foret and La Mer and one about twenty miles away at Hardelot, Les Dunes. They went out to dinner each evening in the town, sampling the delicious French food.

In the hotel were a number of display cases exhibiting products available in local shops. One of these displayed clothes and accessory's from a local golf clothes shop. One evening they visited it. It contained a range of ladies golf clothes which were very smart, very fashionable, very exclusive and very expensive. The females loved them and most of them purchased new golf outfits.

Eventually the time came to go back to England. They drove to the ferry chatting about how much they had enjoyed the break and how easy it was to fit in with their friends from the golf club. They had a meal on the ferry and little over an hour later they were on the M2 speeding towards London.

Bobby noticed that Fran was a bit quieter than usual as they drove home. "Penny for them" he said.

She looked at him and smiled. "We need to have a talk" she said.

"Oh dear, sounds ominous".

"I have been trying to think what is the right time to talk about this and I hope that you will understand but I am going away".

Bobby was taken aback. He felt a sort of hollow feeling in his stomach. "Where, when?" he said.

"Before we got involved, almost a year ago in fact, I arranged this holiday. I will be away for six weeks, the first four I am going to see loads of people who I knew when I lived in the States and for the last week or so I have booked a holiday on the beach in Florida".

Bobby brain seemed to go into overdrive. He suddenly felt jealous. It was out of his mouth before he thought about what he was saying. "Are you seeing your ex husband?"

"Yes, I told you we were still friends. I have planned dinner with him twice. We are only friendly, nothing more". Bobby couldn't understand why he felt so unhappy about her going. He felt that he would miss her but it seemed more than that. They were still talking about it when they arrived back at Fran's house. They went inside. Bobby was annoyed with himself, he felt jealous of her going away for six weeks, about having a life that didn't include him and most of all about her ex-husband. He knew it was irrational which made him even more annoyed.

He started to question her; "where are you going? Who are you going with? What will you be doing?" Finally, "is your husband going on holiday with you?"

Fran burst out laughing. "Nicholas Mead, are you jealous?" Although she was laughing she could see that she had hit a nerve. She stopped laughing, came close to him and put her arms around him. "Believe it or not Nick I love you and I wouldn't do anything to hurt you. This trip was arranged over a year ago and booked months ago, long before we got together. I will not sleep with my ex-husband, and that is 'ex' by the way. I am not going on holiday with him. I am going on my own, that is unless you want to come".

Now it was Bobby's turn to laugh. "I know, I'm a stupid pratt. I was jealous, I am jealous". Bobby felt bad about what had just happened. His life was very complicated and he always knew that he should not get involved with Fran, or anybody, but somehow it had happened. This was a question of heart over head but he still was annoyed that he felt jealousy. Not for the first time when talking to Fran the words were out of his mouth before he thought about them. "A holiday would be lovely. Have you booked your flight?" Fran told him that she had and that she would give him the details so that he could sort something out for himself. She had booked eight nights at the Holiday Inn on Sanibell Island in Florida to finish her trip so she said that she could pick him up from Miami Airport and drive across state. She was leaving at the beginning of June and Bobby would not see her again until almost the middle of July.

Bobby had never felt like this before. He decided that he must have fallen in love with Fran too. He then had an unnerving thought. Nick's passport was due to be renewed in six months time. To visit the US he needed to have a minimum of six months unexpired, he would have only about four, he needed a new passport in the name of Nick Mead. Would his application pass the inspection at the passport office when his new application went there with his, not Nick's photograph? He would soon find out. The next day he had his photograph taken and sent his application off.

CHAPTER 81

B obby's business's were all doing well. The economy was still very buoyant. He decided that as his future was so uncertain he would not get involved in anything new.

They had been back from France two weeks when the club held a ladies challenge match. The six females that had been to France all wore their new golf outfits. They were a talking point, all of the other women liked them. They wanted the address of the shop in Le Touquet where they came from.

The following week in the clubhouse there were some long faces. The Le Touquet shop would not sell on a mail order basis, personal shoppers only. That evening in bed Bobby suggested that he could go to Le Touquet and buy some of the clothes for the ladies, he could take their orders with him. Fran said that he should negotiate a UK agency for the clothes and offer them to other clubs. Bobby was not sure whether it was a serious suggestion and he liked the idea when he thought about it. It would mean that he would have a business interest that he could work on with Fran. On Sunday morning Franick Golf Fashions was formed, Fran and Nick were business partners. Nick would deal with supplies while Fran was away on her break. It turned out that the company was a small retail group, with six shops in France, the head office being at the shop in Paris. Bobby negotiated the UK agency and committed himself to a minimum £50,000 turnover in the first year. The clothes were expensive and stylish so he thought that he would have no problem achieving that level of sales.

Two weeks before Fran was due to leave for her holiday, Bobby got a phone call from Ari. He was tempted to tell him that he was too busy, he wanted to spend all of his free time with Fran. He decided against it because he was afraid of arousing Ari's suspicions.

As it turned out this job was different. The victim was a man who had had an affair with the daughter of a local face. His name was Alan O'Keefe, he was a builders labourer and certainly not good enough for the faces daughter. He had been given a kicking but this had just brought sympathy from the daughter who had gone back to the boyfriend. Again the father had intervened and this time the victim had been seriously beaten up, resulting in a broken arm and three broken ribs. The couple had again defied the father and run away together. They had been discovered after two month living as Mr. and Mrs. Smith in a caravan in Clacton. They had started to refurnish it, bought a cat and the girl was now pregnant. The faces wife had persuaded her husband not to kill the boyfriend for fear of losing her daughter forever. The face had agreed to give him one last chance and that was Bobby.

Bobby was unhappy about this job. For many years he had 'persuaded' people for Ari and his friends. He had somehow managed to switch off his emotions when he was living this side of his life. He had always managed to put it in a separate compartment and if he needed to justify it to himself he did so by telling himself that the people he dealt with deserved it in some way. They themselves were bad or had been very stupid. This man was different. He felt that the victim had done nothing wrong and that they obviously loved each other or else they wouldn't still be together after the beating he had taken. Ari explained to Bobby that he really had no choice. Given what was going on in Watford Bobby gave in without an argument. Again he didn't want to give any reason for Ari to become suspicious about anything. The meeting was arranged for the following week. Stavros with some help would collect the victim from Clacton and take him to the Rainham factory. Bobby asked Stavros not to strip the man or tie his feet on this occasion.

Bobby remembered that sometime in the distant past Ari had mentioned a doctor who had been struck off. It was during one of their meetings that Ari spoke about a friend of his who needed attention after receiving a knife wound but couldn't go to hospital. Ari still had his details and offered to put him in touch with Bobby. Next week Bobby wanted to dissuade the man without hurting him.

CHAPTER 82

Bobby arrived at the Rainham factory a week later. He had spoken to the doctor and Stavros had visited him that day and collected a cardboard box from him which was on the floor just inside the door. The man was seated in the middle of the floor. He was still clothed and his feet were free. Only his hands were tied as Bobby had requested.

As Bobby approached him he said "you don't frighten me. 'e's already 'ad me kicked twice and its made no difference. I love 'er and she loves me".

"Actually I believe you" said Bobby, calmly and quietly, "this is why this is so difficult for me. Firstly let's get one thing clear, I am not going to beat you up, in fact I am here to save your life. To show you how, I am going to I will explain a couple of things to you and let you decide what you want to do next. Now your girlfriend's father is an angry, nasty man who hates you. If it was not for me you would have been picked up tonight, spent a few weeks in agony and then buried in concrete under a road somewhere or maybe in the flower bed at the end of his garden that he pisses in when he's had a few too many beers at a barbeque. Not only that, but his reputation is more important to him than his daughter is, so she would also suffer, and just to make things worse, you would both see each other suffering. After you have been disposed of, she would be next. So let me show you something".

Bobby walked across the floor and picked up the cardboard box. He put it in front of the victim, opened it and took out a cat. Its four legs were all floppy, just strips of fur. Bobby put it down on the floor and it lay on its stomach, unable to move. "This cat is an example. Your girlfriends father knows this doctor. He's a struck off surgeon. He has removed all of the bones from this cats legs so, as you can see it can't move. Other than its head. He can do this to humans too, take the bones from the arms and legs and leave all of the vital organs intact. What will happen if you ignore me is that he will have not only you, but his daughter operated on. He would then put you somewhere like this, and empty factory or warehouse. He will bring his friends and his employees to see you both, to show what a hard man he is and what could happen if anybody steps out of line. So here you both are, your legs and your arms floppy pieces of useless flesh, effectively unable to move, the object of ridicule, with his heavies feeding you because he would want to keep you alive for his amusement, both of you sitting in your own shit and piss with your girlfriends belly getting bigger and bigger with a kid inside it".

Bobby could see that the message was getting home. The victims face was completely white as he looked from Bobby to the cat and back to Bobby again. Bobby continued "then, after a month or two he would become bored. Then he would gather his friends and those employees who he thought may cross him and he would also call for me". Bobby pulled a length of catheter tubing from his pocket.

"Now I've done this before so I can tell you what happens. I push this into your prick, I push it in until the end is in your bladder. I then pump petrol in through the tube. Do you know how much liquid a bladder can hold? About two litres. I then set light to it. The flame goes up through your prick and into your bladder. You will die in excruciating agony just after you see the flames appear as they burn through your stomach". Bobby knew this wasn't true, he would be dead before that, but he knew that the victim wouldn't know that.

"Then there would still be your pregnant girlfriend. A lot of this is to show how hard he is in front of his friends. So he can't let her live can he, especially in her condition, pregnant with a child by a man he hates and having no working arms and legs"? "So what does he do?"

At this point Stavros walked across the floor. As arranged with Bobby beforehand he took out of his pocket a small calibre pistol, held it against the head of the cat and pulled the trigger. The cats head exploded, blood, bone and brains spilling across the floor, some of it onto the trousers of the victim. He threw up.

"Now" Bobby continued in the same quiet, measured voice that he used throughout, "I'm going to let you go. Where you go is up to you. You can go East, towards Clacton where there are people waiting for you and you will be picked up and the outcome will be as I described, or you can go West or North, I would suggest a long way West or North, and never come back. That way you could live a long and healthy life. Bobby moved away. Stavros moved forward and cut the rope around the victim's wrists. He grabbed him by his shoulders and pushed him towards the door. The victim was just leaving when he stopped, turned around and said to Bobby "thank you".

Bobby drove home feeling unhappy about what he had

done to the cat but he hoped that his actions at the cost of the cat's life, would save the lives of three people, the victim, his girlfriend and the unborn baby.

The victim phoned his girlfriend, said goodbye, headed North and disappeared.

CHAPTER 83

Nicks passport arrived back a week before Fran left for her holiday. Bobby had already booked his tickets so was relieved that it had come. He was also very pleased that it was another hurdle overcome in his ambition to eventually become Nick. He now had a complete set of genuine documents in Nicks name.

Bobby took Fran to Heathrow. He went to the terminal with her and she checked in. She was surprised and delighted that she had a business class reservation. Bobby had found out her booking reference and phoned the agent and paid for her to upgrade. "Can't have my lady travelling back in another part of the plane can I? And I'm not travelling cattle class". They had a long lingering kiss. Fran promised to send Bobby postcards and also to phone him every week. They said goodbye and Bobby walked to the car park as Fran went through passport control.

Bobby had decided that he would use this time to see something of Delroy and also get the golf clothes business going. He had stock now, he just needed to sell some. He had rented one of his own storage units for the clothes and was using the office in the warehouse to run things. The warehouse itself had become very successful. He had than eighty percent occupancy so he didn't need to ghost rent any longer and the loan was being paid off at more than double the rate that the bank required.

The next day he started to try and sell. He agreed with the pro at the golf club that he could have some stock on sale or return. He offered a similar arrangement to two other clubs, one in Dunstable and one in Boreham Wood. He targeted the more traditional member only clubs. He managed to sell small volumes to the club in Stoke Poges and Royal Berkshire. After a week he decided that to succeed this would be a full time job. He couldn't spend that much time at this venture. When Fran got back he would talk to her about appointing agents. At the thought of Fran he realised how much he was missing her.

On the Saturday after Fran left, Bobby went to the Dulwich house. He hadn't been there for a couple of months but it seemed busier than it used to. "There's a lot of money around" said Delroy. "Doesn't make them any happier though. They now come here more, these rich, successful men, for a drink, a quick shag and time away from the wife. Here they feel safe and they relax. I'm not complaining" he said smiling at Bobby.

"I hear you had a result the other week" Delroy changed the subject.

"What's that?"

"The persuasion at Rainham, the vic who put Dennis the Menace's daughter up the spout. Word is that Dennis was going to use him as part of the foundations to a patio he was having laid at his mothers house. It was his wife who persuaded him to try using you. She thought if he just did away with the boyfriend she would lose her daughter. Worked too. He's lost in Liverpool and the daughters gone back home crying on mummy's shoulder that her boyfriend has walked out on her. Daddy has persuaded her to get rid of the kid and in return has bought her a nice new car and had her bedroom redecorated and new furniture put in it. Win win brother".

As usual Delroy's chef produced a very good meal and Bobby enjoyed Delroy's company. He was easy to be with and didn't ask any difficult questions. As usual again Delroy offered Bobby a room for the night but as the club was now busier all of the rooms had girls in. As usual Bobby said no, despite assuring Delroy that all of his girls were beautiful. It was now a game they played. As the evening drew on the guests left and soon the club was almost empty. "It's more busy on Saturdays that it used to be but its still an early night" explained Delroy. "I wonder after being here and having had one of my girls, if these guys go home and can get it up to give their wives their Saturday night treat". Both men laughed at Delroys comment.

Bobby headed home to Chigwell. He would spend most of his time there while Fran was away.

He visited all of his car lots and showrooms and also carried out an inspection of some of his properties to see if they needed any work doing on them. Bobby had always kept his rented properties in good condition.

The weeks that Fran was away went slowly for Bobby. She phoned him and said that she missed him but was having a good time seeing her old friends. She didn't mention her husband. Eventually the day arrived for Bobby to leave. He had his flight ticket, passport, driving licence and credit cards, all in the name of Nick Mead. He parked his car in the Pink Elephant business parking area and took the bus to the terminal building to catch the British Airways flight to Miami. He checked in and went to the lounge to wait for his flight. The flight was uneventful, the food was adequate and the service was good. It arrived at Miami only five minutes late. It took Bobby over an hour to get through immigration and passport control, he collected his case and went through into arrivals hall. Fran was waiting for him. They met and held each other for ages. "God I've missed you" said Bobby.

"Me too, welcome to the good old U S of A" said Fran in an American accent.

"You're here for a month and you speak like a native" he said.

"You forget, I've got dual nationality, I was married to an American, so I'm half American, well sort of". They walked out into the humid Florida air with their arms around each other, laughing. Fran had hired a Ford Mustang convertible from Avis. She thought that Bobby would like to ride in an American icon. Fran drove them to the Crowne Plaza Hotel near the airport where they were staying the night. They checked in, had an early dinner and a beer and then went to their room. It was only just after eight o'clock but with the time difference it was the early hours of the morning for Bobby's body clock. They showered and got into bed a cuddled each other.

"You tired?" said Fran.

"Sorry, I am a bit, actually I feel knackered".

"You lay there" she said as she moved on top of him. She kissed him passionately on the lips, then started to move down his body. He was very quickly aroused, despite being tired. She took his erection in her mouth and moved it up and down while caressing it with her tongue. He came in her mouth after only a few seconds. She moved off of him and lay on top of him with her arms around him.

"God I love you" he said.

Fran jumped up a shrieked then squeezed him tight. "You've never said that before Nick" said Fran, " you've never used the L word. Maybe I should leave you for a month more often".

"Don't you dare" he said. The 'love' word had slipped

out without him meaning to but now he had said it he didn't mind, he thought that probably he did love her. "If you go away for a month again I want to be with you".

They lay next to each other and kissed tenderly. After a while Bobby's eyes became heavy and he fell asleep. When they woke the next morning the sky was blue and the sun was shining. Both Bobby and Fran thought to themselves what a lovely day it was. They had breakfast and checked out of the hotel. They left the city and drove north towards Fort Lauderdale. They then took interstate 75 towards Naples, known locally as alligator alley. They had the top down and Fran drove. For most of the time they held hands. They reached Naples and then headed north towards Fort Myers and then across the bridge to Sanibel. Sanibel is a very small island and with Bobby reading the directions they soon reached the Holiday Inn. It was a two story red building in the middle of a residential area. They checked in and went to their room on the first floor. It was early afternoon so they went to the pool bar. Bobby had a burger and a Bud and Fran a club sandwich and a white wine. After lunch they walked to the beach that was just beyond the pool and spent the afternoon lying on sun loungers reading books. Bobby found it a bit difficult to concentrate on his reading, he was distracted watching the pelicans dive for the fish and once he saw some dolphins swimming just off of the beach.

They ate that night in the hotel restaurant and went to bed at about ten o'clock. They made love slowly and passionately and fell asleep in each other's arms.

The next day after a morning on the beach they hired bikes from the hotel and went to explore the island. It was simple to navigate. There was a road that ran down the middle of the island, for the first half it was Periwinkle Way and then it became Sanibel Captiva Road. The Island was shaped like a fish, the main roads being the spine with road running off of the spine to the beaches in both directions. They didn't get too far, a couple of miles to Pinocchio's Ice Cream parlour where they had a huge ice cream cone each and sat outside the shop on a wooden bench and watched the world go by. On their way back to the hotel they went to a small supermarket in Periwinkle Way and bought some bottled water and some fruit. The hotel receptionist told them that Sanibel is a very quiet island where everything closes early in the evening and there is no nightlife, so if they wanted to eat out they should not leave it too late. This was ideal for Fran and Bobby so at six o'clock they were seated in a restaurant that had been recommended, The Island Cow. Bobby had the meat loaf and draught beer and Fran the fish dish of the day and white wine. They both thought that their meals were delicious. By eight o'clock it was pitch dark, they went back to the hotel and lay on the sun loungers that had been brought to the edge of the beach just inside the hotel fence. They lay with just the light of the moon and the stars, holding hands and listening to the sea. Bobby could not remember when he had felt so happy and relaxed. He didn't know it but Fran felt the same.

The days seemed to pass so quickly. They lay on the beach during the day, sometimes going for a quick swim in the pool, and sometimes going out for a ride on the bikes. They visited the lighthouse at the end of the island and came back, stopping at Pinocchio's on the way. They liked the food and the atmosphere at The Island Cow so they ate there each night, sitting outside sometimes and sometimes going inside where they had a guy playing the guitar and singing.

Too soon it was their last evening. They had come back from dinner and as always were lying on the sun loungers in the dark, looking at the stars. "Why don't we live here?" said Bobby.

"Don't be silly" said Fran, "how could we?"

"Why not"? said Bobby. There are some great houses here for sale. OK they are a bit expensive but this is obviously an expensive place to live. The people are all friendly, the climate is terrific, there are golf clubs, the beach, the sea, the city is not that far away, we could get to Fort Myers or Naples in less than an hour. Why is it silly?"

He could feel rather than see Fran sit up and look at him. "You're serious aren't you?"

"Yes. At least I think that it's worth considering. You have to admit this is a lovely place. It would suit us fine. You are already an American citizen so it's no problem for you. I could live here on a six month non-working visa, go to the UK , renew the visa for another six months. While I'm there I can check the business every so often, we could let our houses so we would have an income from them too."

"It would be a bit of a commitment" she said

"So I'll commit. I have made a monumental decision which I think you should know about", now Bobby was smiling. "I've decided that I do actually love you and I think that if you are telling the truth and love me too then we should get married".

Fran launched herself at him and as she did so her lounger collapsed and she fell on top of him.

The next day they flew home. On the plane Bobby told Fran about his idea to get agents to sell the golf clothes. She thought it a good idea and offered to deal with the recruitment. Fran had promised to think about Bobby's suggestion of moving to Sanibell. Bobby had already decided that he wanted to live there. There was only one problem, a large part of his life was still Bobby Parsons and he needed it all to Nick Mead.

CHAPTER 84

Bobby went to his office in Watford the day they got back. Fran went to see her sister. From his computer he was able to check the accounts of all of his businesses and that the rent payments were up to date. All was fine. Bobby sorted out all of the details of the golf clothes, put them in a file and put them on the desk that he had put in there for Fran. He phoned the golf clubs that he had placed the clothes in and was pleased to hear that they had started to sell well. He even took some repeat orders. He phoned Ari to tell him he was back. He had told him he was revisiting the places that he and Nick had been to.

That evening when they had finished dinner Fran told him that she had told her sister about getting married and moving to Florida. She admitted to Bobby that Clare had been her one reservation, she was her only family and she had been getting closer to her of late. Her sister had been enthusiastic about it and said that she should grab the opportunity.

"Is that a yes then?" said Bobby.

"Yes, that's a yes" she replied.

"When?"

"As soon as you like really. As Clare said, we're not getting any younger".

"Nice of Clare" said Bobby laughing.

Fran was very enthusiastic about moving to Florida. She wanted to do it quickly and Bobby encouraged that. He was not yet sure how he would manage to achieve it but he wanted to live the life that he envisaged that he would, if they could get away. Fran gave up the golf clothes before she had started, leaving it for Bobby to deal with. They decided that Fran would go back to Sanibel on her own and look for a house. Having a US passport meant it was so much easier for her to travel to and from Miami. When they had been on holiday they had noticed a light blue, timber clad house for sale that they had both liked. It was on Casa Ybel Road, which was the road that ran from Periwinkle Way to West Gulf Drive, where the Holiday Inn was. Fran booked flight tickets for three weeks time and phoned the Holiday Inn and made a reservation for a week. She asked them if they could ask the local Real Estate company's to fax her details of properties similar to the blue house they had seen. She gave them the fax number of the Watford office. The hotel staff were extremely helpful and said they would arrange it.

The next day details started to come through on the fax. Fran had about twelve properties to look at already, after only one day. Bobby told her to phone him every evening and let him know how she was doing. He also said to her that he would trust her judgment completely so if she saw a house that she really liked then she should buy it.

"Nick, we haven't talked about how exactly we are going to pay for this house. The blue house that we like is $299,000 dollars. We will need to sell one of our places to buy that".

"No we won't" said Bobby. He had been preparing for this conversation. "I was in the army for sixteen years. I retired a Lieutenant Colonel. That's a fairly well paid rank. When I left they offered me an army pension to start when I am fifty or no pension but a cash lump sum. I took the lump sum, invested it as their finance people recommended and now it's sitting in the bank. There is over three hundred thousand pounds there, that's over five hundred thousand dollars. We have plenty of money". In fact Bobby had over seven million pounds in his Swiss bank account.

Bobby advertised for agents for his golf clothing range and also for somebody part time to work in the office as an administrator to deal with orders and dispatch when they left. He had already decided to set aside one of the storage units as an office, fortunately the one next to where the clothes were stored was still unoccupied. He had plenty of applicants for all the positions and decided that while Fran was away he would deal with engaging staff. Although when they had agreed to set up the business the plan was to do it together, Bobby was now in a hurry. He had realised that he did love Fran and that he wanted to be with her and away from his life in England. He wanted to get all of his matters in order as quickly as possible.

CHAPTER 85

Three days before Fran was due to leave Bobby had a phone call from Delroy. It was unusual for Delroy to contact him so he knew it must be serious.

"Hey man, am I glad I got you. There's some trouble you need to know about. We need to meet".

"Can't you tell me over the phone?"

"Better face to face man, Fentiman Road house at ten tomorrow, OK?"

"Fine" said Bobby "I'll be there". Bobby was very anxious about what the trouble was. It was obviously serious for Delroy to phone, it must be very serious for Delroy to insist on a meeting. Bobby had a bad feeling that Ari had found out about his double life, Nick, Fran, the Watford flat, the other businesses. He needed to think fast about what to do. Fran loved him, that he was sure of, but she was an innocent, would her love survive the truth, he feared not.

He arrived at the house just before ten. Delroy was there. "Come in man, have a coffee, tea, something stronger?"

"Coffee would be fine thanks. What's the problem?"

"Lets sit over here", Delroy moved to a settee at the side of the room as one of the women went to get the coffee.

"You know the vic you sorted at Rainham a few weeks ago".

"The bloke who was living in Clacton with some faces' daughter"?

"Yeah, that's 'im. Well after you finished with 'im he pissed off to Liverpool. Appears he has family up there. Well, it turns out that he is some distant cousin of Mad Paddy's wife. You know she's a scouser. Well her relatives want her to get Mad Paddy to sort out Dennis the Menace and he don't want ter know. Until they find out that she's got rid of 'is kid. Now that's a mortal sin in their eyes. You know what these RC's are like. Kill, maim, shag around, deal drugs, go to church and tell the priest you're sorry, say three hail Mary's, go to mass on Sunday and on Monday start doing it all again. Killing the kid though, that's out of order in their books so now Mad Paddy is persuaded, even if its just to shut up 'is missus. He's putting up a team to sort Dennis and everybody else involved".

Bobby sighed. "Fucking hell, I saved the cunts life" he said. "If I hadn't got involved he would be dead by now. He even thanked me just as he was leaving the warehouse. Fuck – fuck – fuck".

"Well maybe 'e's told someone that and you will be OK, But in a month or two, as soon as Mad Paddy has got it together, there's goin' to be a war, or at least a battle".

"Ari hasn't mentioned any of this. Do you think he knows?"

"He knows alright, it was from one of his pushers that my man heard it. I checked with a brother I know in the pool and he confirms it".

"Oh fuck. Delroy I gotta get out of this. Not just this one problem but the whole fucking game. I've really had enough. I just want to disappear".

"I've told you before man, you won't be allowed. You

give Ari his profile, he ain't gonna let you go". Bobby drove home to Watford feeling thoughoughly depressed. Just as he thought that life was getting sorted this comes along. He needed to talk to Ari. He decided that he would wait until Fran had left for America.

The next day he phoned Ari and arranged to meet him in Loughton the following day.

CHAPTER 86

B obby took Fran to Heathrow to catch the British Airways flight to Miami. He waited with he until she checked in and they kissed a long kiss before she went through passport control and out of sight. She promised that she would phone him every day. Bobby went back to the car park, collected his car and drove round the M25 and off at the Loughton junction, arriving at the Loughton house just before twelve.

Bobby went into Ari's office. "Hello Bobby, how are things. Tea, coffee, something stronger?" Ari seemed quite at ease. It occurred to Bobby that he may know nothing about the problem or even that Delroy had got it wrong and Mad Paddy wasn't interested.

"Coffee would be great thanks ArI". Ari picked up his phone and ordered two coffee's.

Bobby started, "Ari I've heard a rumour".

"What about?"

"About the last vic we sorted at Rainham, how he's related to Mad Paddy's wife and how, as the tart he was shacked up with has got rid of his kid, the vic's family has got Mad Paddy gunning for you and yours".

Ari's demeanor changed. "Where the fuck did you hear that?"

"That doesn't matter Ari, is it true?"

"You must have heard it from the black bastard friend of yours. Tell him to keep his fucking black nose out of my business. It's a small problem, I'm sorting it".

"How Ari? If Mad Paddy gets a load of scousers down here who have you got to go up against him?"

"Its not just me, my mate Dennis is the prime target here, him and that slut daughter. All we did was sort it for him. He can supply muscle if it comes to a battle".

"We can't just dismiss it Ari. From what I heard we are involved as well, we were party to him getting sorted in their eyes, therefore we are in the frame too".

"I've fucking told you I'm sorting it. You stick to what you're good at, I'll do the rest".

Ari's demeanor was far more abrupt than usual towards Bobby.

Bobby sat in silence for a while drinking his coffee. "Ari, I want out of all this".

"What do you mean you want out?"

"I want to retire. I'll sell you all of businesses and property and retire somewhere, somewhere like the West Country. I'll disappear".

Ari threw his head back and laughed. "Retire, disappear, you? Don't be so fucking stupid. You're in son, you're in for life. You get involved in this sort of business and there's no way out".

"Of course there is, I just go. Nobody is going to bother to spend time trying to find me. They'll just find somebody else to do something else to persuade the vic's".

Ari suddenly became aggressive. "I would take time to find you Bobby, rely on that. I've made you what you are. Everything you have is down to me. You were a dead end kid in a dysfunctional family when I took you under my wing. I gave you the chances to make the money, live the life, without me you would be fuck all, a big fucking nobody. I've invested in you, you're mine, you don't walk out on me".

Ari stared at Bobby, Bobby stared back. He put down his coffee cup and calmly got up and left the room. He got into his car and phoned Delroy. He arranged to meet him the next day. Bobby was now cool and focused. Ari had turned and shown that he considered Bobby his property.

That afternoon Fran phoned. She had arrived safely. She had just got up and was viewing three houses that day including the blue painted house that they had seen while they were on holiday. She sounded so happy. Bobby was missing her already and hoped that the problems he now had would be sorted before she came back.

The next day he met Delroy. He told him of his conversation with Ari. "I don't know who this Dennis the Menace person is. I'd never heard his name up until a month ago. Has he got a big crew, do you know?"

Delroy knew of him. "He's and old fashioned villain. He was a safecracker, good one too. He graduated into robbing post offices and holding up armored vans, never been convicted. The good side of him is he loves his family, rumour is he's never been unfaithful, even with a tom. That's why he was so cut up about his daughter and why his wife managed to persuade him not to top the boyfriend. Downside is he's a looney. He cracked open the skull of one of mates with a pick axe handle once because he sneezed while they were waiting in the back of a transit to knock off a payroll delivery. He's got a few blokes but they ain't heavy, they're thieves thugs. Constantine's got a few as well but not many. You don't put pimps and drug pushers up against a load of pissed up paddy's. Your mate Constantine had got some that would razor a woman's face to keep others in line but they are all scum who would probably run a mile if they thought they may get hurt".

"I really don't need this Delroy".

"So you said. What are you going to do though? What can you do?"

"Will you buy me out, the car lots, the yard, the showrooms, the property?"

"Look Bobby, that ain't your problem brother. Your problem is the bastard Greek, Constantine. He may or may not own you as he says, but he thinks he does. Not only that, but you are his membership card to high society. Without you he would just be a small time pimp and drug dealer. The big boys wouldn't want to know him. But with you, that lets him in with the big fish. It also protects him. They may want your services one day so they will smile at him and not ruffle his feathers in case they do. You may not like it but your only chance is to get rid of him. You are right, the others probably wouldn't bother to look for you, but he would".

Bobby thought about what Delroy had just said. "I do owe him a lot though Delroy. He is right when he says that the basis of all that I own is down to him. I was part of a dysfunctional family going nowhere when he came along. He did give me the partnership of the Manor Park lot on the cheap………"

"Oh Bobby, Bobby, fucking grow up. For such a bright honkey you sure are fucking dim sometimes. He ain't given you nothing. Starting with your Dad, who fingered him to be in on the scam. The Greek chose him. What about the gambling debts. How much did he say they were? Thousands? Do you think that he would let a loser like Wilkinson run up that sort of debt? Of course not. It was an attempt at theft, pure and simple and he selected your dad as a fall guy. Did the police get the money back? No. Where is it, where did it go? I'll give you one guess. Did you know that all three of them got longer sentences because they didn't recover the money? That's how much he helped your dad. So, good old

Ari Constantine, he finds your mum a house, that he owns. Keeps her under watch and lets your dad think that she and you two kids are being looked after. Just for good measure he gives her a shag once a week to stop her looking around elsewhere. So, your dad comes out, he moves your mum into another of his houses and moves your dad into the flat, finds him a job at one of his business. Everybody is happy, good old Ari looking out for us, good old Ari is controlling everything. But a problem, Holmes and Wilkinson are released. Wilkinson wants pay off. Lets see what Bobby Parsons can do. He's riled up about what has happened, to his family, his job, his life, maybe he will hurt Wilkinson. So, in you come and hey presto, you are a star. So he locks you in, he gets you to frighten somebody else, just a favour Bobby, to help keep the scum in check. Already you are locked in and just to make sure, he pays you more than you can earn in months legit, for just a couple of hours work. Then he makes you a partner. That has three benefits. One, you are indebted to him, two, you can keep an eye on that business without him having to pay you, and three you leave home so you have no support network. He has cut you off and you are more reliant on him. What about Wilkinson? Did you want to clear your Dads name? Have you heard anything from him? Of course not. That meeting wasn't about getting money, it was about seeing what you could do. Wilkinson probably didn't see the week out. He's probably underneath a load of landfill somewhere in an Essex gravel pit. Wake up brother, he ain't your friend. He's used you, your father, your mother and for all I know your sister too. He doesn't care a fuck about you, only what you can do for him. The only thing he cares about is his kids and himself and he will use anybody to do anything to make things better for them. You may be rich boy with your own business and property but to him you are an employee".

Bobby looked at Delroy. "Sorry brother" Delroy said "but you had to hear it. Nobody else is going to tell you. But think on eh? You need to get rid of him, that's the only way you will be free". Bobby drove back to Chigwell. He sat down and thought. He knew deep down that Delroy was right. He had never thought of it before but somehow he knew.

CHAPTER 87

Early that evening Fran phoned. She had seen the blue house. It was very nice, she said that Bobby would love it. She had seen some others but she didn't like them as much. It was morning in Florida and she was off today to see three more on the other side of the island, overlooking the sea but on the Fort Myers side. She said that she would phone Bobby and let him know how she got the same time tomorrow.

Bobby sat up all night, in the dark, thinking about his situation. He considered his position. He thought about his life, looking at situations involving Ari with the benefit of hindsight. He considered various plans and ramifications if they went wrong. At six o'clock he had formulated a plan of action. He went to bed and set the alarm for eleven. He wanted to see Ari to give him one more chance to let go and he know that he was usually at the Loughton house around lunchtime.

He arrived at the Loughton house just before one, he walked into Ari's office. "What do you want, you always phone first?" said Ari, still sounding angry.

"I want to talk"

Ari did not seem pleased to see him. "I told you that

I will take care of it. Now fuck off and leave me alone, I'm busy".

"Ari, I want to talk about my dad".

Ari looked up. He was genuinely surprised. The anger and aggressiveness suddenly disappeared "He's been dead years Bobby, what's to talk about son?"

"Did you help set him up. I mean with Wilkinson and Holmes at the Corporation? Who was it that selected him?"

The aggressiveness reappeared. "Who the fuck have you been talking to? What's brought this up? Get real Bobby. Business is business. You've crocked loads of people and never given it a thought, you haven't cared what effect that would have on their kids or their wives, you haven't even thought if they have kids or wives. Its business. Your old man got caught up in it that's all. It wasn't about him personally, he was the right person in the right place, we had to have a drone, he was that drone. Business. I looked after you though, you and your Mum and sister, while he was inside and when he came out. You think your mum could have afforded the flat in Kingston Road without my help?"

"What was that then Ari. Pay some rent in cash and have a shag for the rest?"

"Don't get fuckin' pure and 'holier than thou' with me son. As I told you, business".

"Is that what I am Ari, business?"

"Too fucking right. So get out of my office and next time you want to see me, you phone and make an appointment. So go home now, enjoy your money that I made for you and wait for me to phone you when I want you to jump for me again. Now fuck off, I've got enough problems without your moaning".

On the drive home to Chigwell Bobby phoned Delroy and arranged to meet him the next day.

Bobby sat in Delroys office at the Dulwich house, the venue that Bobby had requested.

"I've thought a lot about what you said the other day. I met with Ari yesterday and he more or less confirmed it. I agree that the only way that I'm going to be free is to get him out of the picture. However just having him hit won't solve the problem. His business needs to be carried on otherwise if he just disappears the scum will fight over it and I may be dragged into it. So I thought that the best thing would be if you took over all of his and my businesses. If you got them cheap then you could afford to sell some for a low price to keep a problem away. The other thing with this business hanging over him with Mad Paddy, if you own the businesses he will think that you have sorted not only Ari but me too, so you could have a gold star".

He then told Delroy the outlines of his plan.When he had finished Delroy sat back. "Well, now I know why some people think you are clever. That's a good plan and it may work. If it comes off it will make it look like the Greek shit was looking to clear out ahead of the trouble and just got unlucky".

"I think it might work but I need this house with no girls at home, I need you to organise your tame lawyer and I need to borrow some pairs of hands for twelve hours".

"If I come in on this the house and hands are no problem. The lawyer I will have to talk to. He won't like it. I have never shown any video to any member but I may need to show him. I have many good shot of him with the girls, in various positions. You can leave that to me. But first I want to hear your plan in detail. If I am going to be involved I need to be happy with it".

Bobby told him in detail, it took some time. Before they parted they agreed that Delroy would pay Bobby three million pounds for all of his and Ari's businesses and property's. They were probably worth about fifteen million. Bobby was happy with three and the rest would pay Delroy handsomely for his help.

That evening Fran phoned. She had found a house that she loved. It was in West Gulf Drive, the same road as the Holiday Inn. It was about four hundred yard past the hotel and on the other side of the road. Therefore it didn't look out over the beach but the beach was only about one hundred yards away on the other side of the road. Instead the garden ran down to a small steam and beyond that was a golf course. The house itself was similar to the blue painted one but was slightly bigger and although the garden was not as long, it was wider and because it looked over the golf course, the house and garden were not overlooked. Bobby could tell that Fran was in love with the house.

"Buy it then" he said.

"Don't you want to know how much it is? It more than the blue one. They want $320,000 for it but the agents think that they may drop a bit. Don't you think that you should see it before we decide anything?"

"It doesn't matter, I don't need to see it. If you love it, I'll love it. Have you opened a bank account? Let me have the details and I will get $350,000 transferred into it tomorrow". First thing the next morning he telephoned the bank in Geneva and after spending what seemed like ages going through the security questions and passwords, he transferred the money to Fran's account in the US.

Bobby spent the next couple of days sorting out what he needed to do for his encounter with Ari. He was on the phone to Delroy too making sure that his end was being sorted. Delroy confirmed that he had spoken to his lawyer. He said that at first he refused to even discuss it, it was illegal. However after Delroy had shown him a video featuring him with two of his girls and another with him enjoying a third doggy fashion over the end of the bed, he agreed to help. Delroy said again that he had never used the video's before and now that it was known that he had them he expected a drop off in membership. Bobby reminded him how much he was going to make on the deal.

The money arrived in Fran's account and she started the process of buying the house. The owners had not lived there, it was a summer let investment. They suggested that Fran move in, pay a nominal rent and stay there until the sale went through. She had agreed and was to move out of the hotel two days later. Because it had been a holiday let it needed work doing on it but it was mostly cosmetic. She suggested that she stay there a week or so longer and supervise the work. Bobby readily agreed to this. He missed her but right now it was better not to have to explain where he was all of the time.

CHAPTER 88

Bobby was at the Dulwich house mid afternoon. He checked over the documents that the lawyer had prepared. They were exactly what he wanted. The first set was a list of all of Bobby's businesses and property's and a contract selling them to Ari dated a month previous. The second was a list of all of Ari's businesses and property's, at least as far as they could find out, which included all of those that he had got from the purchase of Bobby's. This contract showed that he had sold them all to Delroy two weeks previously. As Delroy had said, apart from him getting Ari's empire for nothing, it would look to the outside world, Mad Paddy and his family, that Ari was planning to liquidate his assets prior to disappearing. Bobby then had a lesson from Delroy so that he could work the various screens and video equipment that Delroy had installed throughout the house. Finally Delroy introduced Bobby to eight of the men that he had arranged to help him. He was introduced to Soloman who Delroy described as one of right hand men. He showed Bobby the walkie talkies that he had got, as Bobby had requested as part of the plan.

It was just after seven o'clock in the evening when Ari was delivered, unconscious, to the Dulwich House. He had been picked up as he left Loughton and chloroformed. He had been driven around in the back of a van for a couple of hours until it was dark and the rush hour traffic had become a bit lighter.

He was tied to a chair next to Delroys desk in his office, secured tightly by his feet and left wrist although his right hand was tied with a piece of electrical cable that would allow him to move his right hand. Bobby sat in Delroys chair opposite him and two of Delroy's men stood by the door.

After about twenty minutes Ari started to come to. It took him a while to focus and then he saw Bobby. At the same time he realised that his hands and feet were tied. "What the fuck....? What is this, where are we? Have you lost your fucking mind?"

"No Ari, I haven't lost my mind, in fact I've come to my senses. You see, I want out of all of this shit and the only way out is to get rid of you and for me to disappear. It has to look good so what you are going to do is sign over all of your property and businesses to Delroy Campbell so it looks like you have flown the coup".

"Over my dead body, give anything to that black shit bag? I'll have you for this Bobby Parsons, you ungrateful bastard".

"You don't understand Ari, you don't have a choice. The only question is how much pain and grief are you willing to subject your family to before you give in and sign these contract which we have here, prepared and witnessed".

Ari said one word, "Bollocks" and sat back and looked at Bobby. There was hatred coming across the desk from him.

Bobby had all of the screens on the desk switched on. He could see what was going on in all of the rooms but Ari could not. Bobby nodded to one of Delroys men standing by the door. He went out, spoke on the walkie talkie and after only about ten seconds returned to the room. Bobby flicked a switch and the interior of one of the bedrooms came up on the two big television screens on either side of the room. Ari turned and looked and saw his wife sitting on a bed looking rather bemused.

"What's going on here?" he said.

Bobby said nothing, he just looked at the screen. They saw three of Delroys men walk into the room. One of them grabbed the woman, threw her back on the bed and pined her down by her shoulders. Another ripped her skirt off and then tore off her knickers and tights. The third pulled down his trousers and exposed an already erect member. The room filled with Ari's wife's scream. The third man forced her legs apart and thrust into her, she screamed again. He pumped away until he arched back, shooting his load into her.

"You bastard" said Ari.

"Sign here and it's finished" said Bobby pushing the contracts and a pen towards Ari. He ignored them and just looked back at the screen. The second man had now removed his trousers and was climbing onto the bed between Ari's wife's legs. He too was already erect and pushed in hard. She screamed again and then started sobbing, crying "no, no, no".

Ari looked at Bobby again. "I'm going to kill you for this, you little bastard. I am personally going to kill you slowly and painfully, you ungrateful little shitbag".

Bobby replied slowly and softly, "you haven't understood have you Ari. You're already a dead man. You won't survive tonight. The question is will you sign these contracts. If not you will still die and we will forge your signature. We would however prefer you to sign them, more authentic. What you must ask yourself is how much pain and grief do you want to impose on those you love before you sign".

Ari looked at Bobby again with raging hatred in his eyes. "Listen to you, what do you know about loving people. You're a social misfit. You've never loved anybody except maybe soldier boy. You lost touch with you mother, you still don't talk to your sister or her kids, your old man committed suicide because his life was crap, and you talk about my loved ones? You haven't got the right."

Bobby was pleased to hear this speech from Ari, it meant that he didn't know anything about Fran or his life in Watford. If Ari didn't know it was likely that Delroy didn't either. Ari looked back at the television screen. Another man had just removed his trousers and was approaching the bed. Mrs. Constantine was now laying there quietly sobbing.

"Delroy's has about fifty of what you would call big black bastards to play with wife Ari. How many are going to shoot their spunk into her before you sign?"

"Dream on nigger lover" was Ari response.

Bobby was surprised. He had thought that Ari would have capitulated by now. He obviously cared less for his wife than he said he did. Bobby nodded to Soloman, who went outside the door, spoke into the walkie talkie and returned.

"I'm bored with this" said Bobby to Ari. "We can come back later and she how she'd getting on". He turned the television screens off. They sat and looked at each other for many seconds before Bobby said "part 2," flicked a switch on the consul and turned the screens on again. This time it was another bedroom and in this one, sitting on the bed was Ari's daughter.

Ari jerked forward to try and get out of the chair. Babbling slightly he said "not her, she's too young, she only fifteen, she's a virgin, she's only a kid".

Bobby pointed to the contracts, "sign then, while she is still a virgin, that gives you about thirty seconds".

Ari hesitated. Bobby nodded to Soloman again and again he left the room to speak on he walkie talkie. "OK Ari, we'll leave her for a while. We can always come back to her later.

Maybe some of the guys who have fucked your wife will have recovered enough to try the daughter by then." He switched monitors again to a third bedroom. He switched them onto the two big screens so that Ari could see his thirteen year old son. Ari face went white.

"What is this?" he said, sounding slightly horse. As he spoke another three men walked into the room. They grabbed the boy forcing his trousers down over his ankles and pulling him face down over the end of the bed. One of the men dropped his trousers. The size of his erect member left no doubt that he liked to rear end boys.

"Stop, stop I'll sign" shouted Ari. Bobby nodded to Soloman who spoke into the walkie talkie. The screen showed the man still advancing towards Ari's son who was held down on the bed. He stopped, turned and looked very disappointed as a voice off camera told him to stop. Ari could see the men leave the room and his son, on his own, sit on the bed crying as he replaced his trousers and pants.

Ari started to sign the contracts. He looked up at Bobby and said, in as cold a voice as Bobby had ever heard, "its difficult to kill somebody, especially in cold blood. You may think that you can do it. You had better make sure that you do a good job on me Bobby Parsons because if I survive this, I will hunt you down. I will make it my life's work to find you, in the West Country or wherever you go. I will make you pay for this. In Greece during the war, the partisans had a way of treating traitors. They would hang them up by their arms and cut through their stomach muscles. Their intestines and stomach would then spill out. The pain is not enough to send the victim unconscious, not then anyway. But when they released the dogs, and the dogs started to eat the fresh meat, then there is pain. Can you imagine what its like to watch dogs eating your insides while you can only look? Well imagine it in your nightmares because that is what will happen to you". He pushed the signed document back towards Bobby with his free hand.

"Do you guarantee my family will be OK?"

"Yes, you have my word. In fact you can watch them be taken back if you like".

All of the rooms had en-suite showers for the girls. As part of the plan, a change of clothes had been brought for all three of Ari's family as a precaution. Mrs. Constantine had showered and was getting dressed in clean clothes when Bobby switched the big screens on again. Ari was sitting looking at the screen. He saw both his daughter, who had been untouched and his son, who had been frightened but not harmed, being shown out of their rooms. Bobby then switched the monitor to the entrance hall where they could see the reunion of mother and children, they hugged and then went out of the front door. Bobby then switched to the security camera at the front door and they saw them getting into a car and being driven away. They were blindfolded as they were led out of the house and sat in the car, but that was all.

"They will be driven home and left there. The house and any money you may have was not part of what you signed, so they should live comfortably without you".

"Don't expect me to thank you, you bastard" said Ari.

Solomon moved forward and placed a chloroform soaked cloth over Ari's mouth and nose. He quickly lost consciousness.

CHAPTER 89

Bobby arrived at the prearranged meeting place on a remote road near Heybridge in Essex. It was by a bend in the road and the land dropped sharply to the side of it. It was two o'clock in the morning. Shortly after he arrived a small van pulled up followed by a dark Audi A4 saloon car which had been stolen in North London a few hours before. Ari, still unconscious, was pulled out of the back of the van and placed in the driving seat of the Audi. Bobby and all of Delroy's men wore latex gloves, the type that surgeons would use for operations. They put the Audi in neutral gear, released the handbrake and pushed it off the road, down the bank towards a tree. It hit the tree and stopped. The Audi driver then got into Bobby's BMW and drove off. The van driver followed Bobby down the bank to the Audi. He took a small gun from his pocket. He wrapped Ari's hand around it and by pressing his finger on the trigger fired a shot into the woods beyond the car. He then reloaded the gun, replacing the bullet and then he put it in the glove compartment. Bobby looked at him, he didn't understand what was going on. This wasn't part of the plan.

"Delroys idea" the man said, "window dressing, confuse the old bill". Bobby got into the passenger seat. Ari had hit the windscreen with his head but as the car was not going fast when it hit there was no serious damage. Bobby fastened Ari's seatbelt. He took a syringe from his pocket. He found a small freckle on Ari's arm and injected heroin into Ari's arm. It was about three times the amount that an addict would take. He then took out another syringe, this one several times bigger than the first. He pulled back the plunger and filled the syringe with air. He then found the same spot on Ari's arm and injected air into Ari's vein. He then got out of the car and stood in front of it by the tree that the car had run into. He stood and waited.

After a very short while the effect of the heroin on his system jolted Ari into consciousness. It was a rush and at first he was disorientated. Then he realised he was in a car. He felt full of energy although he realized that he was slightly hurt, he touched his head. Quickly the events of the day came back to him. He remembered Bobby telling him that he would die. He laughed. He had survived. The idiot had tried to kill him in a car crash and failed, he had survived. He tested his arms and legs, he was free. He looked out of the windscreen and saw Bobby standing there looking at him. "Now I'm going to get you, you bastard" he thought to himself. He was getting hyper as the heroin was effecting his system. He began to move out of the car. He suddenly felt a pain in his chest. He had never felt such pain before. It was so painful that he suddenly couldn't move. He slumped back in the seat. The air that Bobby had injected into his vein had arrived at his heart and Ari had had a massive heart attack.

Bobby walked up the bank to the waiting van and was driven to Chelmsford station. He waited for the first train to Liverpool Street.

The body was discovered the following morning by a man out walking his dog. The police were called and assumed that the car had left the road and crashed into a tree causing the injury. The car and the body were taken to Chelmsford police headquarters where an inspection of the vehicle uncovered a packet of heroin, worth about fifty thousand pounds, in the boot. There was also almost one hundred thousand pounds in cash. The police also discovered the gun in the glove box. Having also found out that the car had been stolen the night before in London they asked for initial autopsy reports as soon as possible. They had found Ari's wallet in which was his driving licence. They had advised the Metropolitan Police of the situation and they dispatched two officers to inform his wife of the accident. There was no answer at the house so the police left without informing her.

The initial autopsy report identified a high level of heroin in the bloodstream but identified the cause of death as a massive coronary. The conclusion was that Ari had been out on business, probably making deliveries and collecting money, had taken heroin, which had brought on a heart attack as he was driving, he lost control of the car and it left the road. As far as the police were concerned it was death by natural causes brought on by drug abuse, investigation closed.

The gun they found had been fired recently, there were three bullets missing and the residue on his hands showed that Ari had fired the gun.

The Metropolitan police had not been able to gain entry to his house all day, despite making five attempts to do so. The following morning a hysterical woman made a 999 call, it was the Constantine's cleaner. She had entered the house and found the body's of Ari's wife and her two children sitting on the settee in the lounge. The police arrived and established that they had all been shot with a single bullet from a small pistol, from close range to the temple. Subsequent tests showed that the bullets had been fired from the gun found in the crashed car and the only finger prints on the gun were Ari's. The police, anxious to close the case, concluded that Ari had shot his family and intended to disappear with any cash he could raise. This was also the story that was accepted by the fraternity of his piers, especially when Delroy explained that he had paid Ari ten million pounds for all of his businesses four weeks previous and had contracts to prove it.

Bobby's car was found in Epping Forest burnt out. He had caught a train to London and then to Watford. He had left his passport, driving licence and everything in the name of Bobby Parsons in his house in Chigwell. He was now Nick Mead. Because the car was burnt out and a BMW 750 had not been reported stolen, the police took no action. It was four weeks before anybody reported Bobby missing. The postman had reported that the mail was not being picked up from the mat. The police broke in and found nobody there, no sign of a struggle, nothing suspicious except a missing person. They recorded that fact.

CHAPTER 90

Fran had arranged to let her house in Moor Park and although the tenants were not moving in until January she had moved all of her personal things into Bobby's flat before Christmas. They had decided not to let that too as they would need it when they visited, if only when Bobby returned to renew his permit and to monitor the business.

Bobby had received a number of applications for the jobs involving the golf clothing company. He had interviewed five applicants from the advert in the Watford Observer for an administrator and had employed Molly, a thirty year old, single mother of two children, the youngest of whom was starting school after the Christmas holidays. She wanted to start work at nine o'clock and finish at three to allow her to take her children to and from school. She was full of energy and Bobby thought she was just right. He also employed three agents to sell the clothing, two men and a woman, all golf fanatics, on a commission only basis. All contact would be through Molly and that would be only on a mobile phone, registered to company in Watford which Bobby owned, so wherever he was in the world he would be contacted using a UK number. That way nobody could trace where he was by tracking his phone.

Bobby had checked his Swiss bank account. Delroy had been good to his word, three million pounds had been deposited.

They spent Christmas with Fran's sister and her family.

One the afternoon of 28ᵗʰ December 1988, the British Airways flight from Heathrow landed at Miami International Airport with Bobby and Fran on board. There were not a lot of people going through immigration so Bobby was through in about thirty minutes. Fran had gone ahead of him on her American passport and organised the car. They drove straight across State without staying the night in Miami. The agent met them at the house, gave them the keys and the documentation proving ownership.

They spent the next couple of days buying some furniture, they didn't need much, the house had been furnished, but they did need towels and sheets and personal things. They also brought a bike each. Every day they walked along the beach holding hands.

They celebrated New Years Day 1989 by having breakfast at a small café next to Pinocchio's ice cream parlour to which they had cycled. They walked along the beach and got home late in the morning. Bobby got two sun loungers and put them in the garden, it was a pleasant twenty-two degrees. They lay there a while reading a book each. Fran got up, kissed him on the forehead, and said "coffee?"

"A cup of tea would be better" said Bobby. She smiled, kissed him again and went into the house. Bobby lay there thinking, he had got away with it. He was with a woman that he truly loved and who he knew loved him. He was in a place that was a wonderful place to live, far away from anybody who might recognize him. He was healthy and happy and he had a legitimate business in the UK earning him an income on which they could both live comfortably and if it needed subsidising, he had millions of pounds in a numbered Swiss bank account.

It had taken years to get to this point, but life was now perfect.

"Happy New Year Nick Mead and a happy new life" he said to himself.

Lightning Source UK Ltd.
Milton Keynes UK
25 August 2010

159016UK00001B/2/P